Charles Higson is writer, producer and performer on the hit BBC comedy *The Fast Show*. He has also worked as a writer for Harry Enfield and a producer for Reeves and Mortimer as well as being the singer in a band, The Higsons, in the early eighties. He is the author of three other novels: *Happy Now*, *Full Whack* and *Getting Rid of Mister Kitchen*.

king of the ants

of the
ants

Charles HIGSON

ABACUS

An *Abacus* Book

First published in Great Britain by Hamish Hamilton 1992
This edition published by Abacus 1998

A CIP catalogue record for this book
is available from the British Library.

ISBN 0 349 11103 0

Printed and bound in Great Britain by
Clays Ltd, St Ives plc

Abacus
A Division of
Little, Brown and Company (UK)
Brettenham House
Lancaster Place
London WC2E 7EN

For Alan

'Fuck off, Caesar!' The dog threw itself up against the wire and the little kid jumped back. He was trapped on the concrete football pitch. The only way out was through the open gate further along. But the problem was the dog on the other side of the fence. The dog belonged to three bigger kids, who were sitting on an old sofa listening to a car radio. Each time, just before the little kid reached the gate, the big kids would let the dog go, and it would race along the outside of the fence snarling and yelping. So the little kid would stop and the dog would try to get through the wire to where he stood shaking and swearing.

The dog was too stupid to know about the opening further along, so where the boy stopped, it stopped. The little kid knew that if he got as far as the gate, then the dog would get through and probably kill him. It was a very simple game, and the big kids looked like they could play it all afternoon without getting bored.

Sean Crawley leant on the wall of the walkway outside his flat and looked down at the enclosed pitch. He'd been reading the paper when he'd heard the dog and had come out to see what was going on. The dog looked like a Bull Terrier, a Stafford, or possibly a Pit Bull. It was an ugly thing, squat and brutal and powerful-looking, with thick bowed legs and a massive head which ended in a short, pig-like snout. It wore an iron-studded harness strapped over its shoulders, under its chest and around its neck, making it look like a monster from the cover of a cheap science-fiction book.

'Look. Fuck off, Caesar.' The kid was trying to sound hard. The big kids laughed and the dog turned its head towards them and wagged its stump of a tail.

'Call him off, Neville,' said the little kid.

'Come on, Caesar.' Caesar trotted back to where his master, Neville, sat laughing and smoking with his mates. Neville was black, maybe about twenty – Sean wasn't too good at judging ages – smartly dressed and wearing expensive sun-glasses. One of his friends was white, and the other looked like a Greek or a Turk.

'You're a chicken, Jason,' said the black guy, roughly stroking the sides of Caesar's head with both hands.

'Fuck off, Neville, I want to go home.'

'Go on, then. Nobody's stopping you.'

'Oh, yeah? He'll fucking kill me.' He was close to tears.

'Nah, chicken.'

'Let me go.'

'Don't be such a spaz.'

'I'm going.' He began to march purposefully along the pitch towards the gate, trying not to run. He was almost there when he glanced back and Neville let the dog go.

'Get him, Caesar. Eat him, boy.' Caesar shot along the fence with ferocious scurrying speed. Jason froze, then spun round and ran back from the opening. Caesar launched himself into the air and smashed against the wire.

'Call him off,' Jason screamed.

'Come on, Caesar.' The Greek kid slapped his thighs to attract the dog's attention. 'Let him go, Nev.'

Jason began to walk away again. 'I'm fucking going,' he said. The dog watched him, snuffled a bit and looked questioningly at Neville.

Neville pretended he wasn't playing any more. He waited until Jason was just about to go through the gate and then whispered, 'Go on, Caesar.'

'No don't, Nev,' said the Greek. 'Let him go.'

Jason thought about his chances, slipped through the opening, then ran like hell. Neville called Caesar back and clipped a hefty chain to the dog's harness. The game was over.

Thank fuck for that. Although Sean had quite enjoyed the show, he hated the sound of dogs barking. The estate was crawling with them. Mangy cross-breeds for the most part, half wild. There were always a few of them about, sniffing round the bins and each other's arses.

Sean went back inside and started to think about what he should wear. Duke's phone call had been deliberately mysterious, and he had no clear idea what the meeting was all about.

Duke the big man. Always wanting to make an impression. Always wanting the upper hand. Duke the boss. He bet Duke had a dog, a big dog like an Alsatian or a Rottweiler.

He remembered when he'd first met Duke. A couple of months back, in Fulham. He'd been doing some decorating at the time, nothing fancy, cosmetic stuff mostly.

So there he was, in a quiet terrace, painting the inside of a tiny converted labourer's cottage, when he went to answer the door, and there stood Duke. He was a couple of inches over six foot, well built, but carrying a lot of excess fat. Thick arms and a beer-gut. A typical builder's build.

'All right, mate?' he said. 'Is Mrs Schafft around?'

'No. She's at work. Are you the electrician?'

'That's me.' Duke grinned. He was wearing a paint-spattered Led Zeppelin T-shirt and jeans, and carrying a tool-bag. He came in and looked around the hallway.

Sean closed the door. 'She told me to expect you.'

'Yeah.' Duke dumped the tool-bag and studied Crawley.

'Painting the place up, are you?' He had long hair tied back in a pony-tail and a scrubby beard and moustache, which he scratched absent-mindedly as he talked. His eyes were covered by a large pair of half-tinted pink glasses.

'She selling, is she?' he said as he inspected the sitting-room.

'Yeah.'

'Bloody typical, isn't it? Lives here for God knows how many years, does fuck-all to the place, then gets it all nice just to sell it. She's a Yank, isn't she?'

'Boston.'

'Boston? I've got an aunt in Boston. What's she asking for this place, then?'

Sean told him and Duke chuckled. 'Silly money, you could get a place like this south of the river for a quarter of that. There's no sense in it, house prices, no sense. So, she got any tea here, or don't she drink the stuff?'

'Yeah, sorry.' Sean made some tea while Duke had a vague look round at the job.

'I suppose if we're going to be working here for a bit,' said Duke as he came into the kitchen to pick up his tea, 'we may as well know who we are. I'm Duke. Leastways, that's what everyone calls me. Don't see why you should be an exception.'

'Sean.' They shook hands.

'You a Paddy?'

'No. I think me mum fancied Sean Connery.'

'James fucking Bond.'

'Well, Sean Crawley.'

'Creepy-Crawly, eh?'

'I've never heard that one before.'

'Yeah, point taken, expect you got that a lot at school.'

'Just a bit.'

'Kids can be right bastards sometimes, can't they? It's like we had this Paki at my place, everyone called him Shitty.'

'Yeah?' Sean said quietly.

'His real name was Shritra, or something, but we just called him Shitty. I expect he'd have been glad to have been called Creepy.'

'Yeah. I expect he would.'

Duke didn't work very hard. He'd potter around in the mornings, ripping up floorboards, swearing at what he found underneath, and taking extended tea-breaks. Then he'd sit in the pub all lunch-time, and in the afternoons he'd often disappear altogether. As far as Sean could tell, he had at least another two jobs on the go in different locations around London.

Sean plugged away at his painting. He didn't like drinking at lunch-time because it made him tired and he couldn't work afterwards, and as he was on a quote and not a daily wage, he wanted to get it done as quickly as possible.

Sometimes, while he was painting, Duke would come in and stand around and offer him advice. Duke had, of course, done a fair amount of decorating, like everything else.

'You'll get away with one coat there, mate,' he'd say. 'Tell her you've done two, she'll never know the difference. You know what they say: what you don't know don't hurt. That's the trick with this game, keep the punter in the dark. There's no great mystery to building and that, but you've got to act like there is, otherwise they'll cotton on and do it for theirselves. It's like this wiring, I give her a price for materials, she don't know what I'm buying, it's all under the floorboards. I mean, she don't know one end of a piece of wire from another. You've got to, like, understand the game, right? Everyone's doing it, she probably does it herself, in whatever she does. It's how the world works, everyone screws everyone else, see? So I reckon you can get away with one coat there.'

Sean just smiled and got on with it, but in the last week the sun was shining and he was winding down, so he decided that if Duke asked him, he'd go for a drink.

Monday and Tuesday, the big man didn't come in at all, and Wednesday he went off with an older man at eleven and didn't come back till nearly three. But on Thursday he put in a normal morning, and at half twelve he came clomping down the stairs carrying a long piece of flex and singing an obscene version of 'Like a Virgin'.

'I don't know what wally wired this place up,' he said when he saw Sean. 'It's chaos. I reckon it must've been some fucking DIY wanker. I'm surprised the whole place hasn't blown up years ago. No wonder Mrs Schafft said she was having trouble with her lights. I tell you, this is the sort of place you turn on the light and the sink fills up. How long's she lived with it like this, eh, for fuck's sake? I tell you I do not understand some people. It's like, by the time I finish here I'm going to have to have rewired just about the whole bleeding place. You might even have to come back and touch up your painting. It's stupid, she should have got me in before you, she's got it all arse about tit. I mean, you've just about done, haven't you?'

'Yeah, I've just got to come in tomorrow and tidy up a bit, and then I'll clear out.'

'Lucky old you. I'm going to be here for days. What do you say to a drink, then? Or are you still little Miss Goody-two-shoes?'

Sean laughed. 'All right, then. You ready now?'

'See, you're learning. I'm ready any time.'

2

It was a beautiful sunny spring day. The air was warm and still, and everything looked bright and fresh. As Sean left the house, he stretched and smiled. He felt good. One more day, and then nothing. Bliss.

'Yeah,' said Duke as they strolled down to the pub at the end of the road. 'You done a good job there.'

'Thanks.'

'I mean, I don't mean to be rude, but what do you do for a living? Don't get me wrong, like, as I say, you've done a good job an' all, but you're not a bleeding painter, are you?'

Sean laughed. 'You noticed.'

'No, it's just when I first saw you, I said to myself, the first day I come in, I said, "He's not your usual tosher." And I've seen you work, slogging away at it. Like I say, you've done it well, but you don't do it for a living, do you?'

'No, not really. I don't suppose I do any one thing in particular.'

'You haven't got a regular job?'

'Not unless you count signing on.'

'Oh, a dole queue scrounger, eh? A dangerous criminal.' Duke laughed. 'I don't blame you, mate. How're you supposed to live on the amount they give you?'

'Yeah, so I do a bit of everything, really. Painting, gardening, bike messenger, typing things into VDUs, bit of leafleting, anything that pays cash, really. So I suppose if you were to ask me what I do, I'd say anything.'

'Right. That's what you need nowadays. The days of your skilled craftsman who could do one thing really well and was bollocks at everything else are long gone. There's so many tools and corner-cutting shit these days, anyone can do anything. So long as you've got half a brain and you're reasonably fit. It's like me and the building game – you name it, I can do it.'

'Yeah?'

'Oh, yeah.'

They'd come to the pub, the Fox, a countrified little place with oak beams and a bare wooden floor. Duke held the door for Sean and they went in.

'What you having, then?' Duke asked, rubbing his big dry hands together.

'Pint of lager, please.'

'Two pints of lager, please, love.' Duke leant on the bar and got back into his stride. 'Yeah, I can do electrics, of course, painting and decorating like you, plastering, carpentry, plumbing, glazing, roofing. I could build you a place from scratch if you wanted, do it all myself, even the labouring if needs be. It makes sense, you see, cut down on your workforce, keep things co-ordinated. That way, instead of having to wait for some wally to turn up before you can get started on what you need to do, you can do it yourself. It's like, she could have got me in to do the wiring, and what you're doing as well. I'm not saying I'd have done such a careful job, but she'd never have known the fucking difference. Mind you, you've got to charge accordingly. If I'm doing three different jobs, I'm going to be paid for three different jobs, you see what I mean? It takes time to pick up those skills. So it doesn't work out any cheaper for the punter. What'd be the point in that?'

The middle-aged landlady put down two pale pints of lager in straight glasses and Duke gave her some money.

'Ta, love.' He gave Sean his drink. 'That's the thing, you see, to be versatile and charge accordingly. I've done it all, not just building, I've done security, you know, night-clubs, that sort of thing, cars, there's money in that if you know what you're doing. Driving work, mini-cabbing, I could go on all afternoon. But that's the trick, you see, these days, do anything, don't tie yourself down.'

Sean smiled. It was funny to be advised by someone to do something that you'd just told them you already did. But if Duke wanted to go one up on his story, then who was he to get in his way?

They went and sat outside the front of the pub in the sun, and Duke took off his T-shirt. His skin was pale and hairless.

'Ah, yes,' he said. 'Yes indeed.' He took a large gulp of beer. 'And work breeds work, you see? Like money breeds money. I'm only thirty-four, but I'm doing very well for meself. Something comes up, yeah, give old Duke a ring. I'm very well placed.'

'Why do they call you Duke? Is that your surname?'

'Me surname? No. Me surname's Wayne. You know, like in John Wayne. And his nickname was, like, Duke, and I'm a big bloke, so I suppose it seemed appropriate and all that. You know, Duke Wayne, Cowboy Builder.'

Sean smiled into his pint.

'What a lovely day,' Duke said, spilling some beer and massaging it into his belly. 'I think I might take the afternoon off and go fishing.'

'Fishing?'

'Sure. Fishing. Magic. If I had the money, I'd retire tomorrow and spend the rest of my life just fishing. You know what my dream is? To own my own piece of land in Scotland, with my own lake, or loch, or whatever they call them up there, and my own stretch of river, full of lovely trout and salmon. Just sit there all day, fishing and drinking Scotch.'

'I'll leave the fish to you, if you don't mind,' Sean said, picking some dried paint off the back of his hand. 'But I'll join you on your estate for some whisky.'

'Nah, there's no need to take the piss. I know I'll never own me own beat, but that's not the point. It's just like, you know, something to think about. I mean, you must have some plans, stupid plans, dreams.' He looked at Sean with a half-amused, half-serious look on his face.

'I don't know.' Sean wasn't committing himself.

'Oh, come on, don't tell me you want to spend the rest of your life sitting around scratching your arse on the dole.'

'That's not all I do.'

'Oh, right, I forgot, you paint people's houses white and all, don't you? Very fulfilling. That's all you ever wanted in life, is it? Don't give me that, there's got to be more, there's always more.'

'Not really. I'm quite happy, as it goes.'

'Oh, fuck off.' Duke shook his head.

'No, it's true,' Sean said. 'I'm fine. I get a lot of spare time, I do what I want. I've generally got enough money to be comfortable. I'm fine.'

'Yeah, right, so if I offered you a million pounds you'd turn it down?'

'No, of course not. But I'm not going to break my back trying to *make* a million pounds.'

'That's not what I meant, though, was it? I'm talking about what you'd like to do in an ideal world.'

'An ideal world, eh? I really don't know.'

'There must be something. You must have some stupid fantasy. Like being a film star or an astronaut.'

'An astronaut? No way.'

'You know what I mean.'

'Really stupid fantasies?' Sean thought for a moment. 'Well, when I was a kid I wanted to be James Bond. I guess that's what comes of being named after Sean Connery.'

'Nah, every kid wants to be James Bond. But I'm not talking about that, I'm talking about now.'

Sean watched the pattern of light on the pavement, refracted through his glass.

'I should think most people's fantasies are pretty similar, really,' he said, 'when you come down to it.'

'You think so?' Duke asked.

'Yeah. You know, money, fast cars, women. Everything you see on the TV.'

'And you're above all that, are you?'

'No, of course I'm not. I'm the same as everyone else. That's what I'm saying. We all want to be like people in films, you know, like, a cowboy, or a cop, or a private eye, or something.'

'Private eye? Who wants to be a private eye?' said Duke laughing.

'Yeah, you know, Philip Marlowe, Mike Hammer.'

'Bergerac.'

'I thought he was a copper.'

'Don't know, I never watch it. So that's what you want to be, is it? A private eye?'

'Nah, not really,' Sean said, leaning back and tilting his face towards the sun. 'But they do seem to have a pretty good time of it with the car chases and the shoot-outs and the beautiful women.'

'You don't need to be a detective in order to get off with beautiful women.'

'I'm not talking seriously, am I?' said Sean. 'I thought we were talking about stupid fantasies.'

'Stupid's the word. You really think about being a detective?'

'Not really, no.'

'Yeah, well, perhaps you could go and detect a pint of beer for us.'

'Sorry, what you having? Same again?'

'Please.'

When Sean returned from the bar with the two fresh pints, Duke was playing wth a young cat and giggling.

'Look at this little bastard,' he said, boxing with it. 'I love cats.'

'It's funny,' Sean said, putting the beers down on the bench. 'I was reading this article about private eyes just the other day.'

'Yeah?'

'Yeah, you know, what it's really like to be a modern private detective.'

'And?'

'Well, it looked dead boring, actually. It's all divorces and kids with their fingers in the till.'

'Yeah, well, everyone knows that. It's not Sherlock Holmes any more, is it?'

'Yeah,' Sean smiled. 'But it did set me thinking.'

'What about?'

'Money-making scheme.'

'Yeah? And?'

'Well, all the companies in this article, all the agencies, made one thing very clear.'

'What's that?'

'They'd never touch anything dodgy, never do anything illegal, always keep within the law, everything above board.'

'They have to say that, don't they?' Duke scoffed.

'No, it's not worth their while to break the law. They wouldn't be able to survive. If they're not respectable, respectable people won't use them.'

'Maybe.'

'But on the other hand, there's bound to be loads of unrespectable people who *did* want stuff done which isn't, you know, strictly within the law. So, what if you set up an agency that only dealt with dodgy work?'

'You're fucking crazy,' laughed Duke. 'How do you advertise? "Sean Crawley Detective Agency, nothing legal considered"?'

'Yeah, I know it's a stupid idea, but there's bound to be some money in it. Clean up on all the dirty jobs.'

'What about ethics?'

'What about it?' said Sean. 'It's a county near Thuthex, ithn't it?'

'Oh, very funny, you stupid twat. But I'm serious. You're talking about breaking the law, becoming a criminal. I mean, what about that side of things?'

'Well, you'd have to have no scruples, obviously.'

'What about you, then? Have you got any scruples?'

'I don't know . . . I just think something like that would be more interesting than painting.'

'You silly wanker. I'll stick to fishing, I think.'

'Tell you what, I'll set up my dodgy agency as soon as you've bought your castle in Scotland.'

'Yeah, and I'll bring you some flowers in the nick, mate.

Or put them on your grave.' Duke picked up the cat and blew into its face. 'I mean, look at you, you're a nice, quiet, decent little bloke, really, aren't you?'

'What makes you think that? You don't know me.'

'I know you well enough.'

'Do you?'

'Yeah. You know nothing about crime, you know nothing about the law, you're a scrawny little sod who looks like he'd come off worse in a fight with this kitten. You stick to painting houses, mate. You may not be a professional, but you get the job done.'

'Yeah, well, maybe you're wrong, Duke. I learnt decorating, I can learn about anything else.'

'Oh, for fuck's sake . . .'

'I'm only joking. I'm not serious about it, am I? I just thought it was an interesting idea. Possible gap in the market. I've got no intention of doing anything about it. I'll let someone else follow it up.'

'Some other nutter.'

'Probably. Look, I know I'm never going to be a detective, criminal or otherwise. But I'm going to do something, I know it. I'm not going to be a decorator all my life.'

'Oh, yeah? Then what?'

'I don't know. I've just got this feeling. One day it'll suddenly hit me, and I'll see the rest of my life mapped out, I'll know what I was always meant to be.'

'You reckon?'

'Yeah, I think so. I mean, at school, they ask you what you want to be, and there's about three options, I don't know, join the army, work in a factory, work in a bank, go to college. It seems such a small choice. But there's millions of jobs out there. I don't even know what half of them are. So how am I supposed to know what I want to be?'

'You better make your mind up pretty quick. You won't be young for ever.'

'I'm younger than you,' Sean said.

'Yeah, but I've got a job. I'm a builder. It was the only

thing I ever considered. See, I'm not such an optimist as you, I'll stick with it and not wait for something else to come along, some magic job. And if I were you, you shouldn't either. It might seem easy now, but believe you me, it gets harder as you get older.'

'Yeah?' said Sean. 'So what do you think I should do?'

'You're not a bad decorator, and there's money in it.'

'Oh, great. One minute you say I don't look like I do this for a living, and the next you tell me to stick with it.'

'No, I mean it, you done a good job. You just don't look like a painter, that's all. If you give us your number when you go, I may be able to put some work your way. That's the thing about contacts, I can get into sub-contracting, make money without even getting out of bed.'

'We all screw each other, huh?'

'Yeah. So give us your number and if something comes up, who knows? Tell you what, give us it now, so I don't forget.' He took a small notebook from his pocket, and Sean told him the number.

'Where's that, then?' said Duke, frowning. 'I recognize that code.'

'Hackney.'

'Hackney!' Duke grinned as if at some private joke. 'Oh yes, I know Hackney.'

3

That was how it had begun. Duke with his T-shirt off playing with a kitten in the sun; Sean, relaxed on two pints of lager, rambling on about his stupid schemes; none of it meant to be taken seriously. Chance. A chain of chance. A million random switches close and you're trapped.

When Sean left the job in Fulham, that was the last he thought he'd ever see of Duke Wayne. On the Friday evening he'd packed up his gear, gone home, got into the bath and slipped into oblivion.

He forgot all about Duke and the job until, five weeks later, as he was struggling into his flat with two carrier-bags full of shopping, the phone rang.

He dumped the bags and picked up the receiver. It was Duke, wanting to know if he was busy.

'Not really, no,' said Sean, slightly out of breath.

'Well, I just might have something for you, mate.'

'What is it? Painting?' Sean felt a bit pissed off; he hadn't wanted any more work for a while.

'Not exactly.'

'Well, what then? Not labouring?'

'No, no. I'll tell you when I see you, all right?'

'See me?'

'Yeah. Where's easy for you?'

'Anywhere within reason, I suppose, but . . .'

'How's Highbury Corner?'

'Okay . . .'

'Great. You know the Cock? By the station there?'

'Yes.'

'Meet me there at seven o'clock, all right? I've got a little proposition for you.'

'What? What sort of proposition?'

'You'll see. But I think you'll be interested.'

'And it's not painting?'

'It's nothing like painting. I'll see you at seven, then.'

'All right, if you want to be mysterious about it . . .'

Duke laughed and hung up.

So now Sean was considering what to wear. He didn't want to dress up in any way, but he didn't want to dress down, either. He had to look normal, like a completely ordinary person. He had no idea what the work might be, so he had to keep up the impression he had tried to give Duke, of someone who could do anything, a blank to be filled in later.

He chose a clean pair of jeans, neither tight nor baggy, slightly faded but not tatty in any way, a green short-sleeved shirt, Nike trainers and a beige zip-up cotton jacket.

He studied himself in the mirror and was satisfied that he looked ordinary enough. His dark hair was cut short, but not too short. His blue eyes were set in an unmemorable face. His skin wasn't pale and it wasn't tanned and he was average height, a little over five ten. He was completely unexceptional in every way. It was perfect.

He looked at his watch; it had just gone twenty past six. He decided to leave so that there was no danger of being late. He wouldn't cycle; the whole impression had to be just right and a lot of people objected to cyclists. He'd get the train from Hackney Central.

He'd eaten straight after Duke's phone call, so that he wouldn't get drunk on half a pint. He was all set. He took a five and a ten from under his shirts in the chest of drawers and then checked that the weather was still fine. There was hardly a cloud in all the blueness; it looked like it was going to be another hot summer. He made sure his windows were closed and left the flat, pulling the door shut behind him. He looked down at the football pitch. The kids with the dog had got in their car and gone. Two boys were cycling between the goal-posts, shouting.

Sean locked the mortice on the front door, dropped the keys in his pocket and walked along to the stairs. As usual they were strewn with rubbish, and filthy pools of water sat on the steps. But he didn't really notice the mess any more, or the graffiti on the yellow tiles, or the constant arguments in the other flats.

He tramped down the stairs, humming something that wasn't a tune, and zipping up his jacket. At the bottom someone hadn't put their bin-bags in the tall drum, and the dogs had ripped them apart. Now a couple of little kids were hitting the spilled contents with sticks, screaming and laughing. They stopped when Sean went past and stared at him in silence, their open mouths ringed with grime.

A black guy was sitting in the front seat of his gleaming car with his legs sticking out the door, fiddling with something under the dashboard. An old woman sat in her doorway on a wooden chair reading the *Sun*.

Sean set off towards the station, but when he reached the end of the block he heard someone hooting at him and he turned to see George in his van. Well, it wasn't really George's van, it belonged to the office supplies company he worked for, but he could borrow it at weekends and some evenings, and so everyone considered it his, even George.

George was a sickly, lazy bloke with thick, black, plastic-rimmed glasses and a bad complexion. He spent most of his spare time getting stoned and watching cartoons and kung-fu films on his video. He was a friend, not a close one, but then Sean didn't really have any close friends, which suited him just fine. George was tolerable, and he had his uses. Sean often got him to carry his gear around in the van, so he was pleasant towards him, and George seemed to genuinely like him in return. The only problem was, he had a habit of dropping round unexpectedly.

'Where you off to?' George leant out of his window and squinted at him.

'Highbury.'

'You want a lift?'

'No, it's all right, I'll get the train.'

'Come on, I'll give you a lift.'

Sean reluctantly got in. There was no point in arguing with George.

George spent the entire trip to Highbury alternately trying to tune the van's radio and find a track on a cassette that he wanted to play to Sean. He never found it, and all the while, over the whining and howling of various foreign-sounding stations, he talked incessantly about the various types of dope he'd been smoking lately.

'I've got this great black at the moment,' he said, hitting the fast forward on the cassette player. 'I tried some in my lunch-hour yesterday and spent the afternoon seeing things.'

'You're an asset to your company,' Sean said sarcastically.

'I know.' George sniggered. 'As a matter of fact, I had a quick blow just now, before I left work. Tell me if I'm driving on the wrong side of the road, will you?' He sniggered some more, and the radio seemed to hiss and crackle with him.

'Very funny.'

'Where you want to be dropped off, then?'

'The Cock.'

'Oh, I'll join you for a jar, then.'

'No, George, I'm seeing someone about a job.'

'Oh, right. What about later?'

'Yeah, maybe. Might see you down the Princess.'

'Okey-dokey. Here, you ever seen *Pink Flamingos*? Borrowed a video off this geezer at work. I tell you, that is one disgusting film, man. There's this bit, right . . .'

Sean stopped listening and looked out at the dirty grey streets of Hackney and Dalston. As usual they were busy with traffic, made worse by the tail-end of the rush hour. Cars and lorries banged along the pitted roads, heading east out of London.

It took them about ten minutes to get to Highbury Corner, and George dropped Sean off at the roundabout.

18

Sean thanked him and with a cheery toot-toot George set off back to Hackney.

'Stupid tit,' said Sean as he turned and headed for the pub.

The Cock was an ugly brick building with no character. Sean went inside and, although he was early, looked around for Duke. It was a large pub and he had to make a complete circuit to be sure he wasn't there. The place was fairly busy for the time of day, office workers mostly, men and women having a few drinks before going home. A group of la-bourers stood around a pool table, and a few old die-hard locals, who still came despite the modernization, were dotted about, drinking alone. Maybe they still had fond memories of when the pub had been gloomy and unkempt and they belonged there.

Sean ordered himself a pint of Foster's and waited at the bar, watching the door. The juke-box was quietly playing an old Rolling Stones song, and Sean found himself tapping his fingernails on his glass. He frowned and put his spare hand in his pocket.

At five past seven Duke came in with another man, late forties, early fifties perhaps, about Sean's height; but stocky and chunky. He had steel-grey hair which came over the top of his ears and almost down to his collar. His sun-tanned face showed the effects of heavy drinking; he looked like a once-strong man gone to seed. He was wearing a slightly too-tight and unattractive seventies-style suit and carrying a brief-case.

Duke was wearing his work clothes, dirty jeans and T-shirt. He spotted Sean straight away and smiled. Sean walked over to meet them and, as he did so, Duke muttered something to his partner and they both smiled.

'Mr Crawley?' said the older man in a not completely successful attempt to sound sincere.

'Hello,' said Sean, shaking his hand.

'This is my guvnor, Mr Mathews,' Duke explained.

'Derek,' Mr Mathews said.

Sean smiled to himself. So the big man had a boss. So much for his freelance trouble-shooting image. He hadn't even hinted at it to Sean before now. Trying to look like he knew it all, when all the time he was working for someone else.

'What're you having then, Duke?' Mathews asked.

'Oh, just a lager, please.'

'And can I get you one, Mr Crawley?'

'I'm all right for the minute, thanks.'

'Go on, you've nearly killed that one. I'll get you another. What is it?'

'Oh, a lager as well then, please.'

'Right, then. There you go, there's a table over there. Grab it and I'll bring the drinks over.'

Sean and Duke sat down while Mathews went to the bar.

'So, what's this all about, then?' Sean asked.

'You'll see.' Duke gave him a big, superior grin.

'What is it, some kind of office work he wants or something?'

'Wait and see. Wait and see. He'll explain it all to you in good time.'

A couple of minutes later Mathews arrived at the table with three pints firmly gripped in his large thick hands.

'So,' he said, sitting down. 'Tell us all about yourself, Crawley.'

'Well, what exactly do you want to know?'

'Duke here's told me a bit, maybe you could just fill us in on the details.'

'Such as?'

'You're a college boy, aren't you?'

'Poly. I never finished.'

'What we used to call a drop-out.'

'If you like. I just thought I was wasting my time. There was no point in it.'

'Where did you study?'

'Here in London. City Poly.'

'You a London boy?'

'No, Reading. I've been here about seven or eight years, I suppose.'

'You know your way around, then?'

'I suppose so. Better than most Londoners, anyway. You know what it's like, people who've lived here all their lives just know their own little areas.'

'Yes, you may be right,' Mathews said automatically. 'And you live in Hackney now, Duke told me.'

'Yes.'

'You live alone?'

'Yes, council flat. I used to share it with a girl, but she moved out about a year ago.'

'Girl-friend?'

'Suppose she was.'

'Got anyone else?'

'Not really, not at the moment.' Sean looked from Mathews to Duke and back again. What the hell was this all about? He hadn't expected a job interview.

'What about family?' Mathews asked. 'Your parents still in Reading?'

'Yeah. Never really see them. Got a sister in Leicester, and a brother working in America.'

'America?'

'Yes. Look, don't think I'm being rude or anything, but what's all this in aid of? I mean, I don't really know why I'm . . .'

'Don't worry, Mr Crawley, I'm just trying to get a general picture of you. You see, the job I might be in a position to offer you is of a rather special nature. I wouldn't offer it to just anyone, you understand? So I want to make completely sure you're the right man before I discuss it.'

'But I don't know what the job is. How d'you know I want it? How do I know I want it?'

'Patience, Mr Crawley. What I'm saying is I've got to be sure of you before I can tell you the first thing about it. If you're not right I won't discuss it, and we'll just sit here and have a nice drink together and that'll be the end of it, okay?'

'Okay.'

'So, after college you've just done odd jobs? No particular skills, no qualifications?'

'Not really. Nothing special. I'm just like all the thousands of other people my age you see around London.'

'Ever been involved in politics? That side of things?'

'Not really.'

'You weren't active in your student union or anything?'

Sean laughed.

'So you're not one of those young people who's always got some cause or other? Gay, black, lesbian, Marxist, single-parent workshops?'

'No, nothing like that.'

'Do you vote? If you don't mind me asking?'

'I haven't done yet.'

'So your philosophy is really looking after number one?'

'I suppose so. Stupid not to. Specially these days. There's no one else going to do it for you.'

'Everybody's screwing everyone else, right?' Duke said, winking over the rim of his glass.

'Yeah.' Sean looked at Mathews; he seemed pretty humourless.

'So any little deal you might get going for yourself is okay, whether it's strictly above board or not? Duke here told me, for instance, about your dole fiddling.'

'Mm.'

'Don't get me wrong. I'd be the last person to put you down. We've all got to do what we can to survive these days, and if you've got to bend the rules a little, all well and good. I'm not talking about bringing the country down, or armed robbery or anything like that. Just a little, shall we say, ducking and diving.'

So that was it. Sean realized he'd have to tread carefully from now on. He didn't want to scare Mathews off.

'I think I know what you're getting at, Mr Matthews,' he said in a business-like manner.

'Good,' said Mathews, similarly business-like. 'What we're talking about is what's right and what's wrong. Where you draw the line. Now, say something was not, in the strictly legal sense, wrong, and yet was, well, antisocial, perhaps. What's the word for that? Er . . .'

'Immoral?' Sean suggested.

'Immoral.' That's it. See, your education wasn't wasted, was it?'

Duke laughed and Sean forced himself to smile. When was Mathews going to get to the point?

'So what's your feelings about that?' Mathews asked. 'About something being immoral?'

'I think in the end it's up to us, really, isn't it? It's up to us to sort out our own system of right and wrong.' Mathews was thinking about that. Sean hesitated. Maybe he'd gone a bit too far.

'What I mean is,' he said, 'you do need order, obviously. It's just, you know, the difference between bending the rules and breaking them. As you say, you wouldn't want to bring the country down.'

'And so' – Mathews leant back in his chair and breathed in heavily through his nose – 'how far would you be prepared to bend the rules, yourself?'

'That depends on what was in it for me.'

'That's your only consideration?'

'I suppose so. As Leslie Crowther once said, "The price would have to be right".'

Mathews looked at his gold watch and straightened his cuffs.

'I can offer you a job, four hundred a week plus expenses, cash in hand. No paperwork. You could even still sign on if you wanted.'

'And I assume that this job is rather . . .'

'Immoral,' said Duke.

'Okay,' said Sean. 'I'm listening.'

Mathews shifted on to his elbows so that he drew close to Sean. 'Now,' he said, 'we've reached the point of no return here. If you're not interested, if you've any doubts at all, I'll stop now. Just say the word and you've never met me. You didn't come here tonight.' He sat up straight and looked towards the bar. 'I'm not in a position to be pissed about.'

'I won't piss you about.'

'I hope so, for your sake.'

'Go on, then.'

'Right. First off, you won't actually be required to do anything illegal as such. So you're safe. You'll just get some information about some things that the general public shouldn't know about.'

At last he was coming to it. Sean felt his throat becoming dry. Things were beginning to move fast, and he had to stay in control. As casually as possible he took a drink.

'So what do you want me to do, exactly?'

'Well, you've got Duke to thank for that, really. You see, a problem came up, and we needed to deal with it. I consulted Duke and he suggested you.'

'And?'

'We want someone watched. We want to know how he spends his time, what he does, who he sees, where he goes.'

Sean nodded his head and tried to look relaxed, like he had this kind of conversation every day, but he felt himself begin to flush. He swallowed hard and studied his beer in a serious manner.

Jackpot.

4

'His name's Eric Gatley,' Mathews explained, laying a photograph down on the table. 'He's an accountant for Hackney Council. Lives just round the corner, Canonbury Road.'

Sean picked up the picture; it looked like it had been taken at an office party. Gatley was holding a plastic glass and leering at the camera. He was bald, with a short beard and moustache, and glasses.

'He's thirty-eight, married, two kids, both girls, thirteen and ten. He drives a Renault 4, but apparently he usually rides a bike to work. One of those health fanatics, you know, vegetarian and all that shit. Oh, and he's got a lodger, young lady, teacher. That's about it. Keeps himself to himself.'

Sean put down the photo. 'And why do you want him followed?' He was pleased with the way his voice sounded, clear and firm. Under control.

Mathews looked into his eyes. 'There's one thing I have to get completely clear before I say anything else.'

'What's that?'

Mathews offered him a smile that wasn't really a smile at all.

'Now this may sound corny, but, like, in films, when the heavy says, "You fuck me around and I'll break both your legs," that's usually the line, isn't it? Well, what I mean is, if any of this goes any further than the three of us here, then I *will* break both your legs. All right?'

'Yeah.'

'I've got some big boys working for me, and if I tell them, you could spend the rest of your life in hospital.'

'I understand,' said Sean flatly.

'Good. There's no need for this to become unpleasant. So back to Mr Gatley. Now, as you probably know, the building trade's a bit of a game, a rough game sometimes, and, as with everything else these days, it's getting harder all the time. So one way or another you've got to give yourself an edge, a little money here, a little muscle there, a favour here, a blind eye turned there. You know how it is. Sometimes corners have to be cut, accountants have to be a little creative.'

'Sure.'

'Now, take sunny Hackney. Where do you suppose most building contracts come from?'

Sean shrugged.

'The council,' Mathews said. 'That's where the money is, council contracts. The place is virtually one big estate, and it's all falling down. But things being what they are, there's a lot of competition for those contracts. So, as I say, you need an edge, a few sympathetic ears in the council, a foot in the door. Now that means a few big drinks for the right people down at the Town Hall. Everywhere's the same, it's not just Hackney.'

'You mean that perhaps your work's not as rigorously checked as it might be,' Sean suggested.

'Perhaps.'

'And perhaps the accounting's not scrutinized in depth.'

'Yeah, and perhaps the materials we charge for are not the exact same materials that get used on the job.'

'I think I know the sort of thing you mean.'

'No great revelation, right? But it might be in different quarters.'

'So what's the problem?'

'Did I say there was a problem?'

'Well, no, but . . .'

'*Potential* problem, Crawley, *potential* problem. Maybe. You see, a few months back our man Eric Gatley starts work there. And him being new and keen, he starts looking into things and finds certain discrepancies. "Hello," he thinks, "this is all a bit fishy." And the next thing you know he's dug a bit deeper and come across a whole steaming lorry-load of fish. He's not quite put two and two together yet, but it's only a matter of time.'

'You can't get to him?'

'Not our Gatley. A little saint by all accounts. We've tried a few casual approaches, but you get a nose for these things. We don't want to push it, no telling what he might do.'

'Isn't he likely to just go to the police?'

'Not yet. He's on a crusader kick, he's seen too many films. This is his one chance to be a hero, to get famous, get his mug on the telly. So he's got to crack the case by himself. He wants to say, "I'm the one, I did it all by myself." Then there's publicity, promotions; he'll be one of the fucking Untouchables.'

'But if you know all this about him, why do you want him watched?'

'We want to know what he's going to do next, in case we want to try and stop him.'

'Stop him how?'

'You've got to find out if he's got any weak spots. If we can't bribe him, we may be able to blackmail him. I want to know what that little bastard gets up to morning noon and night. I want to know him inside out. I want him taped.'

'So why me?'

'I could use one of my boys, but I want to be covered. If anything went wrong, and one of my lot got sussed, it wouldn't look too good for me, would it? I'm not suggesting that anything is going to go wrong, mind, but you've got to play it safe, understand? Now, you, on the other hand, I don't know you, do I? If it comes to it, you can make up any old excuse why you're hanging around Gatley. There's no law against it. You could say you fancied his wife or something. This way we're all covered.'

'I suppose so.'

'No, it's got to be a stranger, someone who could never be connected with me. This is the only time you and I will ever meet.'

'All right. You're on.'

'Good. Duke's rarely wrong in assessing someone. The only thing he's a bit slow on is getting his round in.'

'Sorry, guvnor.' Duke jumped up. 'Same again all round, is it?' They nodded and Duke went to the bar.

Mathews put his hands behind his head and belched quietly. 'You'll report to Duke. Phone only, don't use your real name. Work something out between you. And only get in touch if you've got important news, or it's an emergency, right? Don't suppose I need to tell you not to put anything in writing?'

'No.'

'I'll start you off on a month's pay, in advance. Cash, of course. And that's whether you work for all that time or not. That's to keep you sweet. Keep you on our side. You do all right by us, and we'll do all right by you.'

'Sounds good to me.'

'It's a deal.' Mathews smiled and they shook hands.

Duke came back with the beer and they chatted for a couple of minutes about nothing in particular, before Mathews excused himself and went to the toilet with his brief-case. Duke took this as a sign to leave and he finished his beer in one long swallow.

'All right then, Sean?' he said with a wink. 'It looks like your wish came true.'

'Looks that way.'

Mathews reappeared, dumped his brief-case and a carrier-bag on the seat, and smiled at Sean.

'All set then, Duke?'

'Yep.'

'Come on, then, I'll give you a lift.' Mathews picked up his brief-case and nodded at the carrier-bag. 'That's yours there, Crawley. Don't forget it.'

'Thanks.'

And then they were gone.

Sean was too excited to finish his beer. He picked up the carrier-bag and looked into it. There was an envelope at the bottom, not bulging, but full. He stood up and walked to the toilet. He felt self-conscious, as if he was drunk and trying to pretend to be sober, imagining everyone in the pub was looking at him.

In the toilet he locked himself into a cubicle, sat down and took the envelope out of the bag. What if the whole thing had been an elaborate joke? And when he walked out of the toilet, Mathews and Duke would be standing there pissing themselves.

But what if it wasn't a joke? Everything had happened so fast. What had he got himself into?

He tore open the envelope. There was a wad of notes in it, of various denominations. Carefully he counted them out. Exactly sixteen hundred pounds. He felt himself grinning from ear to ear.

'Fuck me,' he said quietly. 'Fuck me to hell.'

He closed his eyes and tried to calm down. Tried to make some sense out of what had just happened. It was true, then, he'd just been hired to follow someone. Jesus Christ.

He'd followed people before. When he wasn't working and was bored, he'd sometimes go into the centre of town, pick someone at random, and tail them. It was always crowded enough for him not to be noticed, and only someone who had reason to believe that they were being followed would be at all conscious of someone following them.

Most times, the person would disappear into an office and that would be that. But sometimes he'd latch on to someone a little more interesting, and he'd spend hours watching them. Once he even went as far as Brighton, only to lose the woman on the sea-front. But he had never witnessed anything extraordinary or clandestine; it had always been more interesting than exciting. For an hour or two, though, he would become part of someone else's life, lost.

But this was different. He knew something about the person he had to follow and he had to find certain things out. And he was being paid.

Yes. He riffled through the stack of grubby notes. On the whole, he reckoned he'd handled things rather well, like not telling Mathews he couldn't drive. But what the hell, Gatley travelled by bike. No problem.

No problem.

With trembling hands he put the money back in the envelope. And feeling even more self-conscious than before, he left the toilet.

When he got home, he hid the envelope under his bedroom carpet and went to the Princess Alexandra to celebrate.

George never showed up, so he drank alone, sitting quietly in the corner and musing over his new job. It was brilliant. Whichever way you looked at it, it was brilliant. He had sixteen hundred quid and all he had to do was watch some twat from the Town Hall.

So where was the catch? There had to be a catch. But the more he thought about it, and the more he drank, the less he could pin it down. In the end he gave up thinking and concentrated wholly on the drink.

Coming back from the pub afterwards, he suddenly felt horribly anxious. What if someone had broken into the flat? What if he'd been burgled while he was out? It would be hard to find the money, but not impossible.

When he got to his staircase he started to run. It felt easy: six pints of lager deadened any pain, it was like running in a dream, effortless and not quite real.

The light on his walkway had long since packed in, so that the last flight of steps was in darkness. His heart was beating hard and fast, but that could have been caused by the running. He slowed, and stopped. What if the thief was waiting in the darkness? What if he ran past him now, clutching the sixteen hundred quid? What would he do?

Don't be stupid.

There was no burglar.

He had to calm down, relax. Not act like a kid.

He carried on up. There was no one there. There never was. His neighbour's flat was in darkness as usual; he walked past it to his own front door. Exactly as he had left it. Nothing changed. He unlocked the door and went inside, then he pulled back the carpet and tipped out the contents of the envelope.

He laid the notes out on the floor and smiled at them.

'Fuck,' he said, and laughed.

He stood up and looked at himself reflected in the window.

'Bastard,' he said, and the reflection smiled.

5

Sean's mind was too active when he went to bed . . . What did Mathews and Duke really think of him? Was the job illegal? What equipment would he need? Round and round and round . . . In the end it couldn't have been much before five when he actually fell asleep, and when his clock radio came on barely two hours later, it was torture.

He swore and rubbed his face, trying to massage some life into his buzzing head. Then he swore some more before finally managing to haul himself out of bed.

He dressed and ate what breakfast he could, washing it down with foul instant coffee and about a pint of freezing orange juice.

At twenty to eight he gave his bike a quick check and wheeled it to the door. His head ached and his skin felt dead. His eyes were sore and dry, and his whole body felt weak and heavy. Thankfully, though, it was a sunny morning and already growing warm, and when he got outside the flat he felt slightly better. He checked his *A–Z* one last time and put it in his rucksack before locking the door. Then he hoisted the bike on to his shoulder and carried it down the four flights of stairs.

The ride to Islington woke him up and pumped some life into his bones, and in a quarter of an hour he was cycling up Canonbury Road. Large, attractive three-storey town houses lined either side; like most of the previously run-down area, the process of gentrification had long since had its effect.

Sean had no idea how much a local government account-ant earned, but he presumed that Gatley must have bought this place some time ago, as the prices now were getting ridiculous. He slowed down and counted ahead to Gatley's house. Like all the others in its row, it was painted grey with black woodwork and had black iron railings running along the front. As he cycled past he turned and caught a glimpse of the inside, which had been knocked through, so that the ground floor consisted of one large kitchen and dining area. Another window at the back showed a patch of bright green garden. But he also saw the silhouette of a woman, probably Gatley's wife, and it gave him a shock. He sped up and cycled on.

A small pub finished the row of buildings, and he stopped there to try and plan his next move. Although there were plenty of cars on the busy street, and the occasional pedestrian, he felt that he'd be too conspicuous just hanging about and waiting.

Back down the road on the other side was a small public garden. He cycled down and checked it out. It was ideal. From a wooden bench among the trees he had a clear view through the shrubbery to Gatley's house. There was no movement, so he watched some ducks grubbing around by a little pond, looked at the flowers, and relaxed in the sun.

Without realizing it, he dozed off, but he woke with a jerk a few seconds later as his head dropped forward. He cursed and quickly looked round at the house. Gatley was just coming out, so Sean got up and walked over to the railings to get a better look.

He had plenty of time to study Gatley as he got his bicycle all set for the journey. He was short, and stocky in a soft, rather than muscular way. He had small hands and feet, and was slightly flat-footed. His head was bald and pink, his lack of a hair-line made up for by his well-trimmed beard.

Having made sure his bike was prepared, Gatley set about getting himself ready. He tucked his corduroy trousers into his socks, put a small brief-case into one of his panniers, removed his jacket, folded it neatly and put it in the other pannier. Then he cleaned his glasses, waved goodbye to his wife through the window and at last clambered on to his bike. He looked right then left, and sailed off down the road.

'Shit,' said Sean, who had been quite lost in studying him. He dashed back to the bench, grabbed his own bike and manhandled it out of the garden. But by the time he got round to Canonbury Road, Gatley was out of sight.

Brilliant, he thought, I lose my man on the first day.

He pedalled like a demon down to Essex Road, however, and just caught sight of Gatley heading north.

He soon made up the difference and fell in behind him. Sean prided himself on knowing the shortest routes in the area, and he assumed Gatley would have worked out the quickest way to work. He was pretty sure the little man would turn right down Richmond Road towards Hackney, then head straight to Mare Street and the Town Hall; but Gatley didn't take the turning. He didn't take any of the turns towards Hackney. He carried on going north towards Stoke Newington. When he still didn't head east at the Ball's Pond Road, Sean began to get suspicious.

What was he up to?

All sorts of ideas formed in Sean's mind. Maybe he'd found something out already; one day on the job and he was getting results. That wasn't bad going.

The truth, however, was not quite so exciting. As Sean found out, the accounts department of Hackney Council was based at the Town Hall in Stoke Newington Church Street, and not in Mare Street at all.

Sean was embarrassed. Bloody good private eye he was, he hadn't even bothered with the most elementary research. If he was going to carry on like this, he might as well give up now.

But no, the money was too good for that. Besides, who would ever know? He had already decided last night that he could lie to Mathews as much as he liked; he'd never know the difference. And if he was dissatisfied with the job, the worst he could do would be not to hire him again. And he wasn't ever going to do that, anyway. It was a perfect job, really. Perfect.

He watched as Gatley picked up his bike and carried it into the building. And then . . . And then that was that. It was as if a black cloud had passed in front of the sun, and Sean was instantly filled with gloom. What the hell was he going to do all day?

Suddenly things didn't seem so perfect any more.

The more he thought about it, the more ridiculous his position was. How was he supposed to do any real investigation? He had no access to the Town Hall; he wasn't about to break into Gatley's house and have a look round while he was out. Just what was he supposed to do? The only times he could even see Gatley were on his way to work and back, and what was the use in that?

But Mathews must have known all this; he must have known Sean's limitations. So why had he hired him? There was definitely more to this business than he'd been told, he was sure of that. But what? He knew he'd just have to wait and see, and in the meantime he had the whole long day stretching ahead of him. His first day as a private investigator.

It hardly bore thinking about. What was he going to do?

Shopping.

Yes, that was the thing. Do some shopping, be prepared.

This end of Church Street was narrow and quiet, with little shops, a greengrocer's, a charity clothes shop, a flower shop, a couple of down-market antique shops and a pub. It had something of the atmosphere of a village high street. He bought a *Daily Mirror*, a notebook, a packet of Bic biros and a cheap digital watch from a newsagent. Then, after scouting around, he found a camera shop, where he bought a state-of-the-art Polaroid camera, which spewed the photographs out of the front with a satisfying whirr. Although the films were expensive, he bought five. After all, he wasn't short of money and he could claim them as expenses.

He felt self-conscious leaving the shop. All he needed now was a raincoat, a pair of dark glasses and a hat. He told himself not to be stupid; there was no way anyone could know what he was up to.

He tried a few practice shots of the Town Hall. The front of the building was round, rather like a cheap Albert Hall, but it didn't make a complete circle; round the back it was a disorganized jumble, obviously not intended for public view. The building looked even more dreary in the photos than it did in real life.

Next he found a bench and sat down to make his first entry in the notebook. But before he could do that he had to work out how to set the watch, a complicated manoeuvre involving the careful use of two tiny buttons. It took him nearly half an hour of intricate fiddling, but he at last mastered it, and was ready to start.

But still, the first few timings he'd have to guess at.

8.30 (?) Gatley leaves house. Silver bicycle.

And that was that. There wasn't anything else.

He stood up. He wasn't going to give in yet. The next thing to do was get to know the area properly.

Virtually opposite the Town Hall was Stoke Newington church itself, an impressive building whose soft golden stonework had been recently cleaned so that it looked bright and fresh. He looked up at the high narrow spire against the grey sky and felt that he could be anywhere in England. He tried the doors, but they were locked, so he read the notices on the notice-board, most of which seemed to have been there since the church was built.

On the other side of the road was another, smaller, church. It was a strange patchwork affair which had been bombed in the war and repaired with ugly yellow concrete. Behind this church was the green expanse of Clissold Park.

The park was virtually empty now; there were a couple of tubby joggers, the occasional man and woman on their way to work, a schoolboy on a bicycle, a smartly dressed lady exercising a Labrador.

Sean wandered down one of the paths and was surprised to find a sort of zoo, first ducks and geese, and then, over an artificial river, some bored-looking deer behind a fence laced with barbed wire. Further on stood a cluster of aviaries with various exotic birds and, in a nearby pen, about fifty rabbits scrabbled about in the dirt.

Watching the rabbits was a red-faced old man in a flat cap with an excited Jack Russell, which raced up and down the wire wagging its tail. Sean was reminded of Caesar and the game on the football pitch.

He watched the rabbits for a while before returning to the Town Hall. But when he looked at his watch he was dismayed to find he'd killed barely twenty minutes.

He moaned.

Never mind. Press on.

He went to the greengrocer's and bought himself some oranges, then he sat on the bench and ate one of them. After that he got up and went back to have another look round the shops. He had no interest in antiques, but he thought he might be able to find a book of some sort in the charity shop. He sorted through the piles of paperbacks for anything that looked vaguely readable. In the end he settled for *Goldfinger*; it somehow seemed appropriate. He returned to the bench to read it.

It had been sunny earlier, but now thin clouds were congealing across the sky. He was still warm from the ride, but he could feel himself starting to cool down. By half past ten he was starting to shiver and his bones were hurting his buttocks. He walked around and stretched himself, and decided he'd be more comfortable somewhere else.

The pub looked suitable; facing the Town Hall, it had a good view of the front doors. Inside, it had been given the fashionable cod Victorian touch, with bookshelves, imitation gaslights, stuffed animals in glass cabinets, and a fake open fire.

Sean got himself a pint of lager and sat in the wide-bowed window, reading the James Bond book. Every now and then he glanced out at the high semicircle of the Town Hall.

He found himself racing through the book, as it seemed to have been written for a ten-year-old, but it took his mind off his watch.

From about twelve onwards, people began coming out of

37

the Town Hall, and at least half of them made straight for the pub. By one o'clock it was full of men in cheap suits with bad haircuts, standing in little groups around laughing women.

At quarter past one, Sean caught sight of Gatley. He was crossing the road with another bald man, deep in conversation.

Sean quickly drained his pint and got ready to move, but luckily Gatley and the other man came into the pub and went up to the bar.

Sean put his book in his pocket, moved to a bar-stool near where Gatley stood, and ordered himself another drink. He could hear most of what the two men were saying, but they might just as well have been speaking Japanese. It was all internal politics, money, office gossip and council policies.

Sean was soon bored, and when it became obvious that they weren't about to start discussing corruption and a certain builder called Derek Mathews, he returned to his seat in the window and simply kept an eye on them. They themselves moved to a table when it became free, and a barmaid brought them some food. Pieces of pie with peas and chips.

Keeping up a non-stop stream of conversation, they ate their food, and at two fifteen they went back to work.

Unfortunately, the pub didn't stay open after lunch, and by then Sean had got through four pints of beer. He wasn't used to drinking at this time of day, and he was now half drunk. He soon found out that this made everything worse.

He started out feeling mildly happy, then tired. Then, as his stupor wore off, it was replaced by a headache.

The sky remained grey, the air just slightly too cold to be comfortable, and the next two hours were an eternity of growing boredom and irritation, compounded by an unruly bladder.

He walked round the park again, round the shops again, round the Town Hall again. He even read the church notices again. A couple of times he was tempted just to lie down and go to sleep, but instead he unchained his bike and rode as fast as he could round the park. It didn't help.

He finished the book on a succession of uncomfortable benches, and he threw it away. He talked to an old woman about road-works, and to a young mother about *The Simpsons*. He visited the rabbits twice, and the public toilets three times. But each time, no sooner had he gone than he needed to go again. He tried to fight it for as long as he could, but it was no use.

After his third trip, he was standing on the bridge over the man-made river, looking down into the murky water, when he noticed something at the bottom, something pink, the body of a girl, a tiny girl, like a drowned midget.

He realized that it was a doll. The sight of it made him remember something, something that had happened to him when he was a kid. He'd pretty much forgotten about it, but now the memory was suddenly very vivid. He wondered why he should be thinking about it now.

He'd had an ordinary childhood, he supposed; there'd been no family problems, his parents had stayed together. They hadn't been exactly rich, but they'd never been short of money. His father had run a small plastics firm, and his mother had worked part-time in hospital administration.

As the middle one of three children, he'd been neither spoiled nor neglected. He was quiet, and perhaps rather shy, but other boys liked him and he had no problems at school. He was averagely intelligent, average build, completely ordinary.

The particular incident that came into his mind now had taken place when he was thirteen.

He'd been on a boating holiday with his parents. It had been a hateful two weeks. His brother and sister had gone to France to stay with some cousins, and there had been no one of Sean's age around. His parents had asked him if he'd wanted to bring someone along, but he had no close friends, at least not any he'd want to spend two weeks cooped up with on the Norfolk Broads.

The water had been jammed with boats carrying fat men in caps and women wearing inappropriate bikinis, and Sean had moped about by himself, wishing that they'd all sink.

The days hadn't been too bad: when they were on the move, he could steer the boat or go swimming. He was a strong swimmer, and it was about the only physical activity at which he was more than just competent. But the evenings had been hell. There was nothing to do; there wasn't even a television on the boat. He had taken up going on long solitary walks.

One evening he'd been walking along a relatively quiet and empty stretch of water when he'd come across a family having tea on the bank, completely blocking the narrow path.

The father was in a wheelchair, and the mother was a thin, nervous-looking woman with a permanent, unconvincing smile. There were two children with them, a little girl of about six, and a boy of about ten.

Sean had stopped, too shy to push past. He'd stood there, sullenly whipping some weeds with a stick and watching the boy play with an Action Man. It was a talking Action Man, with real hair, and Sean had wished that it was his.

After a while the mother had sent the boy on to the boat for some more milk.

'And don't run,' she'd said wearily, 'you'll slip.'

'I'm all right,' the boy had snapped back as he hopped on board.

'Be careful, Gordon.'

The boy had disappeared below deck, only to reappear moments later clutching a milk bottle. But the deck must have been wet, because he'd skidded into the rail and toppled over the side.

'Gordon!' the mother had screamed, and Sean had watched as the father had instinctively tried to pull himself out of his wheelchair.

'Gordon!' the mother had screamed again as she ran to the water's edge.

Gordon was flailing about in a growing milky cloud, gasping rhythmically. It was obvious that none of the family could swim.

The mother had then become aware of Sean. 'You, boy,' she'd wailed. 'Can you swim?'

Sean had shaken his head without hesitation.

'Oh my God, Gordon.' The mother had run on to the boat.

Sean had watched fascinated as Gordon repeatedly sank and resurfaced, each time weaker than the last. Slowly he'd drifted downstream. The woman had held out a long pole for him, but he either didn't see it or couldn't reach it.

The father hadn't made a sound. Sean saw his terrified eyes fixed on his son, his head shaking from side to side, his lips mouthing something over and over.

The little girl ran backwards and forwards between her parents, crying.

But it was the expression on the drowning boy's face that had really captivated Sean. It was a mask of panic, terror and incomprehension. Chalk-white, gaping, and streaming with snot, he'd bobbed up for the last time, gulped, and was gone.

Sean could easily have rescued him, but he hadn't wanted to. He'd hated the boy, hated him for falling in, hated him for being called Gordon, hated him for having a talking Action Man. In fact, he'd hated the whole family. What sort of people went on a boating holiday when none of them could swim?

But there had been something else, a tremendous feeling of power. By simply standing there, watching, doing nothing, he'd felt he'd had the power of life and death over these people.

He'd soon been forgotten. Become invisible. The mother had waded into the water and stood with her arms stretched out, sobbing. The father had struggled on the bank, in-effectually trying to wheel towards her, while the girl clung on to his arm, crying.

Sean had carefully picked up the Action Man and hid it under his jumper. Then he'd sneaked away down the path.

Nearer his own boat, however, he'd become worried that he might not be able to explain how he'd come by the toy, so he'd thrown it into the river and watched it sink, just as he'd watched Gordon. He didn't mind; in the end the Action Man hadn't been important.

He'd never told his parents about the incident. And when they read the newspaper reports the next day, they'd told him to be extra careful. He said he would be. And he had been. All his life he'd been careful. He'd stayed invisible, waiting for the moment when he'd know what he was and could reveal himself.

He shivered, turned away from the lost doll. There was something bothering him and he tried to work out what it was. Then he realized. He had an erection.

6

Sean spent the rest of the day sitting on the church wall and staring at the Town Hall doors, willing Gatley to appear. He was utterly miserable. Thank God tomorrow was Saturday; he couldn't face another day like this, hanging out in the pub and wandering around the park. If only he'd had a car he could have sat in that.

At last five o'clock came, and Gatley waddled out, his trousers tucked in his socks and his bike at his side.

Sean easily followed him home and tried to convince himself that this was a little more exciting. But as he watched Gatley disappear inside his house, an awful thought struck him.

Was he supposed to watch him all night?

He'd assumed, without thinking, that he could keep regular hours like the accountant. But he realized now that it wasn't as easy as that. He should really watch Gatley as much as possible. What had Mathews said? 'Morning noon and night.'

He felt sick. The detective game wasn't turning out to be quite as much fun as he'd imagined. Decorating was a positive joy compared to this. But he was being paid a fair amount of money. Maybe he should try and be a little conscientious about the job.

Why? Mathews was a crooked old bastard, there were no two ways about it. Why should he bother hanging around here all night? Mathews would never know the difference.

But what if he didn't bother to watch Gatley tonight and he went to the police? Sean would casually tell Mathews that nothing had happened, and then the shit would hit the fan and he'd look stupid. Which was something he had to avoid at all costs. But then, what if Gatley did meet someone? How was Sean supposed to know if it was Chief Harry Snapper-Organs of the Yard, or Gatley's cousin Dave in the deep-freeze business?

There was his camera, of course; he could send pictures to Duke and let him sort it out.

Yeah, brilliant. What about at night? Or indoors? He couldn't exactly use a flash, could he? And besides, Gatley didn't even need to see anyone in person, he could just pick up his phone and give them a ring. Surely Mathews didn't expect Sean to tap the bloody thing.

He sat in the little garden and brooded. The more he thought about it, the more ludicrous his position seemed. He wished he'd thought a bit longer before rushing into it.

To take his mind off things, he brought his notebook up to date.

8.30(?) Gatley leaves house. Silver bicycle.
Lunch: 1.15 to 2.15 (EVERY DAY?)
17.00 Gatley leaves work.
Home: 17.15
Evening?

Stunning.

He tore the page out of the notebook, ripped it up and threw it away. He could remember Gatley's movements, for fuck's sake. They were burned into his mind like acid.

He closed his eyes and tried to sleep, but his head was aching too much.

At about half six he strolled past Gatley's house and looked in. Gatley and his wife and children were sitting down for a lively evening meal. He suddenly felt very hungry. He'd eaten a couple of sausages in the pub, but the beer had left him feeling empty. So he carried on walking until he reached the pub at the end of the row of houses. It was grey and gloomy inside; a few workmen lounged at the bar, and an old local who looked half dead sat alone at a table.

They didn't do evening meals, so he bought himself a beer and a stale ham roll left over from lunch. There were a couple of seats outside and he went out and ate his roll there. The roll was dry and tasteless, and it left him feeling even hungrier than before.

Cars raced past, kicking up dust and leaving a mist of exhaust fumes. Going home, most of them, probably. Sean rested his chin on his hand and drew pictures with his beer on the table. He had a clear view of Gatley's front door from here, but he didn't relish the idea of sitting all night by the side of the road without even anyone to talk to.

He wondered who he could ring up to come and keep him company and decided on George.

Luckily the pub had a phone, and luckily George was in. Sean told him some story about being stood up and George said he'd be right over. That was the thing about George, he could never resist a drink.

Half an hour later the office supplies van clattered to a halt and George climbed out.

'What you sitting there for, you stupid wanker? It's freezing.'

'It was really smoky inside.'

'Well, I'm not drinking out here,' George said, locking the van.

Sean looked down the empty street at Gatley's house. What the hell! What difference did it make?

'Come on,' he said, standing up. 'What are you having?'

Once they'd sat down inside, George showed Sean a brand-new pair of trainers he was wearing.

'What d'you reckon, then?' he said, waggling his feet.

'Very nice,' said Sean.

'This is the first pair of new shoes I've bought in about ten years. I can never bring myself to spend money on clothes, somehow. They're so expensive, and there always seems to be something else more important.'

'Yeah, like dope.'

'Precisely. Dope is a necessity. I tell you, I simply cannot do my job straight. I tried it once after some cunt persuaded

45

me it would be easier, and after two days I was climbing the fucking walls. One day more and I'd have cracked. I'd have been like one of them American bastards, you know, who go into work with a fucking machine-gun and take out the whole office. I tell you, it was getting dangerous. I had to get a sick note in the end, take the rest of the week off, stress.'

'That stuff fucks you up, you know, George?'

'Too right it does, there wouldn't be any point in smoking it otherwise. It's like they say, opium is the opium of the people.'

'So that's it, is it? You'll just fart about in your shitty job, happily stoned for the rest of your life.'

'With any luck.' George grinned, then became serious. 'I'm not like you, Sean, I like a nice regular routine. I don't want to worry about how I'm going to pay the gas bill in three months' time. Never knowing what I'm doing from one day to the next, that's not for me. I've got it just how I want it, no worries. I know what I'm doing tomorrow, well, not tomorrow, tomorrow's Saturday, but you know what I mean. All right, so I hate the job, but so what? I've got no responsibilities, a regular income, and when I'm not at work I can forget all about it. After all, me job's not me life, is it?'

'No. Dope's your life.'

'You think I'm a complete moron, don't you?'

'I never said that.'

'I mean, I do do other things, you know.'

'Oh, I don't doubt it. You've got to buy cigarettes, stick papers together, roll them up . . .'

'Oh, fuck off, Sean. I bet I do more with my spare time than you do.'

'Like what, for instance?'

'Like, for instance, I'm writing a book.'

'A book?' Sean put his beer down and studied George to see whether or not he was being serious.

'Yes, a book.' He *was* being serious.

'What about?'

'Dogs.'

'You're joking.'

'No, I'm writing a book about dogs,' said George patiently.

'Well, what about them?'

'It's not your usual shit, you know, all pedigrees and training and grooming, and dog shows and all that crap. It's more of a philosophical book, really.'

'Oh, yeah?'

'Yes. It's about, well, I suppose it's really about, what do dogs mean? What exactly *are* dogs?'

'What exactly are you talking about?'

'Just stop taking the piss for a minute and I'll tell you. It all started when I was staying at a friend's house. A geezer I knew at college. I don't think you knew him, it was before your time. Dave Scott.'

'No, I don't think I knew him.'

'Dave the biker, he used to be called. Long hair, leather jacket, dirty jeans, British bike, always bust. He married this girl there, Lucy Robinson. She was a bit of a hippy really. Quite posh, motherly type, that sort of robust hippy with muscles, you know, big arms, big sweaters, big blonde hair, big tits, white skin and a pink nose. She'd shagged just about everyone else there, but once she got together with him, that was it. Next day they're living together, and about thirty seconds after that they're married. The works. A kid and everything.

'It was funny, they changed overnight. She became monogamous and he was converted to cycling. Obsessed he was, you know, with that sort of religious zeal of the new cyclist.'

'George, I hate to interrupt this touching saga, but what's this got to do with dogs?'

'All right, I'm getting to that. I just wanted to, like, set the scene. So anyway, last summer they invite me up to their place to stay for the weekend. Right out in the country it was, down in Suffolk. They had this, like, converted outhouse, or something, on a farm, stank of pig shit. It's

47

miles from anywhere, and there's fuck-all to do except get stoned. They had this, like, home-grown stuff, because they're into all that self-sufficiency shit, but it wasn't much cop, really. I don't know, it's not hot enough here, I don't think. Can't get the resin up; it's all a bit insipid. But luckily I had this stuff I'd taken with me, some black, really heavy and sticky it was, like plasticine, you could make faces in it. Right evil shit it was, the like of which has never been seen since.'

'I have a horrible feeling this is turning into one of your getting-stoned stories,' said Sean.

'Well, that's involved, but there's more to it than that.'

'Go on, then.' Sean knew that there was no stopping George once he got started. 'So there you are with your magic black, down on the farm in Suffolk, with Dave the push-biker and Lucy the hippy.'

'Right, well, they'd just been used to smoking their home-grown shit, so they couldn't handle my black, crashed out at about half past eight. So I carry on smoking all by myself, and, like, gazing into the fire, and generally getting mellow, until I've lost all track of time. Well, I've lost all track of everything, really, and I look at the clock, and it's about four in the morning. Middle of nowhere, the wind's howling in the trees, and there's owls, like, hooting, and there's foxes barking, and there's fuck knows what kind of sounds coming from the pigs. And I'm all alone, only I'm not alone, 'cause there's this dog, right?'

'Ah, a dog, of course. I'd forgotten all about the dog aspect.'

'Yeah, well it's a big yellow fucker, a Retriever or a Labrador or something.'

'You're obviously quite an expert.'

'It's not important. The important thing is, it's a dog. Boadicea its name was, a bitch. Fat old thing, and it's, like, lying there on the floor, half asleep. I'm getting more and more arseholed, and I'm getting really conscious of this other being in the room, and I start really looking at it, and every now and then it would sort of look at me, you know, the way dogs do.

'And I tell you, it was the weirdest fucking thing. I suddenly thought, this is a dog, right? It just seemed so dog-like. A real fucking dog. Not just a thing, but a creature, a living, thinking being.'

'I get it, you'd turned into a hippy.'

'Fuck off. It wasn't like that. I'm not saying I discovered something mystical about dogs; all I did was really sort of understand what a dog was. I suddenly had this, like, great insight into the nature of dogs, what they are, what they mean. I sat there, and I looked at Boadicea and I thought, fuck me, it's a dog.'

'George, you're a genius.'

'No, you don't understand. It's like, you know that feeling when you've known someone a really long time, and you've got a mental image of what they look like, and yet you've never really looked at them properly? And then one day, for some reason, you study them and you see that they don't look anything like what you'd imagined. And from then on you see them in this, like, new light? Well, it was like that with me and this dog. I had a revelation of what a dog is. I really began to see things differently. I suppose it's like Dave getting turned on to bicycles. Suddenly the whole world was different; he saw things from a cyclist's point of view. Haven't you ever had that experience when you learn something? How it changes the whole world.'

'Maybe.'

'Yeah, well, it's hard to explain, you'll have to read the book, it's clearer there.'

'I should hope so. Listen, this book, are you sure you've actually written it? It's not just another one of your dope fantasies?'

'Fuck off. I started that night, I've been sort of adding to it ever since, it's getting pretty long now. It's got, like, all different sections, chapters and that, you know?'

'Such as?'

'Well, there's a chapter on barking.'

'Oh, for fuck's sake. This is a joke, right?'

'No. No one's ever really done a proper study of barking.

You know all the different types, the arf-arf, the yip-yip-yip, the howl, the whine, the woof-woof, your standard bark, the yelp. What do they all mean? Can you tell a breed by its bark? Can you tell an individual dog? What are they trying to tell us?'

'They're probably trying to tell you you're a fucking nutcase.'

'No, it's really interesting.'

'I'll take your word for it. What other chapters you got, then?'

'There's shit, of course.'

'Of course.'

'I mean, I've probably seen more dog shit in my life than almost any other substance known to mankind. People in London are experts on it – at least they would be if they bothered to think about it a little.'

'It must be very enriching, thinking about dog shit.'

'The point is, Sean, I'm using my brain again. I'm thinking. It doesn't matter that it's dogs, it could be anything. It's just I happened to get interested in dogs, so that's what I happen to be writing about, thinking about. And it's amazing, when you put your mind to it, when you really do think about something, what you come up with, and your mind feels so much better for being used. I mean, once I started writing I really began to notice dogs. Dogs everywhere. Here in London we're surrounded by dogs, right? Millions of them, it's weird. I mean, when you think of Africa you think of lions, don't you? But if you take a patch of Africa, how many lions actually live there? And yet how many dogs live in London? But when you think of London, do you think of dogs? This is a city of dogs, and we feed them, we look after them, we clean up their crap. They're like a really successful parasite. Can you imagine it? What brilliant evolution, they've developed a system whereby they do fuck-all, and in return we look after them. I mean, if this whole country went vegetarian tomorrow, we'd still have to keep cattle just to feed the fucking dogs. So who's smarter in the long run? Us or them?'

'Us,' said Sean.

'You reckon?'

'I don't know, maybe you're right. You look round this town and it does seem fit only for dogs.'

'Yeah, that's why I smoke. Dope makes me glasses turn rosy-tinted.'

'Makes it all bearable, huh?'

'Yeah. You know, sometimes when I'm stoned, I can stand on my balcony and look out over half of London and it actually looks beautiful, a magical city, something really special. Then I think that in a way it's romantic living here.'

'Romantic? Come off it, George. Look at us. What have we got to be romantic about?'

'You're missing the point, Sean. You don't get it, do you? Romance is important. I need to feel romantic sometimes, I need to feel like that.'

'No, it's you that doesn't get it, George. You see, I like all this. So don't give me any crap about romance.'

'What do you mean, you like all this? Why do you drink, then?'

'I like drinking, it's part of all this. It's part of the shit.'

'And you like that, do you?'

'Yes, I like it. The shittier the better. Nothing's going to change. Everything's falling apart. The quicker the better as far as I'm concerned. The whole world's crap. You might as well see it for what it is. Which is shit, basically.'

'That's a very depressing attitude,' said George, and they fell silent.

Sean looked round at the dusty, smoky air, the dirty windows, the yellow, nicotine-stained ceiling, the rings of beer on the tables, the rips and burns in the seats.

Yes, it was shit, and they were all shit, and he was at home.

7

After the pub, George drove Sean home. They were both pissed, but luckily George didn't hit anything. Sean got out of the van, took his bike from the back and banged on the roof to say thanks and goodnight.

He trudged up the stairs with his bike on his shoulder, and went into his flat. It was very quiet and cold and empty. He slumped into a chair and stared at the wall. He felt slightly sick, and the state of his flat didn't help. It seemed grey and lifeless.

When his girl-friend, Annie, had left him last year, she'd taken most of the furniture with her, and since then he'd got rid of more. He was down to virtually nothing. There were a couple of old armchairs in the sitting-room. A small table. A black-and-white portable television that George had brought round one afternoon to watch the football on and never taken away. There was a gas fire, and that was about it. No carpet, no curtains, no pictures on the walls; only the marks where Annie's had been. He'd sold his record-player and few records when he'd been short of cash, and never replaced them. There were no books. He read a lot but usually threw the books away afterwards. There was a pile of newspapers by the door, but they didn't really count as furniture. His bedroom was similar, except there was a carpet and a blind at the window which he never opened. He had a bed-base with no legs and a double mattress, a few hooks to hang clothes from and a chest of drawers in which he kept the rest of his unimpressive collection of nondescript clothing. It was utterly impersonal, like an empty flat waiting for someone to move in.

He was normally happy there, he had all he needed; but tonight it depressed him. He was tired. He was hungry. He was drunk. He'd had a tedious day.

He decided not to think about it and go to bed instead.

The next day was a Saturday, so he didn't bother setting his alarm. He awoke at eleven, feeling heavy-headed and sweaty.

He ate breakfast in his underpants, and wondered how he should spend the day. It was hot again, and the sun made everything better. He was just considering going for a swim when it came back to him that he wasn't free. He had a seven-days-a-week, twenty-four-hour job.

'Shit,' he said out loud. No sleep for the wicked.

What use was all Mathews's money when he had no spare time?

He told himself to calm down. The job wouldn't last for ever.

As he finished his breakfast, he tried not to think about the journey back to Islington and exactly what he'd do when he got there.

Half an hour later he was kneeling opposite Gatley's house, pretending to inspect his tyres, when Gatley came out of his front door carrying a cardboard box. He put the box in the back of his car and began to rearrange the contents. As he was doing this his two daughters came out, followed by their mother. They were also carrying stuff. It looked like they were going on a picnic.

It was the first time Sean had really seen Mrs Gatley and it disturbed him.

He had expected her to be his idea of a social worker, or teacher, or the wife of an accountant for Hackney Council. But she wasn't. She was wearing faded 501 jeans and a grey V-necked sweat-shirt with nothing underneath. She was slim and fit, with dark hair pulled back and loosely tied behind her head. She had large, very pale blue eyes, and glowing, white, unlined skin. But the focus of Sean's attention was her mouth. She had thick, full lips, pulled down at the corners into a fleshy bow. Her teeth were large, so that her mouth was never quite shut, giving her a disappointed, hungry look. She must have been in her mid-thirties, and she obviously looked after herself, though there was a tiredness about her eyes. She moved slowly and calmly, with a gracefulness that made Sean think that she might at one time have been a dancer. The two girls were arguing, but she fended them off patiently, detached from the turmoil around her.

Sean's throat went dry. What was her name? Had Mathews told him her name? Mrs Gatley just didn't fit her. He couldn't connect her with the gnome.

Gatley, you wanker, you stupid little wanker, you don't know what you've got there. Look at her, damn you! Look at her, you fucker! . . . And look at yourself.

Gatley was wearing jeans as well, but they didn't fit him right. He also had on a short-sleeved shirt with thick yellow and white stripes, and it was pulled tight across his round belly. He fussed around, packing the car, trying to tell the girls what to do.

Sadly the two girls had taken after their father rather than their mother, except perhaps in their loose, sullen mouths. Still bickering, they climbed into the car. Gatley told them to shut up, then closed the back.

Mrs Gatley tilted her head on her long neck and smiled into the sun.

What are you doing, Gatley? On a day like this, you shouldn't be going on a picnic with your brats; you should be fucking that woman.

Gatley put his arm round his wife's waist and squeezed her. She smiled absently at him.

What the hell did Gatley know about anything? And yet what did Sean know? The great detective. Maybe Gatley was a marvellous father, a considerate husband, a sensitive lover, a dynamite lay . . .

Bollocks! He was a gnome, a mole, a twat, a little bald bastard. He had no right to the woman.

Sean pointlessly pumped up his back tyre and watched

Gatley's wife. Then suddenly she turned and looked at him. Her big pale eyes met his and he froze. It lasted an instant, and yet it seemed to happen in slow motion. He tried to make out her expression. Was it a frown? A smile? And then it was gone. She looked past him and he didn't exist.

Everything happened very quickly then. Gatley got in the car, followed by his wife. The engine started and they drove off.

After a moment of indecision, Sean leapt into his saddle and tore off up the road after them. He had nearly caught up by the time they reached the roundabout at Highbury Corner, but he got trapped in the traffic and watched helplessly while they headed down Holloway Road. By cycling recklessly he got round, and the traffic was so slow here that he easily made up lost ground by cutting up on the outside. He soon saw the Renault up ahead, and he was starting to relax when they passed a set of lights and the bottle-neck cleared.

The car began to move faster, and Sean watched it steadily pull away from him. He was cycling like a fool now, the sweat pouring down his back and forehead, standing on the pedals, oblivious to the solid block of pain in his legs. He took stupid risks, dodging between cars, jumping lights, mounting the pavement, but the car got further and further away.

By Archway he had a crippling stitch in his side and he'd lost sight of the car. His throat felt like it had been dried with a towel, he had no saliva and swallowing was torture. He gave up.

He jumped off his bike, pulled it out of the road and kicked its back wheel.

'Shit, shit, shit, shit, shit!' He dropped his head and stood there buckled over, heaving and swearing. His legs were trembling. They felt like they'd give way if he stopped concentrating on them. Then he laughed.

Jesus, what had he been thinking of? The Gatleys were only going on a sodding picnic. He had no real need to follow them.

So why had he tried so hard?

It was her. He didn't want to admit it. But it was her. One look at the woman and he was acting like a madman.

He laughed again. There was no need to be stupid.

He cleared his head, got on his bike and slowly cycled back the way he had come.

He wondered what he should do now. Gatley's house was empty; maybe he should break in? That would impress Mathews. Except he knew nothing about burglary, of course. Yeah, get arrested for house-breaking. That'd really look good. He could have a look, though. It'd be better than nothing.

By the time he got back to Canonbury Road, the sun was high in an unclouded sky. It wasn't like English weather at all. It was hot and heavy, sticky and bright.

He got off his bike and peered in through the front window.

He had glimpsed the room before, but this was his first chance to get a good look at it.

The front was a dining area; near the window was a large old oak table with a few wooden chairs round it. The back of the room was the kitchen. The thing that impressed Sean most was how full it was, how full of life. He could have fitted half his flat into the room, and yet there was no empty space. It was piled high with furniture, toys, coats, books, magazines, posters, papers, boxes, boots and shoes, a vast array of cooking equipment, food, a fish tank, a filing cabinet, a dishwasher, baskets and bags, boxes and plants.

Through the window at the back he could see part of a small garden. It was like a different world.

He wondered whether he should try the front door. Maybe Gatley hadn't locked it. Yeah, and maybe Gatley was a Martian.

He laughed. Best just to go home and forget all about it. Another wasted day.

And yet he found himself staring at the door. Drawn to it. Behind it was Gatley's kingdom. If he could get in, that'd show Mathews.

He stepped closer. It was an ordinary door, exactly the same as all the others on the road. Big and black and slightly worn, with brass fittings. He looked at it, and as he looked at it, it opened.

Sean suddenly went very cold. What was going on? Who was this? He jumped back and yanked himself round. He quickly squatted by his bike and fiddled with it.

Whoever it was came out of the house and walked in the opposite direction. He was shaking, confused. Who was it? Who the fuck was it?

Somewhere in his mind he had the information. He desperately searched for it.

The lodger.

Of course. The bloody lodger. The teacher who lived with the Gatleys. It was as simple as that.

He felt better now he had things under control. He calmed himself down. It was stupid of him to have forgotten.

She was walking away, she hadn't even noticed him. For want of anything better to do, he decided to follow her. He chained up his bike, waited for her to gain ground, then set off.

He felt happy now; this was just like when he used to tail people around town at random. Only this time there was a point to it. It gave him a purpose. There was a certain excitement about it. Where would she go? What would she do? What would he find out? By being with her he shared her life, he borrowed her life, he could forget about everything else.

She was short with sandy, bobbed hair. She was wearing a simple black skirt and a baseball jacket. She had Doctor Marten shoes with no socks and thick, tanned legs.

She walked up to the station and got the overground to Camden. On the train Sean got the chance to study her face. It was unexceptional, small eyes, a small nose, freckles.

In Camden she strolled down to the High Street, busy with young people there for the weekend market, and went into a pub.

Sean was slightly unnerved. He'd always thought of

teachers as old, grown-up, adults, but here was one acting like himself.

Christ, Duke had been right. He wasn't young any more.

He was probably older than she was.

The pub was packed, and Sean watched as she peered around the smoky sun-lashed gloom. Then she obviously saw whoever it was she was looking for, because she smiled and moved deeper into the crowd.

A man appeared, a young man, about Sean's age, with curly red hair and a wooden brief-case. He kissed the teacher quickly and asked her what she wanted to drink. Coffee.

Once again Sean felt deflated. What was he doing here? Who was he trying to kid? He was just wasting his time. He got himself a pint and stood near the young couple, only really half listening to what they had to say.

He didn't learn much. Just names. The teacher's name was Emma, or Emm as the young man called her. Gatley's kids were called Polly and Sarah, and they got on Emm's tits. And Gatley's wife; Gatley's wife was called Susan. That cheered him up, finding that out. He didn't like to think of her as Mrs Gatley. Now he had a name. Susan. Yes, it would do. Susan.

He was looking at Emm now, her mouth moving as she talked, but he couldn't make any sense of what she was saying because he was seeing Susan; she was standing across the room from him and she was naked.

'Hello, Sean.'

Sean turned and saw a girl with bleached blonde hair tied back in a tight plait. She was wearing an American motorcycle-cop jacket, a short grey dress and patterned tights.

It was a moment before Sean realized he knew her.

'Mary,' he said.

'Hi.' She smiled at him. 'What are you up to?'

'Oh, you know . . .' She didn't know of course, she didn't know that he was following someone. How could she?

'So, anyway, how are you?' he said. 'I haven't seen you in ages.'

Mary had been one of Annie's best friends and Sean

remembered that he'd always quite fancied her. He'd also had the impression that she might feel the same way about him, but she'd been one of the wide circle of friends who had slowly drifted away when Annie left him. Drifted away until there was no one left, unless you counted George. And Annie had never liked George.

Mary was with another girl Sean recognized; she was called Sue, or Sarah or something, a quiet girl, rather small, dressed all in black, and wearing a severe pair of old-fashioned, black-rimmed glasses which for some reason were considered stylish in certain areas.

Sean smiled at her.

'You know Sandra, don't you?' Mary said, taking out a pack of cigarettes and offering Sean one.

'Yeah, hi . . .' Sean shook his head at the cigarette. 'So what are you up to these days?' he asked, trying to smile pleasantly.

'Well, as a matter of fact' – Mary pushed a strand of hair out of her face – 'I started a new job this week.'

'You still in the music biz?'

'God, no. Couldn't stand it any longer. No, I'm a housing officer now, for Wandsworth Council. I was just telling Sandra, it's the first proper job I've ever done. You know, with office hours and regular wages and everything.'

'Yeah?' Sean couldn't really concentrate on what she was saying. 'And what about you, Sandra?'

'I work for a film company, videos mostly. I'm a production assistant.'

'Sounds flash.'

'It's not, really. I'm basically just a glorified secretary.'

'Oh.'

'So,' said Mary, after a short silence, 'do you see anything of Annie these days?'

'No, not really. Not since, you know, we haven't kept in touch.'

'Right, I've kind of lost touch myself. What with moving south of the river, and my job and things, I haven't seen her for months.'

'I saw her the other day,' said Sandra. 'She's pregnant.'

'Jesus Christ,' said Sean, almost laughing. 'Annie? Who's the father?'

'She's going to be a single parent.'

'Oh, the stupid idiot.' Sean saw Sandra looking at him with an expression that he took to be a mixture of shock and reproach.

'Can I get either of you a drink?'

'No thanks,' said Mary. 'We were just going.'

'Oh, okay.'

Mary made a move to leave.

'See you, then.'

'Yeah, see you.' He watched them make their way through the crowd towards the door.

It was gone, whatever it was he'd imagined was there between them. She had a new life and there was no way he was ever going to be part of it. It was meaningless, he couldn't connect with her on any level; he felt like a foreigner, lost and alone.

He looked at Tim and Emm, still chatting happily. He tried to focus on their conversation but it was useless. It was just the pathetic small talk of a young couple stupidly in love. They disgusted him. How did people get like that? Become nothing but a couple, vegetables in each other's company. Sean realized that he was getting angry. He had to get out of the pub. Tim and Emm were annoying him, everyone was annoying him. But it was no better outside.

People everywhere. He hated them all. They were foolish, utterly foolish. He was so consumed with anger, for a moment he couldn't move.

All these silly young people in Camden, going about their silly meaningless business, while all around them cars crashed, planes fell out of the sky, fires started and consumed streets, rivers burst their banks, washing away whole towns and villages, volcanoes erupted, avalanches, landslides, mudslides, wars with tanks and machine-guns, missiles, rockets, famine, disease. The whole planet was an inferno of death and destruction, and here were these twittering, empty-headed young people at the calm centre of the whirlpool, foolish, confident and blind.

But not Sean. He knew. He had the power of knowledge, and when the time came he knew which side he would be on. He would walk hand in hand with death and the foolish streets of London would be washed with blood.

And in the meantime?

Well, in the meantime he could only watch and wait.

Emm and Tim came out of the pub and pushed past him, laughing. They didn't see him. They crossed the High Street and went up a side road to a car, an old and beautifully kept green Morris Minor.

Sean watched as they climbed into it and drove off, jolly and quaint.

A beetroot-faced dosser, his trousers undone, emerged from a pile of boxes and shook a can of Carlsberg Special Brew at the departing toy-town car.

'Ah, fuck!' he yelled at it, and lurched into the road. He tried to kick a piece of brick after them, but missed and toppled sideways into a parked Citroën. He slammed his already scarred face against a wing-mirror and collapsed in a filthy heap.

'Ah, fuck!' he said. 'Fuck them all!'

'Quite,' said Sean, and he went back to the pub to get drunk.

8

For the next week Sean wearily staked out the Town Hall in Stoke Newington, putting in shorter and shorter hours every day. And every day was the same. Gatley off to work at eight fifteen. Gatley in the pub at lunch-time. Gatley leaving work at five o'clock. Sean bored, deadly, deadly bored.

That was it. The one exception to the routine was Wednesday, when Gatley left Stoke Newington at one, went home and never came out again. Sean saw nothing, found out nothing. The only thing that kept him going was Susan. The hope that he'd see her again, that she'd look at him like she had done that first time.

At night he'd lie awake thinking about her. Whenever he closed his eyes he'd see her.

She was the same every time. Standing across the street looking at him, her weight on one leg, squinting slightly because of the sun. But the most important part was that one moment when her big pale eyes had locked with his. He hadn't really had a chance to get a good look at her since then and the image was fixed, like the freeze-frame on a video. Something had happened then, and he didn't quite know how to deal with it.

What did her look mean? What was the expression on her face?

Was it curiosity? She saw a stranger across the road, and was curious?

Surprise? Surprise that he was looking at her? Shock, even?

Was she embarrassed? Suddenly self-conscious?

Or was it hate? The hatred that a beautiful woman must grow to feel, constantly looked at, constantly made into an object by all those millions of eyes. Hatred and disgust, to look round and see, yet again, a man staring at you.

But then again, it could have been lust.

That was where he always ended up, and it was ridiculous, but he couldn't do anything about it. Lust took hold, and he'd get on his bike and he'd cycle over to the house . . . and wait.

Saturday came round again at last and he told himself he wouldn't bother. He'd had enough. He tried to put Gatley and his wife out of his mind, but he couldn't concentrate. He fought it all day, but come seven o'clock he found himself sitting staring at the wall with the image of Susan filling his mind.

Twenty minutes later he was sitting in the little garden, willing Susan to come out of the house.

This time he was in luck. At nine o'clock the two of them appeared. Gatley was wearing some kind of God-awful shiny track suit, garish and multicoloured. Susan was wearing jeans and a plain woollen top. Sean felt a rush of excitement.

Luckily they didn't get in the car; instead they walked off, arm in arm, down the road. Sean followed, wheeling his bike. Gatley was evidently telling Susan a long comical story; he was doing most of the talking, and she was doing most of the laughing. Now and then she asked him a question, turning her face towards him and smiling.

They crossed Essex Road and headed down New North Road towards the canal, chatting and laughing all the way. After a while they came to a pub, the Rosemary Branch, and went in, Gatley holding the door for his wife.

The pub was full of plants and old furniture. There were posters on the walls for alternative cabaret and women's groups. They served real ale and real food, to real Islington types, social workers, actors, people in the media and one or two self-styled eccentrics.

It seemed popular and was fairly full, but Susan had

managed to find a table and sat waiting for Gatley to be served at the bar.

Sean studied her as she sat there, calm and relaxed, completely at ease with the world. She tipped back her head, pushed her hair behind her ears, and smiled politely at someone she knew.

Gatley came over to the table and Sean bought himself a drink. Then he found a handy position to eavesdrop. He hoped it would be a little more fruitful than Emm's conversation in Camden last week.

The first surprise was Susan's voice. She had a mild American accent, but it partly explained Sean's feeling that she didn't quite fit in.

At first they just chatted about the girls, Sarah and Polly. Then they talked a bit about Susan's job; she seemed to do some kind of part-time administrative work. Then they talked about Gatley's parents, one of whom was sick. Sean realized that half the time he wasn't even listening, but was watching Susan instead. Watching her mouth as she spoke, watching the changes in her eyes. As he did so, nothing else existed. It was as if he was alone with her, in a silent magical world. Then he'd snap out of it and try to stop staring. But he kept forgetting and would realize that he was once again transfixed by her face.

This went on for at least an hour before Susan said something about Gatley's job, and he went quiet for a while, before saying quietly, 'I've decided I'm going to see that Michael Mead bloke.'

'From the paper?'

'Yes.'

'Are you sure?'

'I'm not really sure of anything, Susan, but Paul seems to think this Mead fellow might be able to help.'

'Are you sure it's not going to get you into any trouble at work?'

'I told you, I'm not sure of anything. But if it all comes to nothing, there's no reason why anyone at work should know.'

'You haven't discussed it with anyone else?'

'At work? No. Not since that first time. As far as they're concerned, I've forgotten all about it.'

'Maybe you *should* just forget all about it, Eric.'

'I couldn't stay there, knowing what's going on, and you know what it's like trying to get jobs these days. No, this is the best way.'

'Well, be careful. Don't let this newspaper guy make you say anything you don't want to. I know what you're like.'

'Yes, dear, I'm not a complete fool.' He smiled at her and she smiled back. 'It's just that this Mead chap is in a position to find out certain things that I never could. Then once we've got together a case, *if* we get together a case, we can go to the police if needs be.'

'Why not go to them now, darling?'

'I can't risk kicking up a stink before I'm a hundred per cent sure of anything. Imagine how it would look if I was wrong.'

'I still think you should be careful. You know what the politics are like in those places.'

'Well, that's exactly what I've been saying, dear. That's exactly it.'

'So when are you seeing this guy?'

'I've told him Wednesday. My afternoon off.'

'Well, don't let him get carried away, and don't give him anything.'

'Oh, come on, Susan. Do you think I'd give council files to some hack from the *Evening Standard*?'

'I don't know, honey. I just hope you know what you're doing.'

'Don't worry. I'm simply going to ask him if he can't find out a few things for me . . . If he's interested. I mean, he might not even be interested.'

'Let's just hope it's a storm in a teacup.'

'Oh, it's all very boring, really. I just want to get it sorted out.'

Sean turned away. He couldn't stop himself from grinning.

This was it. He'd done it. This was better than he ever could have dreamed. He'd actually got some results. It was almost enough to make him forget the days of tedium.

He decided that he'd better leave. He didn't want to become conspicuous. He had to get out while the going was good.

All the way back home, he felt elated. All that hanging around had paid off after all. And it also meant that he didn't have to watch Gatley at all until next Wednesday, when he was seeing the reporter.

When he got home the elation wore off, and he found himself thinking about Susan once more. It was the hope of seeing her again that had made him hang around tonight, and he didn't like that. He didn't want to get involved. Maybe now things were starting to happen, he'd stop thinking about her. She was there, though, in his head, looking at him across the road.

Susan wasn't the only thing that had disturbed him, however. Since starting this job, watching the house, following the teacher, meeting Mary and Sandra, listening to the Gatleys in the pub, he had been given a glimpse into a world that he was no longer a part of. The 'real' world of couples, families, children, proper jobs. A world that Sean had never really understood. He followed people, he watched them, but they had nothing to do with him. It was like watching television.

He'd been part of that world once, however, for nearly three years. But that had ended last December, when Annie had walked out on him.

It'd been fun at first, being together, and they'd drifted into something long-term. Then they became a couple, moved in together when some friends of Annie's moved out of their council flat and offered it to them.

A year they lived there, slowly growing more and more apart. Sean remembered the night when she'd lain in bed with him in the dark and told him she wanted to leave.

'Why?'

'Because you're not there, you're never there.'

'What do you mean? I'm always here. You're the one that works. I'm always here, I'm always in the flat.'

'Oh yes, you're here, don't I know it? Your body's here. But you, there's nothing there, there's nothing inside. You're like a robot or something. I don't even really know you.'

'What the hell are you talking about?'

'You, Sean, *you*. I'm talking about you. What are you? I don't know. I thought I did. Sometimes I still think I do, but I don't know what's underneath it all. Sometimes, when you're not there, I wonder if you exist at all.'

'Oh, fuck off. Don't talk crap.'

'I'm not talking crap. Christ, in three years this is the only time I've ever got any kind of reaction out of you. You don't talk. No, you talk, but never about yourself. I don't know you. I don't know anything about you.'

Sean had turned on the light and propped himself up on one elbow.

'Look into my eyes, Annie.'

'What?'

'You think there's something wrong with me? You think I'm different? You think I'm hiding something? Well, look into my eyes.'

'Sean, I'm being serious. This is serious.'

'I am fucking serious. Look!'

'All right.'

'What do you see?'

Annie had shrugged, sighed and rolled her eyes.

'Well, what do you see?'

'Nothing.'

'Quite. There's nothing there. There's no mystery. I'm not hiding anything. This is it. This is me.'

'For God's sake, Sean.' Annie turned away and lay with her back to him. 'You think that's a good thing, don't you?' she said, with tears in her voice. 'It's like talking to myself, a mirror or something. Well, I've given up. I've given up trying to find out what's behind that bloody mirror. You never show me. I've had enough.'

That had been just before Christmas. It was cold, wet and

miserable. She'd packed her stuff the next day; she'd obviously been planning it. Her brother had arrived with a van and a friend, and the four of them had filled it with an air of edgy politeness.

Sean and Annie had stood in what had been their bedroom, tense and silent. Sean had had a headache.

'Well,' she'd said, 'I'll see you, then.'

'Yeah, take care.'

'Yeah.'

She'd moved to kiss him, then changed her mind. She'd touched him lightly on the shoulder instead and given him a grim, tight-lipped smile. He'd stared at her when she walked out, then watched from the walkway as the van clumsily drove off.

He'd gone back inside, closing the door behind him, and was surprised at how little stuff he had. He'd wandered around the empty flat, and already it had been as if she'd never lived there.

That had also surprised him, how little he felt. He'd always assumed that he was fond of her, but as far as he could tell, apart from the headache he felt nothing.

And now, months later, he felt the same, except the headache had gone.

Since then he'd slept with two or three girls. Well, two to be precise. The first time after a party, at her place. They'd gone to bed drunk and woken up sober and hung over. They'd soon realized that they had nothing to say to each other and that was that.

The second girl, she'd been nineteen, he'd met her at a night-club. She was very young and she'd been speeding. She might have ended up with anyone that night, but somehow she'd ended up with Sean. She wasn't really sure what she wanted, but Sean was pretty sure she'd be better off not wanting him, so he'd never given her his number. And he never saw her again.

He hardly thought about sex any more. If it happened, it happened.

So why was he thinking about Susan Gatley?

He couldn't figure that one out. She was just someone he'd seen, briefly, from the other side of the road, and now he couldn't put her out of his mind.

He lay on his back in bed and gave in to his obsession, but still he had that freeze-frame image in his head, of her looking at him. He couldn't think of her any other way, he had to clear it out.

He ran through all the meanings again, and once more ended up at the same point.

Lust. His lust mirrored in her.

He smiled at the conceit. But why not?

He was young, healthy, not unattractive, and Gatley, what was he? A gnome. Gatley, the little bald bloke who tucked his trousers into his socks and had flat feet. What could she think of him? Could she find him sexually attractive? She'd obviously fucked him at least twice, the girls were proof of that. But could any woman really be satisfied with the waddling accountant?

Maybe she was the bored wife, with the girls at school, the husband at work, trapped in that house. Trapped in that body. What had she been thinking about just before she saw Sean? With her face turned up to the sun, she'd been miles away. What had she been thinking about?

She looks round and there's Sean. She can see the excitement in his eyes, and just for a moment . . .

Sean laughed at himself, but it was too late for rational thought. His hand moved down to his hardening prick and . . .

Susan puts her hand to her head.

'Are you all right, dear?' Gatley asks.

'I just suddenly felt faint.'

'You look a bit iffy.'

'I've got a killing headache, actually.'

'That's all right, dear. I'll take the girls, you have a lie-down.'

She waves as he drives off, then glances once to make sure that Sean is still there and goes into the house.

Sean crosses the street. He knocks on the front door, Susan opens it. She says nothing. Sean walks in and the door closes behind him. For a moment they stand staring at each other and then she puts a hand behind his head and pulls him towards her. That mouth, those lips, that hungry flesh. She drops to her knees, undoes his jeans, takes him into her mouth. All he can think of is the mouth. The curve of it, the fullness of the lips, the teeth.

At last he pushes her back, on the hall carpet, on Gatley's hall carpet. He tugs down her jeans, yanks them past her heels and buries himself in her. It's moving faster now. She looks into his face, grabs him by the shoulders and they fuck.

Her lips drawn back, her teeth bared, her eyes shut. Her mouth open.

They fuck.

Sean came on to his stomach, and the scene dissolved. He lay there breathing heavily through his nose as his mind slowly focused and cleared.

He knew now what the look had meant.

Nothing.

She hadn't even seen him.

9

On Wednesday morning Sean cycled over to Stoke New-ington at eleven. He wanted to make sure he caught Gatley when he left work. It felt good to be back on the job. He hadn't really enjoyed his three days off. He'd been at a loose end, excited about Gatley's meeting with the journalist.

At one o'clock Gatley came out of the Town Hall with his bike, and Sean followed him home. Five minutes later he came out of the house carrying a brief-case. He had taken off his tweed jacket and tie, and put on a brand-new, cardboard-stiff, dark-blue denim jacket with white stitching.

He walked to Highbury, bought a ticket from a machine and went to the southbound platform of the Victoria Line.

There were plenty of people standing around, so Sean didn't have to worry about being noticed.

After a while the train arrived. Sean sat at the opposite end of the carriage to Gatley, but he still had a clear view of him.

Gatley got off at Oxford Circus. The station was busy with determined Londoners and confused groups of tourists. Gatley kept up a brisk pace and seemed to know where he was going. He dodged in and out of people and hurried up and down escalators with practised ease. There was only one slight delay, when a French girl, who obviously didn't know the drill, was standing on the left on an escalator. Gatley got stuck behind her and made impatient faces, but was too polite to say anything. Eventually the girl's boy-friend pulled her out of the way and explained the system.

Gatley made his way to the eastbound platform of the Central Line and rode one stop to Tottenham Court Road.

Sean followed him to the exit through the tunnels with their Mexican-style mosaics and plastic trimmings.

It was a relief to be outside again, even if it was only the sweaty West End with its smog-blackened buildings, its crowds, and its fuming traffic. It was very bright and hot and it took Sean a few seconds to adjust.

Gatley pushed his way down Oxford Street, then turned left into Soho Square and continued south on to Old Compton Street. Half-way along, he looked at his watch and went into a French-style pâtisserie.

There was a counter at the front and several large wooden tables filled up the back. There were pastiche thirties murals of people sitting round tables much like these.

Sean stood at the counter and ordered a coffee. He watched Gatley sit at an empty table and try to catch the eye of one of the elderly waitresses. He was still trying five minutes later, when Sean saw a tall blond man approach his table and introduce himself.

Gatley half rose out of his seat and shook the man's hand. He was very thin, probably in his mid-thirties, and he had developed a slight self-conscious hunch because of his height. He collared a waitress, ordered for the two of them and sat down.

Sean saw that he had very bad skin. His face was red and pock-marked, and there was a rash of spots around his neck.

Gatley opened his brief-case and took out a pink file. For the next twenty minutes they talked. They both appeared serious and animated. Mead nodded a lot and made notes in a small pad. Now and then Gatley fished out various pieces of paper from the pink file and showed them to him.

Sean ate a couple of pastries and drank two cups of coffee. His heart was beating faster than normal. This was it. It was like the films. Mathews would love him.

In the end Mead got up to go. There was a brief discussion, almost an argument, and Gatley did much shaking of his head before resolutely putting the file back in his brief-case.

They left together, and as they stepped out into the sunlight, Mead said something at which they both laughed. They walked down Old Compton Street together. When they reached Charing Cross Road they shook hands again and went in opposite directions.

Sean wasn't sure who to follow. In the end he chose Gatley. He told himself that it was because he'd left his bike in Canonbury Road, but he knew that it was really because there was a chance he might see Susan again.

Gatley went straight home and disappeared into the house. Sean was about to head back to his own flat when he saw the white Renault coming up the street.

It parked a few doors down and Susan got out, followed by the two girls, wearing brightly coloured leotards and carrying little sports bags. They laughed and chattered and danced about on the pavement. Susan smiled at them and shepherded them towards the front door. She too was carrying a sports bag, and her black hair looked wet, as if she'd just had a shower or been swimming. She got the girls inside, and the street fell quiet.

Sean checked the time for future reference, three fifty, then suddenly felt exposed and foolish, standing here in the street spying on this ordinary family.

A wind came up from nowhere. Two teenage girls scuffling along in high heels on the other side of the road shrieked as their skirts flapped about their legs.

Sean shivered and zipped up his jacket, then leant down to unlock his bike.

The key jammed half-way in the padlock, and he had to swear and fiddle with it for several minutes before it finally snapped open.

He was now in a thoroughly bad mood. He untangled the plastic-coated chain from the spokes and wrapped it around his handlebars, then set off down the hill into the wind, swerving now and then as a gust hit him. Near the bottom he turned and glanced back, and thought he saw Gatley and his wife coming out of the house.

He turned away.

So what?

So fucking what?

It was just gone ten past four when he got home and he decided he'd better ring Duke and let him know what he'd found out. He found the number he'd been given, where Duke was working, and dialled it. It rang for ages before someone picked it up. He could hear banging in the background, and a radio playing pop music.

The man who answered sounded slightly awkward and self-conscious, trying to be polite. It was obviously another builder and not the owner of the house.

'Is Duke there?' Sean asked, 'Duke Wayne? He's doing some work.'

'Oh yeah, right, hang on.' Sean heard him call out Duke's name, and then more shouting.

'He says who is it, he's a bit tied up at the moment.'

'I'm doing a job for him. Tell him it's, erm, Mr Connery. Tell him it's quite important.'

He could hear further shouting, then, 'Hang on, mate, he's on his way.'

There was a clunk as the phone was put down.

After a long wait he heard Duke's voice.

'Hello? Mr Connery, is it?' He could picture the big man, with his pony-tail and his tinted glasses and his grubby T-shirt.

'It's me, Sean. I wasn't sure what to say, who it was.'

'That's okay, I thought it must be you. What can I do for you, anyway?'

'Something's come up.'

'Oh yeah? What?'

'I'm not sure if I should discuss it over the phone.'

'Oh, for fuck's sake . . .'

So Sean told him everything: the conversation in the pub with Susan, the meeting with Michael Mead, the pink file. Duke seemed pleased.

'You're not such a useless sod after all, are you?' he said. 'The guvnor'll be well chuffed.'

'So what should I do now?'

'Keep on the case. Let us know if anything else crops up. I'll get in touch with Mathews, let him know what's happened, see how he wants to take it from here. You just carry on as normal, unless you hear otherwise. Keep on his tail, it's more important than ever now.'

'Right.'

'Well, see you then. Keep up the good work.'

'Yeah, see you.' He hung up.

He felt disappointed. Somehow he had expected more.

A full week's boredom for that, a brief phone call with a singularly unexcited Duke.

But what more was there? What more could he expect? This was the reality of his perverse detective game. He'd find out a few things, he'd tell Mathews and that would be that. He'd go back to his old life.

To try and lift his spirits he went to Tesco's and bought himself a four-pack of Stella.

He sat on the steps at the bottom of the flats and watched some kids on the football pitch. They'd rigged up a ramp and were jumping off it on their bikes. To make it more exciting, they had forced a couple of smaller kids to lie next to it so they could jump over them too.

What now? Today had been a peak, exhilarating. He couldn't face going back to the Town Hall tomorrow and just hanging about. Why not take the rest of the week off? Duke was happy. Gatley was unlikely to rush into anything new just yet. In the meantime, he could have a few beers and spend a bit of money, make some use of the sixteen hundred pounds.

He smiled when he thought of the money.

He'd hardly spent any of it yet. Shit, he could go out to any shop and buy whatever he wanted. The only problem was, he couldn't think of anything.

Yeah, well, never mind. The money meant security.

But for how long? How much was sixteen hundred pounds these days?

Say a pint of beer was, on average, a pound. It was

actually a lot more than that in London, but it made the maths easier that way.

How many pints did he drink in a week? Perhaps three a night, more at weekends, say twenty-five pints a week. Then it would take sixty-four weeks to drink sixteen hundred pints.

Shit, the thought of it made him feel sick, sixteen hundred pints.

So if beer was a pound a pint, then he'd drink away the money in just over a year.

That wasn't such good going, especially as beer was more than a pound a pint. It was more than one pound fifty in some places. So, what would that make it? Twenty-five pints a week at one pound fifty made about a hundred and fifty pounds a month. Which meant his sixteen hundred quid would last for just over ten months, or one thousand and sixty-six pints. That was assuming he only drank twenty-five pints a week. If he was going to be honest with himself, it was probably a lot more than that. Say ... Oh, bollocks. He'd had enough maths. Suffice to say, sixteen hundred pounds didn't go very far these days.

Christ, fifty years ago he could have drunk himself to death on sixteen hundred pounds. These days it was barely enough to give him a hangover.

And that was just beer; there was food as well. Even if he cut down to twenty pints a week it'd barely last him six months.

No, when it came down to it, sixteen hundred pounds was not much. There had to be something more to it than this.

There was Susan, of course, with her big mouth and her wide blue eyes, but he might have seen her around anyway, followed her, just her, and not her stupid husband. And it wasn't as if he was ever going to talk to her, ever going to get to know her. He'd never fuck her.

So if it wasn't money, and it wasn't pleasure, what was it really all about, following Gatley? Why was he still excited by the idea of it, despite the reality?

Deep down he knew why. A vague plan was forming in his head. It had been there from the beginning, ever since Mathews had opened up to him in the Cock, and it involved something more than just following Gatley.

On Saturday morning Sean was slobbing about his flat in his underwear when George turned up. He was on his way to Islington for a drink, and he wondered if Sean wanted to come.

'Not bloody Islington,' said Sean, putting on a pair of jeans.

'What's wrong with bloody Islington?' George hadn't shaved; there was a dark smudge of growth over his grey skin.

'Oh, nothing. Are you driving?'

'Yes. You coming or not, then?' George went into the sitting-room and sat reading a paper he'd found on the stairs.

'Yeah, why not?' Sean called from the bathroom. 'What's it like out? I won't need a jacket, will I?'

'Naah, it's like the bloody south of France out there. It's not British, this weather, not British at all.'

George was right; the wind of the last couple of days had died completely and the sky was a hazy deep blue.

'Ah, yes,' said Sean, hefting a rubbish sack out the front door, 'the perfect weekend.'

'I don't like the heat,' said George, looking distastefully at the sky. 'Makes me uncomfortable.'

'You're just a slug, George.' Sean double-locked the front door.

'Give me the winter any time.' George scratched his stubble. 'It's not natural, all this heat.'

He was wearing a black suit with a white shirt and a loose grey cardigan.

'Why don't you try taking some clothes off?' Sean suggested as they clattered downstairs.

'I like wearing clothes. I need to wear clothes.'

'You're a real jerk sometimes, George, do you know that?'

'Thanks.'

When they reached the bottom, Sean hoisted the sack into a rubbish drum while George unlocked the van.

'I just have to pick John up from the Princess first,' George said, clambering in.

'John who?'

'John Buckley.'

'Fat John?'

'Yeah.'

'What you picking that git up for?'

'He may be a git but he's lending me his car for a month while he's in the States.'

'You've got the van.'

'Yeah, well, a car's a car, a van's a van. Only he's left the car in Islington and I said I'd drive him over to pick it up.'

'I hope this isn't going to turn into one of your complicated manoeuvres, George.'

'Nah, don't worry. Trust me.' George winked at him and they set off.

'You been up to anything lately?' said George as they drove out of the estate and on to the main road.

'No, nothing much. Enjoying the sun, you know.' Sean fiddled with his seat-belt, trying to tighten it.

'I wouldn't bother with that,' said George. 'One size fits all.'

He fished out a tape from the mess in the glove compartment and slotted it into the machine. Tinny African music came out of the little speaker on the floor. George sang along with the guitars and banged out a rhythm on the steering wheel.

'What about you?' Sean asked. 'How's the book coming along?'

'Haven't done a lot lately, I've been getting into model-making. You know, plastic kits, like when you were a kid.'

'You're not serious?'

'Yeah, it's great.'

'What, you mean like aeroplanes and that?'

'No, cars. I've made this E-type Jag. It's brilliant, got all the engine parts and everything. Then I found this great paint. Special metallic stuff, I can't remember what it's called, but it gives a great finish, like a real car. I've been painting everything with it. I've got a red radio, a red table-top, I'm thinking of doing me gas fire. It's very therapeutic, painting.'

'I know what you mean. I sometimes miss decorating when I'm not doing it. Hate it when I am, mind you.'

When they got to the pub, Fat John was standing outside drinking on the pavement with a couple of friends.

Fat John lived up to his name; he was fat and called John. He was about six foot tall and five foot wide, with huge sculptured sideboards, and a magnificent black quiff.

He was wearing a T-shirt with a picture of Bob Marley on it and a pair of impossibly large jeans held up with stars-and-stripes braces.

George parked the van and jumped out. Fat John saw him and came over, waving with his pint of beer.

They chatted for a while, then George opened the back of the van and John got in, still carrying his beer.

'Hello, Sean,' he said with the remains of a West Country accent. 'How's it hanging?'

'I'm fine thanks, John. How are you?'

'Cock-a-doodle-doo, mate.'

George got back in and they set off for Islington.

'You should have come last night, George,' John said, leaning forward and jamming his head between the two of them in the front. 'It was fucking hilarious. I got so pissed I tried to pick up this bloke's car on the way home.'

'What?'

'Yeah, I'd dumped me motor and I was, like, staggering along the road and this fucking Mini comes haring round the corner and nearly fucking runs me down. Screeches to a halt, and it's some fucking yuppie on his way home to the

Docklands, or somewhere, with this poncy girl. So he's sitting there going beep beep beep, and I'm standing there going, "Fuck off!"

'Well, anyway, I thought I'd show the bastard, and I grab hold of the front bumper and try to lift him up. I actually thought I could do it. I was convinced. But I just bent the bumper a bit and fell over on me arse, and Noddy drives round me and pisses off.'

'Sounds brilliant,' said George as they pulled up at some lights.

There were two drunks on the pavement having an argument. They were probably only in their thirties but they looked much older. They were clutching cans of Tennants and shoving each other. As the lights changed, one of the drunks punched the other in the face; it was a surprisingly powerful punch and it knocked the other drunk over into the road.

'Shit,' said George, driving round the body. 'Good punch.'

'Fucking hell.' Fat John laughed appreciatively.

'This country's on the way out,' said George.

'Going to the dogs, eh?' said Sean.

But George was serious. 'You wait. You may laugh now, but you just wait!'

'We're all doomed,' said Fat John with a leer. 'It's the end of the world.'

'No, I mean it,' said George, undeterred. 'It's getting like New York, or something. We've all got to get into self-defence, survivalism, it's the only answer. I mean, I live in fear right now, but when I learn self-defence it'll be different. It'll be, "Oi! Four eyes!" "Huh? You talking to me? Well, up yours, scumbag! Wham, bam, you're dead, I'm not." And you can't trace the weapon, 'cause it's my own bare hands. Fucking right. *Hiyeeeagh!*'

George let go of the wheel, flung back his arms and executed a wild karate chop, which sent the van careering across the road.

'Be careful, George.' Sean shook his head. John laughed and took a swig of beer. 'Nutcase,' he said thoughtfully.

Half-way down Upper Street they joined a queue of cars. Nobody was moving; it was deadlock.

'Now what?' said George.

'Must be an accident or something,' said John.

They sat there in the hot sun and waited, fumes rising around them into the shimmering air.

Somebody started to hoot, and a couple of other people joined them. Up ahead somebody got out of their car and looked angrily down the road.

'Look at this,' said George. 'We're witnessing the final collapse of civilization.'

'Oh, not again,' said Fat John. 'Give it a rest.'

'At any moment this traffic jam could erupt into frenzied violence.'

'Either that or it won't,' said John with a little snigger.

'You think what you like, John, but I'm going to be prepared. Self-defence, that's the answer.'

'You already told us that.'

'Kung fu. That, or a fucking enormous gun, big Magnum. Like Dirty Harry, blow a man to shit. You don't mess with a fucking Magnum.'

He held out one hand as if he was aiming a pistol and steadied his wrist with the other hand. Then he took careful aim at the back of the driver's head in the car in front. He pulled the trigger.

'Pshoo,' he said. Then 'Pshoo' again, as he began to pick off various people walking along the pavement. 'It's time somebody set about cleaning this town up. Look at these people. Pshoo. You've got to get them before they get you. Pow. Any one of them could turn nasty at any moment. Bang. Look at them. They deserve to die. Look at that bald bastard coming out of that DIY shop . . . Die, scumsucker! Kapow!'

Sean looked round and froze. Crossing the road towards them was Eric Gatley, carrying a plastic bag and chatting with Susan.

Susan was wearing a pair of tight pedal-pushers and listening intently to something that Gatley was saying. Gatley was gesticulating with a paint-brush.

'Now, you tell me,' said Fat John, 'how a prick like that gets off with a bird like that.'

'Maybe he's got money,' said George.

'Maybe he's a nice person,' said Sean.

'Hah!' said John. 'Don't make me puke He's a twat. Whoever said you can't judge a book by the cover was an idiot.'

'She *is* nice, though,' said George, 'isn't she?'

'Fucking women,' said Fat John, 'they're stupid. Look at him with his little dicky paint-brush, probably talking about politics, or crèches, or something.'

They watched as Gatley and Susan got into their car, which was parked by the side of the road.

'Cunt,' said John flatly.

Sean knew he shouldn't get involved, but Gatley and Susan were his property and he didn't like anyone else talking about them, particularly someone like Fat John. 'You don't know anything about him,' he said.

'I don't need to,' said Fat John. 'When I see a bloke with a beautiful woman like that . . .' He gestured with his pint, slopping beer down the side of Sean's seat. 'I automatically hate them, no matter what they're like.'

Gatley was having trouble getting out of the tight space into the stationary traffic. He was nudging backwards and forwards with a lot of noise and crunching of gears. Then Susan got out and started directing him and the cars in the road.

'I hate him,' Fat John went on. 'And because I hate the bloke, I reckon the woman must be stupid and all. Jesus, look at the arse on her.'

They looked. Sean didn't know what to think; he was trying hard to keep a cool head. But John was right. He'd done the same thing himself; hated Gatley for Susan.

'All wasted on him,' said John. 'Mind you, the good-looking ones never know how to fuck. You get hold of some ugly cow and she'll give you the ride of your life, she knows she's got to make an effort. But the good-looking ones, the ones like her, the stuck-up ones, they think they're too fucking good. They just lie there like a piece of cold fish. They don't need to try; they know that most men would risk their lives just to see them naked.'

'You'd know, would you, John?' said Sean, trying to sound casual. 'You'd know what she's like?' It came out sounding angry and Sean told himself to shut up.

'Oh, he's God's gift to women, didn't you know?' said George.

'That's why I hate them,' said Fat John. 'Because I'm ugly and all, so I never get a chance to shag a woman like that.'

'I thought you just said she'd be no good in the sack,' said George.

'Yeah, yeah . . . I did. I reckon that watching those two at it would be about as exciting as watching two snails fucking.'

'How do you know they're fucking?' said Sean.

'Eh?'

'They could just be friends, brother and sister. Why do you assume there has to be sex involved?'

'Of course they're fucking,' said John. 'Look at the look on his face. He's like a kid in a sweet-shop, he's never had it so good.'

Sean looked at Gatley, stuck diagonally across the road, smiling apologetically at the other cars. What kind of stupid fate had brought them here? He felt that his world had shrunk to a tiny stage: a triangle made up of Hackney, Islington and Stoke Newington, with three players, Gatley, Susan and himself. No, two players; he was the audience.

It was like George and his dogs. Once your eyes were opened to something, you couldn't help seeing it everywhere.

Maybe it was fate. Maybe he was meant to be here today with Fat John and George and Gatley and Susan. He laughed to himself; he wasn't sure he believed in fate, but now they were all here, maybe he could use it to his advantage.

Susan stretched, pulled her shirt tight across her breasts, and Sean knew he didn't want to let her out of his sight. Follow them. Yes, that was obviously what he was supposed to do. And maybe George could help.

'Why don't we find out?' Sean looked George in the eye.

'Find out what?'

'Find out the truth about them. See what he's really like. See if they're fucking.'

'Oh, yeah, and how do we do that? "Excuse me, madam, are you having sex with this man?"'

'No. We follow them.'

'Follow them. Don't be daft.'

'Why not?'

'Why not? Because . . . Well . . .' George looked at Fat John for support; John merely shrugged.

'Why not?' said Sean. 'I've done it before. It's easy.'

'You can't just follow someone.'

'Why not? It might be fun.'

'It sounds crap.'

'No, haven't you ever wondered what it'd be like? You know, tailing someone in a car, like in a film?'

'Listen,' said Fat John. 'I'd love to play silly buggers with you two, but I think I'll get out. I can walk from here.'

'All right.' George got out and opened the back door.

'I'll bring the motor round tonight,' said John, shuffling his huge body out of the cramped van.

'Yeah, see you later, then.' George banged the door shut. Sean watched John drain his beer and put the empty glass on the roof of a parked car.

'He really is an evil fat bastard,' said Sean as George got back in.

'Yeah,' said George. 'But he's got a nice car.'

John waved and sauntered off up the road.

'So what about it?' Sean asked.

'You're serious, aren't you?'

'Why not?'

'Well . . .' George looked doubtful, but Sean knew he had him.

'Well, how do we do it exactly?' George asked with a serious frown. 'How do we know we won't lose them?' He looked at the Renault.

Susan had by now got back into the car which was half

facing the other way; Gatley was waiting to pull out into the opposite lane.

'Don't worry about it,' said Sean. 'If we fuck up, so what? What have we lost?'

A gap appeared and the Renault moved off.

'Well?'

'Hold on.' George quickly glanced behind, then jerked the wheel round, slammed the car into first and cut out into the traffic. He raced across the street and into a dead-end alley.

'Jesus Christ, George,' Sean yelled.

'Relax.'

'Okay, but this isn't a car chase, just remember that.'

George reversed out into the road, then carried on after Gatley and Susan.

'Trust me. Where do you reckon they're going, then?'

'We'll see.'

Gatley was easy to follow; he drove carefully, without taking any risks, neither too fast nor too slow. He always signalled well in advance, never went through anything less than a green light, and never overtook if there wasn't plenty of room. It was textbook stuff.

George soon got the hang of it. He kept a safe distance and supplied a running commentary about exactly what he was doing and where they might be going.

They headed north across town, avoiding the West End, and as they cruised over the Westway Sean asked George about his self-defence.

'What about it?' said George, opening his window and chucking out a half-smoked cigarette.

'Well, do you actually know anything about it?'

'Of course I do. I've seen loads of films.'

'No, I mean, are you having lessons?'

'Fuck off, are you kidding? I went to an evening class once, right? Karate it was, or at least it was supposed to be. So I get there, and there's all these big fuckers, in all the gear, and there's me in this old track suit I had, with the crotch down to me knees. So then the bloke in charge rolls up, right, and he's some ex-army storm-trooper with a skinhead haircut. I mean, I was expecting some inscrutable little Jap with glasses. You know, the small and puny can overthrow the huge and mighty if they turn their strength against them, all that kind of shit. But instead of some saintly, gentle guru, there's this fucking great meat-head with an IQ of four and the sensitivity of a psychotic rhino.

'So, first thing we do is pair off for some preliminary sparring, and I'm paired up with this *thing*, this monster. I swear it was not a human being, and it proceeds to beat the living shit out of me for half an hour. Then, for a bit of a laugh, the so-called instructor announces that we're going to have a free-for-all. I mean, it was a fucking battle. It was fucking war, man. The so-called lesson consisted of everyone just basically trying to kill each other.

'It was not what I'd expected. I thought it was gonna be like, you know, that kung fu programme on the telly, all that "Snatch the pebble out of my hand, glasshopper, walk on the lice-paper", and we'd all be meditating cross-legged. All we got was a fucking pub-brawl. I had bruises all over me. I could hardly walk for a week. I had headaches, dizzy spells. I actually, seriously, lost the use of my right arm. I thought I was gonna be like that for ever, but I went down the hospital, and this crazy nurse yanked it about. Christ, it was worse than the fucking karate, but at least I could use it after.

'But I never went back for any more karate, I can tell you.'

'So how are you ever going to become a master of self-defence if you don't have any lessons?'

'Ah, fuck it. As soon as I get my hands on a fucking Magnum . . .'

They left the Westway at Shepherd's Bush and headed south-west, through Hammersmith, before eventually ending up in Fulham, quite near the football ground at Stamford Bridge. It was also, Sean realized, quite near the house where he'd met Duke.

There was something lifeless about the streets round here, and there was a lot of money in evidence, although the buildings themselves weren't any better than any other part of London.

Gatley spent some time driving around before they eventually found a parking space, and Sean and George realized that they'd have to do likewise.

'Listen,' said Sean, undoing his seat-belt, 'I'll get out, see where they're going, and then I'll meet you back here on the corner.'

'Okay. I think I saw a space just now.'

Sean jumped out and sauntered along the road. Gatley and Susan passed him on the other side, arm in arm. They marched off down the street and in a couple of minutes arrived at a junk-shop. It was the sort of place where bin-men got a price for pieces they salvaged, and builders brought in stuff they'd ripped out of houses.

There were old doors, radiators, venetian blinds, two or three fireplaces, odd chairs and bits of furniture, and the usual stacks of paperbacks, useless records and awful clothing.

Sean hung around long enough to make sure that the Gatleys would be there for some time, then hurried back to find George.

He was waiting for him on the corner, smoking a cigarette.

When they got back to the shop, they found Gatley and Susan sorting through some large mirrors with the owner, a big woman with short hair who was wearing a fisherman's jumper and a pair of high-waisted men's trousers with a leather money-pouch hanging down the front.

Gatley had a tape-measure and he was carefully checking each mirror. They were eventually left with a choice between two, and he let Susan decide. They paid the woman, then half-heartedly browsed round the rest of the shop.

In the cluttered front window were four polystyrene heads wearing hats. An elaborate woman's hat covered with dusty flowers, a couple of nondescript and rather small trilbies, and a white homburg with a black band.

Gatley saw it and put it on. He walked back and studied himself in one of the mirrors. Susan laughed. Gatley smiled at her and bought the hat.

They carried the mirror back to the car, Sean and George trailing along behind.

'It was worth it,' said George. 'Just to see him in that fucking hat.' He sniggered. 'John was right, the guy's a dick-head.'

'I think he looks sweet,' said Sean sarcastically.

'I think he looks like a dick-head.'

'Okay,' said Sean. 'I give in. You're right. The guy's a dick-head.'

When they reached the Renault, Gatley opened the back and put down the seat. Then he double-checked the opening with the tape-measure, and carefully eased the mirror in.

'Is that it, then?' said George.

'What do you reckon?'

'I don't know. I'm not sure I can stand any more excitement.'

'Come on, it wasn't that bad.'

'Hah! We never even found out if they're fucking.'

'What d'you reckon?' Sean asked.

'They're fucking,' said George. 'Married, probably with kids.'

'You'd make a good detective,' said Sean. 'Come on, looks like they'll probably just head back now.'

'Yeah, I'll take you home.'

In the van, Sean thought about his good luck. Okay, so Gatley hadn't got up to much, but you never knew, he might be able to salvage something useful from the day. The important thing was the feeling of power; power over Gatley. The little man really had been behaving well lately. Yes, all in all it had been a good week.

With the beer washing through him, he settled back in the seat and smiled. He felt good about the future.

George was silent now, engrossed in driving, as if he were playing a video game. But as they neared Hackney, he asked Sean if he wanted to come round for a smoke.

'Sure. Why not?'

Why not, indeed? Things were falling nicely into place. Everything was under control.

11

Sean was always amazed at how tidy George's flat was, especially coming into it after riding up fourteen floors in the tiny vandalized metal lift, which always stank of piss. He somehow expected him to live in squalor, but it was a clean white flat, with everything in its place. The sitting-room was large, with a light-grey carpet, and, as well as the comfortable three-piece suite, there was an expensive stereo and a new colour TV and video. Next to them, neatly stacked in a metal unit, were a home computer and a games console, with a well-ordered collection of programmes and games. One wall was completely lined with shelves, mostly full of books on a wide and bizarre range of topics. There were a few house plants here and there, and a low table with magazines on it. Along the window ledge, beneath the massive picture window with its view south towards the river, was a collection of toys.

The only untidy part was an old chipped table in one corner, the top of which was painted a vivid metallic red. George used the table as a work-bench for whatever hobby he was currently obsessed with. At the moment, it was model cars. There were two under construction, and one finished, an E-type Jaguar, painted the same gleaming red as the table-top.

The first thing George did was make a pot of tea. Then he rolled several joints, and the two of them spent a couple of hours smoking them and drinking beers from George's well-stocked fridge. They watched various bits of videos, all the short comedy items George could find. They talked a bit about the afternoon's detective work, but mostly they just giggled.

At nine, Fat John came round with a thin pale girl who looked like a junkie. She was introduced as Helen, and after saying hello she didn't speak at all.

Fat John had brought round his car, an ancient, immaculately preserved, orange Cortina with a black vinyl roof. He took George down to run through its eccentricities before handing it into his keeping. Afterwards they went to George's local, which never shut, and drank until quarter past one. Then they bought some carry-outs and went back to George's for another smoke.

Sean sat on the sofa and felt everything slowly receding from him. At some point in the early hours he passed out, a can of beer between his feet, from which he had taken exactly one sip.

He was woken at eleven by George hoovering the flat. He grinned at Sean and offered him some of his joint. Sean declined, scratched himself and drank some of the beer. It wasn't completely flat.

George had been down to the shop for the Sunday papers and some bacon, orange juice, eggs, and sliced bread for toast. They drank coffee and ate breakfast without talking. In the background, very quietly, some nineteen-forties country swing played on the CD.

After breakfast they read the papers and at half one they went to the pub. For a while Sean perked up as the alcohol reached the optimum level, then he was over the peak and a terrible tiredness settled over him.

He shuffled off to get the bus home. The journey seemed to take for ever and when he got to his flat he collapsed on to his bed and fell asleep.

Just before five he was woken by the phone. He forced himself off the bed, his head pounding, and staggered out into the hall, confused and sick.

'Hello?' Everything was grey and distant.

'Sean Crawley?'

'Uh?'

'Is that you, Crawley?'

'Yeah. Sorry, who is this?'

'Mathews. Derek Mathews. Remember me?'

'Oh, right, hello.'

'Where the fuck have you been?'

'I was out.'

'I know you were fucking out. I've been trying to get hold of you all day.'

'Yeah, sorry. I was, you know, I've been watching Gatley. Did Duke tell you what happened?'

'Yes. That's what I'm ringing about. Listen, I've got an idea, something I want you to do. But not over the phone, all right? I want to see you.'

'I thought you said, I mean, we weren't supposed to see each other.' Sean yawned and scratched his crotch.

'Yeah, well, don't worry about that. Special circumstances. This is something of an emergency.'

'Oh.'

'Don't worry about it. Listen, I'm in Kent, a place called Sevenoaks. I want you to come down here.'

'What, now?'

'Shut up and listen, all right? I'll explain.'

Two hours later, feeling numb and washed out, Sean arrived at the characterless, concrete-and-plastic railway station at Sevenoaks, in the heart of commuter land. He crossed the glass-walled footbridge and came out at the top of the car park which sloped down towards the tracks.

It was a warm, clear evening, very calm and peaceful after the turmoil of Waterloo and the dirty, rattling train.

Sean hadn't been waiting more than about five minutes when a fat, maroon Rover silently drove up and stopped. He recognized Mathews as he leant over to open the passenger door.

Sean got in.

'Train on time?' said Mathews.

'Yes.' Sean fastened his seat-belt, though he noticed that Mathews just rested his across his belly without securing it. 'I just got here.'

'Good.' There was the sweet, warm smell of alcohol coming from Mathews, mingled with stale sweat and the relaxing aroma of old leather seats.

Mathews was breathing noisily through his nose and licking his lips. He looked rumpled, as if he'd been up all night, or had slept in his clothes. Sean was glad he'd had time for a quick, scalding bath before he'd come out.

Mathews put the car in gear and they moved off.

'You sure this is okay?' said Sean, staring out at the wide sedate streets of small offices and neat shops, as the car cruised on without making a sound.

'Don't you worry about it,' said Mathews.

'I'm not worried, Mr Mathews, it was you that made the rule.'

'Right, so I can break it.' He turned and leered at Sean, his face bloated and red. 'I'm the boss, right?'

'Yeah,' said Sean. 'So what is it you want?'

'Patience, Crawley. All in good time.'

'Where we going?'

'You're full of questions, aren't you?'

'It's my job.'

'Yeah, I forgot. S. Crawley, Private Detective.' Mathews started to laugh and it turned into a cough.

He picked up a gold packet of Benson & Hedges from the seat and put a cigarette in his mouth, then pushed in the lighter on the dashboard and carried on speaking, the unlit cigarette waggling between his lips.

'Have you eaten?'

'No.'

'Well, that's where we're going. Chinese all right?'

'Sure.'

The lighter popped out and Mathews put it to the end of his cigarette. He puffed a few times, then, satisfied that it was properly alight, inhaled deeply.

'Look at this fucking place,' he said. 'It's like toy-town. All these old buildings, it's like, if you were going to make a film about England, you'd make it somewhere like this, wouldn't you? Nice. That's what it is, nice. But this isn't

England.' Mathews stared out at the tidy, deserted streets. 'Not the England I live in. Not the real England. Oh shit!'

'What?'

'Bollocks, gone straight past it.'

Without hesitating, Mathews did a U-turn, then sped back down the street and steered into the car park at the side of a modern building whose ground floor was taken up by the Jade Garden, Traditional Chinese Restaurant.

'Here we go, then,' said Mathews, opening the door. 'Flying tonight, velly good Alsation wiv noodle. Hung-Lo, ploplieter.' Laughing wheezily, he clambered out of the car and threw away his half-smoked cigarette.

He looked up and down the road as he locked his door.

'Sunday night in the mausoleum,' he said.

He tightened his tie and put an arm round Sean's shoulders to lead him indoors. Sean looked at the big hand resting on his shirt; it was stained yellow around the fingers.

'Come on, my son,' said the builder, enveloping Sean in a cloud of whisky and bad breath, 'let's get some chow mein down us.'

The restaurant was not even half full and they were immediately seated by an efficient young Chinese man.

'You want a menu?' Mathews asked, thrusting one at Sean. 'I always have the same thing myself. Sweet and sour pork balls, special flied lice, chicken chow mein and a curry. Sounds a lot, but an hour later you feel hungry, eh?' He nodded at Sean as if he'd offered him a startling insight. Sean forced a smile and studied the menu.

'Something to drink?' Mathews asked, leaning back in his chair and looking around for the waiter.

'Just a lager, please.'

Mathews spotted the young man and beckoned him over.

'Two pints of lager while we're waiting, John,' he said, and the waiter noted it down.

They sat in silence until their drinks arrived, then they ordered their meals. As soon as the waiter left, Mathews drained half his glass in one long gulp.

'Ah, that's better.' He loosened his belt and got comfortable in his seat.

'So, how's it going, then?'

'You mean with . . . with Gatley?' Sean said cautiously.

'Yes, Gatley. Look, no one's listening to us here, they've got their own conversations to worry about. Relax, enjoy yourself.' He swallowed some more beer. 'Tell me what's what.'

Sean repeated what he'd told Duke, though in slightly more detail. When he'd finished, Mathews looked thoughtful.

'Does this mean you're in trouble?' Sean said.

'Not necessarily. Not necessarily, no, but that's why I wanted to see you. We've got to change our plans.'

'How?'

'I'm not completely sure yet, but I'm working on it.' He winked at Sean.

'What sort of thing did you have in mind?'

'Well, we need a way of stopping all this getting any further. Ah, good.'

The food arrived, and Mathews ordered two more beers.

'You doing all right for money?'

'Sure,' said Sean.

'Never say that,' said Mathews. 'Never turn down money. If someone offers, you take it. That's what this is all about, really, money, good old money. The root of all evil. That's what they say, isn't it? But it also makes the world go round, eh?' Mathews winked.

'I thought that was love,' said Sean.

'Eh?'

'Love makes the world go round.'

'Bollocks, it's money. Take it from me. You know the song, from that Liza Minnelli film, the one about poofs and that.'

'*Cabaret?*'

'Yeah.' He began to sing. 'Money makes the world go round, the world go round, world go round. Money makes the world go round, in the most delightful way, ting-a-ling. There you are, proof.'

Mathews speared a pork ball, shoved it in his mouth and carried on speaking while he chewed it. 'And all this round here, see' – he gestured in a general fashion with his fork – 'this is where the money is. Now you talk about me being bent, but I got nothing on this lot. They're a million times worse. That's how they got where they are. Thing is, they've got away with it. Yeah . . .'

Mathews sniffed and looked out of the window; he seemed genuinely upset. Sean thought it best not to say anything.

'What's crime, Crawley?' Mathews said presently. 'What's right and wrong? I don't fucking know.'

'No such thing really,' said Sean. 'As you say, people would do anything if they thought they could get away with it.'

'You reckon? What about you, then? How far would you go?'

Sean shrugged.

'Would you rob a bank, for instance?' Mathews shovelled a forkful of food into his mouth. 'If you thought you could get away with it . . .'

'Yeah, if I thought there was no risk of getting caught I would. But the thing is, I would get caught. I mean, I'm not a bank robber, am I? It's too much of a risk.'

'What about mugging, then? Why not mug old ladies? That's easily done. You ever thought of that?'

'Of course,' Sean said. 'You see some old dear cashing her pension, frail, weak, scared little thing, you think, all I've got to do is grab that bag and leg it. But then you think some more. What if someone sees you? What if, just as you grabbed the bag and pushed her aside, a police car comes round the corner? I wouldn't last five minutes in prison. No, it's not worth it for what, twenty quid? Thirty quid?'

'That's sick, Crawley. People who mug old ladies are the lowest form of scum.'

'What about you?'

'What d'you mean?'

'What about your substandard buildings in Hackney?

97

What about all those old ladies' homes you fuck over and botch up? Put in the wrong radiators, wind whistling through cracks in the walls, repairs needing doing after six weeks. What about that, eh? How's that different?'

'Well, I'm sorry, but it is different. They're not terrorized, they're not beaten up. Have you seen some of those pictures? It's sick.'

'It's the same, it's exactly the same. They get draughts, they can't afford the heating. You know the joke, what's blue and fucks old ladies?'

'Hypothermia,' said Mathews, and he laughed.

'Quite,' said Sean. 'Hackney's falling down around them, they get depressed, they die.'

'It's not that fucking bad.'

'It is, though, in the long run. You see, in the end you're just part of the chain, with muggers at one end, stockbrokers round here at the other, and hypothermia as the end-result. Whose money do you think you're ripping off, for fuck's sake? Little old ladies'.'

'It's still not the same as beating the shit out of them.'

'It's connected. Everybody screwing everybody else, as Duke would say.'

'So I'd be stupid not to join in.'

'Yeah.'

'And you reckon all crime's the same? Mugging's no worse than cooking the books?'

'Right, the end-result's the same.' Sean looked at Mathews. When was he going to get to the point? He didn't like his habit of endlessly skirting round the issue. His brain felt battered from the weekend; he was coping, but he felt detached; everything was slow and fuzzy.

'Okay, then,' said Mathews carefully, the words seeming to take for ever to come out. 'If all crimes are basically the same, if that's what you're saying . . .'

'Yeah.'

'Then that would mean that murder's no worse than stealing?'

'Sure.'

Mathews laughed. 'So you'd be all right about murdering someone?'

'Under the right conditions, yes.'

'And what are the right conditions?'

'Okay. One.' Sean perked up, things were moving again. 'There would have to be no possible chance of my getting caught, or even suspected.'

'Right, we've covered that.'

'Then I'd have to be sure I was physically safe. I wouldn't want to put myself in any danger, from the victim or anyone else who might be around. So I'd have to be in a guaranteed superior position.'

'What, you mean stronger?'

'One way or another. Better weapons than the enemy, surprise, whatever . . .'

'Okay.'

'Right. Four . . .'

'What happened to three?' said Mathews with a frown.

'We've done three.'

'What was it?'

'It doesn't matter. Three, then, which is probably part of number two, actually. I'd have to be a hundred per cent sure I could actually carry it out. It would have to be a sure-fire method of killing.' Sean paused. 'What number am I at?'

'Fuck knows,' said Mathews. 'You lost me round about three.'

'We'll call it five. Point five, a reason. A reason why I was going to kill.'

'Such as?'

'It could be anything: revenge, self-defence, reward . . .'

'Reward?'

'Yes, if there was a sufficient personal reward for doing it.'

'We're back to money, then?'

'Not necessarily. It could be power, pleasure, I don't know, to prove a point . . .'

'And motive's the last consideration, is it?'

'The order's not important. But I'd have to be completely covered. I mean, the best way is, of course, random. Like, say, you're walking down Oxford Street on a Saturday afternoon, and you just stick a knife in a passer-by and walk on. You're immediately lost in the crowd, and how could you ever be linked to the victim? The main problem with that, though, is there's no real reason for doing it.'

'Would you do it if someone offered you five thousand pounds, say?'

'No. Not enough. Not worth the risk. I could earn that in six months if I took a permanent job. An ordinary, safe job.'

'Ten grand, then? I mean, what price would you do it for?'

'Certainly not less than fifteen, it wouldn't be worth it. Twenty, maybe.'

Mathews looked at him, picking his teeth with his tongue.

'For twenty grand you'd kill someone? Just like that?'

'Yeah. Why not?'

12

As they were leaving the restaurant, Sean realized that the fuzziness was gone, his mind was clear. He'd passed beyond drunkenness; he felt detached and cool, as if his body was on automatic and he was a pilot, sitting back inside the skull, watching the world go by.

'Fancy a pint?' Mathews asked. Sean inadvertently glanced at the car.

'I can drive the bastard with my eyes shut.' Mathews opened the door. 'Come on,' he said, 'I'll show you something.'

Sean said nothing and got in the passenger side.

Mathews belched, then cleared his throat as if he was getting ready to spit. He swallowed and exhaled loudly, then started the engine and quickly reversed into the road.

They drove through town in silence. The engine was so quiet and the streets so empty, it was a while before Sean realized just how fast they were going.

They were heading into a more residential part of town. After a while they turned off into a tree-lined road with a park on one side. Sean looked at the name: Blackhall Lane.

There was a row of smaller avenues off to the left, and Mathews drove up one of them.

'This is it,' he said. 'This is the money.'

Those houses that Sean could see, set back behind tall hedges, in orderly gardens, were large, expensive, English family homes, each one different, some red-brick, some mock-Tudor, some plain-stone, all solid and traditional.

'Twenty grand to kill someone,' said Mathews, 'but one of these bastards would set you back half a million. Do you know how many people you'd have to knock off to buy one of these?'

'I could always invest my money wisely.'

'Yeah,' said Mathews, 'you could put it in a building society.' He shook with laughter. 'But do you really think,' he asked, once he'd got over his joke, 'do you seriously think you'll ever live in a house like this?'

'Who says I'd want to?'

'Don't give me that shit. Everybody wants to be rich, live in a big house, not worry about things. I know the sort of dump you live in, I grew up in something like that. Don't try and tell me anyone actually wants to live in one of them places. Christ, what do you think all this is about? It's about the difference between your shit-hole and a fucking castle round here. I mean, to look at me in this suit and this flash motor, you'd think I've never had to worry about money, but you'd be wrong, see? I mean, I don't talk posh or nothing, so I suppose that's a bit of a give-away, but we were poor when I was a kid, dirt poor, and in them days poor was poor. Now that does something to you.'

He looked out at the parade of houses, as they silently cruised the maze of roads.

'Everyone was poorer then, of course, and the war didn't help. Grew up in the blitz, Isle of Dogs. Me old man was a docker, worked in the docks all through the war. Too important, see, too important to go and fight. And the fifties weren't much better. Worse, probably. Terrible time to be growing up, no money, no food, nothing. It was like they said, what was the point of winning the war if you had to live like that afterwards? I didn't get much schooling, I'd bunk off all the time, hang around the docks. That's all I wanted, see? To be a man, like the other men.'

Sean looked at Mathews. He wasn't really talking to him. He was drunk and nostalgic, talking to himself, driving aimlessly around.

'But one day, I must have been about fourteen, me dad caught me, should have been in school, gave me the hiding of me life. Then he told me something, something I'll never forget.'

Mathews stopped the car and turned off the engine. It was almost dark outside, but the street lights hadn't come on yet. Sean was alone with Mathews's voice.

'I can remember him, walking among all those big ships. It was like the centre of the world to me, but he saw something that I didn't. "See this, see all this?" he said. "This whole place is dying, rotting. You can smell the stink of it. It's over. It's over and I'm glad."

'This is my old man telling me this, a docker born and bred. Our whole family, for as long as anyone could remember we'd lived there. All the families was like that, proper little community it was, and here was my own father telling me it was finished.

'"There's no future here," he said. "Hitler started it, but it'll be finished one day. It may be ten years, it may be twenty, it may even be fifty years, but it's going." And he was right; what Hitler started, the LDDC is finishing. They're building a whole new city on top of the place.

'He used to tell me it was the best education a man could have, working there, and it had taught him one thing, I suppose, that it was all changing, the world was changing, and it was the working man who was gonna be shat on, as usual.

'"Ray," he says to me, "you've got to get out." And I was shocked, I didn't know what to think. Everything had been so clear-cut, I knew it all. Then suddenly, I knew nothing. I'm standing there with a fucking stranger.

'You've got to understand, you see, Crawley, in those days you'd no sooner leave the Island than you'd marry a nigger. This was all new to me.

'But I left, I did what I was told and I never looked back. 'Cause he'd shown me a very important thing; things change, and you've got to change with 'em. You can't sit still and expect the world to go on the same old way, day in, day out. You can't rely on nothing, or no one. And that's what I done. I done it myself, Crawley, I made myself.

'I left the Island, started up labouring. Got to know the business. Worked me way up. Soon I had me own business, doing well. I didn't get married straight away like some of them. I worked. Twenty-four hours a day, seven days a week. Plus I wanted to have me fun, there was birds everywhere in them days. No, didn't marry till later. Three kids, two girls and a boy. Me eldest daughter's going to university. I've done all right. You should see my place. It's not like one of these, but it's big; four bedrooms, big garden, kids need that. Plus I've just bought a place in the country, Suffolk, very nice. It's falling down but I'm working on it, old farmhouse. And when it's done, me and the wife will . . . me and the wife will . . .'

Mathews fell silent. He looked straight ahead, momentarily lost in private thoughts, seemingly transfixed by a house down the road. A big, solid, English house, with a pointed red roof and picture-book windows. Sean wondered if perhaps their drive here hadn't been completely random after all. He looked at the house for clues, but there were none.

Then Mathews came out of his trance, rubbed his face with his hands, took out a cigarette, pushed in the lighter and started the engine.

'Come on, let's go and have a drink,' he said. 'It stinks round here.'

They headed back towards Blackhall Lane.

'A working man, Crawley,' Mathews said, shifting up a gear. 'That's me. My whole fucking life working, building up a business. A bloody good business. A bloody good life I got now, a family. And I don't intend to just –' he paused, then went on, his voice distorted with anger and bitterness '– to just throw it all away!'

'You mean Gatley?'

But Mathews evidently hadn't heard. He turned to Sean; there were tears in his eyes. 'They can't do this to me. It's not right. They can't treat me like shit. After all these years. Well, I'm going to fix them.'

'That's what I mean. You want me to do something about Gatley?'

'Gatley?' Mathews was momentarily confused. Then things clicked into place. 'Oh, yeah. Gatley.' He accelerated into Blackhall Lane, and sped along the narrow road. 'Don't you worry,' he said, 'we'll fix them.'

At the end of Blackhall Lane they came out on to a large unkempt green surrounded by woodland. On one side there was an old pub, the White Hart.

Several expensive cars were parked outside, and smart young people sat around wooden tables.

Mathews flamboyantly swung the Rover into a space and switched off the engine.

'Once more into the breach,' he said, closing his window, and they got out.

They pushed through a loose gaggle of well-spoken youths discussing cricket, banks and the sixth form.

Inside, the low ceiling was supported by authentic-looking black beams, and on the walls hung the predictable horse brasses and hunting gear.

More well-dressed people, of all ages though mostly young, sat around on velvet seats.

Mathews bought the drinks and they managed to find an empty table near the fruit machine.

'Gatley's your problem,' said Sean.

'Yeah . . . Gatley,'

'Obviously you'd prefer it if he'd never started work at the council.'

'Obviously.'

'And now you'd prefer it if he no longer did.'

'Yes, obviously.'

'And you were wondering if maybe I had any ideas as to how he might be persuaded not to work there any more?'

'That's the gist of it.'

13

'Let me tell you a story, Crawley. Once upon a time there was this girl. She was a lovely sweet thing with the face of a little cherub. She was eighteen, though she looked about fifteen. I met her about ten years ago; she was looking for a job, secretary. Well, she was no fucking use as a secretary but she had other uses, and, I don't mind telling you, I fell head over heels in love with her. I'd have done anything for that girl. But it was difficult, you see. She lived at home with her family and I was, well, I was married, wasn't I? But, you know, we was going through a difficult time, you understand. There was nothing wrong with what I was doing. She was so nice and innocent, it was just like being, well, it was like being young again, like a teenager. But there was nowhere for us to go to, like, you know, sleep together. I didn't want to go to a hotel, it would have been, you know, sordid, 'cause it wasn't like that with her.

'Anyway, to get to the point, one night I couldn't wait any longer, so I arranged with one of the lads who worked for me that I could borrow his place. Pretend it was mine, you see?

'So I get the keys, and take Sam back there. Samantha, the girl, you understand? But when we get there, there's this fucking dog, a little mongrel thing, and he's jumping up and yapping and wagging his tail. And, well, Sam starts paying more attention to him than she does to me. But at last I get her into the bedroom and I start in on her, but the fucking dog starts barking his head off and, like, scrabbling at the door, and Sam starts giggling, and everything's going wrong. So I go out and I whack the little fucker and tell him to shut up, and he goes off whimpering into the corner with his tail between his legs. I go back in to Sam, all smiles, but no sooner is the door shut than he starts up again, scrabbling and scratching, and going yap-yap-yap. So I get up and boot him into the kitchen, but it's only a small place and he's barking louder than ever. Well, fuck him, I think, he's only a dog. So I go out, I pick him up, and I break the fucker's neck, snap, just like that. And I go back and I have one of the best nights of my life, 'cause that Samantha turns out to be a right dirty cow.

'But that's the point of my story, you understand? Sometimes, to get what you want you've got to be a little bit ruthless, and if there's some insignificant little wanker in your way, you sometimes have to remove them. Like the dog, and like Samantha, 'cause I tell you, she was a fucking hopeless secretary. That's how I've lived my life, and that's why I'm still around today to tell you about it. But it's not wrong, is it? Because, in the long run, there's things more important.'

'Yeah,' said Sean, and he smiled.

Money and death, sex and shit, power and destruction. It was a pretty small world, really. He looked round at the other people in the pub; they were miles away. They were a bad soap opera he was watching. Their loud voices blathered on, but they were stupid, they didn't see the heart of things.

He excused himself and went for a piss.

There was a bloke in the toilet, younger than Sean, in a white tuxedo and crisp Italian jeans. He was leaning against the wall, swaying slightly, and pissing in bursts and dribbles.

'Bloody hell,' he said without looking up. His voice slurred.

'Yeah,' said Sean quietly.

'Whooh! There goes all my money,' said the boy. 'Lovely, lovely money, down the drain. Tinkle-tinkle.'

'Plenty more where that came from, eh?' said Sean.

'Plenty more, loads more, loads and loads of lovely money, and I shall be drunk for ever. For ever and ever.'

Sean did up his flies, walked over to the boy, hooked his foot around his shin and pulled away his support.

Still pissing, the bloke yelled and slipped down into the gutter.

'Whoops-a-daisy,' said Sean. 'You want to watch yourself.'

He washed his hands, checked himself in the mirror, and went back to Mathews.

'Feel better for that?' Mathews asked.

'Much.'

'We understand each other, don't we, Crawley? Enterprise and initiative, mind your back and sod the rest of them.'

Sean watched as two young men went into the toilet, laughing.

Mathews went on. 'Thing is, you've done good for me, good work, and now I'm in the position to offer you a pay rise; a promotion, if you like.'

'What sort of pay rise might we be looking at here, Mr Mathews?'

'Well. The figure of twenty grand has been discussed, but I'm afraid that's out of the question. I can't go that high.'

'How high can you go?'

'Ten.'

'I explained my conditions. Make it fifteen.'

'That'll be difficult.'

'It's a difficult job.'

'Not for a man of your talents. It's a cinch. Twelve.'

'No less than fifteen.'

'Twelve – all right, thirteen, that's a lucky number.'

'Yeah. I like the sound of that.'

'It's a deal, then?'

'All right. When would you want it done?'

'A.s.a.p., obviously.'

'And the money?'

'Five now, the rest when you do it. How does that sound?'

'What do you mean by "now"?'

'Tuesday. It'll take me a day to get the cash together.

Now, you're sure you understand the exact nature of your employment?'

'I think so. There's a barking dog you want dealt with.'

'That's about the length of it.'

The two blokes that Sean had seen going into the toilet now came out again, no longer laughing. They were supporting the drunk between them. He was soaked all down the front and right-hand side, and his head was bleeding.

He was crying and his eyes, which had become very small in his white face, were unfocused. His head lolled round as if he was trying to see something, and then he caught sight of Sean.

'That's him there,' he mumbled.

He tried to stand upright and break away from the other two. He lurched against Sean's table.

'Is he all right?' Sean asked one of the embarrassed friends.

'You b-bastard, I'll kill you.'

'What happened?' Sean said.

'Dunno,' said one of the friends. 'He's drunk.'

'He was asleep on his feet when I was in there,' Sean said. 'Is he okay?'

'You f-fucking maniac,' the drunk shouted. By now everyone was watching.

'Come on, Julian,' one of his supporters said. 'We'd better get you to a hospital.'

'Not in my car,' said the other friend. 'He stinks.'

'We'll take his car, then.'

Julian tried to break free and have a go at Sean. 'He did it, he fucking did it!'

'Come on, Julian. Sorry about this, mate.'

They left, surrounded by friends and girl-friends, excited and concerned, half serious and half laughing, shaking their heads.

'What was all that about?' said Mathews.

'Must have fallen over in the toilet.'

'That's the trouble with kids these days, they all drink too much.'

On the way to the station they organized Sean's payment. Tuesday lunch-time he was to go into the Blue Posts on Tottenham Court Road. Mathews would be in there with the money in an envelope, but they wouldn't talk. At two o'clock, having first made sure it was empty, Mathews would go into the toilet. Sean was to follow him in. The envelope would change hands in the toilet, and Mathews would leave first and walk straight out of the pub. Sean was to stay for at least a quarter of an hour. If either of them had a problem, they shouldn't turn up.

It seemed straightforward enough; Sean had by now consumed so much alcohol that everything seemed perfectly reasonable. He hardly noticed the journey back to London. The beer had finally got the better of him, and his mind was working overtime.

He'd started planning the job already.

The first problem was how to do it.

Certainly not with any weapon that could be traced. The best thing would be to use something he found at the time, perhaps even something of Gatley's.

Right.

When?

Wednesday would be the best time. It was Gatley's afternoon off; he'd go home to an empty house.

That was providing, of course, that Gatley's actions always followed a set pattern.

Of course they did.

Sean had watched the bloke long enough to realize his whole life was habit and routine. Just over two weeks, and he felt as if he'd got to know everything there was to know about this uncomplicated man.

So Gatley could be relied on. That was the one thing he was sure of.

Wednesday, then. He would do it at home, Gatley's home, not out in the open.

What about Susan?

That was a mistake. He immediately wished he hadn't thought about her; it always caused his thinking to go rushing out of control. All he could see now was her face, as he had done that first day, but now the look was anger, hatred, the look of an enraged parent, telling him off, scolding him, superior.

You silly boy, you silly little boy. Bad. Bad. Bad.

He tried changing her back into a sex object, but she had the better of him.

Don't think about her, stick to the point.

It was too late, his confidence had gone. Things didn't seem so clear and easy. Doubts crept in.

He remembered before, in the stillness of Mathews's parked car off Blackhall Lane, a moment of confusion. Mathews had said something, something about his childhood, which had disturbed him. What was it? Something his father had said to him. He couldn't think, he couldn't recall it.

He'd drunk too much. He wasn't thinking straight; it was stupid. He had to take control. Things were going too fast. It was a bobsleigh run through the dark.

Since starting the job, he'd been drinking a hell of a lot more than usual. But sod it, he could do what he wanted. There was no Annie there to give him a hard time when he rolled home pissed, or to make snide comments if he ordered an extra pint when the bell sounded for last orders.

He was his own man, no one was watching him; he was responsible to no one.

Least of all Susan.

Jesus, Gatley. I hope you're fucking her now. Make the most of her while you can.

Because in three days' time you'll be dead.

Why?

Sean had a headache.

Hard as he tried, he couldn't stop the question from sneaking into the front of his thoughts.

Why did Eric Gatley have to die?

Sean knew why he wanted to kill him, his reasons were sound, but that wasn't the same thing. And he knew why Mathews wanted him dead. That made sense as well.

But what reason was there for Eric Gatley himself to die? What had he done to make it inevitable? What was there in him that made him deserve it?

He'd stumbled across a scandal. So what?

He was too dull and unattractive for his wife. But was that enough to die for? After all, he seemed to be a good husband and father.

There had to be a good reason for everything. He just couldn't think of one at the moment. Not one good strong reason.

Shit, what difference did it make? These things happened.

Gatley wasn't significant. Who cared if he lived or died?

Sean would find a reason. It would come.

Sooner or later it would come. It had to.

14

He awoke on Monday in a depression of anticlimax, with a black hangover. He couldn't properly wake up, yet he felt a crazy compulsion that threatened at any moment to break out into frantic activity. He wanted to do everything now, he couldn't wait. He felt that if he didn't move quickly and get it over with, he'd never do it at all.

He told himself to slow down, to take things steady. Do it properly. There were still things to be done, loose ends to tie up.

One thing at a time.

He wouldn't bother with Gatley today, his fate was sealed. Today he had to check on Susan. She was the only unknown factor.

He cycled to Canonbury Road and waited for her.

She came out just after eleven, wearing a man's grey suit and carrying a worn leather brief-case.

She walked and he followed, the pain of the hangover drifting away.

Susan, with her hair tied up, her hips swaying, walking fast in the morning sunlight.

Gatley, your wife walks out in the world, and you don't know it. There's a body beneath those clothes, skin and flesh, muscles and bone.

What is it like when you both stand naked? Can you bear to compare your flesh?

Look at her. She was the best thing you ever had.

Forget him, forget Gatley for today. Look at Susan.

Susan swinging her hips, Susan skipping down from the

pavement into the road. Susan leading him through the back streets of Islington, his eyes on her back. Susan baring her teeth as she comes.

In a few minutes they arrived at a converted church behind Essex Road.

There was a dirty, faded banner strung up above the entrance, white letters on a red background: 'St Luke's Theatre'.

Susan went inside and Sean hung about to wait and see what happened. When she hadn't come out after a few minutes, he went in.

This part of the church functioned as a reception area. A thin man with a trim beard sat behind a counter sorting through a pile of papers.

There were posters and leaflets everywhere, for theatres, galleries, women's self-defence groups, concerts. All small, and local, and struggling for money.

Sean loitered for a while, then picked up a leaflet for their current production and went back out into the sunlight.

On a bench opposite he sat down to read the leaflet.

The play was *Agamemnon*, performed by an avant-garde German theatre group. But Sean wasn't interested in that; he was searching through the names of the theatre's staff printed at the end of the hand-out.

And there was Susan's.

Susan Gatley, Assistant Finance Director.

How easy it was, he thought, being a detective.

He basked in the sun, idly scanning the rest of the hand-out, and wondering whether he should wait for her. She only worked part-time, that much he knew, but he had no idea what her hours might be.

He decided to have a look round the area, perhaps pick up some of the things he needed for Wednesday.

He walked down to Essex Road and bought a small bottle of Lucozade. He drank it strolling along until he found what he was looking for, a Help the Aged shop.

He went in and poked around among the drab piles of

clothes and unwanted junk. The first thing he found, in a large box at the back, was a white, slightly scratched crash-helmet. He tried it on; it was a bit loose, but that didn't matter.

He took it to the old woman at the cash register.

'I don't suppose you've got any gloves to go with this, have you? You know, like motor-cycle gloves, gauntlets.'

'I don't know, dear. I'll have a look for you.'

It was agony, watching her slowly sort through all the places he'd just looked, but he didn't like to say anything.

To kill time he browsed through the usual selection of books.

In the end another old woman appeared, and they had a conference. Then the second old woman went out the back and reappeared with a large pair of sturdy, imitation-leather gloves, which she gave to the first old woman.

'Are these what you mean, dear?'

'Yes, they're ideal.' Sean picked up a copy of *Diamonds are Forever* and took it over to her. 'How much for the lot?'

After a few moments' deliberation she gave him a price, and he paid.

'Do you want a bag? Or are you going to wear it?'

'A bag, please, if you've got one.'

She found a large Dickins & Jones carrier-bag and carefully fitted the helmet, gloves and book into it.

He bought himself a turkey salad roll in the sandwich shop next door and sat outside at a little round iron table, watching the cars go by.

There are some days when you just feel happy; no worries, no problems. You can just sit down somewhere and feel great, at one with the world.

It was turning into one of those days. His blood was hot, still laced with alcohol, his muscles lazy. Idle thoughts of Susan flicked through his mind. He wondered if he should go back to the theatre.

Yeah, he could buy some cans and go and read the book on the bench.

Twenty minutes later, he was popping the ring-pull of a

can of Foster's. He took a long cold swallow, then put the can down, stretched out his legs, tilted his head back in the sun and rested his hands on the bench, palms upward.

He had no idea when he fell asleep, but it was nearly five when he woke up again.

He felt awful, as if he'd been shut up in an oven. His skin was itchy, his throat dry, his neck agonizingly stiff.

He swore and rubbed his thighs, and a wave of nausea passed over him. He dropped his head between his knees.

Then he heard footsteps and looked up.

It was Susan; she passed about two feet in front of him.

He blushed and became drenched in sweat, even though there was no reason why she should have noticed him.

He waited for her to get well ahead and then followed her home, cursing himself as an idiot. All good feelings had gone. He just wanted it over and done with.

He watched her go into the house.

He'd had enough; he felt tired and dirty. He went home and had an almost unbearably hot bath.

As he lay in the steaming water, the happiness he'd felt earlier soaked back into him and he sweated the blackness out. He was calm again, but he knew he'd have to do something about his wildly varying moods.

After his bath he put on a pair of track-suit trousers and had something to eat.

His next thought was to go to the pub, but he fought the impulse.

No more drink. He had to get himself straight. He must be clean, healthy, and clear-headed.

Yes, get fit.

He did thirty press-ups and thirty sit-ups, with his feet jammed under an armchair.

Then what?

He read some of the James Bond book.

Time passed very slowly. In the back of his mind was the constant thought of drink.

He needed a drink.

Shit, he wasn't an alcoholic. He could do without it.

But he *did* want a drink.

Forget it. It'd pass. It had to pass. Wait for the alcohol to drain out of the system.

He looked at the phone and willed it to ring. If only George would call, ask him to go down the pub, take the decision out of his hands.

It didn't ring.

He watched television, but there wasn't much on.

He watched a science programme about DNA. He didn't understand it.

He wanted a drink.

Ten o'clock, ten thirty. At last, eleven, no chance of a drink.

He drank a pint of water and went to bed.

He read for an hour or so, then turned out the light and tried to sleep, but he couldn't stop thinking; it was like someone had turned the volume control of his brain full on. His head was crowded out with thoughts. One thought led to another, then back, then round, mad circles and spirals, worries amplified out of all proportion, memories, mathematical problems, shopping lists, DNA, beer.

No beer!

James Bond.

He turned the light back on and read some more. The book became more and more preposterous. He became more and more furious.

In the end he threw the book aside and turned out the light.

He tried to sleep again, but immediately the whirlpool started up again. Eventually, however, he found that he could keep everything quiet by concentrating very hard on just one thing. The best was the DNA chain, turning endless colourful computer-generated spirals in his brain. At last he sank into oblivion.

The next day he felt worse than ever. Utterly weak. He couldn't wake up, he couldn't get out of bed, he couldn't get dressed, he couldn't wash, he couldn't eat. But most of all he couldn't face going to Islington, or Stoke Newington.

But he ought to check. Did Susan go home for lunch?

Fuck it, she worked part-time, she wouldn't necessarily follow the same routine from day to day anyway.

He had to stop thinking about it or he'd never do it.

In the end it was getting on time to go and meet Mathews and pick up the money. He forced himself out of the flat and walked down to Mare Street, where he got a 55 into town.

He was early, so he went to an arcade and spent an hour playing Nemesis. He flew his spaceship, picking up more and more weaponry and blasting enemy ships and gun emplacements, but there was one point he couldn't get past. Huge Easter Island heads appeared, spewing out fireballs. Every time he got trapped, and clusters of fireballs would home in on him from all sides until he was overwhelmed. With no way out he would disappear in a flash of white light. He had to stop himself in the end, or he'd have been there all day, growing more and more frustrated and irrational.

The Blue Posts, at the south end of Tottenham Court Road, was a small, dark pub with a low ceiling and a mixed clientele of office workers, shop workers, labourers, fashionably dressed young people and one or two drunks.

Sean went in and ordered a pint. He knew it would upset his non-drinking regime, but this was work.

As he stood at the bar he casually looked around for Mathews. He soon saw him sitting in a booth with an open brief-case on the table, studying some papers.

Sean played the fruit machine for a few minutes, then sat and read his book.

At just after two Mathews packed up his stuff, finished his drink and went into the toilet. Sean waited a minute, then followed him.

Mathews was at the urinal, having a piss. He nodded as Sean came in.

'All right?'

'Yeah.' Sean decided he might as well take a leak as well, now that he was here.

'Tomorrow,' he said without looking round at Mathews.

'Good.' Mathews shook himself off, did up his flies and took a battered brown envelope from inside his jacket.

'I had a bit of a problem getting the cash. It's not quite as much as we talked about. Just cash-flow, you know, nothing to worry about. I'll get the rest for you all right.' He thrust the envelope into Sean's hand with an ingratiating grin.

Before Sean had a chance to say anything, someone else came into the toilet and Mathews hurried out.

Feeling like a mug, Sean washed his hands and went back to his drink. Mathews had already gone.

Well, there was nothing he could do about it now. He'd just have to trust him.

He stayed in the pub another half-hour, then went down to Oxford Street, where he bought a Big Mac and chips.

He sat at one of the tables to eat, but didn't really taste it.

When he'd eaten he went into the toilet, locked himself in a cubicle and opened the envelope. It contained two thousand nine hundred and five pounds in mostly large denominations. It was over two grand short, but it would have to do to be going on with.

He thought he might have a look round, see if there was anything he wanted to buy with all this cash, but everywhere was packed, and he couldn't face going into any of the stores.

There were still things he needed for Wednesday, however, so he headed towards Charing Cross Road. As he made his way through the underpass beneath Centre Point, he noticed an old black derelict and an idea came to him. The derelict was shouting incoherent obscenities at a couple of tourists, following them the length of the miserable concrete tunnel. Every now and then he turned his back on them, bent over, flipped his dirty grey coat up over his arse and made farting noises.

He was ideal.

Sean held back, waited. The tourists scampered up the steps at the other end. There was no one else around. He hurried over to the derelict.

'How'd you like a couple of quid?' he asked.

'And fuck you, you bastard,' the man spluttered and leered at him.

'Shut the fuck up, you stupid old twat.'

'Ah, you cunt. Bugger off, you white cunt. You whore. I'll fuck you.'

'Here.' Sean held out two pound coins in the palm of his hand. The drunk bowed his head and peered at them.

'Fucking coins, white fucking coins. White shit.' He reached out for them.

Sean grabbed a handful of the old man's hair and tugged.

'Hey!' The man backed off and swung at him. 'You fucking Satan. God'll fucking see you, you white whore. You cunt.'

'Here,' said Sean, 'take the money.' He shoved it into the man's hand and walked off.

'God knows you,' the man yelled. 'And the Holy Mother Mary with the white tits.'

Sean went up into the noise and light of the street and bought a box of matches. He emptied out the contents and carefully replaced them with the few tufts of black hair.

A little further down the road was a shop he remembered. It sold work clothes and camping equipment. He bought a shoulder bag, two pairs of black army boots and two sets of identical blue nylon overalls, complete all-in-one suits which buttoned up at the front.

Now he was ready. Despite the set-back over his payment he felt confident and prepared. When he got back to his flat, however, he started thinking about drink again. It was crazy to keep on drinking at lunch-time and then trying to give up in the evenings. It was important to take control of his life.

Tomorrow everything in the world was going to change; he had to try and remain sober. Surely it wasn't that hard not to think about having a beer.

But the evening seemed to be coming on slowly, and he saw it stretching out in front of him, and then the long night, and then ... And then Wednesday. He felt like a little kid on Christmas Eve, waiting an eternity for the next day.

He thought about eating, but couldn't face doing anything about it. He watched television instead. The pictures swam about meaninglessly and the words all seemed to be in Martian.

He got up, turned the set off, left the flat and went to the nearest off-licence. He bought eight cans of lager and drank them steadily until it was time to go to bed.

But he couldn't sleep.

Dammit. Tomorrow was Wednesday, he had to sleep, but his mind wouldn't let him.

He swore, and tried every comfortable position he could think of. Then, just as he thought he might be getting somewhere, a loud pounding started in the block of flats opposite.

It was a party, with a DJ announcing the records over a mike and encouraging everyone to have a good time and dance.

Sean became more angry with each record; each shattering beat seemed louder than the last. He felt like he had done when the fireballs came at him, frustrated and irrational. All he wanted to do was destroy, kill and kill again. If only he had a Nemesis spaceship now, he could blast the party off the face of the earth. Boom!

He was filled with hate, but he was impotent; there was absolutely fuck-all he could do about it.

After an hour or so the music was turned down, and Sean relaxed.

'We're taking it down a bit,' said the DJ, and Sean got comfortable in the bed. 'There's some police outside.'

In the comparative silence Sean got near to sleeping, but then he heard a car drive off and the music returned, louder than before.

This happened twice more, each time filling Sean with false hope. He twisted and turned in the bed and became a horrible, mad thing in the rumpled sheets.

Some time after four someone got hold of the mike and

started rapping, his voice droning on over the repetitive beat.

Of all nights, of all the fucking nights. Not tonight.

He felt that the state he was in he could do anything and get away with it. All rationality had long since fled.

Anything was permissible, he realized now, everything was justified. He could go and slaughter everyone at the party and be hailed as a hero by the whole fucking estate.

15

He must have fallen asleep eventually because he woke at seven, his whole body throbbing and stiff with tension. There was no thought of going back to sleep now. He was wide and painfully awake.

He went into the bathroom and filled about a third of the bath with cold water. He climbed in and lay flat. He gasped as it took his breath away, and his whole body became rigid. Then he turned on the hot water, and waited as the bath gradually filled and warmed. It was like returning from the dead. His muscles tingled, unknotted, relaxed in the steadily increasing heat. Eventually it was as hot as he could stand and he turned off the tap and rested, staring up at the peeling paint on the ceiling.

For a while he felt peaceful, and he tried to clear his mind, but then his stomach twisted and lurched, and every few minutes a terrible panic would crowd in on him.

He couldn't eat breakfast, but he drank countless glasses of cold water.

He tidied his flat, did the washing up, anything to keep occupied, to keep himself from thinking of the day ahead.

Gatley wouldn't be home from the Town Hall till at least one fifteen. Which meant that he had about five hours to kill.

At quarter past eight he bought a newspaper and a Mars bar. He went back to his flat and ate half the Mars. He looked at the words in the paper, but they didn't mean anything.

He stormed about the flat, looking for something to do,

then lay on his bed and pounded it with his fists, saying, 'Fuck it,' over and over again.

He told himself that he didn't have to go through with it.

Of course he had to go through with it. What would Mathews think? Or Duke?

Fuck it. Fuck them. Just forget the whole fucking thing. Leave this crazy world and return to real life. Jesus, Mathews could find someone else.

If he just forgot all about it, returned the money, then it would never have been real.

But it wasn't that easy. He knew too much. About Gatley, about Mathews. He was in too deep. Mathews would never leave him in peace.

Besides, he had it all planned. There was no risk. It felt good. He knew that he could do it. He knew that he would do it.

Jesus, if only it was time now. If only he didn't have to think about it any more. It was the waiting that was doing him in.

He went into the sitting-room and arranged his gear on the floor, laying it out in an orderly, symmetrical fashion.

First the helmet and gloves, then the two sets of overalls, then the two pairs of boots, the dosser's hair in the matchbox, the shoulder bag. He sat for a while looking at it all.

There was a comforting sense of order about it.

He tried on one set of overalls, with the boots, helmet and gloves. He decided to keep them on for a while, to get used to wearing them, so that he wouldn't feel too self-conscious later.

The overalls were rather hot and they swished when he walked. The helmet made him feel cut off from the world.

He looked at himself in the mirror. He could be anyone.

He sat for a while in his outfit, then got bored and took it all off again. All except the boots.

He decided to do his washing. He took his clothes down to the launderette on Well Street. He'd been meaning to do it for days and, in case anyone remembered, he wanted to appear like an ordinary, untroubled person going about an ordinary untroubled day, with nothing on his mind.

While his clothes were washing he did some shopping. He spent as much as he could in as many shops as he could. Then he went back to the launderette and had another go at reading the paper.

He was home before eleven.

Still at least two hours to go.

He put his clean clothes away, then packed the shoulder bag. He put the other pair of boots in the bottom, then the overalls, then the gloves. Finally he jammed the helmet in down one end. It only just fitted and it was a bit of a struggle doing up the zip.

He'd had just about enough of his flat, so he walked over to Hackney Town Hall to get a bus to Islington. He hoped he'd have to wait for a while, waste some more time, but unfortunately a 38 came along almost immediately.

On the bus he couldn't stop himself from thinking about Gatley. He still couldn't work out what it was about Gatley that marked him for what was going to happen. He needed a reason.

Why Gatley? Why you?

The bus passed the end of Canonbury Road and he looked up it. It looked exactly as it always did. There was nothing remarkable about it today; there were no portents, no warnings.

He felt better in Islington. Among the crowds he was invisible again, he could get things back into perspective. He was surrounded by a million secrets, a million crimes. Nobody would notice him; he was nothing special, Gatley was nothing special, it all meant nothing.

In a hundred years everyone here would be dead, and so would he, and so would Gatley.

His stomach was making obscene noises and trying to eat itself. He ordered a pizza in PizzaExpress, but could only get through half of it.

Afterwards he just wandered around. He had a look in a couple of shoe shops, a bookshop; he even poked around the antiques shops in Camden Passage.

Then, at quarter to one, he went into a pub on the

green. In the toilet he slipped into a set of overalls and then put on the gloves and helmet.

It would normally be only about a quarter of an hour's walk to Gatley's from here, but he walked slowly. He didn't want to be waiting around for him outside the house.

He tried to walk casually, neither too fast nor too slow, without showing anything. But he found that if he thought about it, it became impossible to do it properly, and he began to walk in a very strange way.

In the warm swishing overalls and the helmet, he was cocooned. It was like a dream.

When he got to Canonbury Road he was out of breath, exhausted by his efforts to walk normally, and his throat was dry. But he couldn't risk stopping and getting himself together. He knew that if he stopped he might never start again.

He turned the corner and sauntered up the hill.

The road constantly veered between being endless and being ridiculously short. He didn't want to ever get there, but he couldn't stand the waiting any longer. The edges of the helmet made him feel as if he was in a tunnel, with Gatley's house at the end of it.

With each step it was harder to turn back. Yet, if he wanted, he could turn at the last moment, at the door even. Turn and go home. Forget all about it.

Half-way up he heard a bicycle, and out of the side of his vision he saw Gatley struggle past. Sean's insides froze, but then he saw the hat. The stupid white hat that Gatley had bought on Saturday.

The twat was actually wearing it. Sean was overcome with anger. How could anyone actually wear such a stupid fucking hat? Didn't he realize what a complete fool he looked?

His wife was always immaculate; she cared, she thought about herself, she was beautiful. And here was Gatley, his trousers tucked into his socks, tie flapping in the wind, his glasses slightly steamed with exertion.

And on top of all that, the hat.

He was actually wearing it.

A great peace passed through Sean. The final cog had turned. Everything made sense now. He quickened his steps. He had a reason at last. He thanked Gatley.

Anyone who wore a hat like that deserved to die.

He slowed down, watched Gatley stop, dismount and carry his bike indoors.

He hung back a minute, then approached the door.

He was at the edge of the cliff; once he knocked, that was it.

His heart was hammering inside his chest like a drum-machine. Would he even be able to speak? He wanted to be sick.

Fuck it. Fuck it.

He knocked. His hand was shaking slightly.

Don't answer, you fucker, don't open the door. Don't be stupid all your life.

The door opened and there was Gatley's face, with a quizzical look on it.

Wrong number. Tell him you've got the wrong number, then go. It's not too late.

'Oh, hello, Mr Gatley,' Sean said amiably. 'Is Emm in?'

He was hoping that Gatley would vaguely recognize him, register on a subconscious level, assume he'd seen him with the teacher. He must have noticed him around, after all.

'No, er, I'm afraid not. She's, erm, she's teaching today, actually.'

'Oh, typical,' Sean tutted. 'I thought Wednesday was her half-day.'

'No.'

'God. Trust me to get it wrong.' His voice was tight, threatening to crack. Did Gatley notice? Oh, Jesus. Leave it there, go away. Forget it.

'Listen, would it be all right if I left a message for her?'

'Surely.' Gatley stood in the doorway. He had to get inside.

'Erm, I'm sorry. Do you have a pen and paper?' he asked.

'Oh yes, of course. Come on in.'

Fuck it, he's said it, it's his own fault.

Sean crossed the threshold. He had to finish it now, he'd never get another chance. He noticed that Gatley's trousers were still tucked into his socks, though he'd taken off the hat.

They pushed past Gatley's bike in the hallway, and a jumble of kids' toys, coats and boots.

The kitchen was as he'd last seen it through the window, full of stuff yet still, somehow, ordered.

He casually looked around as Gatley tried to find some paper.

The remains of the family breakfast were still on the table.

There was a child's painting of a cat stuck to the tall fridge-freezer.

There was a box of paints in the middle of the floor.

It was strange being this close to Gatley, in his house, standing there, an alien.

Gatley was leaning over a drawer, his bald head gleaming in the fluorescent light.

'There should be a pen here somewhere. The blasted girls never put things away properly.'

To his left was a row of glass jars full of rice and pasta, and next to them there were some old-fashioned iron scales, with a collection of weights.

'Ah, here we are.'

Sean picked up the two heaviest weights in one hand and stepped towards Gatley.

'Right, then.' Gatley straightened up and was turning as Sean swung. The weights caught him just above the right eye.

He said, 'Ow,' very loudly and backed into the work surface. He put a hand up to his forehead as blood began to pour out of the deep gash.

'What the bloody hell?' he muttered and groaned. Then it struck him that he was in danger. He looked at Sean with a mixture of fear and incomprehension. He put his hands up for protection.

Sean threw the weights, which were too light, at Gatley's arms, and picked up the scales, trying not to think about what was happening.

'Please,' said Gatley.

Sean hefted the scales into the air and crashed them down on the top of Gatley's head.

He said, 'Ow,' again and fell to his knees. A chunk of skin and bone had been taken out, and a huge bump was quickly developing to one side of the dark hole.

Whimpering, Gatley started to crawl across the floor, one hand clutching his head.

Sean hit him again with the scales and knocked him flat. He lay still now, except for one foot which was twitching like a sleeping dog.

Sean knelt down and inspected him. He was obviously still alive. But he couldn't face beating him to a pulp with the scales. There was already blood everywhere, and a steady stream of it was pumping out of Gatley's head.

He wanted to just leave him. Let him bleed to death. But what if someone came back?

No, he had to make sure. He'd gone this far, only a little further now.

No risk. Do it right. Finish him off.

He had an idea. He pulled Gatley into the middle of the room and carefully positioned him in line with the fridge.

By the cooker there was an old radio clock, the type whose numbers flipped over rather than the more modern LCD ones.

He turned it on; it was tuned to Radio 4. He twiddled the dial until he found some music, an old Beatles song. He turned up the volume, then had another look at Gatley.

He had sat up, his feet out in front of him, a dazed look on his blood-streaked face.

He looked sad rather than frightened, a little boy lost in the big world. His glasses had fallen off. He looked up at Sean with small, soft eyes.

'Lie down,' Sean said quietly. 'Don't worry, it'll soon be over. Lie still.' He laid Gatley back on the sticky tiles, then tested the fridge; it had a heavy freezer at the top. It would do.

He knelt down next to Gatley. 'Where's your hat?' he asked quietly but firmly, like a nurse.

Gatley was shivering. He turned his face towards the big table, and Sean saw the hat on a chair with his brief-case.

He went over to get it. He looked out into the street; there was no one about. He returned to Gatley. The Beatles were singing about love.

'What?' said Gatley.

'Shh,' said Sean. 'Go to sleep now.' He hid Gatley's face with the hat and tipped the fridge over.

It came down with a rush of air and a thud.

Gatley didn't move at all now. His head and shoulders were completely hidden by the fridge.

Making as little noise as possible Sean scattered papers, food, books, pushed over furniture, pulled pans out of cupboards.

Then he turned down the radio, retuned it to Radio 4 and checked the time. It was twenty-three minutes past one. He set it forwards to quarter past two, then yanked it out of the wall. He put it on its side in the middle of the floor.

He took the matchbox from his pocket, dipped the hair in Gatley's blood, then sprinkled it over his outstretched hand.

He opened Gatley's brief-case, took out the pink file, then closed it again and tossed it into the corner.

He took off his blood-spattered overalls and his boots and put them in a plastic bag. He then took off his gloves and changed into the matching set of overalls and packed away the dirty stuff in his bag with the file.

He rinsed the helmet under the tap, just to be sure, and put his gloves back on.

He took one last look at Gatley lying under the fridge. It wasn't a pretty sight to come home to. Gatley looked so pathetic. He couldn't leave him like this.

He knelt by him and untucked his trousers from his socks. That was better.

It was done.

Finished.

Sean walked into the hallway.

He froze by the front door, remembering that time when he'd been on the other side and Emm had come out unexpectedly. What if someone opened it now?

No, don't even think it. Don't think anything. Just go. Get out of there.

He opened the door and turned in the opening as he went out.

'Well, thanks, Mr Gatley,' he said cheerily. 'Maybe I'll call back this evening.'

He waved, pulled the door shut and wandered off up the road.

Half-way to the tube, he realized he was crying.

16

It was shit. Everything was shit. Shit, shit, shit. Round and round in his mind. Shit. God, Gatley had been so full of shit, lying there, and the shit had all come out. Lying there dead, stuck dead.

The cars were too loud; they rushed at him. Yelled as they went past. Stinking cars. Nobody on the street, just in the cars. He couldn't see them, he was alone now. He wasn't in their world any more. He was by himself.

His hands, in his gloves, in his pockets, were clenched tight, so tight that they hurt, to prove that pain wasn't so bad. There were worse things.

There was a dog up ahead, pissing against a pile of builder's rubbish. A long, dark stream of piss was snaking down the pavement. Sean closed his eyes and saw all the blood. He felt sick. How could there have been so much blood? Blood everywhere.

The redness of the blood was fading to brown. Shit.

The sky had gone dull, and the colour was draining out of everything. Everything becoming dirty, dusty, old, dark and obscure. The world was turning yellow, like a page from a magazine found under a rotted carpet.

The dog looked up at Sean; it was far, far away, going away. Growing smaller and smaller. Small. Shit. Dog shit.

The dog ran off.

Next thing he knew he was at Highbury and Islington station, buying a ticket. Then he was on the train and he took off his helmet.

The carriage was packed. Everyone was ugly, malformed,

yellow, dead. At King's Cross someone sat next to him with a Walkman. Sean could hear the faint rattling music from the headphones, like a fly buzzing in his ear.

He didn't want to get off the train; he wanted to stay on it for ever, stay in limbo. He had no energy. Just stay here and forget everything.

No, act normal. It had all gone well so far, don't fuck up now.

At Oxford Street he hauled himself out of the seat and somehow made his way out of the station, pushing, half blind, through the crowds.

The streets were full of crazy people and derelicts.

He walked towards Piccadilly.

He passed a restaurant. A heap of boxes and bags was piled against the wall, stuffed with bones and skin, discarded meat.

He looked inside at the people eating.

Life went on.

It meant nothing, what had happened; it would never mean anything to these people.

He grinned and, as he turned to leave, he nearly bumped into a man with thick, tight, yellowish-grey curls and a purple face with deep lines in it. He was wearing about three coats.

The man was grinning, too, in an exaggerated way, fierce and desperate. Sean frowned; the man frowned.

Sean tried to take hold of his rising anger, and the man looked furious. It dawned on Sean that the man was impersonating him.

He didn't know what to think. The man looked confused.

'Here,' said Sean, 'take this.'

The man made garbled sounds, but the tone was right, the meaning was there. He took the crash helmet from Sean and stared at it.

Sean mimed putting on the helmet, and the man put it on.

A motor-bike messenger passed them, slowly weaving in

and out of the traffic, and the nutter ran off alongside him, mimicking his actions.

Sean watched him as far as the traffic-lights, where a woman with a camera took over his attention.

He felt a little better. A part of the other person was gone. The person who had done the thing. The person in the helmet and overalls.

He found an off-licence and bought a half-bottle of Teachers.

He needed to go somewhere quiet and hold himself together. He wandered through the narrow tangled streets of Soho, going nowhere in particular, and then he came across a cinema, advertising four non-stop triple bills of sex films at a reasonable price.

He walked in through the glass doors. A young Pakistani in uniform looked at him without interest.

An older Asian woman sat behind the ticket and refreshment counter, reading a magazine. Sean bought a ticket for Screen Two. Then he made his way down a well-lit corridor to where another young Pakistani, with a thin moustache, was waiting to tear up his ticket and point him to a door marked 'Two'.

Sean went in. For a moment he couldn't see anything in the dark, then he slowly got his bearings. It was a small, dingy room, and he was conscious of several rows of well-spaced men. He felt his way up the gentle slope until he found an empty aisle seat. Just along from him an old guy was asleep in his chair, snoring quietly. Another derelict, another homeless ghost.

Sean sat down and looked around. About half the punters were old men who probably spent all day there; the other half were a curious mixture, young men in ones and twos, a few businessmen, and a party from the Far East, all sitting in reverent silence.

The film showing had once been hard-core, but it had been cut. All the explicit fucking, sucking, wanking and cum-shots had been removed. There was only about half the film left. There were endless build-ups to sex, a bit of obscure

foreplay, and then . . . and then nothing. It was an inter-
minable prick-tease, incoherent, meaningless, and ultimately
pointless.

Whoever prepared these films for the British market had
come up with a lot of semi-ingenious tricks to make the
films up to something near feature length. Sean had come in
at the tail end of a film, probably *Hot Lunch*, and was just in
time to watch a surreal master-stroke. A couple were evidently hard at it on a bed. The woman was very graphically
telling the man what to do, while the man described exactly
what he was doing. It sounded like fun, but the men in the
audience weren't seeing any of it, because a table lamp had
been superimposed over the rutting couple. As the camera
moved around the bed, the enormous lamp hovered in the
foreground, obliterating everything.

And then the film suddenly stopped, and the lights came
up.

No one complained, no one said a word, though the
party from Japan looked rather confused.

In this unreal environment Sean found himself winding
down.

The guy from the foyer came in with a refreshments tray
and was completely ignored. After a few minutes he went
out and the next film started, *Hot Legs*.

This was a European film, and they had tried an array of
techniques to fill it out. For a start, all linking scenes, when
there was no dialogue, were slowed down. The early shots
of the plump heroine floating around town in a stately
underwater fashion were like a bizarre endless nightmare.
The ritualistic qualities were further brought out in the sex
scenes, where non-explicit sections were repeated, and sometimes reversed, to try and con the audience into thinking
that they were different shots. As the sound-track progressed,
the picture would keep getting stuck in little whirlpools. So
that, to moans of passion, a hand would endlessly circle and
recircle a navel, or a face would move, over and over again,
towards a groin. It was like an avant-garde video installa-
tion. There was a weird, masochistic, Christian logic to it:

temptation, pleasure, self-denial, sin and punishment all combined in one neat package. And at a very reasonable price.

It was just what Sean needed. In another state of mind he would have become bored and angry, but now he found it hypnotic and soothing.

He sat in the darkness and let it bathe him with its monotony.

Near the end of the film he moved along the seats, took off his gloves and slipped them into the sleeping man's pocket. Then he got up and went to the toilet.

The toilet was a mess; graffiti covered its ochre walls, a bare bulb was screwed at an angle into a socket in the ceiling, half of the mirror was missing. There was the cloying stink of disinfectant.

Sean went into the single cubicle and locked it. He sat down and looked at the door. Someone had written, 'I will lick any cunt', and someone else had drawn a penis and round hairy balls spitting three little drops of semen into a girl's gaping mouth.

Sean unscrewed the cap on his bottle of whisky and drank as much of it as he could. Then he closed his eyes. He could hear dripping water, the comforting roar of the air-conditioning, the whoosh and clank of the plumbing, the general engine hum of the cinema.

It was okay. Everything was okay.

He felt more like himself again. He could face the world. He smiled. Everything was going to be good from now on.

He took the pink file out of the rucksack and put it in the carrier-bag with the whisky. Then he took off his overalls and stuffed them into the shoulder bag with the other pair.

As he opened the cubicle door he glanced at the mirror, but quickly looked away again. The person in the mirror had seemed to be looking at him.

The exit from the cinema took him down a dim concrete corridor to a push-bar. He came out on to a car park at the side of the building a different man to the one who had gone in.

A nearby building was being demolished; there were

clouds of dust in the afternoon sunshine. At one side of the car park sat a large half-full skip. He dumped the shoulder bag in it beneath some pieces of rotting lino.

He strolled down to Shaftesbury Avenue and got on a bus for Hackney.

It was only after he'd sat down upstairs and bought his ticket that it struck him that it was another 38. It would take him right through Islington, right past Canonbury Road. For a moment he was seized by panic. But he sat still and looked out of the window at the crowds, and it went away.

He had to be normal. He was safe, he'd done nothing. His life would go on as before.

It was like what they always said about riding a horse; if you fall off you should get right back on again, or you never would. He could hardly spend the rest of his life avoiding Islington.

But what would it be like?

Would the body have been found yet? Would there be police cars? An ambulance? Crowds of reporters?

And if the body had been found, then, by whom?

Susan? The girls?

What if they came home, laughing and dancing, full of stories to tell Daddy, and they found him, in the kitchen, under the fridge.

Well, at least his face was hidden. He'd spared them that.

But he wouldn't have been found yet; he would still be there, all alone in the empty house. Sean could get off the bus, run up the road, go to Gatley, maybe he was still alive, maybe he could . . .

No.

Not alive.

Shit. I'm sorry.

I'm sorry. I'm sorry. I'm sorry.

Susan, I'm sorry. But I had to do it.

He could ring the police, tell them, get them to find the body, spare the family.

No.

Stupid.

He was safe. He had to stay that way.

Think positive. Act normal. Nothing had happened.

The bus sailed past Canonbury Road, and it looked just as it had done the first time he'd been past it today, a busy, unexceptional road of pleasant, quiet, town houses. There weren't any police or avenging angels. The world hadn't changed. Just him.

But no one was to know that. As far as they were concerned, he was Sean Crawley, unemployed, on his way home from an uneventful day in town, a bit pissed, perhaps, but normal.

He just had to keep telling himself not to think about anything. But whenever he closed his eyes he saw Gatley sitting there, looking up at him without his glasses, blinking. Still alive. For the last time, alive.

If only he could go back to that moment, apologize, say it had all been a mistake. Leave.

Why?

It was what he'd wanted. Why change it? It was done now.

After all, who was Eric Gatley? Why should he care about him? Susan was better off without him.

What did it matter?

And down came the fridge.

Wham.

Hackney hadn't changed, either. It was a bit yellow, perhaps, and he noticed the dirt more than usual, but that was it. He sluggishly made his way down Morning Lane, feeling like he'd been awake for years. He was tired, all of him was tired, deeply, deeply tired. It was like he was pushing his way through knee-deep shit.

When he reached the stairs up to his flat, he stopped. Someone had dropped an ice-lolly, raspberry or black-currant, or whatever flavours they had these days. It had melted and left a sticky red pool, which was oozing down the steps.

Sean thought he was going to puke. His head started to whine; everything went away from him. The yellowness tightened, entered into him. He tried to move but his head hurt; it was full of shit. He was stuck there. It was like the point you can't pass in a dream. But he had to fight it. It was stupid to be stopped by an ice-cream; he forced himself forward, stepped over it, then ran up the four floors to his flat, the stink of blood burning his nostrils.

He threw himself down on to the bed. And something broke inside him. He soaked the sheets with tears, snot and saliva.

It was then that everything started to go wrong.

17

There was a brief item on the BBC regional news that evening, but the story didn't properly break till Friday. 'London man brutally murdered'. Sean watched as the story grew. On Saturday a couple of the papers ran pictures of Gatley and Susan. It was an old one of Gatley, and not very good, but the ones of Susan seemed to have been taken recently, outside the house. She looked tired and old. He didn't like to look at those pictures. He hated the journalists for chasing her. Why couldn't they just leave her alone, for God's sake? She'd had a hard time.

He hardly went out. In the mornings he'd hurry down to the shops for the papers, the *Guardian*, the *Telegraph*, the *Sun* and the *Mirror*, and any relevant local ones. Then every evening he'd go back out for the *Evening Standard*, and stock up on any food he needed.

He tried to be as quick as possible, so that he'd be in when Mathews got in touch. And he spent the rest of the time sitting by the phone, waiting.

Every morning he was awake long before the postman was due. He came twice, once with a reminder from the dentist that it was time for a six-monthly check-up, and once with a postcard for the people who'd lived in the flat before. Sean wasn't too worried about the post. He didn't really expect Mathews to write. But he did want him to ring. He needed the rest of his money.

Sunday was quiet; a tiny piece in the *Observer*, and a slightly longer, more graphic account in the *News of the World*. But it seemed like none of the papers had much to go on, except for the very basic facts: that Eric Gatley, an accountant for Hackney Council, had been battered to death in his home, by a person or persons unknown, for reasons unknown.

But then, on Monday, the bomb dropped. The front page of the *Evening Standard* carried Michael Mead's exclusive story, in which the name Derek Mathews was frequently mentioned. Sean had put the crater-faced journalist out of his mind when nothing had immediately appeared, but now he thought about it, it was inevitable that Gatley's death would lead to an investigation of Mathews. Rather than keep him safe, it had only put him into worse trouble.

The headline, in massive black letters, said, WHY WAS THIS MAN MURDERED? Then a picture of Gatley, quite a good clear one, and the paragraph, 'Exclusive, from our reporter, Michael Mead, who spoke to the victim about council corruption only days before the murder.'

There was a picture of Mathews. It was worse than the one of Gatley the other papers had been using; it hardly looked like him at all. Sean wondered where they'd got it from. Underneath it said, 'Derek Mathews, builder. Under investigation by murdered man.'

Sean felt sick; he'd been dumb enough to forget about Mead. Why had they both been so fucking stupid? Sean, playing the hard-guy assassin, had been so preoccupied with the job that he hadn't looked at the wider implications. Mathews was well and truly in the shit now. No wonder he hadn't been in touch.

He looked at Mead's name and pictured him that afternoon in the pâtisserie. He wondered why it had taken so long for him to say anything. He supposed that he must have been checking and double-checking his facts, pestering the police, being pestered by the police, pestering Susan.

But when Sean reread the story he realized what Mead's problem was. Although the article was certainly sensational, it didn't quite go all the way; it couldn't quite say that Mathews had anything to do with the death of Gatley. Despite some melodramatic stuff about Gatley's fears that he was being followed, and a missing file of evidence he'd been collecting, there was little real substance to the article. Mead had been waiting for something more, something to definitely tie Mathews in with the killing. He hadn't got it, but he obviously couldn't wait any longer.

Nevertheless, Mead might have nothing now but his article could stir up all kinds of shit. Sean was thrown into a panic. The police would be bound to talk to Mathews now. What if they gave him a hard time? Would he tell them anything?

No. No, he couldn't. He must know that as long as he kept his mouth shut, nothing would happen. He was safe. He'd known when the killing was planned for, he must surely have sorted himself out some decent alibis. There was no reason why anyone should know about Sean. They were all safe so long as no link could be made between the two of them. It was his security. If Mathews dropped him in it, then he could drop Mathews in it. As long as Mathews remembered that and didn't do anything stupid, they were in the clear.

But the next few days were agony, as the news spread to the other papers and across television. The house in Canonbury Road was 'besieged with reporters'; wild stories began to fly about. Mathews couldn't be found. Susan, the 'attractive dark-haired Canadian wife', went into hiding. The police spokesmen worked overtime. But still they couldn't fit the whole thing together. When it came down to it, there was still no positive connection between Gatley's death and Mathews.

And at Sean's end only silence. No one came round, no one phoned. He knew it was probably too risky but he wanted the rest of his money; he couldn't be penalized for Mathews's lack of forethought. He knew he was a fool not to have demanded it all up front. If only he hadn't been so eager.

When it came down to it, he'd been a complete bloody wanker about the whole business.

But he wanted that money. He didn't necessarily need the

cash itself; it was the principle of the thing. He was owed ten thousand pounds. He'd risked a lot to kill Gatley, and he wanted to be properly rewarded.

He could wait, but not for ever.

For several days he saw no one, but then on Wednesday evening, a week after the killing, George showed up. He seemed quieter than usual, thoughtful. He stood in the kitchen as Sean made some tea, and they chatted about nothing much. And then George came out with it.

'That bloke that was murdered in Islington.'

'What? That accountant geezer?'

'Yeah, from the council.'

'What about him?'

'That was the bloke we followed that day, wasn't it?'

'Fuck, that's exactly what I thought. You think it's the same guy, then?' He washed a couple of cups.

'Yeah. I wasn't sure at first, but it was the wife really.'

'Yeah, I know what you mean. It's weird, isn't it? Like synchronicity or something.' Sean grinned at George. George didn't smile. He was chewing the cap off a biro.

'It said in the papers he thought he was being followed.'

'Yeah, I know.' Sean laughed. 'D'you suppose he meant us? Do you think he saw us, thought we were, like, spies, or something?'

'I don't know. It's just, well, you know?'

'Weird?'

'Yeah, a bit frightening.'

'Bollocks. What, you reckon the cops are after us? The two mysterious men in the white van?'

'No, I mean, you'd never followed him before, or anything?'

'Before?' Sean put a tea-bag in each cup.

'Yeah. It's just, in the van, I thought now and then that maybe there was something more. Something you hadn't told me.'

'Like what?' Sean poured boiling water over the tea-bags and got some milk from the fridge.

'I don't know.'

'For fuck's sake, George, you're not seriously trying to tell me that you think I've got something to do with that bloke being brained?'

'No, of course not. I was just thinking about it.'

'As you would. I've been thinking about it, too, and it's freaked me out a bit. But it's just some stupid coincidence.' He gave a cup to George and they went through to the sitting-room.

'You shouldn't think too much, you know, George,' he said as they sat down. 'It doesn't do you any good.'

George soon perked up, and in half an hour he was his old self again. Sean relaxed. Now it would be just another amusing story to tell his mates when they were having a drink and a laugh.

Sean had been seriously frightened that George might know something, and somehow he couldn't face that. If George knew about his killing Gatley, it would be awful.

They were friends, nothing deep, nothing too personal; they got stoned together, got drunk together, they had a laugh together. They were two ordinary blokes with ordinary lives. It would fuck everything up if one of them turned out to be a murderer.

And Sean hadn't changed. He was really still the same person; he'd always been this way. He just didn't want to have to answer any questions, to explain what was for him quite straightforward.

No, it was best not to think about it. He was okay about things now. He'd got over the shock. He felt a bit sorry for Susan, he had to admit that; he even felt a bit sorry for Gatley. But he didn't want to take it any further than that, because he could sense a mounting wave of danger, a tidal wave climbing higher and higher, darker and darker. Something was wrong; he'd jumped from the plane without a parachute, and the world was rushing towards him.

He stared at George, sitting there chuckling at a joke, and he wanted to be like him. Simple and unconcerned.

He tried. They played chess but he couldn't really concentrate, and George beat him quicker than usual, then asked if he wanted another game. Sean said he wasn't into it, so they went to the pub instead.

But drinking didn't help. He couldn't get drunk; he'd reached a permanent numb state, tired, irritable and dull. He couldn't think, he couldn't sleep.

The next morning he felt more impatient than usual. He needed something to happen; he wanted the free-fall to end one way or another. He needed to speak to Duke or Mathews, find out what was going on, find out where his money was, what they were doing, what the police were up to. He knew he couldn't ring, though, so there was nothing he could do about it. He just had to wait. And, while he waited, the silence built up around him.

He stopped reading the papers; they weren't any help. He hardly ate any more, but he kept the fridge full of beer.

He knew that, outside, things were happening. Policemen and journalists were going about doing their work. Somewhere Mathews was sweating and, like Sean, waiting. But in his flat, nothing.

The whole thing was a complete balls-up.

Thursday passed into Friday, Friday merged into the weekend. George came round. They drank some more. George went away again.

Sunday crawled along. The night came; he lay in his bed. The family in the flat below were having an argument. He was half awake and half asleep.

Monday came and he could see the rest of the week stretching away into nothing. And after that? Another week. A month. The rest of his life. Nothing.

Maybe this was it, then. Maybe it was all over. He'd not be paid, he'd never hear from Mathews again, he'd forget all about the killing. It would all be like it had never happened. He'd go on doing odd jobs here and there. His world would go back to normal.

But that still didn't mean that one day a copper wouldn't turn up, and it'd all be over. And if that happened, he at least wanted something to show for what he'd done.

Mathews would never get in touch. He knew that now. There was no reason why he should. So he had to get in touch with him. He had to put the pressure on from his side.

Yeah. That was the only way.

Fuck you, Mathews, I'm taking what I'm due.

Yes, do it, do it now. Ring the bastard.

He grabbed the yellow pages and flicked through the Mathewses in the area. There was no builder named Derek. That meant he'd have to try all the other London areas. He'd have to go to the library. But at least he'd be doing something.

He was locking his front door when the phone rang.

It was probably just George, or someone. But he'd better check. He quickly unlocked the door and went back inside.

'Yes?'

'Sean?'

'Yes? Duke? For fuck's sake, I've been . . .'

'Shut up and listen. The tea hut in Regent's Park, you know it?'

'Yes.'

'Well, be there at two o'clock, then. You've got some talking to do.'

'*I've* got some talking to do . . .?'

Duke hung up.

Just before two, Sean was getting off his bike at the Camden side of the park when an American couple with a map asked him which way Regent's Park tube was. He pointed them through the park, then followed, wheeling his bike.

He stopped for a while to look at the wolves inside their little enclosure. After a couple of minutes he carried on up the gentle slope towards the café.

Tourists sat around on the brilliant green grass in untidy colourful groups. Young couples strolled hand in hand among the trees. A group of unfit-looking men in shirts and ties played football.

Sean was soon at the café. The wooden tables on the terrace

were surprisingly full, seeing as it was only a Monday, but it was hot and sunny. Big white clouds drifted across a bright blue sky.

Sean looked around and saw Duke before he saw him. He was standing drinking a can of coke, watching an Asian family playing cricket.

The big man was wearing jeans and trainers, and a grey, Coq Sportif T-shirt stained under the arms. He turned as Sean approached him and his tinted glasses flashed in the sunlight.

'Hi,' said Sean.

Duke crushed his can and dropped it into a bin.

'Always on time, eh?' he said.

'What's wrong with that?'

'Nothing. Never said there was.' Duke stared at him, showing no emotion.

'Well?' Sean asked.

'Well what?'

'Well, what do you want to talk about?'

'You ever been to the zoo?'

'The zoo?' Sean leant on his bike and frowned.

'Yeah, the zoo.'

'Years ago.'

'Meet me there by the monkeys in twenty minutes.' Duke started to wander off.

Sean followed him. 'Look, can't we just talk here?' he said impatiently. 'What's wrong with here?'

But Duke wasn't listening, he was purposefully walking back the way Sean had come.

'Twenty minutes,' he said, and Sean let him go.

18

Sean soon found the monkey section. The buildings were some of the newer ones in the zoo, with large wire-meshed enclosures outside, connected to the brick-lined indoor quarters through large plastic cat-flaps.

Duke was standing with a crowd of people laughing at a couple of baby chimps. He was pointing and shouting, almost child-like.

Sean pushed in next to him. 'What are we doing here, Duke?' he said, looking at the apes.

'It's nice here,' said Duke. 'All fenced in. Nice and safe and secure. Nature behind bars. Next best thing to seeing it on the telly. I've been meaning to come here for ages.'

'Come on, what's this all about?'

'I had to make sure I wasn't being followed. I had to make sure you wasn't being followed. And I needed to speak to you somewhere private.'

'Private?'

'Well, there's no chance of our bumping into anyone we know in here, is there? Come on, what do you want to see first? There's a lot of new bits since I was here last.'

'I don't fucking care. Look, Duke, I'm fed up, okay? I'm in the fucking dark, and I've had enough. There's things I need to know. And Mathews owes me.'

'If you don't want to play with the big boys, you shouldn't try and join in their games, should you?'

'Yeah. Well, your team keeps changing the rules.'

'Maybe it's just that you don't know the rules well enough.'

'All right. Then explain them to me.'

'That's just what I intend to do.'

Before Sean could say anything else, Duke walked off and consulted a map. Sean followed him, shaking his head.

'You know what happens when people go to the zoo?' The big builder rubbed his scrubby beard.

'What?'

'They always end up trying to work out what animals their friends are most like. It's usually monkeys, of course. But I reckon we can do better than that, eh? Use a bit of imagination.'

Duke winked and turned from the sign to find himself face to face with a gorilla. He was an enormous silver-back, with sad black eyes. Duke turned to Sean and mimicked the gorilla's intent and hopeless expression.

'What do you think?' he said, hunching his shoulders and wobbling his head.

'Eh?'

'Him and me?'

'I can't see it myself.'

'You're learning. See? Just because I'm big, it doesn't make me a gorilla, right?'

'No, the gorilla looks more intelligent.'

'Very funny. You're a funny man. But the point of the game isn't just to insult someone, you've got to really find the right animal. You can't just call me a hippo, or a warthog, or a sodding toad, or something, just to try and get at me. Not unless you really do think we're the same.'

'Duke?'

'What?'

'Oh, never mind.' Sean resigned himself to playing Duke's game.

First they tried the big cats, most of which were asleep in their spacious landscaped pens. Duke inevitably fancied himself as a tiger, one of which paced up and down behind a glass wall, only inches away from them. But Sean reckoned that if Duke was a cat, it was more likely a lion. Lions had always struck him as being slobs. But Duke couldn't make a decision because all the lions were dozing in the part of their compound which was hardest to see.

So they tried the elephants and rhinos. Inside their cramped concrete house there was an overpowering smell of shit, and the high cement walls magnified and echoed the grunts and bellows of the huge, shuffling, mad-looking beasts.

'What d'you reckon?' Duke asked, resting his elbows on a thick iron railing, watching a rhino piss like a fire-hose.

'Well, they're certainly big. But they're a bit too dignified, I reckon.'

'All right, then,' said Duke, 'I can see you're enjoying the game, but we've got to find some animals for you. These are all too big. I think of you as being essentially small.'

'Some of the monkeys were small.'

'Yeah, but you're too quiet and self-controlled for a monkey. We'll try the reptiles.'

'Okay.' Sean was relaxing. Maybe Duke had good news. He certainly seemed friendly enough now.

They walked towards the reptile house.

'Yeah,' said Duke, 'there's something of the lizard about you, a bit slimy, you know? Always watching and waiting, sort of camouflaged. You know, that's the funny thing about you. When I was waiting for you to show up, I was trying to remember what you looked like. And I couldn't.'

It was dark and humid in the reptile house. They wandered from one glass-fronted box to another, but none of the creatures seemed quite right; the snakes were mostly immobile, and none of the lizards had the exact qualities that Duke was looking for, though he did stop for a while at the chameleon, which flattered Sean.

Sean saw something of Duke in the alligators; if only they'd been a bit more boisterous they'd have done fine. They were ugly, sly-looking, pot-bellied and seductive. And they grinned in the same way as the builder, with their teeth showing.

Duke had found a tank with some hatching snakes' eggs in it. He stood with his nose pressed against the glass, fascinated.

Sean looked at Duke's reflection in the window. 'You don't really like me, do you?' he said.

'I haven't ever given it much thought.' Duke moved along to another tank. A grey slow-worm moved slowly out from under a rock. 'I'll tell you one thing, though, I don't trust you. You're a liar; everything about you is a lie. You're devious. Underhand. I wouldn't trust you as far as I could fucking throw you. Not even half as far, seeing as how I could probably throw you a fair old distance.'

'Why do you need to trust me?' Sean asked. 'Surely the question is more whether I trust you?'

'Is it?'

'I'd say so, yeah.'

'Tell me about it.'

'You tell me,' said Sean angrily.

'What?'

'When am I going to get paid?'

Duke tilted his head back and roared with laughter.

'What's so funny?' Sean asked.

'You are. You're fucking hilarious.'

'Why?'

'You come on the big man, the big fucking detective, the cool operator, big tough guy. Got it all sussed out, haven't you? But you're pitiful. You're a stupid little cunt who's wandering around completely out of your fucking depth. You're like this worm here, slithering around, king of the fucking jungle, when all the time you're in this piddly little tank, being looked after by a fucking keeper. Well, you've crawled into a big tank now, haven't you? And you've eaten a little mouse, and you think that makes you a fucking anaconda. But there's some real big snakes in this tank, with big fucking teeth, and they're going to gobble you up, sunbeam, gobble you up.'

'Look, Duke, I don't really care what you think about me. It's just that I did a job and I want to be paid. That's fair enough, isn't it?'

'Fair enough?'

'Yes, I did a job. I was meant to be paid.'

'You did a job? You did a fucking job? You stupid little wanker. Open your eyes.'

'And what? Look at what? Lizards?'

'You don't know, do you?'

'Know what?'

'What the fuck's going on.'

'I don't care. I know what I've done. And I know what I'm owed.'

'Oh, you poor miserable little fucker. I thought you were quite smart when I first saw you. But for a snotty-nosed little college boy who reckons he's got it all taped, you're fucking stupid.'

'So I'm not getting paid, then?'

'Come on, let's get out of here. I don't want these poor lizards to see a sorry sight like you.'

It was disorientating to return to the bright sunlight after the gloom of the reptile house, and Sean realized he'd been blushing. He was hot and sweaty now, his heart was beating heavily and he was grinding his teeth.

'Fancy a look at the bears and the pigs, then?' Duke said amiably, as if the two of them had never been in the reptile house, had never had the conversation.

But Sean wasn't going to let it slip away.

'Duke, just tell me,' he said. 'Why did you want to see me?'

'First the bears, Sean. I've always been told that I'm a great bear of a man.'

'For God's sake.'

'Fuck off, Sean. Just shut right up, okay? I want to see the zoo.'

'Fuck you,' Sean muttered.

But the Mappin terraces were closed, so there were no bears, goats or wild pigs to be seen. Duke was disappointed. 'You interested in giraffes, zebras and that?' he asked.

'No,' said Sean, 'not really.'

'Good. Me neither.'

They passed under the road through the tunnel decorated with imitation cave-paintings and headed for the Charles

Clore small-mammal pavilion instead. Once there they strolled among the cages, looking at the various scurrying, hopping, eating and cowering animals.

Duke led Sean down into the nocturnal world, where day and night had been reversed. Most of the animals didn't appear to be fooled and were sleeping anyway.

A tape played various jungle sounds.

'We can talk here,' said Duke.

'At last.'

'Yeah, at last.'

'And?'

'It's like in films, isn't it? You know, at the end, when the villain suddenly explains the whole plot to the trapped hero. And then he escapes and kills everyone.' Duke laughed.

'Is it?'

They were standing by the fruit-bats cage. There were twenty or thirty of them, with their black leathery wings, clambering on the ceiling or flapping up and down chittering.

'Only in this case,' said Duke, 'I'm not the villain.'

'Yeah,' said Sean, in a non-committal fashion.

'Listen, we had a great little scheme going, a great secret, a great lie. But you should have been told a long time ago. Because now you've gone and screwed it all up.'

'Told what?'

'You still don't see it, do you? You're blind, blind as a . . . a fucking bat, right? You don't see it because you don't want to fucking see it. You're in your own little James Bond world and you don't want to see what a stupid bastard you've been all along.'

'See what? Just tell me what you're talking about, will you?'

'You've been taken for a ride, Sean, you've been had.'

'Yeah, I'm beginning to see that.'

'Why d'you think we hired you in the first place?'

'Why? Because if anything went wrong I couldn't be connected with you.'

'Right so far. And?'

'Well, because, I don't know, you thought I could do it, I could do the job. I was keen, had no particular scruples. Shit, I don't know. I was unemployed; I guess you thought I needed the money. Why else?'

Duke had begun laughing again, quietly at first, but louder with each word Sean spoke.

'Sean, you poor, sad, little fuck,' he said at last. 'We hired you because you were crap.'

'What?'

'Because you were a clueless little turd, who'd be about as good at being a detective as I would at being a ballerina.'

'What do you mean?'

'Well, what do you fucking know about being a detective? About finding things out? Following people? All that shit?'

'Well, I . . .'

'You know fuck all. I mean, you haven't even got a fucking car. We watched you a couple of times on your fucking push-bike, and we fucking pissed ourselves. Come on, Sean, you were fucking useless. That was the whole fucking point.'

19

Duke was looking at Sean now, but Sean couldn't look at Duke. His eyes were fixed on the fruit-bats.

'What do you mean?' he asked quietly.

'Gatley was *supposed* to know that he was being watched, being followed. You see? That was the plan.'

'Why?'

'Why? Why? We had a problem. My boss, that is, he had a problem, right? A rival, a bloke he hates, a bloke that he's always been competing with, a bloke that always beats him and all. Always gets the choice contracts. And it pisses him off. And then he finds out that this other geezer's got his fingers in the Hackney pie. The other guy, right? Not my boss. You get it?'

'I don't know.'

'What do you suppose his name is? Not my boss, the other guy, the guy he hates, the guy he wants to screw?'

Sean thought about it, and it suddenly all became clear. 'Derek Mathews,' he said flatly.

'Precisely. It's simple. My guvnor wants to land this Derek Mathews right in it, see? So he looks around for a way to do it, and he finds out about this new accountant, fresh-faced, eager and upstanding, a regular little saint, Eric Gatley. And he manages to get someone on to Gatley, drop a few hints, but Gatley moves too slow, won't take any risks. And so my guvnor says to me, "How can I put a rocket up this Gatley fellow's arse?" And that's when I think of you. What if old Gatley gets paranoid, starts thinking he's being watched? Sees the big footprints of one of Mathews's men in the flower beds? Thinks he might be in danger, even? That'll make him jump. He'll put his skates on now, won't he? Maybe even go to the police. And you're perfect, he's bound to notice you. So we hire you, as a sucker, and that was supposed to be that. If anything ever came of it, we didn't know you, you'd been hired by Derek Mathews. Not us.'

'Thanks,' said Sean. 'For telling me, I mean.'

'You'd have found out sooner or later.'

'And you thought that wasn't enough. So you got me to kill him, really make it look bad for Mathews.'

'No, I did fucking not. That was never part of the plan. That's what this is all about. That was way out of order. That was fucking stupid. I'd never have agreed to that. No way, that was Ray's brilliant idea.'

'Ray?'

'My guvnor, the bloke you thought was Derek Mathews. Ray.'

'Oh.'

'You see, the thing about Ray, he's an ignorant man. He's ignorant and he drinks. Oh, he's a good builder, he's sharp all right, he runs a tight business, but outside work he's a cretin. Stubborn, reckless, hot-headed, ignorant. Anything that requires serious thought, he's a menace. So I cook the plan up for him, help him out, and it all goes swimmingly, until, well, until Ray fucks up.

'Let me tell you about Ray and Derek. They was close once, started out together in the business. But Derek was always the smarter of the two, and he could talk. Oh, Ray can talk all right, talk shit, but Derek made sense. He had the gift. He was always the most talented of the two, not that Ray would ever admit it. But there was one thing neither of them could handle. Women.

'You see, most people, when they get a hard-on, it's blood, right? That little valve opens, and your limp sponge fills with blood; turns your dick into rock, if you're lucky. Well, it's not like that with Ray and Derek. When they get a hard-on it's not blood in there, it's their brains; they get sucked right out of their heads and into their cocks. And that's that, they're fucked, charging around like a couple of fucking robots. They can't fucking handle it.

'Well, anyone could see it was always going to end up in trouble for one or the other of them, or both.

'And that's what happened. The shit finally winged its way into the fan. They both fell for the same bird, just some fucking peroxide barmaid, but they both had to have her. So they fought; and they fell out, and, I don't know, they tried to fucking kill each other. And in the end, it was inevitable, I suppose, Derek got her, married her. The two of them wouldn't speak after that, not for years. Broke up the business, went their separate ways.

'They've had the odd reconciliation since, but it's impossible; they always end up arguing. Ray married someone else in the end, Zara, nice looker, but stupid. That was the best time. Derek was at the wedding. But it didn't last, they fucked up again. Fell out as per usual.

'And then a couple of months back, Ray tells me he wants to fuck up Derek once and for all. They'd had some poker game, and somehow Ray had beaten Derek, and Derek had got pissed, started needling Ray, really laying into him. Well, Ray comes to me, and he says he wants to fix that bastard. And that's where you come in. It was perfect, really; he paid you out of his winnings, exactly sixteen hundred quid; he thought there was some kind of justice in that. So he hires you, and everything goes like clockwork, and that should have been that. But something happened.'

'What?'

'Well, far as I can tell, Ray gets suspicious of Zara and he gets pissed and he gets the detective bug and all. Decides to follow her, and it looks like she's up to no good. He follows her out of town, and all the way down to a place called Sevenoaks.'

'Sevenoaks?'

'Know it, do you?'

'Yeah.'

'Thought you might. And Ray knew it, too, he knew it very well, because that's where good old Derek lives. In some big posh house down there. Ray was always jealous of that house. But Derek was always just better at making money.

'So Ray watches her, Zara, his lovely wife, go into the house, and she doesn't come out, and he flips his fucking wig. Derek's only gone and done it again, hasn't he?

'I can't believe those two. Where women are concerned, they're just fucking kids, thick. Not that their women are any brighter. I don't know what Zara's playing at. I don't know what any of them are playing at.

'So, anyway, far as I can tell, he sits there all night in his car, and watches the house, and drinks, and plots, his little mind turning away, and come Sunday he's thought up this brilliant scheme to really screw old Derek once and for all. He completely forgets we only hired you 'cause you were useless, gives you a ring, and down you trot. If only he'd talked to me, but no, he talks to you instead.

'I'm surprised the stupid sod didn't just ask you to kill Derek, but I suppose poor bloody Gatley was the next best thing. He wasn't thinking straight, he was confused, his brain was in his dick and his guts were full of brandy. But you, what's your excuse?'

'I don't know.'

'You don't know. Marvellous. You killed a bloke and you don't know why.' Duke laughed humourlessly. 'The whole thing's a crock of shit, and I've got to pick up the pieces.'

'I'm sorry.'

'*You're* sorry? You're fucking sorry? You're worse than him; where's your fucking brains? You're supposed to be educated. You don't just go around killing people.'

'Fuck it,' said Sean. 'Let's get out of here.'

Before Duke could say anything, Sean walked towards the exit. Duke didn't try to stop him.

Sean walked up the stairs into the light and back into the real world. He wandered among the cages trying to get things straight in his mind, and Duke kept away from him.

After a while he left the small-mammal house and sat on a bench in the sun. A few minutes later Duke came and sat next to him.

'Don't you see, Sean?' he said. 'If you'd just followed Gatley, as we'd planned, then there was nothing wrong, we'd done nothing wrong. He gets worried, spills the beans, Derek's snookered. But you kill him, and everything changes; Derek gets suspicious. Now, I know Derek, and he's not going to sit around on his arse doing nothing. He's not about to go down for murder, is he? And he knows full well who's behind this tragic little scheme. In short, mate, we're all in trouble.'

Sean jumped up.

'Well, why didn't you tell me before? Instead of just taking the piss? How was I supposed to know?'

'You weren't supposed to know.'

'Well, don't blame me, then.'

'But, Sean! You killed someone. What the fuck do you think you were doing?'

'I don't know, all right? I don't bloody well know.' He walked off, and this time Duke stuck with him. 'Come on,' he said. 'Up there.'

He nodded towards the insect house, an old brick building at the edge of the zoo. They clanked up the iron staircase and went inside.

In the rows of dusty glass cages were huge spiders, gleaming black scorpions, millipedes, centipedes, locusts, stick insects, beetles, a bizarre collection of alien creatures. Utterly unknowable. So specialized and stripped to the barest of essentials that they were frightening in their simplicity and casual brutality.

There were no dilemmas here, no jealousies, no greed or lust, no rivalry, no guilt, no conscience. Just survival in its purest form.

There was an elderly couple at the far end looking at some snails.

Sean stood in front of Duke and watched a spider slowly spinning its web.

'Ugh,' said Duke, 'I hate spiders.'

'Big man like you, frightened of spiders?'

The elderly couple wandered out and they were alone.

'Listen,' said Duke. 'I mean it, you're in trouble.'

'Why? It's over. No matter what Derek does, no matter what the police do, as long as I'm kept out of it, there's no problem. You set it up right from the start. Mathews doesn't know me, you don't know me, we've never met. As long as I can't be traced we're safe. So it looks like we're just going to have to trust each other, doesn't it? For all our sakes.'

'Bollocks. You're not listening. We're not dealing with normal people, we're dealing with Ray and Derek. You don't know what they'll do. Derek's men are already nosing around. It's only a matter of time before someone finds you, or until Ray fucks up. There's only one way to be completely safe.'

'How?'

'For you to disappear.'

'What do you mean?'

'That's what I've come to tell you. You did it; in the end they'd have to have you for anything to stick. So you've got to be out of the picture. No chance of Derek or the coppers getting hold of you.'

'For fuck's sake, Duke, no one will find me. You keep away from me and we're all safe.'

'I want you away from here. I want you gone.'

'Now you listen, Duke, I'm not going anywhere until Ray gives me what I'm due. If I get my money, then I'll disappear, okay? But I did it for the money, and I intend to get it.'

'He never meant to pay you, you wanker. What was it? Thirteen grand? Don't make me laugh. Why should anyone pay you thirteen grand to do anything?'

'But I did it. And I want paying. And until I get that money I'm here, and I'll cause a fuss if I need to, but unless I . . .'

Sean stopped. Duke had grabbed him from behind, put his massive arms around his chest and begun to squeeze.

Sean could feel the hard muscles in his arms, feel the massive strength of the man.

'Duke . . .'

'You listen, shit-head,' Duke whispered in his ear. 'You're nothing, right? Nothing, you understand? You're just a little twerp who's got involved in something he should have left well alone. You don't tell me anything, right?'

As he spoke, he slowly increased the pressure, and lifted Sean off his feet.

'You'll get no money. You've had all you're getting. Which, let's face it, is too much already. You'll get no more money, and you'll disappear. I don't want to ever see you again, right? You'll shrink away to a little speck of shit and then you'll be gone. I don't care where you go, as long as it's far away, and for ever.'

Sean couldn't breathe at all now; colours and spots danced in front of him. The rest was black and white, and growing small. His ears whined, his lungs felt like they were full of acid. And still Duke squeezed, harder and harder.

'I could kill you, you know? I could kill you, and I wouldn't even have broken sweat. I could crush you, snuff you out as if you were a little kitten, and who would know? It'd all be over. As you say, nothing to link you to us. Just remember that; one more stupid move, one word out of place, and you're dead. As simple as that, and we're in the clear for good. You're the danger, *you*, talking. If you don't exist, then there's no danger. If you disappear, then you're no longer a threat. And there are two ways for you to disappear: one is to leave the country, the other is to die. Take your pick.'

Duke's voice sounded like it was right inside his head. He was no longer aware of anything except that voice, that quiet intimate murmur. The rest was pain.

'So you be sensible and get out of it, leave me alone. Forget everything, all right? Do I make myself clear? I think I do. You want to live? Then live in Spain or somewhere.'

He let go. Sean fell to the ground. He felt like his chest was exploding, mushrooming outwards, splitting him open.

The air rushing into his lungs felt like scalding steam. He moaned as oxygen was pumped back into his brain. For a moment he blacked out; when he came to, he was retching and gasping. Before, all he'd wanted to do was be allowed to breathe, but now it was agony. He wanted it to stop, he tried to make it stop. He pulled himself into a corner, tears sliding down his face.

Duke carried on looking at the insects.

Gradually Sean regained his control, slowed his heart and lungs. He dried his face and stood up, rubbing his aching ribs. Duke called him over.

'Look at this,' he said amiably. 'I've found it.'

'Found what?' Sean shuffled over to him.

'I've found you,' Duke said. He was standing by a long window, behind which was an enormous ants' nest, built on two islands surrounded by water and connected by a little bridge. It was a turmoil of manic, ceaseless activity, as a million ants went about their business. On one of the islands a large magnifying glass was focused on half an orange, where scurrying ants studiously collected food.

'I should have known, really,' said Duke. 'You're an insect, aren't you? You're a creepy-crawly, a bleeding ant. We should have come straight here. This is you, you see. Look, see? That one there looks just like you.'

'Yeah,' said Sean without feeling. He nodded his stiff neck. 'Maybe you're right.' He didn't feel like arguing now.

'So you're going to fuck off, then?'

'Tell me one thing first.'

'What's that?'

'The picture in the paper, of Derek Mathews. Why does it look like Ray?'

'Why?' Duke smiled at Sean. 'Simple. Ray and Derek are brothers.'

'Brothers?'

'Yeah, twins. Identical fucking twins.' Duke roared with laughter.

'Oh.' Sean watched the insects for a while.

Duke made a move to leave, but Sean stopped him.

'Look,' he said. 'There's two ants here that look the same.'

'They all look the bleeding same.'

'No, look there. They look just like Ray and Derek. And there, see that one dead in the water?'

'Which one?'

'The one that looks like Gatley. You're right, Duke, we should have come here first.'

'Dah, they all look the fucking same to me.'

'Oh, no, Duke. They're all different, just like people. And see that big one there, shifting that dead body. It looks just like you, Duke.'

20

'No,' said the old woman, and she laughed with the check-out girl in a dirty conspiratorial way. 'I got children. I got grandchildren. I got great-grandchildren. I'm sixty-seven, I am. Ha, ha, ha, but I don't know.'

She was a big wheezy woman in an even bigger dress which jacked into big stiff folds when she moved and allowed her off-white underwear to poke out here and there. She was holding two large plastic bottles of bitter in her naked, fat, pink arms.

'Are you going to give me some money, then?' the girl asked in a good-natured way.

'Here you are, love,' said the woman, paying the girl. 'It doesn't go far these days, does it? But I've got me pension.'

'Not for much longer, if you carry on like this.'

'Oh, I've got to have me wallop. I like a nice glass of beer.' She laughed again, winked at the girl and shuffled off.

The check-out girl started to ring up Sean's shopping.

It was all food. No drink. He was back on his health kick. He couldn't face being in a trance any longer.

Cycling home from the zoo, he'd nearly crashed twice. His mind had been spinning like the wheels in a fruit machine, wheels which never all quite stopped at the same time.

Should he run? Should he hide? Should he fight? Should he give up? He'd got home and just sat until it got dark, sat and tried to stop the wheels from spinning. Then, before going to bed, he'd done some press-ups, as many as he could, forcing himself on through the pain. He'd managed fifty before he collapsed on to the sitting-room floor.

When he'd woken up things hadn't looked so bleak, but he knew he had to take control. No more drink, no more dope, no more pissing about.

He'd fixed himself a routine.

In the mornings he'd set his alarm for nine o'clock, then either go for a run round Victoria Park or a swim in Highbury. He ate a light lunch every day, and in the afternoons he went to the sports centre for a work-out on the multi-gym.

He'd been reading a lot, and in the evenings he sometimes played chess with George, slowly improving as his concentration became sharper. Now and then he'd have a couple of cans of weak beer, but he didn't smoke any dope. Much to George's disgust.

He was sleeping better now, deep and full of dreams. His mind was generally clearer, quicker, tougher. He felt properly alive and back in the real world. But he was conscious of waiting. Waiting for one of the Mathews brothers to make a move. One of them had to take the next step; he was strongest in a defensive position.

He'd been a jerk, thinking he knew it all, when in fact he knew nothing. They'd used him and he hadn't seen through it. Well, it wasn't going to happen again. He was sure now. He knew what he was going to do. One way or another he was going to get his money. He wouldn't run. He'd wait and, if necessary, fight somehow. He'd find a way. After all, just as he didn't know them, they didn't know him. He was playing to different rules. They couldn't know what he was going to do next, that was his one advantage. Just as he was an outsider in their world, they were outsiders in his. They couldn't understand him. None of them could ever understand him. So maybe if he did things his way they couldn't touch him.

And it wasn't as if he didn't have any resources. He'd dealt with Gatley, he could deal with them. He just had to calm down and think things through. He just had to think.

He had to think what he could use against them.

To start with there was Gatley's pink file. That was a useful bargaining tool.

Yes, he was thinking now. He mustn't let them freak him.

He paid for his shopping and sat on one of the benches on the little terrace outside Tesco's to read the newspaper. It was a week since he'd seen Duke at the zoo and things were nice and quiet.

There wasn't anything in the paper about Gatley, for instance. Already people were forgetting all about him.

He'd been sitting there for about five minutes when he looked up and saw a man staring at him.

He was a fat, square man with white hair and a fat, square, suntanned face. Sean thought he vaguely recognized him; maybe he was one of the regulars from the pub. He was certainly dressed like them, in immaculate jeans and a brightly coloured ski jacket.

He went back to his paper. But when he looked up again the man was still there, leaning on the railings, staring at him.

Sean got up, picked up his bags and headed for home. The man followed. He didn't come up the stairs, however, and when Sean looked back down from the walkway he'd gone.

Was this the next step? The man had been too blatant to be a policeman, so was he working for Mathews? And if so, which one?

Had he been sent to scare him?

Hah! That was Sean's job, hanging around and making people paranoid.

There was no point in worrying about it. He just had to be a little more alert from now on.

That night he went down to the pub for the first time since he'd killed Gatley. He'd been reluctant to go at first, but it was George's birthday, and he thought he'd better make the effort. He told himself it was all part of getting back to normal.

Fat John was still in America and a couple of other people had promised to show up but never did, so there were just the two of them. It was a decidedly gloomy affair. Sean drank slowly to start with, but somewhere along the line he forgot, and by ten o'clock he was gone.

They hadn't spoken since half past nine. George was slumped at the table reading a beer mat for the tenth time. Sean was studying the patterns of foam round the sides of his beer glass. He decided to attempt some kind of conversation.

'How's your book coming along?' he asked.

'I was having a look at it at the weekend, as it goes.'

'It's funny,' said Sean. 'Since you told me about it, I've been noticing dogs a lot more. I know what you mean about this being a city of dogs. We've even got an Isle of Dogs. Hah!' His comment hung in the air for a few moments before collapsing.

'You been down there lately?' said George. 'On that new railway they've got? It's like Disneyland.'

'No.'

'I went down there a few weeks ago with Chris. Stupid cunt actually thought it was a real island.'

'Oh.'

'Maybe I'll write something about it in my book. Dogs and place names.'

'Maybe I should write a book,' said Sean.

'What about?'

'How about ants?'

'Ants?'

'Yes, ants. You've been thinking about dogs, I've been thinking about ants.'

'Who's interested in ants?'

'I am. They're weird bastards, all insects are weird. But ants are the weirdest. Ants are organized. Ants have got society.'

'What, like Noël Coward?'

'No, listen. I listened to your shit about dogs, now you listen to my shit about ants, all right? I happen to have been thinking about ants a lot in the last few days.'

'Yeah, all right. Ant society.'

'Right. Each ants' nest is like a little city, you see?

Everything running perfectly, with every ant knowing his place. They've all got a function and they just work, all day and night, work, work, work. And what for? Not for themselves, as such, but for the whole nest, for society. It's like one single being, like a body. The fingers and toes can all work, but they're nothing without each other. You take a single ant and separate it, it's lost, it'll probably die. It becomes meaningless, it needs the other ants; it needs the whole ant society.'

'That's absolutely fascinating.'

'Ah yes, but look around you, George, that's what all this is, England. It's a fucking ants' nest. Each person pootling about reckoning he's the centre of the fucking world, but they can't see, can't see that everything's connected, and they're nothing, nothing without the other ants. I mean, do you know how to mend a telephone? Do you even know how a telephone works? What about a car? Could you make a car? Could you make spaghetti? Plastic? Bread? What about cotton? You couldn't even weave wool. Jesus, I bet you couldn't even rub two sticks together to make fire.'

'I've got a lighter.'

'That's precisely my point. We've got a co-operative society, that's how society works. We're all little cogs, we all make our own little contribution.'

'And what's your contribution, then?' George said, looking up from his beer mat.

'Well, I used to think I wasn't part of it. That I was outside the nest looking in.'

'Oh blimey,' George laughed. 'Sean Crawley, ladies and gentlemen: the classroom malcontent, the adolescent existentialist, rebel without a frigging satchel. Grow up, Sean, this is the real fucking world, and you're up to your arse in it.'

'That's precisely what I'm saying, George, if you'd let me finish.'

'Go on, then.'

'Well, as I say, that's what I used to think: that I had no part in all this. But now I realize what my function is . . .' He stopped himself just in time.

'What?'

Jesus, he was drunk. He'd nearly said it. What an idiot. He tried not to blush.

'What?'

'Well, you know . . .'

'No, I don't know. What?'

'Something, I don't know . . . I guess I'm just an ant, like other people.'

'Oh, Jesus Christ, Sean. You aren't half a wanker sometimes.'

Don't I know it? he thought. Don't I bloody know it? He'd nearly told George he was a murderer. That his role in society was killing people.

He really did have to stop drinking.

But he didn't.

Eleven o'clock came and went. The landlord bolted the doors. Half eleven. Twelve . . .

Sean wasn't sure exactly what time it was when they finally decided to leave. A barmaid unlocked the door for them, and Sean stepped out into the cool night air. For a moment he was slightly dizzy. Then, as the fog cleared, he saw the white-haired man leaning against a factory wall up the street.

Sean ducked back inside just as George was coming out.

'Goodnight, then,' he said.

'Eh?'

'See you around.' He hurried through the pub, into the other bar, and let himself out by another door.

There was no one around. He jogged down the street without looking back.

He'd have to go home in a wide circle, but there was nothing for it. The white-haired man had definitely been waiting for him.

As he trotted round a corner someone called his name, and he turned round without thinking.

It was Duke. He grinned at Sean, put two fingers in his mouth and whistled. Sean tried to make a run for it, but Duke grabbed him by the arm and held him tight with one meaty fist.

'Good evening, Sean,' he said in a mock-friendly way as the white-haired man sauntered up to them.

Sean grunted.

Now what?

Duke studied Sean without any show of emotion. 'This isn't your way home,' he said.

'I was going for a take-away,' Sean said, trying not to sound drunk.

Duke released him. 'You were going for a take-away?' he said sarcastically. 'Come on, you can do better than that.'

'All right. What do you want, Duke?'

'I told you. I want you to fuck off.'

'I'm owed money.'

'Fuck off.'

'No.'

Duke threw Sean back into the arms of the other man, who held him by the elbows. Duke slapped him twice, very quickly and very hard, then jabbed a forefinger in his face.

'Listen, pal. I'm pissed off with being pissed about. I've had enough. I want you gone. I never want to see you again.'

'You pay me and I'm gone.'

'Never. I'd top you first.'

'That wouldn't be a very good idea,' said Sean, trying to control the shake in his voice.

'And why is that?'

Sean jerked his head back over his shoulder at the other man. 'How much does he know?'

'Turner? Enough.'

'So you're telling everyone now?'

Duke slapped him again, whipping his head right round.

'All right, just listen,' Sean shouted. 'If you read the papers, then you'll know that when Gatley was killed, his file was stolen.'

'And?'

'His file of evidence. Evidence against Derek Mathews.'

'Yeah, well, that evidence's no good now, is it? Mathews is already in the shit.'

'That's not what I mean. What I mean is it's evidence of another sort now; it's the only link with the murder. It could be very incriminating if it ever turned up. Especially with some notes of my own in it.'

'What are you trying to say?'

'You know the line, you've seen enough films. Do you want me to spell it out? Okay. If anything happens to me, then the file comes to light, all right? It's hidden now, safely hidden. If you want it to be found, fair enough. If not, then you'd better leave me alone.'

'You little bastard.'

'I'll do a deal with you.'

'What kind of a deal?'

'I'll give you the file, if you give me the money.'

'We're back to the money, are we?'

'We never left it. Once I'm paid I'll clear out.'

Duke thought for a while. 'All right,' he said in the end. 'Meet me in the park tomorrow at one.'

'Same place?'

'Same place. And bring the file.'

'You'll pay me?'

'If that's the only way you'll fuck off out of it.'

'It is.'

'I'll bring some cash then.'

'Ten thousand.'

'Ten thousand . . .?' Duke stared at him, then seemed to come to a decision. He smiled.

'Ten grand. Tomorrow at one. And then you disappear.'

'Fine. See you then.'

'See you.'

'And don't bother looking for . . .'

'Oh, fuck off.' Duke shook his head. The white-haired man laughed and the two of them walked back up the street to where a white transit van was parked. They got in, slammed the doors and drove off.

21

Sean leant against the wall and let out a long slow breath. He was shaking, and his knees were weak. He didn't feel up to walking just yet. He stood there breathing heavily and swearing quietly to himself.

He no longer felt drunk. His system was flooded with adrenalin and he felt painfully alert. So they'd made their next move and he had control of the game.

Now what?

He was about to start back to the flat when he saw George walking slowly towards him.

'What the fuck's going on?' George asked when he was near enough.

'Oh, it's nothing. They owe me some money.'

'*They owe you?* It didn't look that way.'

'Yeah, well, they dispute the fact, don't they?'

'You're telling me.'

'They don't want to pay me. I keep asking, they get angry.'

'What's the money for?'

'Oh, it's very complicated. Sub-contracting and all that. They're builders, I did some work for them. They claim I cocked up the job.'

'Is it a lot?'

'Yeah. You could say that.'

'If you ask me, I don't think you're going to get it.'

'You may be right. Listen, George, I've got some stuff, paperwork and that, contracts, receipts, you know? It proves I did the work. I've told them I'm going to a solicitor. I think they might try and get it off me. So, just to be on the safe side, would you mind looking after it for me?'

'Sure.'

'Would you take it now?'

'If you like.'

They set off for Sean's flat.

'How come you're still here, anyway?' Sean asked.

'I didn't know what was going on, you going back through the pub like that, so I went after you. Then I saw that big bloke running down the road, so I followed. I saw it all. But I didn't fancy my chances if I got stuck in.'

'Thanks anyway, mate.'

There was no one about; the streets were quiet and empty. It was a pleasant, warm night and Sean relaxed a little.

Once in the flat, he fished the file out from under the carpet where he'd put it with his money. Then he found a large jiffy-bag in the cupboard in the spare room, put the file in it and taped it shut.

He tried to give George some money for a taxi home, but he wouldn't accept it.

'Thanks again, George,' he said at the door. 'I never thought I'd be happy to see your ugly face.'

'Ta.' George set off.

'Oh, and by the way.'

'What?'

'Happy birthday.'

Sean double-locked the door, shifted his chest of drawers in front of it and went to bed. But he didn't sleep until it was almost light.

He woke late, feeling dry and groggy, had some breakfast and, at twelve o'clock, cycled over to the pool.

The roped-off section was full of the usual types, methodically swimming up and down. Sean joined them and as usual his mind drifted.

It was perfectly clear that Duke had no intention of giving him any money today, or any other day for that matter. He'd probably just have grabbed the file and walked off with it. And there would've been nothing Sean could have done about it.

Well, fuck you, Duke. Sean looked at the clock and smiled. One fifteen. By now it would be obvious to Duke that Sean wasn't going to show up.

The pool was starting to get crowded with office workers on their lunch-break, so he changed and cycled over to a café on Morning Lane where he had a huge fry-up. Afterwards he went to Victoria Park, stretched out on the grass in the blazing sun and dozed.

It was nearly four when he got home.

He carried his bike up the stairs, and hardly noticed the weight at all.

The bottom half of his front door had been kicked clean off. The top half was still secured by the two locks.

He left the bike outside and went in. The place had been torn apart. What few belongings he had were strewn everywhere. His bed was torn open, furniture smashed, the curtains pulled down. The contents of the kitchen cabinets, the chest of drawers, the cupboard in the spare room were on the floor. All his personal documents and his clothes had been ripped up, the television booted in. They'd even smashed the toilet.

The bedroom carpet was up, and somehow they'd managed to tear it nearly in half. All his money was gone.

He had nothing. No flat, no belongings, no money. He sat on the floor and stared at the piles of rubbish.

He stayed sitting there, unmoving, as the afternoon passed into evening, and slowly the wild tangle of emotions quietened down and dissipated into nothing.

A sort of calm came over him. He had nothing, so he had nothing to lose. It was true, he really didn't have anything to lose. After all, he'd killed someone. He'd committed the worst crime there was. Anything else he did now would mean nothing. So here he was, he'd slipped right out of the bottom of society.

That was all very well, but it didn't help. The first problem was somewhere to sleep.

George.

He looked for the phone.

He found it under the remains of his mattress, the receiver yanked from its cord.

He had a few coins left, so he took his bike downstairs, chained it to the railings and went round to try the pay-phone behind the flats. It wouldn't accept his money. He wandered from phone-box to phone-box, but they were all either busted, converted to card phones, or there was such a long queue that it didn't seem worth waiting. In the end he thought that he'd gone this far, he might as well carry on and walk to George's.

Ten minutes later he was riding up in the piss-stinking lift, trying to work out some sort of plan. But nothing presented itself.

The door to George's flat was half open, and a terrible sick feeling grew from the pit of Sean's stomach as he pushed it back and went in.

Shit. They knew about George.

They must have seen the two of them together last night.

Shit.

The mess here was worse, because George had more stuff and because it had always been so orderly. The stereo, the neat shelves, the computers, the toys. Sean could hardly bear to look. He felt responsible. Fuck it, he *was* responsible.

A mixture of fury and guilt joined the sickness.

He stood, unable to move for a while. And then he saw the footprints. The red outlines of boot-tread coming from the bedroom. In the terrible, dead silence his heart sounded amplified, like something in a horror film. He gripped his head in his hands, squeezing it tight.

'Oh, no,' he said.

He took a deep breath and followed the footprints to their source.

It looked like a bomb had gone off. The room was trashed. And worst of all was the sickening red splash on one wall, and the horrible sticky patches on the bed and carpet.

Sean ran into the bathroom and threw up.

The bastards. The bastards. The fucking bastards.

He sobbed and dribbled into the toilet. 'I'm sorry, George. God, I'm sorry.'

And then he was scared.

How long ago had this happened? And if they'd done this to George, what would they do to him?

He ran out of the flat and down the emergency stairs. He couldn't face the lift.

He reached the ground and kept on running.

He ran and ran until he found himself back home.

He hadn't really meant to come here, he hadn't thought. But now he needed a plan.

First he needed a weapon.

He went into the spare room and rummaged through the pile of rubbish they'd spilled from the cupboard.

He'd been on a job once where they'd replaced an old sash-window, the type where the windows were counter-balanced with long lead weights on thin ropes. Sean had salvaged the weights, thinking that he might be able to get a bit of money for them, and they'd been in the cupboard ever since.

He found them. He picked one up and tested it. It was certainly solid and heavy enough. He practised swinging it like a club. It would do for the time being.

In a heap of clothes in the hall he found a raincoat in reasonable condition. He put it on and slipped the weight up one sleeve, holding it in place with his cupped hand. He walked into the bathroom and looked at himself in a piece of broken mirror. You couldn't notice the weight.

He let it slip down into his hand, and then he swung it at a wooden chair. It splintered. It felt good smashing the chair, so he hit it a few more times until he was satisfied.

But he didn't want to have to hold it all the time.

He sorted through the pile and found a length of twine and a knife. He cut off a length of twine and tied one end to the weight, then tied the other end round his shoulders with a slip knot, so that the weight was dangling in the sleeve. By releasing the knot with his other hand he could let the weight drop.

He worked at it until he had it just right.

He left the second weight and the rest of the twine by the door and set off down the stairs.

Now what?

He stopped. It was eleven o'clock at night. He had nowhere to go, his only friend's flat looked like an abattoir, he had no money and he had no plan.

All he had was a stupid sash-weight up his sleeve and about two pounds in his pocket. That was it.

Why hadn't he run when Duke told him?

How could he possibly hope to achieve anything against two rival groups of builders, and the entire police force?

He sat on the steps at the bottom of the flats and began to sob.

He was still crying, twenty minutes later, when he heard footsteps and voices and looked up to see the white-haired man, Turner, coming towards him with a younger guy.

Sean jumped up and ran for it. Turner yelled.

Sean knew the area better than his pursuers and he soon shook them off. He was in a part of the estate where low-rise housing blocks were mixed with small factories, warehouses and sweat shops with names like Zhanco Export and Goldpower Limited. The streets were badly lit and completely deserted. He kept close to the walls and in the shadows as much as possible. He stopped and listened. Not a sound.

The weight in his sleeve was getting heavier, and the rope was cutting into his shoulder. He felt rather foolish and considered getting rid of it, but decided to keep it, just to be on the safe side.

He needed transport; maybe he could skirt back to the flats and get the bike. Would they expect him to do that? Or would they expect him to be miles away by now? The only problem was, he had nowhere to go, but if he had the bike he'd be in a better position, he'd be more mobile. Yes, that was the best bet. Carefully, he started back. Still he saw no one. He crept from block to block. He came to the community hall near his flat and edged round it. A tall street-light threw a yellow pool on the ground. He crawled along and was almost past the light when the massive bulk of Duke slid in front of him, and one big hand came up and rested gently on his chest.

Duke looked tired.

'What?' said Sean.

'You know what.' Duke pushed with his fingertips and Sean staggered back against the wall of the community centre.

'You never showed with the file. What are you playing at?'

'I knew you wouldn't give me any money.'

Duke sighed.

'What are you going to do, then?' said Sean. 'Kill me right here in the street?'

Duke sighed. He took off his glasses and wiped his eyes. 'Why do you have to make everything so melodramatic? So over the top?'

'Me?' Sean protested.

'God, I am pissed off with you.'

'What am I supposed to do, eh? You don't give me any options.'

'You're supposed to go away.'

'How? I've got no money, have I?'

Duke took an envelope out of his pocket. 'In here there's your passport, a ticket to Almeria, and a hundred quid in Spanish money.'

Sean reached for it.

'No. You've got to learn your fucking place first.' Duke slapped him, knocking his head back against the wall.

'This is your last warning. I'm not playing any more, okay? I've had it up to here.' He punched Sean in the guts.

Sean doubled up and wheezed for breath. I've had it up to here, too, he thought. But he'd seen the blow coming and had managed to move away from it and tense up slightly. He pretended it had hurt him worse than it had.

Bent over, he looked at Duke's shoes and saw a red stain on one. He remembered the ugly splash on George's wall and released the knot under his arm. He felt the weight drop down into his fingers. He held it behind his back as he straightened up.

Duke slapped him again.

'Next time I see you,' he said, 'you'll be in a coffin, all right?'

'Fuck off,' said Sean, and he swung.

Duke, expecting some feeble misdirected punch with no weight behind it, simply rocked back slightly and lifted a forearm to ward off the blow, a look of irritation on his face.

He didn't realize about the extra length until it was too late. The wide arc of Sean's swing came round, so that, as his elbow met Duke's arm, the sash-weight came sharply in and hit the big man above the ear.

His head rung with a clanging sound, as if Sean had struck a rock, and the lead bar bounced off it.

Duke reminded Sean of a character hit on the head in a cartoon. His head wobbled and his eyes went out of focus. His face lost its animation, it seemed to blur, with one image laid on top of another. Sean half expected to see lines spiralling around his head, with little stars and twittering birds.

Duke stepped back drunkenly, his arms out for balance. He tried to look at Sean.

Sean swore, and as he did so Duke snapped out of it. He came back into focus and looked straight into Sean's eyes.

Sean immediately moved round, away from the wall, and, putting all his weight and strength behind the blow, he aimed the bar at the same spot.

This time it was more like hitting an egg. Duke's skull crunched as the lead sank into it and sticky liquid splashed out.

Duke gave a tiny shriek and toppled sideways against the community centre, as if his spine had suddenly been yanked out of his body.

He slipped to the ground and lay on the pavement among the dog shit and Kentucky Fried Chicken boxes. A pile of rags and dead meat.

Sean picked up the envelope containing the money, passport and plane ticket, then saw Duke's wallet sticking out of the back pocket of his jeans. He gingerly pulled it out and opened it. Inside were two ten-pound notes and a five. He put the wallet in his pocket, then slipped the sash-weight up his sleeve, turned, and walked away from there.

Nausea and fear bubbled up inside him.

He felt faint.

He was back in the yellow world.

22

He seemed to have been running all day. He was tired, but he couldn't stop. He had to get away. Turner was still around somewhere. And then there was the body. Another body. Two now. This time he'd really done it. There really was no going back.

He was in Victoria Park. The sky was clear, and it was nearly a full moon. He slowed down. There was no one following.

He reached the canal and looked at the black water; it was flat and smooth. He took off the raincoat and put the weight in one of the pockets. He took out Duke's wallet, carefully wiped it, then put it in the other pocket. He bundled it all up with the twine and dropped it in the water. It sank.

He checked the rest of his clothing for blood. It looked okay.

He started walking westwards along the canal, towards Islington. It was fine as long as he kept moving. If he walked for long enough it would be morning. He could change the Spanish money, get out of London, maybe go to Reading, stay with his parents. Yes, that was an idea. Start again from there.

He lost the canal in Islington, and took the Pentonville Road down to King's Cross, heading vaguely for the centre of town, where he wouldn't be so conspicuous.

It had just gone midnight when he passed King's Cross station and saw a group of about fifteen young people marching along with carrier-bags. It could only mean one thing, a party of some sort. He tagged along with them, and no one paid him any attention.

They made their way into the tangle of grim little streets behind the two stations, and eventually arrived at what appeared to be an old warehouse.

There was a short queue of people at the entrance and the sound of loud music.

Sean joined the back of the queue. Up ahead a huge black guy with glasses was taking money. Everyone in the queue was white.

Sean paid ten pounds and went up the narrow stairs towards the noise.

On the first floor he came to a large, bare room. It was horribly hot and damp, packed with people milling about in a dim, yellowish light. Some danced, but most just talked, despite the fact that the music made things very difficult. It was a sort of electro-industrial funk hybrid, much of it sounding home-made. A basic backing of raw drum-machine with various sampled sound-effects over the top, interspersed with the odd early seventies disco track.

Sean thought his best chance for a bed was to find a girl, so he prowled the room looking for someone suitable. After about ten minutes he saw Mary with her little friend, Sandra. He hadn't seen them since that Saturday in the pub. He decided to try Mary.

He didn't fancy his chances much, but it was better than nothing.

'Hello, Mary.' She was wearing a short, high-waisted, dark-green leather skirt and a black cotton polo-neck. Her blonde hair was loose tonight, tossed about in no particular style.

She smiled at him. 'Sean. What are you doing here?'

'Oh, you know.'

'Don't usually see you at this sort of thing.'

'I don't get about much really these days.'

'Have you got a drink?'

'No. Is there anywhere here I can buy some?'

'Here, do you want a can?'

'Great, thanks.'

Mary leant down and picked up the plastic bag at her feet, from which she took a can of Red Stripe.

'It's not very cold, I'm afraid.'

'That's okay.' Sean opened the can and drank some beer. It felt hot, but he was glad of it.

'There's a guy selling some at a table over there,' said Sandra.

'Oh, right, thanks.' Sean smiled politely.

They chatted for a while, but Sean couldn't get any sexual tension going; the more they talked, the more they seemed just friends. Perhaps not even that.

It didn't help that Sandra hung around, occasionally making some offhand remark to Mary. Sean wished she'd bugger off, but there didn't seem much hope of that happening.

It was funny how different the two girls were. Mary showing off her legs, smiling, open, all blonde hair and tanned skin. Sandra small and skinny, black hair, white skin, black clothes, severe, black-framed glasses.

Sean started to get worried that he was wasting time. If he wasn't going to get anywhere with Mary, then he should be trying elsewhere before it got too late. It was just that he didn't really know where to start with someone else; he was too long out of practice. He knew from experience that the more you wanted something, the less likely you were to get it. The harder you tried, the harder it was. If you went out looking for a girl, you usually ended up drunk and frustrated. But if you went out happy with your life, not searching for something new, they threw themselves at you.

Well, he had to try.

He made his excuses and wandered off into the crowd. Mary didn't seem exactly sorry to see him go. He found the table in the corner where they were selling beer and bought four overpriced cans of Foster's.

It was hopeless, he didn't know anyone. There were no single women. He'd never been any good at picking girls up this way. Shit, they probably weren't out trying to be picked up, anyway.

He queued for the toilet, and in the end shared the single bowl with a drunken Scouser moaning about London.

Buttoning his flies on the way out, he recognized someone coming up the stairs, a slightly stocky girl with a bob. His hopes rose, but he couldn't place her. He followed her into the main room, trying to remember how he knew her. He looked down at her thick legs and the Doctor Marten shoes she wore with no socks. God, she was familiar. Only one thing for it, he'd have to take the plunge, say hello.

He touched her lightly on the shoulder and she turned.

'Hi!' he said cheerily. She looked at him, puzzled. He ploughed on.

'Aren't you . . .' And then he froze. He'd remembered her name.

It was Emm, the teacher, Gatley's lodger.

'Oh, er, sorry . . . I thought you were somebody else. Sorry.'

He shrank back into the crowd. London could be a ridiculously small place sometimes. He felt very conspicuous now; he needed to hide. He realized there was no chance of Emm knowing who he was, but he was feeling desperately vulnerable. If he could find Mary again, talk to her, appear normal, that might help.

He moved round the edge of the room, keeping an eye out for both Emm and Mary. Luckily he saw Mary first. She was talking to Sandra and a tall bloke in a baggy suit.

He walked over to them, grinning casually.

'Here,' he said, and gave her two cans of Foster's. She gave one to Sandra.

'Thanks. Enjoying yourself?'

Sean shrugged, and that was it, he couldn't think of anything else to say or do.

The tall bloke asked Mary to dance, and she said yes, so that was that. He watched them jigging about, and leaning close to each other to talk above the noise. There was something between them that had been missing between her and Sean.

He sat down on a sort of low wooden stage, on which the DJ's equipment was set up. Sandra sat down next to him.

'You're not drinking?' she said.

'No, I ran out.'

'Here,' said Sandra, and she gave him back the can which Mary had given her.

'Thanks.' The simple gesture made him feel a whole lot better, and he slightly revised his opinion of the girl.

'What do you think of the music?' she asked.

'I don't know. Some of the old stuff's all right, but it's a bit loud. I think I must be getting old.'

'It's not exactly easy listening, is it?' The track they were playing now seemed to be made up of sampled road-drill noises.

'To tell you the truth,' said Sean, 'I hate it.'

'I know what you mean. This whole thing's a bit of a bore really. I only came because Mary wanted to, and now look at her. I won't be seeing much more of her tonight. She's been after him for ages.'

They sat in silence and watched Mary for a while.

'I think I'm going to go, actually,' said Sandra. 'Hang on.' She got up and went over to Mary and shouted something in her ear. Mary laughed and nodded, waved to her. Sandra came back.

'Are you going to stay?' she said, picking up her bag.

Sean shrugged.

'You don't look as if you're really enjoying yourself.'

'No.'

'Come back for a drink, if you like. I only live round the corner.'

Sean half frowned and half smiled, and a warm feeling settled in his stomach.

'Yeah?' he said.

'Yeah. Come on, then.'

As he followed Sandra down the stairs, he started to see her in a new light. She was actually quite attractive underneath it all, and though she was small she wasn't too badly put together. Her body looked more shapely than it had before. Of course, he told himself, her invitation didn't mean anything, she was just bored. But if he played his cards right, he should at least be able to sleep on her sofa.

Once outside they walked in a business-like way, briskly and purposefully, and without saying much.

Sandra lived alone in a one-bedroom flat just off Euston Road. It was decorated in a tasteful monochrome and had all the modern conveniences you could want: a CD with tiny powerful speakers, FST television, video, word processor, washing machine, microwave, dishwasher.

'You do okay in the film business, then?' Sean asked, settling on to the black leather sofa.

'Video.'

'Yeah, well, I thought these days everyone wanted to make films.'

'We do have a film production department, ads mostly, but I'm in video. Bloody pop music.'

'And you do all right?'

'I do all right. But I got a lot of money when my grandparents died.'

'Oh.'

'Do you want a drink?'

'Sure. What you got?'

'Hmm. I've got some gin left, I think.' She knelt down by a low table and sorted the bottles. 'Some vodka, a little bit of Black Label, you know, Johnnie Walker. Some beer in the fridge.'

'Johnnie Walker would be great. If that's all right.'

Sandra had the same.

She put on an old Miles Davis album and joined him on the sofa.

She rolled a joint, and they smoked and chatted, and drank some more, then after a while he kissed her, and after that they went to bed.

But in the darkness of the bedroom Sean became disorientated. Without her glasses on he wasn't sure of Sandra's features, and in the half-light they kept shifting and changing, until all he could see was Susan's face. Her big pale eyes, her lips, her teeth, her long neck. And when he closed his eyes it was worse.

As he tried to shake her off, she changed again. Her features became ugly and twisted, as if she was angry or terrified. He felt like he was raping Gatley's wife. He tried looking down at Sandra's small breasts, and it helped a bit, but his eyes kept on being drawn back to her face. He couldn't come and in the end he had to stop.

He lay on his back, staring at the ceiling, and held Sandra's cool naked body against his.

'That was nice,' she said, and he kissed her.

She fell asleep long before he did.

Sandra had to be up early for work. She showered and had breakfast, and then explained to Sean how to let himself out. She was relaxed and friendly. They said they'd see each other again some time, and she smiled at him as she left. She had a nice smile.

Sean dozed till about eleven, then got up and washed.

While he ate breakfast he considered what to do. His mind had been working all night, but not in a very productive manner.

All he·knew for sure was that he mustn't go anywhere near his flat.

The first thing to do was go to the exchange at King's Cross and convert the Spanish money into English. There was no way he was going to Spain just yet. For the time being he'd go to Reading. He'd get a train from Paddington once he had some money.

Yes, that was the safest bet.

Don't go anywhere near the flat.

But as he thought of it an image flashed into his mind. He could vividly picture the second sash-weight sitting on the floor by his front door, next to the splintered chair.

Bollocks.

No, it wasn't a problem. Forget it. Don't be stupid. Why would anyone even look in the flat?

Okay.

He pulled Sandra's door shut and set off towards King's Cross. Another sunny day, the streets looked tired and dusty.

They *would* go to his flat. The police would go to his flat. First thing after finding Duke's body they'd do a door-to-door inquiry; check every flat. Find out if anyone saw anything. And then they'd find his flat. The broken door, the signs of violence, the sash-weight, the chair he'd attacked.

All the more reason not to go back. Stay away. He was safe as long as he stayed away.

He came out on to Euston Road and turned towards the station. Cars, taxis, buses, lorries, hammered past him. People bustled on the pavement. The world went about its business.

Even if the police did put two and two together, the flat wasn't in his name. The neighbours didn't know him; he never saw them.

He crossed over the road to the bureau de change and handed over his money. A hundred quid's worth, Duke had said. He watched the cashier count it out. Better than nothing, even though this time yesterday he'd had nearly four grand.

Okay. Now the underground to Paddington.

But what about his documents? In the flat. They were torn up, but they still had his name all over them.

Okay. Stay calm. What if he got the bus home? Removed all traces of himself, threw everything out, ditched the weight, burned all his documents? Then it'd just look like an empty flat that had been vandalized.

No. Too risky. He had to get away. He had to get to Reading.

Fuck Reading. He didn't want to go to bloody Reading. He didn't want to go anywhere, there was nowhere to go. He had to finish this thing.

On the bus he felt purposeful again.

He couldn't escape; his life had shrunk to this vicious little circle and he was at the centre of it, like a man in a spotlight. If he tried to move, the spot would follow him. He had no choice really; he never had, not since that first phone call from Duke, sending him to Highbury to meet Mathews. Ever since then, the whole thing had been mapped out.

He had no choice.

The estate was unchanged; no police cars, no marauding gangs of builders. There was crime and violence here all the time. Why should anyone think that his crimes were any more interesting than anyone else's? It was all routine, and it was arrogant of him to think otherwise.

His bike was still chained to the railings where he'd left it. That was a good start.

When he looked at the remains of his flat again, he was sure that his plan to clear everything out was the best one. It was the only way he could be sure he was safe. All he had to do was empty it completely and no one would know he'd ever been there.

It didn't take him long; he didn't have much stuff. Everyone else just left their rubbish and old furniture on the stairs, so he did the same; apart from the shattered chair which he carted off to a rubbish bin on another estate, along with the sash-weight. Finally he burned all his paperwork.

When he was done he surveyed the flat. There was nothing to show he'd ever been there. That was it, then, it had all come to this. Nothing. He was broke and George was dead for nothing. It was over.

He felt numb as he went downstairs and unchained his bike for the last time. He got in the saddle and took a final look at the miserable estate.

Then he noticed a white transit van slowly driving along the block.

Jesus Christ.

He spun the bike round, stood on the pedals and took off in the opposite direction. Behind him, he heard the van accelerate.

He forced the pedals down with all his weight, moving swiftly up through the gears. He sailed down to the end of the building and skidded round the corner, heading deeper into the estate. Up the pavement, down a footpath. He switched ratios and felt the gears drop into place and the satisfying pull as he sped up. He hammered up an alley between two blocks, not daring to look back. They could follow him, but it would be difficult, he was more manoeuvrable than them. His fitness regime of the last couple of weeks had paid off; he was pumping along almost effortlessly, and with the adrenalin flowing he felt no pain. He could ride for ever, faster and faster.

He had no route in mind, just the idea to cycle through the most inaccessible places. He sped past a couple of small factories, along a car park, across a patch of grass, down a stretch of road pitted with craters, and then he was on Well Street, going the wrong way up the one-way street past the market stalls. Someone shouted at him, but he couldn't slow down now.

Tesco's came into view. He could go left there, head up towards the park.

Then a mother with two little girls stepped out from behind a market stall. He swerved across the road and skidded on a pile of damp cardboard and old newspapers. His front wheel hit the kerb, and he was in the air.

He crashed over a stall selling Portuguese jeans, and his head hit something.

Instead of coming up to meet him, the ground seemed to be going away. Sounds echoed in his head. The world went grey on him. He could taste rusty metal. He sank into a huge pool of warm blood. And then nothing.

23

'I love the sound of money. I love the sound of money.'

Sean could hear voices. His head was tingling and fizzing. There were people staring down at him. He didn't know any of them.

'Do you want a present?'

'What?'

There was something warm and sticky clinging to the left-hand side of his face. He retched.

'Do you want a present?'

It was a parrot, a mechanical talking parrot, inside a glass box. It winked at him.

'I love the sound of money. I love the sound of money.'

Someone knelt down, a raw, bony man, with close-cropped hair and a tight beard and moustache. He stared at Sean with small bright eyes.

'Are you all right?' His voice was husky, quiet.

'Yeah.' Sean lied. He was sitting on the pavement, outside a pet shop. The ring of people were still watching him.

'Can you get up?' the man asked. He had a Northern accent, Newcastle maybe.

'I think so.'

The man helped him up. He was slightly smaller than Sean, but he had a reassuringly strong grip. He led Sean away from the crowd.

'Thanks,' said Sean. 'I think I'm okay now. I think I can manage.'

The white van was waiting round the corner. The fat man, Turner, opened the doors at the back.

Sean tried to break away but his head hurt, and any sudden movement was agony.

The husky man held him firmly by the arm and shoved him into the van. He lay on the metal floor, trying not to think. Turner and the other man got in, and the door clanged shut. The van started to move.

So that was it, then, they'd got him. He found that he didn't really care.

He closed his eyes and studied the pain. His left arm felt stiff, and it hurt when he moved it. There was a rip in his trousers, and a sore graze on his knee. His head was bleeding from a shallow cut up in the hair somewhere, and he could feel a lump growing. He wiped some blood from his face. The worst part was the headache.

He tried to get up, but Turner put a foot on his back.

'Stay down there,' he said. Sean stayed down. The van smelled of oil and paint. There was sand on the floor and a few old newspapers and dirty rags. Nuts, bolts, screws and nails rattled about, rolling backwards and forwards. Sean stared at a small hole by one of the rear lights; through it he could see the road.

After about ten minutes the van stopped, and Sean heard the driver get out. They waited for perhaps a quarter of an hour. Neither of the two men in the back said anything. Then the driver got back in.

'What's he say?' asked the bearded man.

'Got to go to his place in Suffolk, wait for him there.'

'Sod that,' said Turner. 'I'm not buggering off all the way up there.'

'Shut up, Ken,' said the bearded man. 'We don't want any more cock-ups. We'll do what he wants.'

'Any more cock-ups? Oh, that's rich, that is. He's the one that's caused all the cock-ups.'

'Go on, then, Carl,' said the bearded man to the driver. 'Let's go.'

The engine started and they were off again. The van boomed and thundered as they picked up speed. It was like being inside a drum.

A while later they stopped at a McDonald's, and Carl, the driver, got out again for some food. They didn't give Sean any. He stayed on the floor.

By half two they were out of London and on a motorway. The bearded man nudged Sean with his foot.

'You might as well get up,' he said. Sean was happy where he was, nursing his headache.

'Nah,' said Turner. 'Leave him down there.' He chuckled. 'Come on, get up.'

Sean got up, wincing as he moved his bruised muscles. He shifted on to one of the wooden benches that ran down either side of the van and sat facing the two men.

It was his first chance to get a proper look at Turner. He had a typical labourer's build, big and meaty with thick arms and legs, and a big block head. His face was evenly tanned and scored with deep seams, and he had a wide mouth with fat lips and large, well-spaced teeth. He was wearing jeans and a pale-lemon sports shirt. Despite his white hair he was probably only in his forties.

The bearded man was several years younger than Turner. Although he was small, he looked like he was made of granite. There wasn't a trace of fat on him. He had a short overhanging forehead and very thick, black eyebrows above his gleaming red-rimmed eyes. Beneath them his nose was flat and bent. There was nothing soft about him, nothing frivolous; he was like a big brawny man put through a car-crusher and compacted into this small, hard thing. He was wearing grey trousers and what looked like a military shirt, khaki, buttoned up to his neck.

To avoid looking at the two of them, Sean turned and stared out of the front.

'Trying to find out where we're going, are you, Sherlock?' Turner laughed. Sean looked back down at the floor.

'Bung the radio on, would you, Carl?' Turner called out, lighting a cigarette. 'There's a good boy.'

Sean could just hear a DJ's voice over the din of the van, and then a record started. It sounded like the Bee Gees.

Shit, he thought. Oh shit.

He'd never been brave, but usually when it came down to it he could just accept things as unavoidable. It was the not knowing that was getting to him now. That was the frightening part. Once something started then it had to end, and while it was happening you were usually too caught up in it to think. But before it started, then you could only wait and imagine. Maybe if he concentrated on his headache he wouldn't get so scared.

Turner reached under his seat for a carrier-bag and took two cans of Heineken out of it. He handed one to the hard man. There were two little hisses as they opened them. Then Turner began to sing.

'Didn't we have a loverlee time the day we went to Bangor, la-diddy taa-titty tum-ti-taa, and the wheels went round.' He laughed and drank some of his beer.

'Look at him,' he said, wiping his lips. 'Sean Crawley, the great detective, or should I say Connery? Here, you know what? I talked to him on the phone once, on that Islington job. He rang up Duke, right, when he was playing Sherlock Holmes. He called himself "Mr Connery", can you believe it? So's no one would know who he was. Ha, ha. What a clever dick, eh? Must have taken a long time to think that one up, eh? Clever bastard. College boy, are you? You should join the police force, Mr Connery; they need clever dicks like you. A great detective mind like yours would be an asset to the force. No, tell you what, you should join the secret service. Sean Crawley, 007, licensed to ride a push-bike!' Turner found this very funny, and he laughed accordingly.

Sean wondered whether he should probe a bit, see if he could get them to tell him what they intended to do. He hated just sitting there doing nothing, knowing nothing. Maybe if he provoked them they'd open up a bit. Yeah, but what else would they do?

'What are you going to do, then?' he asked.

'We'll see,' said Turner.

'Are you going to kill me?'

Turner just laughed again.

'Duke threatened to kill me. But he might just have been trying to scare me.'

'Shut up about Duke,' the wiry man snapped, and glared at him.

'You know, I might kill you,' Turner said, taking another swig from his can. 'If I feel like it.'

This was getting nowhere. Turner wasn't taking the conversation seriously. Sean had to push it further.

'I don't think you could.' In fact, the more he thought about it, the more he thought he was right. That cheered him up a bit. 'And if you're not going to kill me, then I'm not bothered, so this is all just a waste of time.'

'It's that, all right. We should be at work, not poncing around the countryside with a twat like you.'

'No. You're not a killer, are you, Turner? I mean, I should know, I . . .'

Suddenly, with frightening speed, the hard man leant across and grabbed Sean by the front of his shirt. He yanked him out of his seat, and he crashed forward on to his knees.

The hard man held him a couple of inches in front of his face, and glared at him with his cold little eyes.

'Shut the fuck up.' His husky, high-pitched voice was utterly lacking in feeling of any kind.

He held Sean with one hand, and formed the other into a solid, red fist.

'I could break your fucking neck,' he said quietly.

Sean tensed, waiting for the blow, but it never came. Instead the hard man relaxed his grip, opened his hand, held Sean by the face and flung him back on the floor.

Sean fell on his bruised shoulder and his whole arm went numb.

With as much dignity as possible, which wasn't a lot, he picked himself up, knocked the filth off his clothing and sat down.

'Sounds like I'm missing out on all the fun back there,' Carl shouted from the front. 'Save some for me.'

'So you're just going to beat me up, then. Is that it?' Sean asked, rubbing his bad arm.

Sean realized that he was speaking with a very faint Geordie accent. He did it all the time; took on the speech patterns of whoever he was talking to. He did it as a form of defence, as a way of trying to fit in. It was very subtle, but he was acutely aware that he was doing it now. Overdoing it. He was so tense he was going too far. He told himself to be careful, to calm down.

'Why don't you do as you're told, and shut up?' Turner said.

'What difference does it make? If you're going to beat me up later, you might as well beat me up now.'

'Fucking will, if you don't shut up.'

'Go on, then. Do it. Do it now, it's all the same to me.'

'Oh, yeah?'

'Yeah. It's like going to the dentist, really.'

'You what?'

'You worry about it beforehand, but it's never so bad as you imagine. All you've got to do is tell yourself that tomorrow it'll all be over. Pain doesn't last. You can't remember pain.'

Sean realized he was raving, verging on hysteria. Why didn't he just do what they said, and shut up?

'Yeah,' said Turner. 'It'll be just like going to the dentist, we'll take out all your teeth. Then what, eh? It'll all be over tomorrow, all right, but you'll be eating through a fucking straw for the rest of your life.'

'I could buy false teeth.'

Turner snorted scornfully.

'Thing is, I'd still be alive, wouldn't I? So it wouldn't scare me. I mean, you could spend the rest of the year beating the shit out of me, but I'd still be alive at the end of it. You'd have to stop one day. And then, after that, it's just another memory. So, you see, unless you're going to kill me, I'm not worried.' Well, he almost had himself convinced, anyway, and as long as he talked, then he didn't have to think.

'You're not scared of being beaten up, then?'

'That's not exactly what I meant. But, in the end, no. It passes.'

'How about if we cut your bollocks off?'

'I'm sure you could get used to it. I mean, you should know.'

Sean realized he'd gone too far, and he wished he hadn't said it. It took a second for it to sink in, and then . . .

'You little cunt.' Turner launched himself across the van and knocked Sean sideways with his forearm. 'You smart-arsed little cunt. You're gonna fucking regret that.'

I already do, Sean thought. His ear was singing, and the side of his face felt very hot. He waited for more, but Turner left it at that. And that was a good sign.

Sean straightened up and shuddered. He rested his face in his hands.

'Come here,' said the hard man.

'Uh?' Sean hesitated.

'Come over here. Sit here next to me.'

Sean thought it was probably best to do as he was told. He was wary of the hard man. He couldn't tell what he was thinking; he couldn't tell what he was going to do. He wasn't as transparent as Turner.

As he sat down on the seat the man grabbed his left arm, his bad one, and twisted it up behind his back. Sean doubled over and gasped.

'Does that hurt?'

'Aah.'

'Does it?'

'Yes, of course it bloody hurts. Ow!'

'Are you thinking of tomorrow? Eh? Are you? When the pain won't be there any more? Or are you thinking that it hurts, and that you'd like it to stop? Right now.'

Sean was trying not to think, but the pain was incredible. The hard man forced his arm further up his back. It was the simplest things that hurt the most.

'What if I break your fucking arm? How about that?'

Sean was sweating all over, but he felt very cold. He could hardly breathe, it was hurting so much.

And then it happened. He managed to clear his mind completely; he was away.

He pictured a statue, very vividly. A man of stone. Where was it? Yes, Florence. He was with Annie, on holiday, walking round a museum in Florence. He couldn't remember the name. They'd visited hundreds of the bloody things. For some reason they'd had an argument about the statue. Something to do with emotion in art. That's right, he'd said he thought it was interesting how you could make a statue show emotions, when it was only really a lump of rock. And he'd wondered whether all emotions were just superficial, meaningless posturing. He'd wondered whether deep down inside we weren't all just lumps of rock, without feeling. He knew he never really felt any emotion about anything. He hadn't really meant it, had said it as much to tease Annie as anything else. But she'd got very angry, stormed out of the museum.

That holiday was about the last time when they'd been happy together. Something had happened. Too long alone with each other, they'd realized they didn't have that much to say.

Funny.

Just a silly little incident, a marble statue, a stupid row. It was funny that he should think about it now, with his face pressed against his damp knees and a cold bolt of pain tearing up his spine. Sitting there, weeping, while some maniac tried to break his arm.

Shit. He was back. He'd almost got away. But now he was back in the dentist's chair.

'So you don't mind getting beaten up, eh?' The hard man gave him one more tweak, and then dropped him to the floor. Sean slowly moved his arm down.

'You're full of shit,' the hard man said.

Yes, thought Sean. You're right. I am full of shit.

'No balls, eh?' said Turner, and he kicked Sean in the crotch. There's no other pain like it, really.

First of all the wind was sucked out of him, as if he'd been flung out of an air-lock in space, and then the pain came. He curled up into a ball, hugging his sides. It felt as if an icy hand had been shoved up his arse and was squeezing his guts. The pain filled his whole body.

'You know what?' said Turner. 'I don't think I will cut his balls off, I think I'll just give them a good kicking every now and then. He'll wish I had cut them off by the time I've finished with him. Stupid little twat.'

Sean was trying very hard not to be sick. The pain had dimmed to a general dull ache and he struggled up on to the bench and sat leaning forwards, looking at his shoes and holding himself tight.

This'll pass, he said to himself. This will all pass. It can't go on for ever. Man of stone.

Annie. She was living a different life now. He'd maybe never see her again. It was as if she no longer existed. In a way, standing in that gloomy museum, he'd convinced himself too well that he had no emotions, started to question what he felt for her, question his own capacity to love. And once you stop and look too closely at something like that, it no longer makes any sense.

Best, really, not to think about anything, not know anything, not say anything. Not if it meant being hit, and he'd decided that he'd been hit enough for one day. He didn't say anything else for the rest of the journey. He just closed his eyes and listened to them talk.

They chatted about work, mostly, and about the people they worked with. The only thing Sean found out was that the hard man was called Becket – he didn't seem to have any Christian name – and that he'd been brought in to replace Duke as Mathews's second-in-command. He mentioned Sunderland a couple of times, so Sean assumed that that was where he was from.

They must have driven for nearly three hours in all, and it was late afternoon when they arrived.

Carl parked the van, came round the back and opened the doors for them. Sean was bundled out. He stood, blinking and coughing. After the claustrophobia of the van, the alien sounds and smells of the countryside were overwhelming.

They were in what looked like it might once have been a farmyard, but it was more like a building site now. There were piles of bricks and sand, gravel and bits of planking, a wheelbarrow, some discarded tools. There was no one else around.

This must be the place Ray Mathews had told him about, his little place in the country.

On one side of the yard was a house, which looked empty and cheerless. But Becket prodded Sean in the opposite direction, towards an ugly new breeze-block and concrete building that was some kind of storage shed, by the look of it.

Becket unfastened a padlock, pushed the heavy metal door open, went in and turned on a light. The others followed.

Inside, it was one large, windowless room, with grey walls and a bare cement floor. There was a table in the middle with a couple of empty beer bottles, an old newspaper, an electric kettle and a broken mug. The only other furniture consisted of two wooden chairs next to the table.

There was an out-of-date calendar on one wall, and a coiled length of thick, plastic tubing in one corner.

'Carl,' Becket said, picking up one of the chairs, 'there's an old piece of foam mattress out in the barn. And get a couple of blankets from the house. You know where the keys are?'

'Behind the drain-pipe?'

'Yeah.'

'Okay.'

Carl left. Becket and Turner set about emptying the room of its few contents. Soon there was nothing left except the calendar and the newspaper.

Becket went and fetched a brief-case. He told Sean to give him his watch and his belt and to empty his pockets.

Sean did as he was told. He passed him his keys, a comb, a bus ticket and an envelope containing his passport with the plane ticket and the money he'd changed that morning at King's Cross.

Becket took it all without saying anything, and carefully packed it into the brief-case.

Carl came back with the mattress and chucked it on the floor with two dark-blue blankets.

'Goodnight,' said Turner, and they locked him in.

Sean walked around the room. It was completely silent; he might be anywhere.

He looked at the calendar. It was from a building suppliers, and was full of cheaply printed pictures of naked girls. It was for the year before last.

The newspaper was a six-month-old *Daily Star*, its pages yellow and dry. He read what there was to read in it, sitting with his back against the wall.

Then he arranged his bed, turned out the light and lay down.

The light coming under the door slowly dimmed until it was pitch dark.

He had so many aches and bruises he couldn't get comfortable. Worst of all, the headache was still there.

He couldn't remember when he had ever felt worse.

He cried for a while, then just lay there, neither awake nor asleep.

If only he knew what was going to happen.

24

He awoke some time in the morning. There was a crack of light under the door. It was very cold. He lay on the foam mattress and waited. His left-hand side was very stiff, and he tried to exercise the muscles a little. Thankfully his headache had gone, though his head was sore and swollen where he'd hit it.

He had no idea what time it was when the door was unlocked. He sat up as a blast of sunlight and noise was let into the room.

Becket came in first, carrying a length of thin rope, and turned on the light. He was followed by Carl and Turner, then, finally, Mathews, Ray Mathews. He had a cricket bat and a bottle of whisky. He smiled when he saw Sean.

'Hello there, Crawley,' he said. 'Sleep well?'

Sean stood up and leant against the wall, saying nothing.

'How d'you like our little hotel?' Mathews indicated the room with the bat.

'I need a piss.'

'Oh dear, the gentleman wants to go wee-wee. Show him the bathroom suite, will you, Carl?'

Carl took him outside and shoved him forward along the side of the concrete building. Sean was temporarily blinded by the sun; he stumbled and nearly fell over. Carl giggled.

Carl was younger than Sean, somewhere in his early twenties. He was fairly muscular, but you could tell that in a few years he would be covered in a layer of flab. He was dressed in designer sportswear and had a round, unexceptional face.

Tacked on to the end wall were the beginnings of a toilet, unfinished brick walls with no roof. The door scraped on the ground and only closed two thirds of the way. There was no seat, and the bowl was cracked and standing at an angle.

Sean felt better after the piss. He flushed the toilet, did up his flies and went out. Carl was standing there, lighting a cigarette. For a second Sean considered trying to make a run for it, but he knew it would be a waste of time and would only make them angry. He'd decided after his treatment in the van not to try and provoke any of them. He'd be quiet and co-operative; maybe come to some kind of deal with them.

Inside, someone had brought the two chairs back in again. They stood facing each other in the middle of the floor. Mathews had put the whisky and the rope on one of them; he told Sean to sit in the other.

Sean did as he was told.

'Are you a cricket man, Crawley?' Mathews asked.

'Not really.'

'Expect you played a bit at school.'

'A bit.'

'Used to play a lot in my younger days,' Mathews said. He practised a few strokes. 'Used to be pretty good. Probably could have played for a decent team if I'd put the work in. It's golf now, though. Great game, golf.' He used the bat as if it were a golf club and swung at an imaginary ball, then he shaded his eyes and followed the ball into the distance.

'Magic game. I'd give up working tomorrow if I could spend the rest of my life playing my way round the great courses of the world. Gives you time to think, golf does. I've been doing a lot of thinking lately.' He stood and studied Sean for a while.

'And?' Sean said.

'Tie him up, Ken.' Mathews turned away, practised another couple of shots. 'No, I didn't really think I'd have much use for this old thing any more.' He showed the bat to Sean. It was a dark, old-fashioned model, heavy and well used.

'But you know how it is, you hang on to things, don't you? Things from your past and that. Comfortable?'

Sean said nothing.

'Ken's very good with knots, aren't you, Ken?'

'Used to be in the boy scouts, Mr Mathews.' Ken looked up from his work and grinned.

The ropes didn't feel tight, they didn't cut into him anywhere. But when he tried to move, he realized that he was firmly secured.

'What do you actually want from me?' he asked.

'Good question, very good question. But you see, the thing of it is' – Mathews sat down and rested the cricket bat across his knees – 'we don't actually want anything from you any more. To tell you the truth, we don't even want *you*. What we'd like is for you to just vanish off of the face of the earth.'

'But you hired me, for God's sake.'

'Shut up!' Mathews snapped, suddenly angry.

'I did exactly what you told me to do.'

'I never told you to kill Gatley,' Mathews shouted, jumping up.

'You did.'

'I never did.' Mathews looked round at the others. 'And – and what about Duke, eh? What about that? Eh?'

'He was going to kill me. It was him or me.'

'He was trying to frighten you, that's all. He was trying to make you disappear. Why didn't you just go?'

'You owe me money. You never paid me for the job.'

'You ballsed it up.'

'How? I got rid of Gatley, that's what you wanted.'

'Yeah, well, anyway . . .' Mathews looked flustered. Sean wondered if he was drunk. He suddenly turned and yelled, 'You've got us all in the shit, Crawley! And I've got to do something about it. I've got to do something about you.'

'Why?'

'You know too much. If you fell into the hands of the police, I'd be well and truly up the fucking creek.'

'But that's ridiculous. I'm not going to go to the police, am I?' Sean said. 'I mean, I'm in a slightly worse position than you are when it comes down to it, aren't I? I'm the one that killed him.'

'Yes. And Duke. You're a nut. You're a bloody maniac.'

'Just let me go. I'm the last person to go to the police. Can't you see that?'

'You don't have to go to them. Sooner or later they'll come to you.'

'How? There's no clues. The only way they could ever find me is if you tell them.'

'But you're the one that did it. Without you, they can't prove nothing.'

'They can't prove anything now. I mean, everyone knows they never solve crimes. It's not like the TV.'

'They're suspicious. They're giving me a hard time. They know who to work on. They can shake things up until something falls out, and that something would be you. Without you around, I'm safe. But they could get to me through you, and vice versa. I can't risk that.'

'Then let me go. This is stupid. What if they followed you? Can't you see this is only making things worse?'

'Then there's the little matter of Duke.'

'I told you, he tried to kill me.'

'I don't give a fuck what happened. Duke was my friend. You topped the poor bastard, and I can't allow that. These men here are his friends. And now we've got to bury the bastard, and the cops are crawling all over me like rats. Everything's got too complicated. But there's one simple solution. Get you out of the way.'

'That's crazy. I mean, don't you think that killing me might just make things a little more complicated?'

'Who said anything about killing? We don't need another body. My hands are clean. The only killer here is you, and I want to keep it that way.'

'So you're going to let me go?'

'We were going to. Duke gave you the ticket, it was all set. And then you cunted the whole plan, didn't you? You killed the bastard.'

'You could still do it, you could still let me go.'

'No, I don't think so. I've considered it, but I couldn't trust you to keep your mouth shut.'

'Well, what, then? What *are* you going to do?'

'It's difficult, you've made everything so difficult. Maybe if Duke was still around we could sort something out. He had a good mind, a good clear mind, but he's gone, and you've got to be taught a lesson for that.'

'It was an accident.'

'Shut up!' Mathews motioned to Becket and Turner to come outside with him. Sean was left alone with Carl. Carl looked excited, nervous. He lit another cigarette, then had a good look at the calendar.

Sean didn't feel too happy. The whole muddled drift of Mathews's thinking had worried him. The man was stupid and confused; he might do anything.

'What's going on?' he asked Carl.

Carl didn't look round, just shrugged.

Sean's nose was itching. It was getting on his nerves.

The others came back in. Becket and Mathews looked serious, but Turner was grinning and shaking his head.

Mathews picked up the whisky bottle, unscrewed the cap and handed it to Carl.

'Give him a drink.'

'Okay.'

Carl sniffed the bottle, raised his eyebrows in appreciation. Then, with a look of childish concentration, he shoved it in Sean's mouth and tipped it up. Sean choked, coughing out whisky and saliva.

'Hold his nose, you spastic,' said Ken, laughing, and Carl did as he was told.

Sean was forced to gulp down several mouthfuls. He hadn't eaten since yesterday morning, and the whisky started doing strange things to him.

He sat with his head bowed, panting and sniffing, retching every now and then and shuddering.

'More,' said Mathews.

This time, when it was over, Sean convulsed and began to puke. Carl had to jump back out of the way.

It was difficult being sick, sitting bolt upright in the chair, and the foul liquid went everywhere. For five minutes he gasped and spluttered, heaving spasmodically. It was mostly whisky, but he coughed a lot of it up his nose and it burned like acid.

'Ugh,' said Carl. 'You dirty animal.'

Sean's eyes were streaming, his stomach contracting and opening like the gills of a beached fish.

'Get a bucket of water, Carl,' said Mathews, pulling the other chair away from the mess and sitting down.

'You see,' he said, 'what we really need is for you to disappear. That would be ideal. No body or nothing. Just, poof! But unfortunately I'm not a magician, and Paul Daniels doesn't do that kind of work. But then I had an idea. What if you were dead, but not dead? What if your body was walking around, same as ever, but everything inside it was dead? Wouldn't that be nice?'

Carl came back and emptied a bucket of water over Sean. For a few moments it made him feel much better, then he began to get very cold.

'Let me tell you a story, Crawley.' Mathews tipped his chair back and rocked it on two legs. 'Do you remember Sammy Thompson, Ken?'

'Poor sod,' said Turner.

'He was a great bloke, Sammy Thompson, right Jack-the-lad, always had a laugh and a joke with you. And a good worker, too, old-fashioned type, actually believed in putting in a good day's work. Not like these lazy sods you get these days.' He looked at Carl and Carl blushed. 'He was a flash bugger, too. Always had a couple of birds on the go, didn't he, Ken?'

'He was a right dirty bastard.'

'He had the mouth, you see? Could talk the knickers off a nun. Well, it must be about six years ago now, I've got him working on a site up in Walthamstow. Some crappy new homes we were putting up, and we've got one of them big cranes up there, shifting these girders for the roofs. Big long steel fuckers, on the end of this, like, chain.

'Well, Sammy's just, like, standing there talking to someone, you know, not really paying attention, when one of these girders catches on something. Hooked underneath, you know? And I guess the driver must have, like, jerked it or something, because suddenly it comes free, and it starts spinning. Not even that fast, like, only it spins round and catches Sammy on the back of the head.

'Now, I don't need to tell you, of all people, what a blow on the head can do, but it's not always fatal. At least it wasn't in Sammy's case.

'He'd probably been better off it it had been. Certainly it would have been better for Ruthie, his wife, like.

'You know what they call him now? Sammy the Spaz.'

'Sammy the Vegetable,' said Turner.

'Yeah. There's any number of names for him. He's gaga, simple; you can't understand a thing he says. I don't reckon *he* even understands most of it. He's a different person, really. I visit him now and then, as it goes, for old time's sake. He's in this home now, just sits there, looking at the wall and dribbling. Not even fifty, might as well be dead.' Mathews settled the chair on its front legs, and leant forward, using the bat as a prop.

'Sammy Bollock-Brain,' said Turner. Carl sniggered.

'Yeah,' said Mathews. 'It's terrible what a blow to the head can do. And do you know what? I read somewhere, some article about drinking, they reckon it's even worse if you're pissed. Something to do with the blood and that. I mean, it deadens the pain, but it fucks the brain.

'So what I thought is,' he said, standing up, 'I'd try a little experiment. I thought I'd try to turn you into a vegetable, an alkie vegetable. Be like one of them cunts you see wandering around town.'

'For fuck's sake,' said Sean. 'That's one of the most stupid things I've ever heard.'

'Oh yeah? Who's going to pay attention to some shuffling pissed-up headcase? No, I think not.'

'But you can't just turn someone into a vegetable, or a drunk for that matter. You can't just . . . I mean, just like that.'

'Tell that to Sammy. Now you've very conveniently hit your head, which a lot of people saw, when you fell off your bike, so that's a start. But we don't want any more marks. Carl, tear a strip off that mattress, would you?'

'Okay.' Carl took a knife from his pocket and picked up the mattress.

'You're fucking mad,' Sean yelled, but Mathews ignored him.

'I'm just going to get some string from the house,' he said, and strolled out.

Sean watched Carl cut off a foot-wide length of foam.

'Sean Crawley on the outside, Sammy the Spaz on the inside,' Mathews said as he came back a couple of minutes later.

'Sean Bollock-Brain,' said Turner.

Mathews took the foam and carefully wrapped it round Sean's head, then checked that he was getting enough air, and tied it in place.

It was like being a kid and hiding under the sheets. There was a soft glow of light filtering through the foam, and it was warm and secure. He felt like he was both hidden and hiding. Everything was far away. He could hear the blood in his head, his breathing slow and close.

He sat there for a while, just sort of drifting, and then suddenly there was a massive jolt. He felt his head snap forwards, and he heard himself grunt. His brains sort of rearranged themselves, like cornflakes being shaken in a box. There was a flash of white, and then a dull pain spread inside his head, followed by a throbbing pressure, as if his brain was swelling. He slowly straightened himself up and rolled his head. He felt like he might have pulled a muscle in his neck.

Well, at least he wasn't a vegetable yet. He waited. Was that it? He wasn't sure he could take another blow like that. Was the experiment over?

Then there was a second jolt. Worse than the first. This time he actually had a moment of unconsciousness, a tiny split-second in which he thought he was falling, and then a disembodied ache, as if they'd knocked his head clean off. He didn't know when the third jolt came. Everything was dark and swirling and distant.

And then the lights came back on, and the sound was turned up. He was looking at four yellow faces; he didn't know them, they were staring at him. He didn't know where he was.

Christ, he was in Well Street, outside the pet shop. Yes, he'd crashed his bike. Jesus, how long had he been out? He must have imagined the whole thing. God, it was embarrassing, he'd wet himself. Maybe they wouldn't notice. He tried to stand up, but he couldn't. Fuck it, what if he'd broken his back?

'What do you reckon?' said Mathews, removing the foam, and it all came flooding back. He was in that dreary room, tied to a chair.

He began to sob. He sniffed. His nose was bleeding.

Carl was holding the bat, so he assumed that it was him who'd been hitting him. He looked a bit apprehensive. Ken was grinning and shaking his head again, and Becket had that blank, snake-like look about him.

Mathews was smiling without a great deal of humour.

'Have a drink.' Mathews put the bottle to his lips. 'If you're a good boy and have a drink, then I'll get you some nice breakfast.'

Sean drank, and this time he wasn't sick.

25

They gave Sean some food, a couple of cheese sandwiches, and left him locked in the room for the rest of the day. He lay on the remains of the mattress, curled into as tight a ball as he could make, moaning rhythmically.

They'd taken away his money, his home and his friend, and he'd made the mistake of thinking that there wasn't anything else, that he'd reached the bottom. But he was realizing now that he could fall a whole lot lower yet. They were trying to take away his mind. And that was intolerable.

How clever he thought he'd been, and how dumb he really was. He thought he'd made a series of perfect moves, but in fact, whenever he'd been offered, he'd unfailingly made the wrong choices. He'd rushed at them, snatched them impatiently, and now here he was. And it wasn't nearly over yet.

His head hurt like hell, a relentless shattering pain, as if something inside his brain was screaming. And every time he tried to move it was worse. Like every hangover he'd ever had rolled into one.

It wasn't so bad while he was still drunk, but as the whisky wore off the pain mushroomed up inside him, and he felt more and more sick. He wished his heart would stop pumping; the throbbing of his blood was unbearable.

He was soaked, and the floor was still wet where Carl had thrown the water over him, but with no air circulation and little warmth it wouldn't dry and he became chilled. He couldn't force himself to do anything about it; he stayed curled up and let it seep into him.

There was only one good thing; the pain obliterated everything else. Thinking was virtually impossible. Now and then a gap opened up and he considered his position, and that was frightening. It was almost a relief when another wave of pain engulfed him and he could no longer think.

He stared at the crack under the door and didn't bother putting the light on.

Day passed into night. At some point. Becket and Turner came in. Becket took him to the toilet, and Turner made him drink the rest of the bottle of whisky. He was glad of it. Then they gave him some fish and chips and left him alone.

He ate a few of the chips. But he wasn't really hungry.

The alcohol had deadened the pain and he started walking around to warm himself up and fight off the stiffness. He circled the room, as near to the walls as possible. As he walked he studied the room, looking for a way out. He thought that maybe if he just kept walking he could think of a plan, an escape.

He tired in the end, and took the calendar off the wall, then lay down with it on the mattress.

He masturbated.

He could feel the whisky beginning to ease off again, and the terror started creeping back in. He turned out the light, wrapped the blankets around his shivering body and tried to sleep. But it was no good. For hours he just lay there until he reached a half-way stage, a feverish waking dreamworld. The images of the naked calendar girls were all confused in his mind with Susan Gatley. She kept coming to him and teasing him, tormenting him. She was big and strong, and he was a little kid. She'd parade around with massive tits, leering, while he writhed around in his own shit, unable to get a hard-on.

Becket brought him some more sandwiches for breakfast, and a chair to sit on while he ate.

The pain had dimmed to a general vague numbness, but he was breathing unevenly, and swallowing was difficult. He still wasn't really hungry; he just thought he'd better try and eat.

Becket stood in the doorway and looked out at the yard. It was a dull day, but Sean was glad of the fresh air.

'How long am I going . . . how long are you keeping me here?' he asked, his voice hoarse and cracked.

'Until Ray's happy,' Becket said without turning round.

'You mean, when you've fucked my brain. When you've completely fucked my brain.'

'It looks that way.'

'This is crazy.'

'It's nothing to do with me. I'm just here to look after things.'

'Why don't you let me go?'

'Don't talk shit. I've got a job to do.' He locked the door and an hour or so later Turner came in with a fresh bottle of whisky. Sean drank as much as he could, which was quite a lot. Turner was impressed.

For some reason he was happy for the rest of the day. It was quiet in the room; he could forget about things. The whisky had made him nicely warm and drunk, and as long as he didn't move too quickly the pain was okay.

He spent much of the afternoon rocking backwards and forwards on the mattress, sort of singing, and looking forward to the next half-pint of whisky. Maybe they'd give him more this time. Yeah, that'd be nice.

It was good being shut away, he could make his own world out of the grey nothing of the room. He could tell himself that it was all over, that they wouldn't beat him any more. Maybe they'd forgotten about him altogether. Maybe they'd had enough.

It startled him when they opened the door that evening. He actually jumped. It was like being woken from a particularly deep and peaceful sleep by a harsh alarm.

They brought in the rope and the chair and the bat.

Mathews wasn't with them.

Becket watched as Turner tied Sean up, and then Carl fitted the strip of foam round his head. They argued as he did it, and he had to start again twice to get it just right. Sean felt a rising panic, but he was helpless to do anything about it.

Wrapped in the suffocating darkness, he struggled against the ropes. He clenched his teeth. Screwed up his face. It didn't come straight away. He yelled at them to get it over with, his shouts muffled.

And then there was a horrible thump. He let out a scream and his head shot forward. He jerked against the ropes.

Three blows. Last time it had been three. Would it be more this time? Less, perhaps? Would they be satisfied with one? He wanted to brace himself but his neck was sore and he could hardly move.

He didn't really register the second blow. He just felt a kind of general shock, as if his whole body had become one huge raw nerve and they'd prodded it with an electrode. He heard himself moaning.

They hit him four times in all, and by the end he was virtually unconscious. When they untied him he fell to the floor and lay there shaking. Someone gave him some more whisky, and they left him alone.

He spent the night with his forehead pressed up against the cool cement wall. His body was raging hot. Susan came back. This time she was fat and had a penis. She was yelling at the top of her voice, right in his ear. He wanted her to stop. But she kept on, all night. He thought that was a bit unfair, and kept telling her so.

He was sick in his sleep, and woke up in it. When Carl and Ken came in in the morning they enjoyed themselves with a powerful hose.

They gave him breakfast and more whisky, and he ate on the floor in silence, like an animal. Carl laughed at him.

When they'd gone he took off his clothes to try and dry them, but the whole room was damp. He crouched on the floor, wringing the soaked clothing, and talking to it.

That evening they came in with the equipment and found Sean in just his underpants. He ran round the room, trying to get away from them. Ken and Carl chased him, shrieking with laughter. They got him in the end, and his beating was worse than before.

When they took the foam away from his head, his hearing was still muffled, and his ears were ringing like a fire alarm.

He developed a full fever in the night, and became completely delirious. He kept thinking that he was back in the flat arguing with Annie. She kept on about the woman in his bed. It was Susan. By now she was enormous, like a queen ant, too big to move, caked in make-up, stuffing herself with food and swilling back whisky. Sean tried to explain, but Susan kept yelling obscenities, which didn't help.

Annie didn't understand. He tried to talk to her, but she got more and more angry. If only Susan would shut up for a moment. If only the two of them would give him time to think.

Becket found him in the morning tangled in the damp blankets, shuddering and muttering garbage. He took him out into the yard and dried him out in the sun, then exercised him like a dog.

Turner brought the whisky out to them. Becket wasn't sure about giving it to Sean in his state, but Turner insisted. Sean drank it greedily. Then Becket gave him some Disprin, which Turner found highly amusing.

In the evening they beat him again, and that night the fever got worse. He could hardly breathe. That was Susan's fault. She was lying on top of him. She'd got so huge she was suffocating him, and she was so hot he felt like he was melting. He tried to claw her off, but she was like a jelly; his hands sank into her soft moist flesh. He couldn't get a hold. Her skin was all gooey and sticky, it started to ooze into his nostrils, down his throat. When Becket opened the door in the morning she exploded as the light hit her. Sean lay on the mattress coughing and spluttering. Beckett took him out into the yard again, but he could see that Sean was sick. Later on he took him into the house and wrapped him in a blanket. Sean was very weak, he couldn't walk very well and he wasn't speaking any more. Just grunting, if he had to communicate at all.

Ken and Carl were watching television. They were drunk and in high spirits.

The house was minimally furnished and a complete mess. There were take-away cartons and empty bottles and cans everywhere, as well as dirty magazines, playing cards, overflowing ashtrays, an abandoned game of Trivial Pursuit, video cassettes and several days' worth of newspapers.

Turner tied Sean's hands behind his back, and he and Carl threw chocolates for him to try and catch in his mouth.

Becket convinced them that it wasn't a good idea to beat him that night, but they still locked him up in the shed again, having made sure he had enough blankets, and that the room was reasonably dry.

The worst part of the fever was over, but it had settled down in his chest and he'd developed a feeble croaking cough.

He turned the light on when they'd gone. By now he had pretty well lost all track of time. He just drifted. The next thing he knew, Becket was coming in with some food for him. There was daylight outside, so he assumed that it was the next day. Becket gave him a chair to sit on, and Sean thought that he was going to be beaten again, but instead Becket got the other chair and sat in the doorway.

Sean nibbled at the food and watched Becket as he rolled a cigarette and smoked it in a serious manner.

Sean understood the other two, but Becket was different. Of all of them, Becket was the only one he really feared. There was something alien about him; you couldn't read his little red eyes.

After about half an hour Becket said quietly, 'I could do without this.'

Sean looked up. He wasn't used to being spoken to. He tried to think of something to say. He ran through several possibilities, but in the end he realized that it had been too long, so he went back to his food.

'What do you think of it now, then, eh?' Becket ground out the cigarette he was smoking and looked at Sean, blowing the last lungful of smoke out of his nose.

'What do you think of your trip to the dentist? Will it still be all over in the morning?' He gave a quick grunt of something that was a little like laughter, and picked up the whisky bottle from between his legs. He took a swig, then handed it to Sean.

'You should see yourself.' He watched Sean drink, then shook his head. 'What am I doing here,' he said, 'pissing about in the middle of nowhere?'

He took the bottle off Sean and drank some more. 'This is a waste of time. I told Mathews, told him I didn't think this was a good idea, but he's the boss. I said to him, what if we kill you? What then? You know what he said? "C'est la vie." Don't think he even realized he'd made a joke.' Becket lapsed into silence. Rolled another cigarette. Didn't start talking again till it was lit.

'He doesn't know what he's doing,' he said. 'I tried to find out if he's got any kind of plan, any idea what he'll do if this doesn't work. If you don't get brain damage, or whatever it is he's trying to do. He just said he'd think of something, and in the meantime, keep batting. It's stupid ... But I don't know, maybe it is working. Look at you. Are you faking, or are you really as fucked up as you look?'

Sean stared at the whisky bottle, waiting for Becket to pass it back.

'Have you cracked?'

The whisky looked so good. If only Becket would hurry up and give it to him. He coughed. He was coughing a lot now, and his lungs hurt.

'Have you?'

Sean reached out his hands for the bottle. Becket shook his head and gave it to him.

'You know what?' Becket said. 'I haven't hit you yet. Don't get me wrong, I couldn't care less if you lived or died. I just don't think any of this is a good idea.'

He watched as Sean gulped down several mouthfuls of whisky. Didn't even know if he was listening or not.

'Carl does it mostly. He enjoys it, I think. He's a mindless fucker at the best of times. And Ken has a go now and then, when he's pissed, which is most of the time these days. He's as bad as you. Christ, you think you're having a hard time; you should try being holed up with those two morons.' He got up and stood in the doorway, rubbing the back of his neck.

'This is a shit job.' He went out and locked the door.

Sean still had the bottle. He drank steadily. Becket talking to him had started some part of his brain working again, and he felt cool and calm. He could step outside himself and see what was going on. It all became very simple; he could concentrate on the things that mattered.

He realized that Becket had only been sounding him out, seeing how far gone he was, but the human contact cheered him up, helped him look at something he'd been skirting round. It had been gnawing away at him since he'd first been brought here, and now he let it slip into the centre of his mind.

Was he being punished? Was there some external justice behind all this? Was he being punished for the death of Gatley? For the death of Duke? Did he, in some way, deserve to be here?

Was it God swinging the bat? Was Sean, in actual fact, in hell? Was this hell? This cold, bare, concrete cell? Stinking, airless and damp.

He pulled a blanket round his shoulders and rocked backwards and forwards.

Was he guilty? That was the question, really. Was he guilty? He'd been afraid to ask before, but now that he looked at it, it crumbled and faded away. A light cut through the pain and filled him with happiness.

Of course he wasn't being punished. Of course this wasn't hell. Of course he wasn't guilty. God had no hand in this. How could he? He didn't exist. It was as simple as that. This wasn't punishment, it was just revenge. Mathews was caught like a rat in a hole, and he was desperate, striking out at the nearest thing at hand, and that was Sean.

Not guilty. Never guilty.

Gatley and Duke were dead. So what? People died every day.

Not fucking guilty. Which meant that Mathews had no right, no right to keep him here.

Fuck him. Sean wasn't going to put up with it any longer. He didn't deserve it. He wouldn't accept it. He was going to do something about it. It was time to fight.

He hadn't cracked; he was saner than he'd ever been before. They'd simply knocked some sense into him.

Yes. He was still alive. Existing. Functioning. Functioning on the lowest level, but on that level he might win. They hadn't made him weaker; they'd made him stronger.

He whimpered with pleasure at the knowledge.

He threw off the blanket and began to crawl around the floor, keeping close to the walls. The whisky felt good. The hard concrete beneath his hands and knees felt good. The pain felt good, his pain, his own sweet pain, inside, keeping him warm. Giving him something to hold on to. Something to focus on.

He realized he was talking to himself. He grinned. There wasn't anyone better to talk to in the whole world.

'You're dead you fuckers all dead you shit-fuckers. Crawley will win Crawley is strong Crawley is the killer you are not the killer you cunts you shit-filled scum you fuck-head cunts. Crawley is the killer. You cannot stop him. Gatley was first Duke was second you cannot stop him. Turner is not the killer Turner is fat Turner is soft Turner is weak Turner is flesh. Flesh is weak. Carl is shit Carl knows nothing Carl is not the killer Crawley is the killer Carl will die. Gatley was first Duke was second you cannot stop him. Becket is scared shit-scared-of-death it makes him weak all you fuckers you skin-covered cunts. All weak. All flesh. All soft. Mathews is weak Mathews is already dead you are all already dead do you understand? Crawley is strong Crawley is hard Crawley is the insect Crawley is God. The Ant God. You can cut him shit-heads but it only makes him stronger shit-heads because all you cut away is simply human Crawley doesn't need that he doesn't want it you can kill that for Crawley because underneath is what is strong underneath the human which only fucks you up underneath is the beast and it is strong. It has no mind. It has no fear. It cannot be stopped. It is the insect. It kills without thinking it rips with its claws with its teeth it rips all flesh rips it all to shit it rips all humans all shit-bags all fuck-heads all soft-sacks all-skin-all-blood-all-flesh. So come all you fuckers come to Crawley. Gatley was first Duke was second the Ant will feed you fuckers Crawley will be strong. So return to the shit you fuckers where you belong you fuckers. I am the Ant you fuckers. I am the insect. I am the mindless fuck. I am the head-case. I am the killer. I am the teeth and I am the claws. I am the Ant you fuckers you hear me? The Ant.'

He tilted his head to the ceiling and howled. Howled and howled.

26

Days came and went. Sometimes they beat him, and sometimes they didn't. Sean hardly noticed any more, as he
slipped deeper and deeper into the ant-world. He had no
dreams at night; it was just black. Deep, dead, black. He
slept on his back, his arms at his sides, unmoving, like a
corpse laid out on a slab.

His damp clothes had been left screwed up in the corner,
and they'd grown mould and begun to rot. In the end
Turner took them away and burned them. Sean didn't care;
he was happy in just his underpants. After all, insects didn't
wear clothes.

He talked to himself all the time and was quite happy.
They didn't bother him during the days much, but one
afternoon he was woken by the door being pulled open, and
Becket came in to collect another empty whisky bottle.

'You want a piss?' he said flatly.

Sean got up without saying anything and went outside.
The sun was blinding. He shuffled to the toilet, squinting.
He couldn't see any colours.

Carl and Ken were sitting on the two chairs, drinking
cans of beer. When Sean had finished in the toilet Becket let
him sit with them in the yard. They all ignored him. Becket
and Carl read newspapers, while Ken fiddled with an old
radio.

That was good. Sean sat in the dirt and nodded his head.
Yeah, that was good. They weren't scared of him any more.
They'd forgotten he even existed. They'd slipped into a
routine. They thought that because he was no longer human,

he was no longer a problem. He sniggered and carried on nodding his head.

Ken laughed at him. 'Look at him now. Smart-arse. He looks like a bleeding mong.'

He got up from the chair and stood over Sean. 'All right, smart-arse? What's two and two? What's the capital of France? Ha, ha, ha. Phew, you know what? You fucking stink. You should look after yourself. Here, have a shower.' He poured the rest of his beer over Sean's head and laughed some more.

Sean looked up at him, dumb and faceless. A mong. Is that what they thought? They just couldn't see, they couldn't see past the shell. They didn't know he was an insect. Inside, behind the eyes, behind the face, inside the head, the ant was dancing up and down, jeering, howling, showing his arse and farting at them. You're dead, Ken, fat Ken full of beer, you're fucking dead, you silly fucker.

Ken found a stick and held it under Sean's nose.

'Here, boy! Nice stick.' He threw it away. 'Fetch, boy. Go on, fetch the stick.'

Sean sat there warming in the sun. Dead people, he was surrounded by dead people. It was comical, very comical.

'You know what, Carl?' Ken said. 'I had a dog that was more intelligent than him. Fuck, I won a goldfish at the fair that was more intelligent than him. He's just got shit for brains. I reckon it's worked, you know. Fucking crazy plan, but it's worked. Look at him. He's bleeding dog-meat.' Ken kicked Sean in the ribs and knocked him on to his side.

Sean convulsed in an ecstasy of coughing, which shook his whole body.

'Leave it out, for fuck's sake, Ken,' said Becket angrily. 'We're not supposed to mark him, remember? You thick bastard. State he's in, you're liable to kill him.'

That was good. Keep it coming, you dead people, you'll soon find out you can't kill me. Nothing can kill me.

He began to moan; at least, his body began to moan. The insect inside was just watching, enjoying the show.

'What's the matter with him now?' Ken sat down and scratched an armpit.

'Get him some whisky,' said Becket.

'Yeah, go on, Carl,' said Turner. 'Go and get another bottle.'

'Okay.' Carl went up to the house.

'It's pitiful,' said Ken, picking up the radio. 'How much longer is this going to go on for?'

Becket said nothing.

Squabbling corpses. Why didn't they see that there wasn't any point? They were already dead. Nothing could change that.

Carl came back and gave a bottle to Sean. It was about half full of beautiful golden whisky. Sean looked at it, swirled it round and held it up to the sun, captivated by the lights in it. Then he opened it, smelled it, felt the fumes fill him up like a balloon. He closed his eyes, put the cool glass of the neck between his teeth, tilted the bottle and sank into the whisky dream.

What a glorious day.

The liquid hit him and exploded. Hot needles snaked through his body; he could feel them tickling his balls, surging into his dick, as he drank and drank, lost to time.

He belched, and then he was ready.

He smashed the bottle on a brick, jabbed the broken stem into his neck and began to pull it round.

'What's he doing?' Ken yelled.

'Stop him, for fuck's sake,' hissed Becket.

Carl jumped forward and pulled the broken glass away. It cut his hand and he swore. Becket held Sean down and looked at the wound. It wasn't deep, nothing major had been severed, but it was bleeding heavily.

'Get the first aid kit, Carl,' Becket snapped.

'He cut my hand, the bastard.'

'Get the fucking kit!'

Sean looked at Becket. Scared now? Ha, ha, ha.

'What the fuck?' Ken didn't know whether to laugh or what.

Quarter of an hour later, Sean and Carl had been disinfected and bandaged and things were back to normal.

Sean barely noticed the new pain, but Carl kept whingeing about his hand.

Ken had gone back to his radio. Becket was the only one paying any attention to Sean; he sat there and scowled at him.

Sean waited. There wasn't any hurry. The sun continued to shine. Shadows crept across the yard, and slowly they all relaxed.

Sean watched Becket now; he'd take his cue from him. Once he went off guard, then that would be the moment to strike again. At last Becket picked up his paper and started to leaf through it. Sean grinned, then jumped up and started to run.

'Now what?' said Ken irritably.

'Stop him!' Becket made a grab for Sean.

'Bastard's trying to get away,' said Carl, setting off after him.

Don't be stupid. Trying to get away? Not any more. No, he wasn't running. He was fighting.

He ran straight at the toilet wall. He didn't try to go round it, or jump over it, and they couldn't get to him before he got to it.

He ran straight into it.

He knocked himself out. Only for a second or so, and it was nice, like being hit by the bat.

Susan came to him while he was unconscious, and she kissed him gently. She wanted to look after him. She asked if he could forgive her for her behaviour of the last few days. He was in a generous mood, so he did. She began to undress and he came to.

Becket was kneeling over him, and he could hear Carl and Ken laughing uncontrollably.

'Shut up!' Becket snapped. 'Look at him now.'

'Did you see that?' Carl was almost weeping. Sean could feel several new points of pain about his body, and there was warm blood on his face.

'Silly sod's trying to kill himself,' said Ken, still laughing.

'That's a very clever deduction,' said Becket.

'All right, all right, keep your hair on,' said Ken. 'You've got to admit it was fucking funny.'

'I'll have to ring Mathews,' Becket said, standing up and brushing the knees of his trousers. 'Now, you *watch* him. Don't let him move.'

Morons, dead morons. Didn't they see that it was them he was killing, not himself? But how could they see? They didn't have insect eyes. They had dead human eyes that saw nothing.

Turner took him inside and tied him to a chair, but he rocked himself over and crashed to the floor, so they had to take him off the chair. They tied his hands and feet and left him on the mattress.

After a while Becket returned. He didn't look too happy.

'Right,' he said. 'Someone's got to stay with him at all times, all right? Ray doesn't want him damaged any worse than he is. Jesus, look at the state of him.'

'It wasn't our fault,' said Ken.

'That's beside the point. It's happened, and we don't want it to happen again. Ray's coming up.'

'Great,' said Ken without much enthusiasm.

'Which means that you've got to go and pick him up in the van, Carl.'

'Oh, what?'

'Don't argue, Carl, I've had it up to here. Just do it, all right?'

'Why can't he drive himself up?'

Becket let his breath out very slowly. He looked tired. 'He's smashed his car up, hasn't he? Pissed. Fucking idiot. Took a swing at a copper. So he won't be driving for a while.'

'Oh, what?'

'Yeah, so you're to pick him up from the yard.'

'Why doesn't he just get a fucking train, or something?'

'Just do it, Carl,' Becket snapped.

Carl sloped out, but in a second he was back, grinning and holding up his bandaged hand.

'I can't drive, can I?'

'Why?'

'My hand, it's all swollen up. I can't hardly move me fingers. And it hurts like fuck. I'm serious; I'll never be able to change gear like this.'

Becket let out another long sigh and turned to Ken.

'Don't look at me, mate. I'm too pissed.'

'Bollocks,' said Becket. 'Fuck the lot of you. You're fucking hopeless.'

'Well, we didn't know he was gonna . . .'

'Christ, if you two clowns fuck up . . .' He stared at them and they looked at the floor. 'Don't leave him alone for one minute, you understand? And don't touch him. No treatment, nothing. Just leave him. I want everything to be just right when Ray gets here. Everything ready. He wants to finish it tonight.'

'Thank Christ for that. I . . .'

'Shut up, Ken.' Becket stormed out.

'Keys are on the telly,' said Carl.

Ken did a Nazi salute, and the two of them tried to laugh without making any noise.

A few minutes later Sean heard the van drive off, and he smiled inside. One down, two to go.

The rest of the day passed slowly and quietly. Carl brought the table in and he played cards for a while with Ken. Ken carried on drinking, and dozed off late afternoon, so Carl took his chair out and sunbathed in the yard.

Sean waited. He knew he mustn't push things. It would be a few hours before Becket was back with Mathews. The time would arrive; he just had to wait for it.

Some time in the early evening Ken woke. He was in a bad mood, bolshy and hung over. When Carl announced that they'd run out of beer, his mood darkened.

'What about whisky, then?' he said, and belched.

'He had the last of it.' Carl jerked his head at Sean.

'Shit. We'll have to get some more.'

'How?'

'How? How do you think? We'll buy it, you stupid wanker. There's an offie in the village.'

'Yeah, but we're not supposed to leave him, are we?'

'We won't leave him. One of us can stay here.'

'I don't know.'

'What's he going to fucking do? Eh? Come on, we're only protecting him from himself. I can deal with him all right. Besides, you heard what Becket said; how d'you think Mathews'll react when he finds out we haven't got any whisky for his pet nutter?'

'Yeah, but . . . I don't know.'

'What you don't know, won't hurt.'

'Eh?'

'Come on. Off you trot.'

'Why me?'

'Because I'm in charge, you dick-head. Now go.'

'How?'

'Shanks, me old son.'

'Oh, Ken . . .'

'Go on, it'll only take you about half an hour.'

'Oh, all right.'

'Here, take some money.' Ken handed him a couple of notes. Go. Yes, go.

Two down. One left. Big, fat Ken. The juiciest grub of them all.

Sean lay on the mattress and watched him, poring over the insides of the radio like a little kid, the tip of his tongue stuck out from between his lips. He finally got it working about ten minutes after Carl had gone. He tuned it to Radio 1 and sat back in his chair, watching it as if it was a television. Inane music and chatter echoed round the concrete walls.

Sean began to whimper.

'Oh, shut up,' said Ken, and he turned the volume up.

Sean carried on.

'Shut the fuck up. What's the matter with you?' Turner turned to look over at him.

'Shit,' said Sean, squirming on the mattress, straining against the ropes.

'Shit in your pants. No, on second thoughts, it stinks bad enough in here already.'

He untied Sean's feet and pulled him upright. Then he dragged him outside and shoved him in the toilet.

Sean nodded down at his filthy pants.

'Oh, fuck,' said Ken. 'I'm not touching them.'

So he untied Sean's hands and waited outside while he had a shit, then he hauled him back inside and flung him down on his bed.

The radio began to go out of tune, and Ken went over to try and sort it out.

At last. All ready.

Now, Sean thought. Now.

This was the moment. He'd been given one chance, he'd never have another. If he didn't move now, that would be it, dead and gone.

Now.

Turn your mind off. Shut out that one last bit of human still in there. No more thinking. Just do it. Act. One chance to live, everything else is the end.

Nothing else. Now, go now.

He looked at Ken, leaning over the radio.

Now. Do it now.

Sean hurled himself across the room.

'Hey,' said Ken, and he brought up his hands, but he might as well have tried to stop a train. He tried to turn away, and Sean slammed into the side of him, sinking his teeth into his neck.

Ken crashed over on to the table and the air was pumped out of him with an 'oof'.

Sean concentrated his whole being into his jaws. Nothing else mattered. They were jammed deep into the soft flesh between Ken's ear and his shoulder. His teeth were well through the skin, but he didn't want to take a shallow bite, he had to force them in further, and not close them until he could take out half of Ken's throat.

It was like biting into very thick, raw steak. He could feel the sinews and muscles, and there was stringy flesh in the gaps between his teeth, cutting into his gums.

He was well embedded now, and going deeper all the time.

He became half aware of a sound like a kettle whistling, and he realized that it was Ken, screaming in a horrible high-pitched ululating way.

Neither of them was really human any more. Ken was flapping and flailing about on the table like a landed fish, but the more he tried to shake Sean off the deeper his teeth sank in, the tighter his hold became.

Ken was pounding Sean, tearing at his face, his feet scrabbling on the floor. He kicked a chair over and it span away across the room.

But Sean didn't know any of this, he was just teeth, his body was a rag dangling from those massive choppers. He'd shut out everything else. He didn't know that his fingers were tangled in Ken's hair, that his knee was pressed hard into his flabby, beer-sloshing stomach. He didn't know that he was growling, that the strain was making him groan, a long relentless bass note, which, through the blood and the flesh and the clenched teeth, was coming out as a snarl.

He didn't know any of this.

Ken did. Ken felt as if a white-hot gin-trap was clenched about his neck. And he couldn't shift it, couldn't get it off no matter how hard he struggled.

He rolled off the table and thudded on to the floor, Sean beneath him. But still he couldn't shift the pain.

His scream rose a pitch, battling with the wittering radio. The DJ was talking to someone over the phone, flirting.

With Ken's weight on him, Sean seemed to be squeezed into his own mouth, and he felt his teeth slide in further. He could feel Ken's skin against his tongue, he was so close, so intimate, his lips pressed against him, a love bite, a blossom on his flesh.

Ken shrieked. Sean was almost choking on his blood now; it swilled around his mouth, gurgled in his throat. He bit harder.

Do you really think you're going to live, Ken? Still think you'll get away? Hasn't it sunk in now that you're going to die? Do you still think there's a God? Are you praying? Well, you can pray all you like, you cunt. But there is no God.

Escape? No such luck, Ken. This is it, the teeth at your throat, the end. This is it. Give up. This is where you fuck off.

Just die now, right? Die. Drop. Stop.

Fuck off, and die.

Ken wriggled and Sean bit harder still. Then he felt something give.

It was like an eruption in his mouth, as if he'd bitten into a hot-water pipe, a gush of salty metallic fluid spurted out. He choked, but wouldn't let go.

Soft-shite. Bite, and bite again. Piss, you cunt, fuck off.

Ken snapped like a whip, arched his back, and jack-knifed across the slippery floor. Sean's jaws finally came together and he was thrown clear. He careered into a corner and spat out a mouthful of meat and chewy cords.

He scrambled to his feet and set off back towards Ken, but when he got there he saw that it wasn't necessary.

Ken's face was grey, distorted, like something in a crooked mirror, all pulled out of shape. His eyes were yellow and bloodshot, fixed wide with enormous black pupils.

His body was twitching, but it was all over. The side of his neck was a wide, jagged crater and he was drenched with blood.

Sean, naked except for his filthy underpants, crouched over him, tense, gore round his mouth like jam and smeared over his body.

He crouched there, watching and waiting, while slowly his senses returned.

One eye was now almost closed, where Ken had gouged it, and his left side was numbed from when they'd fallen off the table.

The music stopped and the DJ said something about Russians and summer holidays.

The room, suddenly tiny and black and white, began to close in.

It stank worse than ever. Blood, sweat, food, beer, piss and shit. At the last moment Ken had shat himself.

Sean sank to his knees and threw up.

It was good. Everything came out, even the whisky.

He knelt there for a while, breathing painfully and trying to get his strength back, but it wasn't over yet. He still had to get away. Away before the others returned.

But away where? He didn't even really know where he was. Somewhere in Suffolk, that was it, and he had no clothes, no money.

The house. Could he risk going to the house and looking for some stuff? Clothes and money. Did he have enough time? The option was hiding out in the woods, naked. So he didn't really have a choice; it had to be the house.

He limped to the door of the shed and peered out. It was late; the sky was dark. He shivered; now was when it got difficult. But he couldn't stop, he had to keep going.

He hobbled across the yard to the house. The front door was open and there was a light on inside. He went through to the sitting-room. It was in an even worse state than before, but he hardly noticed. He needed clothes and he needed money. And there was no time. Carl would be back from the village soon. And Becket, how long had he been gone? How long before he came back?

He went round the room throwing everything out of his way, newspapers, bottles, videos. There must be something here. And then, at last, under a pile of coats in one corner, he found something, the brief-case. But it was locked. He rattled it. There was definitely something still inside. He tore at the clasps but couldn't shift them. He was just about to look for something to rip it open with when he heard a noise.

He froze.

And then he heard it again, louder this time.

The distinctive roar and rattle of a transit van.

27

No. He'd been so close. It couldn't happen like this; to come so far and then . . . No. He wasn't going to lie down and let them shaft him now. He struggled into one of the coats, picked up the brief-case and decided to try and make a run for it away into the woods.

He could hear the van getting nearer; he had to get out of the house. He raced to the front door. There wasn't time to look for another exit.

He wrenched the door back and hurtled out into the night. He hadn't gone three feet when the van thundered into the yard and he was caught in the headlights.

'Fuck you,' he yelled, and looked round for a weapon. The only thing he could see was a pile of masonry. He picked up a lump.

Come and get it, then.

It was all over. But he didn't really care any more. He crouched in the light, panting.

Come on.

Come and get it.

The van skidded to a halt in the loose gravel and Sean threw the lump of masonry. It was a good shot; the wind-screen shattered.

The driver's door flew open and Becket leapt out, his impassive granite face finally animated into a mask of fury.

Sean scurried away, out of the beam of the headlights, glancing round wildly for another weapon. Next to the toilet wall he found the length of thick yellow plastic tubing which had been thrown out of the shed when they'd first got there. He grabbed it and moved back into open ground, swinging it round his head so that it sang and whistled in the air.

The passenger door opened and Mathews stumbled out of the van, his face bleeding.

Good, you fucker.

Becket moved in warily. Sean wanted him to come in a rush, get it over with, but that wasn't Becket's way. He was circling him, waiting, like a snake. Sean was losing momentum. Come on. He increased the speed of his swing and had just decided to attack Becket when something strange happened.

More lights, the roar of another engine.

Who now?

Something orange came tearing into the yard. Mathews flattened himself against the side of the van, but Becket couldn't get out of the way in time. There was a thud, and Sean watched Becket's body spin away through the air, like a doll thrown by a baby.

It was a car, an old orange Ford Cortina with a black vinyl roof. It tried to pull round and its rear wheels began to slide. Its back end caught the toilet wall and knocked it down.

Mathews was on the move again. He looked confused, but he was determined to get to Sean. Sean swung again and the tubing slapped him flat.

The car came back under control and stopped next to Sean. The driver leant over and pushed the door open.

'Get in,' George yelled. 'Get in.'

Sean fell in and tried to pull the door shut. It bounced off the seat belt, which had fallen out and swung free. The car sped off. A chariot, a fucking chariot from heaven, with a dead man at the reins. An orange chariot with a black vinyl roof, all thunderclaps and glory.

The last thing Sean saw before he passed out was Carl, standing open-mouthed in the road, clutching two plastic carrier-bags. As George swerved round him, Sean kicked the door out. He heard the bang and the shout as Carl was knocked into the bushes and he embraced oblivion.

'Do you want a present?'

'Eh?'

'Look at me.'

'Sorry.'

'There now.' It was Susan, very elegant in a black evening dress, her lips immaculately painted with blood-red lipstick, diamond ear-rings hanging from her white ears.

She offered him a glass of champagne, and they stood on the balcony looking out over the sea.

'You've been a good boy. Do you want a present?'

He kissed her and it became very dark. She was some kind of cat, a panther. They tore at each other with their teeth, spinning, tangled in each other's claws, in a howling black whirlwind. Red streamers snaked out around them, gold spots bubbled and boiled. But he couldn't go on, he shouldn't be doing this, it was too dangerous, he had to get away. Something huge, so huge it couldn't be seen, was swinging towards him like a planet on a pendulum, big enough to destroy everything. He could hear it scream and whistle.

'Do you want a present?'

It hit him and the lights came on.

He was in the concrete room, tied to the chair. Mathews was standing over him with the bat, leering.

'Hello, Sean.'

Ugh.

He woke up with a jolt.

'Shit,' said George, 'you frightened me. Are you all right?'

'Yes.' He still wasn't quite sure where he was. He looked around, trying to take it in, and slowly his senses returned. He was away, he'd got away. He let out his breath and closed his eyes. Instantly he was back in the whirlwind. He snapped them open again.

'Jesus Christ,' he muttered.

The car had stopped and it was still night outside. Rain spattered down against the roof and washed over the wind-screen. George sat smoking a joint, staring straight ahead into the darkness.

'You're dead,' Sean said, trying to shift upright in his seat.

'What?'

'You're dead.' It was painful to speak, and his voice was a geriatric croak. 'They killed you.'

'Yeah?'

'I went to your flat. They'd wrecked it, there was . . .'

'Sean. What the fuck do you think you're doing?' George's voice was flat and lifeless.

'Well,' Sean half laughed, 'it's kind of a long story.'

'I know.'

'What?'

'I looked at your file.'

'Oh.'

'Sean, this whole thing's a bit shitty, really, isn't it?'

'Yeah.' A sudden jolt of pain shot down Sean's back and he winced. George took another drag on his joint.

'I'm sorry,' Sean said. 'But, just how? I mean, I don't really know what's going on. How come you're not dead? I saw the blood in your flat.'

'It was paint.'

'Eh?'

'It was red paint, my red paint. They threw it everywhere. It was just paint.'

Sean started to laugh again, but stopped when he discovered that it hurt too much. He could barely move now for the stiffness and it was like his body wasn't his any more. His brain had been put into another person's frame, and it didn't fit. It was a monster's body, hacked up and sewn together, and his mind hurt inside it. It felt cold and battered.

He snorted. 'Paint, shit, I knew it. They weren't killers, none of them were killers.'

'You look terrible.'

'I feel terrible.'

'We'd better get you to hospital or something, I suppose.'

'No way, George, no fucking way. You read the file.'

'Yeah. Maybe you're right. So what are we going to do?'

'God knows. Where are we?'

'Middle of nowhere.' George drew a circle on the fogged glass of the windscreen.

'How did you get here?' Sean asked.

'That's another long story. Listen, Sean, if you want me to help you, you've got to tell me everything.'

'You said you'd read the file.'

'Yeah, but that's not everything, is it? Like, what was going on back there?'

'No, you wouldn't believe it.'

'Try me.'

'Well, if you really want to know, they were trying to give me brain damage, actually, George.'

George didn't say anything for a while. He just yawned. Then he drew a smaller circle inside the other one. 'You'd better start right at the beginning, Sean, tell me the works, everything.'

'You mean it?'

'Come on.'

'Look, I'm sorry, George, I shouldn't have got you into all this.'

'Yeah, well, I'm in it now, and I want to know exactly what it is I am in. So stop saying you're sorry and start talking.'

So Sean talked, there in the little cocoon of the orange car, as the rain fell all about them from a black sky.

He told George about meeting Duke, his stupid conversation about fantasies. He told him about Mathews, Gatley, the kitchen weights . . . the fridge. And then, afterwards, the silence, the zoo, the realization of just how crass he'd been, then the helter-skelter fall towards Duke's death, and finally the farm, and the outhouse, the cricket bat and the whisky. And Ken, squealing like a stuck pig.

The only thing he didn't tell him about was Susan. That was personal.

By the time he'd finished the rain had stopped and it was growing light. A silver mist had wrapped itself about them, as if the rest of the world had ceased to exist.

'So Ken Turner's dead as well, then?' said George.

'Yeah, and I thought I was, too. I thought it was all over, and then you turned up, like a miracle. Jesus, I thought . . . I don't know what I thought. How the hell did you find me?'

'I followed the van.'

'How?'

'Well, I knew you weren't telling the truth when you gave me the file. Shit, well before that. I thought there was something funny going on right from when we followed Gatley that day.'

'Yeah, that was stupid.'

'I mean, I never thought you'd actually topped him, or anything like that, but I knew something was going on. And then, on me birthday, when I saw you talking with those two guys.'

'The bastards must have followed you,' said Sean. 'Broken into your flat when you were out. And now they've got the file.'

'Nah.'

'What?'

'I took it into work. I knew you were lying about it. I thought it'd be safer there, locked it in me cupboard. It's still there.'

'Hah! Brilliant!'

'Yeah, brilliant,' said George sarcastically. 'I get home that night and the place is trashed. I didn't get back till late, I'd gone out after work for a drink, must have got there just after you did. Couldn't fucking believe it, mayhem. But they hadn't taken anything, so it wasn't no ordinary burglary. They were looking for something, that was obvious, your bloody file.

'So I went round yours, same state as mine, great. Well, I'd seen those builders, I didn't fancy sticking around to meet them again, so I fucked off round to Fat John's. I had his keys, he wanted me to water his plants while he was away. I've been there ever since.'

'But how did you find me down here?'

'First I read your file. I couldn't really believe you'd killed

Gatley, but there it was in black and white. I realize just how deep the shit is you're in, so I take the day off work. Go sick. Get the bus round to your place on the off-chance you might show up. Just as I get there you come down the stairs without a care in the fucking world. And then the van shows up. I didn't have time to do nothing, I was on foot. Lost the lot of you.

'You don't show up again, the van doesn't show up again. By now I'm thinking I'd better be sick for the whole week. Then I look up Mathews's address in the yellow pages, and start hanging around their yard.'

'How long ago was all this?'

'How d'you mean?'

'What day is it?'

'Friday . . . well, Saturday morning now.'

'So I was there for . . .'

'It's ten days, Sean.'

'Ten days?'

'Yeah.'

'Jesus.'

'If I get into trouble at work because of you . . .'

'That's the least of our worries,' Sean said, rubbing his left arm.

'Oh, ta,' said George angrily. 'It may be the least of your fucking worries, Sean, but that's my living. I'm not some kind of freelance, I don't know, mass murderer, like you.'

'I didn't mean it like that.'

'Yeah, right, well, just you remember. The real world still exists out there, life goes on as normal.'

'All right, I'm sorry.'

'I kind of think it's gone past being sorry, Sean. You've killed three people, and I'm involved. Three people, Sean. I can't fucking believe it.'

'What are we going to do?'

'I suppose we'll just have to go back to Fat John's and take it from there.'

'No,' said Sean. 'Not London, not like this. Not me or the car. We'd just get stopped.'

'We'll be all right.'

'Not London. I can't face London. I need somewhere quiet, somewhere I can get myself together, somewhere to hide, somewhere safe.'

'Oh, right. We'll just have a little look for Shangri-La, shall we?'

'George, I've had enough. I've been kicked in the balls, hit with a bat, jumped on, crushed, my left-hand side's half numb, my neck's still bleeding. Jesus, I think I might have broken some ribs, you know? And my head. It's my head that's worst. I've got a killing headache, and it won't go away. It's like my brain's too big for my head, all swollen up or something.' Sean began to cry.

'We've got to go somewhere,' George said irritably. 'We can't just sit here for ever, can we?'

'Yeah, but not London, okay? I can't face London. They'd find us. They'd fucking find us. We've got to hide. They found your flat, they can find Fat John's.'

'Well, where? Tell me that!'

'I don't know. I've been trying to think. All I've got is my parents or my sister, but I can't go to either of them, not like this. Haven't you got any friends anywhere?'

'Not that we can just turn up at, no. "Can we stay for a while? We're hiding out from the police and a gang of crazed builders!" Come off it.'

'You must know someone.'

'Yeah, well, I don't, all right? I mean, even if I did, what then? You hide for a while, get better, then what? You can't stay there for ever, can you? You're really in trouble, Sean, I mean it. Jesus, you've killed . . .'

'I know, I know, three people, don't rub it in.'

'Come on, Sean, this is serious.'

'Yeah . . .' Sean fell silent. He watched George rolling another joint. 'What do you think about that?' he said after a while.

'About what?' said George quietly.

'My killing Gatley. Not the others, that was self-defence. But what about Gatley? What do you think about all this?'

'I think Fat John's going to be mightily pissed off about his car. I had a look at it while you were asleep. It looks like I've driven into a tree . . . Only it wasn't a tree.'

'George, I . . .'

'I don't want to talk about it, all right?' George snapped. 'It's just too crazy a thing to think about. I can't believe any of it's really happening. I just can't understand why, Sean. Why?'

'I don't know. I haven't really thought, never have. Since this all started, it's been just, like, one thing after another. It's just happened. There seemed a reason for it at the time; it all seemed logical, perfectly straightforward, so I went along with it. But, looking back, I don't know why I killed Gatley. I really don't know.'

'You must know.'

'It just felt right at the time. It just happened.'

'"Things just happen." That's no answer,' said George bitterly.

'But things *do* just happen, that's the point. People don't really plan things. They don't know what they're going to do with their lives; they don't map it out with a plot like a film . . .'

'Fuck you,' said George. 'Fuck you. Sitting there with all your fucking theories, all your bullshit. You know the trouble with you? You think you're something special, you always have. You're an arrogant shit. Is that why you killed Gatley? To prove it? To prove you were special, different from the rest of us poor bastards? Is that what all that shit about ants was about, that night in the pub?'

'I hoped you'd forgotten about that.'

'You have a habit of saying stupid things that stick in my mind.'

'Sorry. Look, if you hate me so much, why'd you . . .?'

'I don't hate you, Sean. I'm just confused.'

'This isn't going to do you any good,' said Sean quietly, 'helping me. You could just turn me in.'

'Yeah, I suppose so, but I guess I'll help you because you're my friend, and there isn't much else, is there?'

'Thanks.'

'I mean, you're the same person you always have been. I just don't know why I ever listen to you.' George wiped the windscreen.

'You're the only person I can talk to, I suppose,' said Sean.

'But what are you saying?'

'I don't know. I really don't know. Let's not try and understand it. Stick to dogs.'

'Eh?'

'You know, your book on dogs. Dogs are nice and easy. Just devote your life to trying to understand dogs, and leave it at that. I mean, you said it, you had a flash of inspiration that night in your friends' farmhouse, and you understood dogs. That's enough for one lifetime. Forget about everything else. Dogs are nice and straightforward.'

'You're telling me.'

'Of course!' Sean said suddenly. 'Shit!'

'Now what?'

'The farmhouse, your hippy friends.'

'Eh? What have they go to do with anything?'

'The farmhouse, where you wrote that fucking book.'

'What about it?'

'Well, where was it? We could go there.'

'No, Sean.'

'Where was it?'

'Suffolk.'

'See, things happen, things present themselves. Suffolk, brilliant. Hippies, they'll look after us. Our problems are solved.'

'No, Sean.'

'Why not?'

'We just can't. What would we say?'

'We'll think of something. We'll make something up. But hippies, they're perfect.'

'No.'

'Why not? Why the fuck not?'

'Well, they might not even be there still.'

'Ring them up.'

'They haven't got a phone, or at least they never used to have one. No phone, no telly, nothing.'

'Perfect.'

'Christ, it was so boring when I was there last. It wasn't even that much fun getting stoned. I think that was why I started writing that book.'

'Never mind about all that, let's just go there. I need it, George, I really need it.'

'They've probably moved.'

'We can try. Look, have you got a better idea?'

'Yes. No.'

'Please.'

'All right, but if it feels wrong we're not staying.'

'Oh, thank you, God.'

'But we'll have to do a few things before we get there.'

'Can't we just go, George?'

'No. First up, you get cleaned. Then we've got to get you some clothes. You're not turning up in a pair of Y-fronts and a dirty old mac.'

'I see what you mean.'

'We'll have to do some shopping. But I'm not taking you anywhere looking like that. You can hide in the boot.'

'Oh, come on, George.'

'You come on. You want to be arrested?'

'No. But can we at least make a start?'

'I'll have to look at the map.' George got an ancient road atlas out and studied it.

'By the way,' said Sean, 'you never finished telling me how you found me.'

'Well, as I said, I went round Mathews's yard, tried my hand at being a detective like you. Spent as long as I could there. Nothing all week. I was just about to give up when, today, yesterday, up drives the van, and I recognized the bloke driving as one of the ones who'd chased you that day in Hackney. So it sits there for a while, and then Mathews comes out and off they go. So I follow them.'

'All the way up here?'

'Yeah. Right, I think I know where we're going.' George put the atlas away and started the engine.

'How far is it?' Sean asked.

'About fifty miles.'

'Let's go.'

George pulled away into the mist.

'All the way from London?' said Sean. 'How d'you manage that?'

'Well, I've got you to thank for that, haven't I? Ever since that Saturday following Gatley I've been practising. It helps me relax. I get stoned and follow someone. I'm pretty good at it now, so they didn't see me. It was a piece of piss till we got off the main roads, then I had to stay so far back I nearly lost them loads of times.'

'You followed them all this fucking way? Fantastic!'

'Yeah, it was pretty good, wasn't it? Luckily it got dark, you see. That helped. They had a dodgy back light which I could follow from way back. Once we got on the country roads I had me own lights off most of the time. That got pretty hairy, I can tell you. Then they turn off the road down this private drive, so I go down as far as I dare – remember, I still don't know if I'm on a wild-goose chase – and I park under some trees and go the rest of the way on foot. And when I get down there, I see you looking like a fucking lunatic, or a ghost, or something, standing there in that coat swinging a pipe round your head. So I ran back, jumped in the car, and hared down there like Stirling fucking Moss. And I hit that bloke, Becket, so now I'm probably in the same boat as you, aren't I?'

'You didn't necessarily kill him.'

'God, it felt horrible.'

'It looked fantastic.'

'I felt sick. Good timing, though, wasn't it?'

Sean laughed despite the pain. 'It was miraculous timing, George. You're a genius, a fucking genius.'

28

It was getting on for half ten when they turned off the road into the driveway of Morewood House. It was a cold, grey, drizzling morning and the Suffolk countryside looked bleak and sullen.

Morewood House itself was a rather unexceptional, squat, brown affair, badly rebuilt at one end. It was set in untidy grounds littered with farm machinery, and it looked empty and deserted.

Lucy and Dave Scott lived in the old stables behind the house. There were flowers in the windows, but no one was about.

George parked and stared glumly at the row of restored stone buildings.

'Look, maybe they don't live here any more,' he said, turning off the engine.

'I'm dying here, George. Go and knock on the door.'

George got out and strolled half-heartedly up to the front door. He knocked twice and waited. He looked back at Sean, slumped in his seat, and rubbed the back of his neck. He knocked again, and peered through the letter box.

He was just about to give up when the door was opened by a small boy with close-cropped hair and a dirty face.

'Yes?' He looked like he was about five. He was wearing baggy jeans and a very old, faded 'Free Nelson Mandela' T-shirt.

'Hello, Luke,' said George. 'Remember me?'

'No.'

'I'm George.'

The boy stared at him.

'Er, is Lucy or Dave around?'

The little boy turned and shouted over his shoulder into the dimly lit interior. 'Mum!'

After a while a woman appeared. She was wearing a long, loose dress and her blonde hair was twisted into an approximation of dreadlocks. She frowned at George for a second, then began to laugh.

'George,' she said with a perfect Home Counties accent. 'What the hell are you doing here?' She threw her arms round him and hugged him.

'It's a long story, Lucy. How are you?'

'Great.'

'Er, listen, I've got a friend with me. He's been, well he's a bit, he's rather badly hurt.'

'Hurt?' Lucy frowned again and looked over at Sean sitting in the car. 'Have you had an accident? What's happened?'

'We were up in, er, Colchester, you know? Some squaddies attacked us. It was a nightmare.'

'Beaten up?' Lucy walked over to the car. George followed.

'We didn't want to go to the hospital, you know? The whole town was crawling with them.'

'I know.'

George opened the car door and Sean smiled at them.

Lucy grimaced when she saw him. 'Are you all right?' she asked, but she could see that he wasn't.

His forehead was bruised and it had ballooned out, so that he looked something like the elephant man. He had a black eye so huge and brown and perfect that it looked like it was stuck on. A tiny slit across its middle oozed a thick sticky gunge. His other eye was red and blinked continuously. A shallow gouge ran from it down to his thick upper lip, which was cut in two or three places. His nose was puffy and swollen, with a yellowish bruise half-way down. The wound on his neck, where he'd cut himself with the broken bottle, was raw and inflamed, and, despite George's efforts, there was still blood all over him.

'He doesn't feel too good,' said George unnecessarily. 'We just got in the car and drove away from there. Bad vibes, you know? We should have gone to a hospital, I suppose, but you know?'

'Hospitals are no good,' said Lucy. 'They just give you a lot of drugs and chemicals.'

'Yeah. But I think he's quite badly hurt.'

Lucy knelt in the mud next to the car and held Sean's hand. 'I'll give you some homoeopathic treatment. You'll heal in twice the time.'

'Thank you,' said Sean limply.

'We'd better get you inside.' She stood up and turned to her son, who was studying Sean intently.

'Luke, can you go and make up the spare bed, dear?' Luke tutted and disappeared into the house.

Lucy and George helped Sean out of the car, but he had stiffened so much that every movement was agony. He stood in a funny way, as if all his bones were out of joint. Slowly they shuffled into the house and up a narrow wooden staircase.

Sean kept apologizing and saying thank you, until George told him to shut up. They manoeuvred him into a tiny, neat bedroom and eased him down on to an ancient iron bed with a very thick mattress.

'Can you undress?' Lucy asked.

'Yeah,' said Sean, 'that's all right.' He tried to take his new shirt off, but he got his arm stuck and tears came into his good eye.

So Lucy and George stripped him off and rolled him under the clean white sheets, which felt almost unbearably cool and luxurious against his skin.

Lucy left the room to go and get something, and Sean grinned at George. George shook his head and smiled back. 'You don't deserve this, you know? You bastard.'

The window was open and Sean could see trees under a grey sky. There were birds singing and the occasional sounds of insects.

'I tell you, George, I've died. I've died and gone to heaven.'

'I thought you didn't believe in all that stuff.'

'I'm ill, I'm allowed to be inconsistent.'

Lucy came back in with a small bottle of pills. She took out three and made Sean swallow them. They were white and hardly bigger than grains of rice.

'Arnica,' she said, 'to help you heal. And here, take some of this.' From another bottle she tipped a couple of drops of tasteless liquid on to his tongue. 'That's for shock.'

'Thank you,' said Sean.

'You're in a terrible state.'

'I know.'

'Get some sleep now. When you wake up I'll have a look at you, and maybe you can have a wash.'

'Yeah.'

Lucy and George left him alone, and before he knew it he was asleep.

He slept all day, and woke in the early evening when Lucy brought him a bowl of soup.

He sat up and smiled at her.

'This is very good of you,' he said.

'That's all right. It's nice to have visitors, even if they are in a bit of a mess. We're a bit cut off here, you can get tired of the quiet life. Now then, I'd better take a look at you. If there *is* anything serious, you *will* have to go to a hospital.'

She peeled back the sheets and began to examine him. She seemed to know what she was doing. She gently prodded and probed, feeling his bones and muscles. She looked in his mouth and his eyes as best she could, and did a few rudimentary intelligence and co-ordination tests.

'You'd make a good nurse.' Sean's voice was hoarse and strained.

'I used to study alternative medicine,' said Lucy, putting the sheets back and tucking him in. 'I did a couple of courses. It's basically all just common sense, really.'

'So, will I live?'

'You'll live. You're not as bad as you look. Apart from your nose, there's nothing broken. When you're better you should have a doctor check it for you, see if you're breathing

247

okay. It might need to be reset. Other than that, it's bruises mostly. Cuts and bruises.'

'Are you sure? I feel like death.'

'A bruised muscle often feels worse than a break.'

'What about my ribs?'

'They seem okay; it's hard to tell. But even if they were broken, there's nothing you could do about it except rest, which you've got to do anyway. That's the thing about ribs.'

'You're not just humouring me? I mean, I really do feel crap.'

'You will for a while. You've been knocked about quite a bit.'

'And you're sure there's nothing serious?'

'Well, I think if there was any internal bleeding we'd know about it by now. You're quite tough, really, aren't you? The only thing we've got to look out for is your head.'

'Well, I can tell you, it hurts like buggery.'

'Yes, being hit on the head's no fun. You'll have to be very careful. The biggest danger is haemorrhaging. We'll just have to watch out for any signs of that, but of course by then it'll be too late.'

'Fantastic.'

'No, you'll live. In the meantime, just rest, drink a lot of water, eat what you can and let me give you some treatment.'

'Don't worry, you can give me all the treatment you want. I'm in your hands.'

Lucy laughed, and George knocked on the door. A moment later he came in, carrying a mug of tea.

'How's our patient?' he said, sitting down.

'Not so bad. But he'll have to stay here for a while. He shouldn't be moved.'

'How long?'

'At least a week, probably more.'

'I'm going to have to shoot off, though,' said George. 'I've got things to sort out.'

'George,' said Sean, 'what are you gonna do?'

'I'll leave you to it,' said Lucy, taking out the empty soup bowl. They listened to her going downstairs.

'I've got to go back to work, Sean.'

'But I thought we said we weren't going to London.'

'You're not going to London. I am, I've got to work.'

'What if they find you?'

'We'll see.'

'George!'

'They don't know where I work and they don't know where I'm living, or they'd have found me before now, wouldn't they?'

'I don't know, George. At least be careful, then.'

'That's rich, coming from you. Listen, they haven't got a phone here, but Lucy can phone from the village if there's a problem. I'll leave you John's number, and you know me work number. I'll come back up next Saturday. And don't worry, I'll make sure I'm not being followed, or any shit like that. All right?'

'Yeah, all right.'

'I'll see you, then.'

'Yeah. And thanks again, George.'

'Oh, will you fuck off with the thanks.'

George left him and he quickly fell asleep again.

Over the next couple of days Sean drifted in and out of sleep. He would have slept permanently if he hadn't been woken by two things, the pain and the dreams. Of the pains, the headaches were the worst, pounding and incessant. But he preferred the headaches to the dreams. When he dreamed, he dreamed he was back in the concrete cell with the foam around his head, waiting for the bat. The tension would build up and up as he willed it to come, but it wouldn't, and the pressure would grow, expand inside his head, and he'd wait and wait, until he could bear it no more and he'd wake up screaming, to find himself drenched in sweat and tangled in the sheets.

But as he rested the pains dimmed and the dreams became less frequent, until Lucy announced that he had to start on a healing regime. So, despite his protests, she woke him every morning at nine and made him eat breakfast. Then she coaxed him out of bed and forced him to take some exercise, so that his bruised muscles wouldn't seize up. The exercises were Chinese, mostly, and at first Sean felt stupid, doing the stork and the tiger and the water lily, but they did help.

After his exercises, if it was fine she'd take him into the garden, because she said that sunlight was a great healing power. As Sean wasn't averse to a bit of sunbathing, he didn't argue.

She gave him various homoeopathic pills, and strange teas, and foot massages, and pressure point manipulation, and aromatherapy, and she tried to make him meditate and do yoga routines, but unless she was there to make him do it properly he wouldn't bother.

She made decent simple vegetarian food, and although he was never hungry, he ate what he could. Slowly he felt better. The stiffness eased, the bruises hurt less, the headache dulled and his black eye opened.

The main problem was that Lucy wouldn't allow him to drink anything. She was very down on alcohol and said that it would be the worst thing for Sean, the state he was in. Some nights he longed for a cool pint of lager. And sometimes, when he woke sweating from a cricket dream, he could taste whisky in his mouth. Despite everything, he ached for a shot of the stuff.

One evening, as he lay in bed resting after an exercise session, Lucy came in to put some things in the wardrobe.

'Oh, yes,' she said, bending down to pick something up from the bottom of the cupboard. 'You had this when you arrived. I just slung it in here. What do you want me to do with it?'

It was the brief-case, the one he'd found at Mathews's place. He'd forgotten all about it.

'Right,' he said, trying not to appear too excited. 'I've lost the keys for it, actually. It's just some stuff, you know? You haven't got something I can try and get it open with, have you?'

'What, a key, you mean?'

'No, something to pick the lock with, or force it. A screwdriver or something.'

'It looks like a good case.'

'Nah, I picked it up in a junk shop. It's no use without the keys, anyway.'

Lucy shrugged and went to fetch him some tools.

He'd got to know her quite well, and Luke; he read to the boy sometimes, when the headaches weren't too bad, and he went along with his little games and fantasies.

Dave wasn't around; he was away working in America on a farm. Lucy admitted to Sean that she never really expected to see him again. She wasn't too bothered, she'd got used to being without him; she had her own life now. She made a reasonable income knitting for a London company who sold fashion knitwear at exorbitant prices in designer stores, and she had Luke, so she was happy.

Sean liked talking to her. She was from such a different world than the one he'd been in lately, it helped him get things into perspective.

Presently she came back with an old kitchen knife, a hammer and a screwdriver. He waited until she'd gone, then tried them out. In the end he managed to smash the clasps off with the hammer and get the thing open. It was more than he'd dared hope for.

Inside was the passport they'd taken off him, the plane ticket they'd bought, and most of his money from the flat, over three and a half thousand pounds. He closed his eyes and held the notes to his face.

He slept well that night for the first time. He had no dreams.

In the morning, as he couldn't risk using it, he burned the plane ticket.

After that he found that he could think again. So he started to plan his revenge. He started to plot the final downfall of Ray Mathews.

He wondered sometimes what Lucy would think of him if she knew the truth, if she knew what he'd done, how he'd really got like this.

But he tried not to wonder too much about that sort of thing. It wasn't healthy, and healthy was everything. He was back on course and mustn't be diverted. A great peace settled over him and he was filled with a strange, intense joy. He'd escaped from his prison, and now he had the upper hand. He knew he could do anything, because he had already broken every law there was. When he left Morewood House he would know what to do, and he would go out and do it.

He could feel power surging into his body, into his mind. He felt like he was becoming Superman.

On Friday night, when Luke had gone to bed, he sat in the kitchen with Lucy at the big scrubbed oak table, drinking camomile tea and chatting.

'What happened to your dog?' Sean asked after a while.

'What dog?'

'George said you used to have a dog, a big Labrador or something.'

'Oh, Boadicea. She died, run over.'

'That's a pity. George wrote a book about her, you know?'

'What?'

'Yeah. I was just thinking, he started it in this kitchen. A book about dogs.'

'I don't believe you.'

'It's true. He was stoned. Well, when I say "wrote a book", he only started it. I doubt he'll ever finish it. He'll be here tomorrow, won't he? You can ask him about it then.'

'Mmm, do you want to do something? We could all go somewhere.'

'You're the doctor. You tell me, am I well enough?'

'A miracle recovery.' Lucy laughed.

'Seriously.'

'Seriously. You looked a lot worse than you were. On the outside, at least. I can't vouch for the inside.'

'So I could go with George, when he leaves?'

Lucy looked thoughtful. 'I should think so, if you want to. But you're welcome to stay as long as you want. It's nice having someone around. You don't get in the way.'

'You say the nicest things.'

'No, I mean it. You don't have to get back for anything, do you?'

'I can't just stay here for ever, can I?'

'I could get you some work if you wanted. They need someone to clean the place up. Up at the house.'

'It's tempting, but there's things I've got to do. I should get back.'

'Yes?'

'Yeah, you know, things to do.'

'What?'

'Oh, you know . . .'

'Not really, no. I don't really know anything about you, as a matter of fact.'

'I've talked to you, haven't I?' said Sean, smiling.

'Oh, we've talked, but don't you think it's been a bit one-sided?'

'Well, what d'you want to know?'

'What kind of a question's that?' Lucy laughed.

'Okay. I've got a sister, a brother, two parents. I do various odd jobs, decorating mostly, and I live in London.'

'Sean?'

'Yes?'

'You haven't really been telling me the truth, have you?'

'What do you mean? It's true. I've got a sister, a mother and a father . . . No, no, you're right. I never told you about my guinea-pig.'

'Very funny. But I'm not talking about that. I mean, you haven't really told me the truth about what happened to you, have you? How you got like that.'

'Colchester, you mean?'

'Sean, I saw you when you got here. You were wearing a brand-new shirt and trousers, no blood on them, and no underwear. You were filthy. Someone had beaten you up, but some of those injuries were more than a day old. I didn't say anything before, because you haven't been well and it was none of my business, really. If you wanted to tell me a story, that was your concern. But I've got to know you a bit since, and I suppose I quite like you a bit, and I just, well, there's something going on, isn't there?'

'Like what? What d'you mean?'

'That's what I'm asking you. I could tell as soon as you got here, the shifty way George was behaving . . .'

'He just wasn't sure of turning up like that.'

'Sean, please, don't lie any more. If you don't want to tell me the truth, okay, but don't lie.'

'Okay, I'm sorry. But it really is best you don't know. I'll go with George on Sunday, and I'll probably never see you again. It's best you just forget me.'

'I wouldn't like that. You can keep in touch at least, can't you?'

'I may not be able to. You see, I may have to go away. Go abroad, or something.'

'Why?'

'Look, there's some people, not very nice people, and for one reason or another which I don't really want to go into, they don't like me very much. It wasn't squaddies beat me up, it was them. They'd do worse if they could, so I'm going away. I can forget all about them, and they can forget all about me. Over, end of story.'

'You're not going to tell me any more?'

'No, I can't. Honestly, Lucy. It'd just make things worse.' He studied the pattern of lines scoured into the table top.

'It's okay.' Lucy put her hand on Sean's. 'I shouldn't have asked. It really isn't any of my business.'

'Isn't it?' Sean pulled his hand away and angrily flung himself back in his seat. 'Jesus, I come here, you've never seen me before in your life, you look after me, feed me. And I . . . ' He stopped and rested his face in his hands. 'Listen, Lucy,' he said quietly. 'I can't tell you how much I appreciate what you've done for me. I couldn't begin to thank you. God knows what would have happened to me if I hadn't come here.' Sean fell silent, listened to a clock ticking.

'Jesus, I could do with a drink,' he said.

'And I thought I'd cured you of all that?'

'In a week? I was drinking a bottle of whisky a day before I came here.'

'That's ridiculous.'

'Yeah, and I guess it's a habit I don't want to get back into. But one glass of beer wouldn't hurt.'

'You want a bet?'

'You're a hard woman, Lucy.'

'Am I?'

'No, you're fantastic. It's a shame I couldn't have met you under different circumstances.'

'Under different circumstances you might not have appreciated me.'

'Yeah, well, I probably wouldn't have met you at all, I suppose. You know a lot of people end up marrying nurses who've looked after them.'

'A lot of men.'

'Yeah.' Sean got up from the table and stretched. 'So you think I'm better, then, do you?'

'You'll do. You should take it easy for a while, though. I wouldn't do any decorating for a week or so. And if your headaches continue, then you really ought to see a doctor, just in case.'

'So it's okay to take exercise?'

'Of course. It's good for you.'

'How strenuous?'

'Well, don't try the decathlon or anything like that. Do the sort of things I've been showing you.'

'Yeah, only I was just wondering.'

'What?'

'Well, you know, I've got to know you a bit, and you know I like you.'

'I should hope so.'

'No, I mean I *really* like you.'

'You *really* like me.'

'Yeah. Really.' Sean moved round behind her and leant on the back of her chair.

'And?' she said, turning round to look at him.

'And, well, you know, I'd really like to, I'd quite like to, you know, go to bed with you.'

'I bet you would.' Lucy laughed and stood up. 'You've just got a nurse fixation. Now go to bed, and I'll see you in the morning.'

She kissed him quickly and sent him on his way.

29

Sunday night George drove into King's Cross with Sean and pulled over near the station. He'd patched up Fat John's car and sprayed it black. It looked almost as good as new.

'There you go, then,' he said. 'Good luck.'

'Cheers.'

'You're definitely not going to tell me your plan, then?' George turned off the engine.

'I get this finished, I cover myself and I clear out. That's all you need to know.'

'And you're not telling me who you know in King's Cross?'

'Nope.'

'In case I fall into the hands of the Gestapo, and they torture the information out of me.'

'Something like that, yeah.'

'I don't know, Sean; either you're taking this all too seriously or you're treating it all like some big game. I can't quite work out which.'

'I'm just doing what's got to be done, George.'

'A man's gotta do what a man's gotta do. You and John fucking Wayne.'

'John Wayne's dead. I killed him, remember?'

'You killed him, did you? And I always thought it was cancer.'

'Nah, it was me, with a sash-weight. Duke Wayne. Never knew what hit him.'

'Oh, very funny.'

'I'm sorry, I'm just in a good mood. I've got a feeling this is all going to work out fine in the end.'

'You're insane. You know that?'

'Am I?' Sean grinned and opened the door.

'Wait a minute.' George touched him on the arm. 'You haven't told me the most important thing.'

'What's that?' Sean closed the door.

'Did you fuck her?'

'Who?'

'Lucy.'

'No, I did not fuck her.'

'Oh, come on, don't give me that. I saw what you two were like this weekend; she was all over you.'

'We're just good friends.'

'Bollocks. You fucked her, didn't you?'

'No. She's a very nice person and I respect her, and I appreciate what she did for me. I wouldn't have made it without her. I like her a lot, I enjoyed being with her, but I did not fuck her.' He sniffed and looked out of the window. 'She wouldn't let me.'

'Ha! You wanker, I knew it.'

'Yeah, well, I don't want to hear any more about it.'

'I reckon she'd be a good sack artist,' said George thoughtfully. 'The healing hands. All that healthy country flesh. I was sure you'd fucked her.'

'Is that it, then?' Sean went to open the door again.

'What?'

'Are you finished?'

'No. One more thing.'

'What?'

George leant over into the back of the car and picked up a carrier-bag. 'I got this for you. To look after yourself.' He reached into the bag and took out a pistol.

'Jesus Christ, George, where did you get that?'

George shrugged. 'It's only a model.'

'What?' Sean took the gun off him. It was plastic.

'Good, isn't it?' said George proudly. 'You can't tell the difference. I got meself one and all.'

Sean laughed and tried the trigger mechanism.

'You know what type it is?' George asked proudly.

'No, I don't know anything about guns.'

'It's a Walther PPK, same as James Bond. I thought it would be just right for you. And this,' he said dramatically as he pulled another gun out of the bag, 'is my little baby.'

'It's enormous,' said Sean. 'What is it?'

'What do you think?' George leered. 'It's a fucking Magnum.'

They burst into laughter.

Sean was still laughing ten minutes later when he stopped outside Sandra's flat and rang the bell.

When Sandra opened the door she smiled at Sean, though she was obviously surprised to see him.

'Hello,' she said.

'Are you doing anything?' Sean asked.

'Not really. Come in.'

Sean followed her into the sitting-room.

'To tell you the truth,' Sandra said, sitting on the black leather sofa among a pile of Sunday papers, 'I didn't really think I'd be seeing you again.'

'I haven't been around.'

'What have you been up to?' She looked at him properly for the first time. 'Shit, what happened to your face?'

'I got beaten up. I've been in hospital.'

'Who was it?'

'Just some drunk on the tube. He was hassling some girl and I tried to stop him.'

'It looks really nasty.'

'It looks worse than it is.'

'Does it hurt?'

'Not now. So how are you?'

'Okay.'

'I would have rung or something, but I didn't know your number. And, you know, well, it wasn't really your problem, my being in hospital, and that. So, anyway, listen, do you fancy going out for a drink?'

'Sure.'

Sean sat on the sofa and watched television while Sandra got ready. It was strange; he hadn't watched any television for what seemed like months. The programmes were all so cosy, and bland, and smug, as if they were from a different planet to the one he'd been on. He felt very detached.

Sandra was ready in a few minutes and they walked to a nearby pub. Once there Sean kept her talking, so that she wouldn't ask him too many questions. It was the first drink he'd had since the concrete room and it was acting on him quickly. He had to watch himself, he didn't want to get too drunk. He managed to keep the conversation largely on her work, and the video and film industry in general, even though he hardly ever went to the cinema.

In fact they had to leave the pub early, because there was a film on television which Sandra wanted to watch. It was a Swiss film about a waitress and Sean couldn't really concentrate. He nearly fell asleep a couple of times and was very relieved when it finally finished and they could go to bed.

It was better with her this time; he seemed to have got Susan out of his system, and he could relate to Sandra a bit easier. Afterwards, as they lay in the dark, they chatted about nothing in particular until Sean worked his way round to asking Sandra if he could stay for a few days.

She hoisted herself up on to one elbow and peered at him in the half-light.

'You see,' said Sean, 'it's my flat. While I was in hospital someone broke in and wrecked it, smashed the toilet, everything. I can't face it right now. I just need somewhere to stay until I get it sorted out. I mean, I meant to ask earlier, but it just didn't seem to come up.'

'It's okay, you can stay,' she said flatly.

'Shit, I know this looks bad.'

'Yes.'

'But that's not the reason I came round. I did want to see you. I mean, I was prepared to sleep on the sofa if you'd wanted.'

'That's very noble of you.'

'Honestly, Sandra.'

'Don't you know anyone else?'

'Yeah, but I didn't want to stay with them. I wanted to

stay with you. I like you, I like talking to you, I like going to bed with you.'

'I quite like going to bed with you.' She kissed him. 'But it's not permanent, okay?'

'Two or three days, that's all, I promise. I need to get my place cleaned up, get the council round and that.'

'I should really kick you out.'

'Yeah.'

'But I won't. Goodnight.'

Sandra settled back down and turned on to her side to sleep. Sean stayed awake for a couple of hours making sure that he was clear what he was going to do. The end was in sight, he just had to follow it through.

He slept well and had no bad dreams.

Sandra was gone when he woke up on Monday morning. He had some breakfast and went shopping. From a sports and camping shop he bought a full-face balaclava, a small nylon rucksack and another pair of nylon overalls. Then he went to a bike shop and bought a cheap second-hand racer.

He piled everything into the rucksack and took the bike for a trial run.

It was strange to be cycling again and he took it easy at first. He rode aimlessly around London. It was comforting to see it going about its business as it had done for so many years. He meant nothing here; he could cease to exist and it wouldn't make the blindest bit of difference. The city was a huge mindless machine, utterly oblivious of him, and that, to Sean, was freedom.

The parts of the machine continued to whirr and click, the cars and vans and taxis and dirty red buses, the motor bikes and push-bikes, the pedestrians, black, white, brown, grey, the filthy air filled with radio signals, TV signals, the buzz and hum of millions upon millions of voices, the shops and the litter, the miles of wires and cables, the sewers and tunnels, the huge buildings and the endless tarmac. It was exhilarating.

But it was also rather sad. Sad to think that he would

soon have to leave all this, the ugly shapeless city which was his home. But then, if it all blew over, he could come back. One day he could return and it would only be superficially changed. Underneath it would still be the same, an old fucked-up city. The best place in the world.

He cycled to a library and chained his bike to the railings outside. Then he went in, found the relevant phone-book and looked up Derek Mathews's address and phone number in Sevenoaks.

After that he went back to Sandra's and had something to eat. He watched television until half five, then he rang Sevenoaks.

A woman answered the phone.

'Hello,' said Sean. 'Can I speak to your husband, please?'

It sounded like the woman laughed and it was a moment before she replied. 'He won't be back till later. Can I take a message?'

'No, that's all right. I'll ring back.'

He left a note for Sandra, saying he had to go and look at a job way out in West London and would be out late. She'd given him his own set of keys so he could let himself in.

At six o'clock he went to Charing Cross and bought a ticket for Sevenoaks. From Sevenoaks station he took a cab to the White Hart, the pub Ray had taken him to out of town. That all seemed like years ago, another life.

He bought himself a half of lager and waited for the phone to be free.

A fat woman was on it. She was very anxious about something and had a small pile of coins, but Sean could wait.

Eventually she finished and Sean rang Derek Mathews's number again.

This time a man answered and Sean hung up straight away.

He left the pub and set off for Blackhall Lane. It was a pleasant evening and he quite enjoyed the walk. There was hardly any traffic, just a few commuters coming home from work. The big, well-spaced houses were quiet, but there were a few people out walking their dogs. He smiled at them, and mostly they smiled back.

It took him about half an hour to find the house, and he wasn't surprised to see that it was the same one he'd sat outside with Ray while he told him his life story.

It looked like the sort of house a child draws. A red roof, chimneys, leaded windows with little tidy curtains, a flower-lined path leading up to the bright front door. All it needed was mummy and daddy standing next to it with a happy little dog.

Sean hurried up the drive and slipped down the alley-way separating the house from a matching double-garage. There was a side door here with a window. Sean peered in. It looked into a much-enlarged kitchen. The lights were on, but it was empty. He moved round to the back of the house. There was an unexpectedly large back garden and he could just make out a tennis court and the ghostly blue of an illuminated swimming-pool.

Sean crept along the back wall, past the kitchen. There was a set of french windows giving on to a paved terrace with a built-in barbecue and a few plants in tubs. The curtains were open and he could see the distinctive flickering light of a television.

He decided to go back and try the side door.

It was unlocked. He put on the balaclava, and took the gun from his pocket. Then he carefully pushed the door open and slipped into the kitchen.

He padded across the spongy lino towards the sound of the television. There was chase music and the wail of an American police siren. For a couple of seconds he listened at the door which led through to the sitting-room, then he quickly opened it and walked in.

Two heads turned to look at him. The nearest belonged to a fortyish woman, who was sitting on a sofa reading a magazine with her legs tucked up under her. She was well turned-out and wearing glasses. When she saw Sean she showed no expression, but took her glasses off.

Sitting in an armchair on the other side of the room was

Derek Mathews, holding a large tumbler of whisky and frowning.

For a few moments nobody said anything.

Sean kept the plastic gun on Mathews and moved out of the doorway.

'Don't worry,' he said, trying to keep his voice flat and neutral. 'I don't intend to use this.'

There was another silence. Sean fought to keep down his excitement and stared at Derek. It was strange seeing him in the flesh; he was so like Ray, and yet so unlike him.

'What do you want?' Derek said at last.

'I'm not a burglar or anything.'

'What is this? Is this a joke?'

'Not really, no. This is to do with your brother.'

'I might have known Ray was behind this. What's the silly fucker want now?' He shook his head and the woman giggled.

'He doesn't know I'm here. I've come to do a deal with you.'

'Oh, yeah? And who might you be?'

'That doesn't matter.'

'What's with the gun, then?'

'That's just to make sure you listen.'

'Go on, then. I'm all ears.'

'I used to work for Ray, in as much as he hired me to sort out that accountant, Eric Gatley. Which, I'm sure you know, was only done to make things look bad for you, drop you in the shit.'

'I had gathered that, yes.'

'Good. Well, I didn't realize at the time just what a cunt Ray is, and a stupid cunt at that. He hadn't thought things through.'

'What else is new?'

'Thing is, you see, it wasn't enough for him to screw things up for you; he wanted to drop me in it and all. First of all he never pays me, then he tries to knock me off, to get me out the way.'

'That sounds like Ray, all right. No head for business.'

'Yeah, well, as he never kept his bargain with me, I'm in a position to go elsewhere. To get what I'm owed, and to put myself in a safe place.'

'So what, exactly, are you proposing?'

'I've got him after me, I've got the police after me, and I doubt if you're sitting around on your arse doing nothing.'

'Too right I'm not, sunbeam.'

'Well, I can't do a deal with the police, and I've learnt all too well that I can't reason with your brother, so that leaves you.'

'Yeah. So, as I say, what exactly do you want me to do?'

'Well, you seem a bit smarter than Ray.'

'Yeah, yeah, all right, get on with it, will you? I was watching this programme.'

'The police think you killed Gatley. You and I know that it was Ray.'

'Yes.'

'Well, I'm offering to fix it so that the police know for sure that it was Ray all along, and that you weren't involved at all. But I have to make sure that it's done in such a way that no one knows about my involvement in it all, and I can only do that with your co-operation.'

'Go on.'

'You'll co-operate?'

'Course I'll fucking co-operate.'

'Okay. Briefly, it's like this. You tell the police that you've known all along that it was Ray trying to frame you, but you didn't want to say anything because of family loyalty.'

'Well, I wouldn't be lying there, would I? I don't like the police interfering in family business.'

'There's no other way, it's him or you. People are dead, the police need a result. They're not going to just fade away, are they?'

'Yeah, but I can't risk this going to court. Ray could start spouting all kinds of shit. He'd make damn sure if he was going down he'd take me with him. We're close like that.'

'If we do it my way it won't go to court. I'm offering to get Ray out of your hair for good.'

'Oh yes?' Derek settled back in his chair and smiled. 'Now you're talking.' He turned the television off with a remote control. 'Can I get you a drink?'

30

'No drink,' said Sean. 'And I'm not putting the gun away, or taking off the mask, or any crap like that. You look too much like Ray for me to trust you. I'm just hoping you're a little bit more intelligent than him.'

'You should have come to me before. We could have saved each other a great deal of bother.'

'Probably.'

'Well, if you're not having one, do you mind if I have another? A celebratory libation.'

'Go on, then.'

Derek got up and went to a well-stocked drinks cabinet.

'You want one, love?' he asked the woman without turning round.

'I don't suppose you've got any champagne?' They both laughed. 'So I'll just have the usual.'

Derek poured out a couple of drinks, handed one to the woman and sat down.

'Right, then,' he said. 'Let's hear what you've got up your sleeve, shall we?'

'All you've got to do is tell the police exactly what we've just talked about. That you've had enough, you're not going to go down in his place, and you're willing to tell them what you know about the case.'

'Which is what?'

'That Ray paid one of his men, a bloke called Ken Turner, to kill Gatley, in order to frame you.'

'Ken Turner? He used to work for me. I sacked the drunken cunt.'

'That's good, that fits nicely. So Ken kills Gatley, but then he starts shooting his mouth off, demanding more money and that, so Ray gets Duke to try and shut him up.'

'Duke Wayne?'

'Do you know any other Dukes? So Ken and Duke fight, and Ken comes out on top.'

'How am I supposed to know about all this?'

'You don't have to tell them everything, whatever you think's best. Tell them you've got friends in Ray's organization, tell them you've pieced it together from what they've told you and what you've read in the papers. I mean, you know that's how the police function, informers. They don't care how it's solved as long as they've got a plausible story. And don't worry about the evidence, I'll supply that.'

'Yeah, all right. Do I need to know anything else, then, or is that it?'

'No. Ray takes Ken up to his place in Suffolk, and Ken never comes back.'

'Poor old Ken.'

'And naturally Ken's mates are a bit upset about this.'

'Naturally.'

'So they go on the warpath. You know, the criminals fall out, all that kind of shit.'

'Sounds exciting.'

'Just make sure that you've got good alibis for the rest of the week, particularly the next two or three days. You and anyone close to you. There mustn't be any danger of you being connected with what happens now.'

'Don't worry about that.'

'And don't go to the police. Wait for them to come back to you, or it'll look funny. And whatever you do, don't say anything to them before Thursday.'

'It's very good of you to take all this interest in my welfare.'

'I don't give a shit about you, it's just that you're the best person to keep me out of this. Mutual protection. With any luck the police will have it all nicely wrapped up and they can pat each other on the back and get promoted. It means that you'll still be left with what Gatley stirred up in the first place, but that's your problem. Let's face it, though, it's better than murder.'

'Everything's better than murder, son.'

'And besides, I'm sure with your contacts you can sort that side of things out.'

'I'm already working on it. If you can really make sure the Bill know it was all Ray's doing, I can get the rest forgotten. Might even be able to do a deal, eh? Co-operate with the police for a price.'

'Right. But there's one other thing. Ray's your brother.'

'Is he?'

'If I deal with him, I've got to know that you'll let things lie. You won't suddenly change your mind about him and get an upsurge of brotherly love.'

'There's only one reason I'd have to come after you, my son.'

'What's that?'

'If you balls it up. Now why don't you sit down and put that gun away? You seem like a very sensible lad.'

Sean ignored him. 'It's a deal, then?'

Mathews laughed. 'Son, I'd pay you to get Ray off my fucking back. I don't know why I didn't think of it before.'

'Yeah, well, I was just coming to that.'

'What?'

'Money.'

'Ah.'

'As I said, Ray never paid me.'

'I think I see what you're getting at.'

'Good. When this is all over, I'm going away, and I'll need a bit of capital.'

'I'll see what I can do.'

'I want it now.'

'Now?'

'I can't risk seeing you again. So I want it now.'

'What, cash?'

'Well, I don't want a fucking cheque, do I?'

'You can have whatever's in my wallet, but it's hardly a fortune. Might get you as far as Southend.'

'Don't piss me about, Mathews. I've had enough. A bloke like you deals in cash all the time. Now, you're not going to tell me you haven't got a little something stashed away here.'

'I haven't. It's not safe. But I can get you some.'

'Bollocks, fuck off! Don't lie to me.'

'But what can I do? If you just give me a little time I can get you as much as you want.'

'You haven't been paying attention, Derek. I told you, I don't trust anyone, okay? I've killed three people so far, so I don't have to listen to promises. Now this gun says give me the cash now or I'll make it look like poor old Ray finally went completely berserk and had you two done in.'

The woman looked at Mathews. 'Give him some money, Derek.'

Derek smiled. 'Oh sod it, why not? You're doing both of us a favour, after all. I've got a few hundred in the safe, but that's it. I really don't like to keep too much about the place.'

'Yeah, all right. Just get it!'

Mathews put down his glass and got up.

'Wait,' said Sean. 'We'll all go.' He indicated that the woman should get up as well.

The three of them trooped out of the sitting-room, across a large hallway and into a very tidy and unused-looking study. Mathews sat down at the desk, took some keys from his pocket and unlocked a drawer. Inside the drawer was a fitted safe. He twiddled the combination lock and opened it.

'Here you are.' He took out a wad of notes and quickly flipped through it. 'There must be nearly a grand here.' He slapped it down on the desk top and looked at Sean. 'It's all yours,' he said unenthusiastically.

'Come on, Derek,' said the woman with a grin. 'It's worth it.' She turned to Sean, 'Blimey, I wish I had some money I could give you, love. It's worth every penny if it means you'll get rid of that bastard Ray for us.'

'Oh, I'm sorry,' Mathews said to Sean, as he relocked the safe and pushed the drawer shut. 'I should've introduced you. This is Zara Mathews, Ray's wife.'

It was nearly half eleven when Sean got back into London, and getting on for midnight when he got off the tube at King's Cross.

It was still fairly busy round the station. There was a blaze of light from two or three fast-food places and an amusement arcade, and people were milling around waiting for buses or just hanging out. Sean crossed the road and headed off into the back streets. The pool of life around the station didn't extend very far, and the streets quickly became badly lit and for the most part deserted.

As Sean walked towards Sandra's flat he became aware of someone behind him. He didn't think anything about it at first, but it was soon fairly obvious that he was being followed. He tried to keep his pace down and not look panicked.

He wondered which one of them it was. Carl or Becket? Or Ray even? It couldn't be the police, surely. Whoever it was, he wasn't going to show them he was worried. He was just about to turn and confront them when a voice said, 'Excuse me, mate,' and whoever it was drew level with him.

He turned, but instead of the expected burly labourer he saw a slim black teenager.

'Have you got a light?' he asked, reaching into his pocket.

'Sorry,' said Sean, 'I don't smoke.'

The youth brought out an open knife and fixed his eyes on Sean's. He looked a bit nervous.

'Oh, for fuck's sake,' said Sean and he snorted with laughter.

The kid frowned and held the knife up in what he took to be a menacing fashion.

'Give me your fucking money, man,' he said.

'You've got to be fucking joking,' Sean replied.

'Hey, I'm not joking.' The kid jerked the knife. 'Now give me your money or I'll cut you.'

'Oh, why don't you piss off?' said Sean.

The teenager gritted his teeth and slashed the knife rather tentatively towards Sean's face, but Sean was ready for it and jumped back. Then, before the kid could come back at him, Sean took his gun out and pointed it straight into one of his eyes. The eyes widened.

'Now look here, you wanker,' Sean said quietly, 'I asked you to piss off.' The youth said nothing. 'But now I think I'll blow your fucking brains out.'

'Come on, man, you wouldn't.'

'Try me.'

'Jesus, all right. Jesus.'

'You picked the wrong person tonight, shit-head. See this gun? Now you may think I'm some kind of vigilante fucker, out to clean the streets of muggers and scum. Huh? No way, I'm something far worse than that, I'm a fucking head-case. I just don't give a shit, you get me?'

'Yeah, all right.'

'Police don't bother me, killing don't bother me, you don't bother me. Okay? Anyone tries to fuck with me, I'm apt to just blow up, you understand? Just fly right off the handle. That's *my* problem. Now, what's your fucking problem? Huh?'

'No problem.'

'No problem? Now that's a matter of perspective. You're standing there looking like a dick with someone pointing a gun in your face and you tell me there's no problem. You're something of an optimist, I'd say.'

'Leave it, man.'

'Why?'

'Come on, I wasn't going to cut you. I just wanted some money.'

'Why are you doing this? Tell me that. You broke, or just enterprising? Because I can tell you a lot about enterprise. The spirit of self-advancement in modern Britain. I've done a bit of it myself.'

'You're crazy.'

'Yeah. And that's why you should be a little bit nervous. Look at you. You've believed the adverts, haven't you? You want it all and you want it now, and God help anyone who stands in your way. Well, good luck to you, but it's tough these days for the self-employed small businessman. In the modern economic environment you've got to be always one jump ahead of the opposition. Huh? Do I make myself clear? You see, even the most vicious and professional mugger can come up against a complete fucking nutter with a gun who can blast their fucking head clean off their fucking shoulders. Because *he just doesn't care* any more.'

'What you fucking talking about?'

'I'm talking about the risks involved in a free-enterprise system based entirely on the individual, shit-head.'

'Fucking hell.'

'Now I've learnt some things from this system, and I'm passing on some of this valuable knowledge to you, you understand?'

'Huh?'

'The main lesson is this, the person with the biggest weapon wins, and if you've got a weapon you've got to use it first. And you, you fucked up all round, so drop that knife.'

The knife clattered to the pavement.

'Now go home.'

The boy looked sullenly at him.

'Go!'

The boy sauntered off, still trying to look tough. When he was a little distance away he turned back and yelled.

'You white bastard. You fucking racist.'

Sean took aim and the boy fled.

Sean kicked the knife down a drain and carried on to Sandra's.

She was still up, lying on the floor watching a video. She greeted Sean coldly, so he kissed her and apologized for being out all evening.

'Look,' she said, 'it's okay. I mean, you can do what you like, just don't treat me like a hotel.'

'Yeah, it just came up today, the job. I needed to get in there quick. It's big money. They even gave me an advance. I can give you some money for food and things if you want.'

'No. That's not the point. I don't know. Look, this is stupid.' She smiled at Sean and he lay down next to her on the grey carpet and slipped an arm round her shoulders.

'Let's not get into all that domestic crap, okay?' she said. 'I'm not used to this.'

'What?'

'Living with someone.'

Sean laughed. 'I've only been here a day.'

'Yeah, but, I don't know, it's all so unexpected. I don't know if I was ready for it.'

'I'm not so awful, am I?'

'It's not you, Sean. It's me. It's nice having you around, almost too nice. That's the problem. I didn't want a relationship, anything permanent. And now I find that I like it. What I don't like is being made to feel like a married woman, or something. You know? "Where were you all night?" I don't like feeling like that.'

'Well, don't, then.' He kissed her again. 'I don't think of you as a married woman.'

'I don't know what you think of me, Sean, I hardly know you.'

'And I hardly know you, but I like you. We've got plenty of time to get to know each other, we can take it as quickly or as slowly as you like. In the meantime I'm happy to know you simply in the biblical sense.'

'God, you're a prat sometimes.'

'Yeah, but you must admit you like getting biblical with me.'

'It's your scars. They're very sexy.'

'Hah! You're only interested in my scars, I knew it!' They laughed again, and kissed again, and were soon in bed again.

Just before they fell asleep Sandra turned to Sean and stroked his face, feeling him in the dark like a blind woman.

'Sean,' she said.

'Mm?'

'What I was saying earlier. I didn't say it very well. What I meant to say was, you can stay as long as you like. I mean, I'd like you to stay. Okay?'

Sean leant over and kissed her on the forehead. 'Okay.'

Sean rang George in the morning and arranged to meet him

for lunch. Then he packed all his stuff into his new rucksack and carefully went round Sandra's flat removing all traces of his presence. He even wiped most of the surfaces to remove fingerprints.

He double-checked, then wheeled his bike out, locked the door, cleaned the keys and put them back through the letter box.

At one o'clock he was in a pub on Farringdon Road. It was packed with office workers, and there was a strong smell of beer, cigarettes and pub food.

George came in late, got himself a beer and sat down.

'What's new?' he asked.

'I'm going for it,' said Sean.

'What?'

'I'm finishing it.'

'Yeah? Well, good luck. I won't ask.'

'You still haven't seen anything of them, then?'

'Nah, not a sausage. I'm all right.'

'Good. Have you got the file?'

'Of course.' George plonked Gatley's pink file down on the table, and Sean quickly checked inside.

'I'll be going away after,' he said.

'Yeah?'

'So I probably won't see you for a while. And I just want to say thanks for everything. You know I wouldn't have made it without you.'

George shrugged, and Sean passed him an envelope.

'What's this?' George asked.

'It's for . . . for all you've done.'

George looked inside the envelope and blushed. 'Oh, no,' he said, pushing it back across the table towards Sean.

'Fuck off, George,' Sean said angrily. 'You're taking it. There's two grand there, okay?'

'Oh, come on, I don't want this.'

'It's the least I can do. Now shut up. Because of me your flat got trashed, you had to fuck around at work . . .'

'Don't worry about me flat. It was insured up to the rafters. I'm gonna make a killing on that.'

Sean laughed. 'I'm the one who's made all the killings. And because of me you're an accomplice to murder and God knows what. So take the money.'

'Yeah, and then I'd be handling stolen goods.'

'That's not stolen, George, that was earned. And it's yours, you earned it. I still don't know why you've done all this for me. I know we were friends but . . .'

'For someone who thinks he's so bleeding smart you're fucking thick, you know that, Sean?'

'What d'you mean?'

'You really don't know why I helped you?'

'No.'

'Look at you. You think you're so bleeding unique; you think you're the only person who might have got a kick out of all this. I enjoyed it, you moron. I fucking enjoyed it. It's been brilliant.'

'But George, you could go to jail.'

'I could go to jail for smoking dope, Sean.'

They laughed. George put the envelope in his pocket and the subject was closed.

An hour later George had to leave to get back to work. They walked out of the pub and quickly said goodbye in the street, and then, for some reason, they shook hands.

'Have a nice life,' George said.

'And you.'

They went their separate ways.

Just before three, Sean wheeled his bike down one of the platforms at Liverpool Street station and loaded it on to an eastbound train. Then he found a relatively empty carriage and settled down for the long journey to Ray's place in Suffolk.

It was after nine when he finally arrived. It was a dark, cloudy evening, and on the unlit country roads he had the feeling he was the only person left in the world.

He got off his bike at the top of the drive and hid it well back in the bushes. Then he started down towards the house between the high, old trees. As he drew nearer he walked

276

more cautiously, in case there was anyone around, but the buildings were unlit, angular black shapes against the dull sky, and there were no cars or vans parked in the yard.

Everything was as he remembered it: the concrete out-house, the untidy yard, the dilapidated sheds. Only the out-side toilet had changed, where George had ploughed into it in Fat John's car.

The padlock on the outhouse was unlocked. He pulled open the door and went in. He felt a familiar pain starting in the back of his head, and he fought to keep memories from creeping in. Inside it was empty and scrubbed; there wasn't even a stain to show what had happened there. The chair was gone, the table, his bed, the old calendar.

He stayed there as long as he could, then let out a long breath and headed for the house.

The front door was locked, but he remembered Becket saying something about there being a key hidden behind the drainpipe. It didn't take him long to find it.

Once inside he tried the lights. The power had been left on, and from somewhere inside the building he could hear a faint electrical hum. But there was a deserted, desolate feel about the place.

He wandered from room to room. Most were empty and there were dust sheets over the few pieces of furniture. The sitting-room had been cleaned out; there were no signs of the debris left by Ken and Carl, the food wrappings and over-flowing ashtrays, the discarded cans and bottles. The tele-vision was still there, but the video machine had been taken away.

Sean left the room and continued to explore the ground floor.

Off the hallway, at the foot of the stairs, was a spotless kitchen. Apart from an old-fashioned kettle which sat on the old gas cooker, it looked like nothing had ever been used. He quickly checked the cupboards. There was a pile of yellow newspapers in one, but other than that they were empty.

A door at the other end of the kitchen opened into what

must once have been the pantry. It was a cold, stone-floored room with another door leading outside. The only things in it were a large deep-freeze and two pairs of black wellington boots. It was the deep-freeze which was making the buzzing sound he'd heard when he'd come in. That must be why the electricity was on; Becket and the others must have left some food in it.

He unlocked the external door and looked out, but it was too dark to see anything, so he decided to check it out in the morning.

He was just about to go and have a look around upstairs when he realized that he hadn't eaten anything since lunch-time, when he'd had a sandwich in the pub with George. So he thought he might as well see what was in the deep-freeze.

He lifted the lid and looked inside.

It wasn't quite what he'd expected. Inside was a single large object wrapped in black bin-liners. He couldn't think what it might be, so he ripped one of the bags back to have a look at what was underneath.

It was Ken, his face mottled blue and grey, the dull eyes yellow and staring, his teeth bared in a snarl.

There was frost in his thin white hair, and the wound in his neck looked hideous, as if something had burst out of it.

Sean wrapped him back up and closed the lid.

'Goodnight, Ken,' he said. He couldn't help smiling. This was perfect; they couldn't have made things easier for him if they'd tried.

All he had to do now was phone Ray and set the final cog in action.

31

Sean couldn't find a phone downstairs, but he knew there was one in the house somewhere; Becket had used it to keep in touch with Mathews. He went up to have a proper look around on the first floor.

There were five doors off the landing. One was for the bathroom, one for a large airing cupboard, and the other three were bedrooms. Two of these bedrooms were completely empty, but the third looked like it had been used at some point. There was a large double bed with no sheets, a carpet, fitted cupboards with a few oddments of clothing in them, an armchair and a dressing-table with a collection of dusty photographs on it.

Sean studied the photos. There was one of Ray and his wife, Zara, the woman he'd seen with Derek. It was an old photo and the two of them looked young and happy; they were wearing swimming costumes and Ray had a beer-gut. There was a photo of three children, two girls and a boy, and another showed Ray standing with a man Sean didn't recognize. There was something strange about it; it didn't quite fit the frame and Ray was right at the edge of the picture, as if half of it had been cut off.

Brotherly love.

By the bed was a phone. Sean sat down and checked that it was connected, then dialled the number he'd got off Derek before he'd left Sevenoaks, Ray's home number in London.

The phone rang for ages before anyone answered it. It was a man's voice, sounding distant and irritated.

'Hello?'

'Ray?'

'Who is this?'

'Is that Ray Mathews?'

'It might be. Who's that?'

'Hello, Ray.'

'Yeah, all right, now who is this?'

'It's me, Crawley.' There was a long silence. Sean looked at Ray's photo on the dressing-table, looked at his round sunburned gut, and grinned. 'I've got an offer for you,' he said affably.

Mathews exploded. 'Crawley, you little cunt, where the fuck are you?'

'Shut up and listen for once, Ray. I want out and I need your co-operation.'

'My co-operation, you bastard, after what you've done?'

'Shut up, Ray.'

'Where are you?'

'Now, I'm not going to tell you that, am I? Just listen, okay? I want this thing over and done with just as much as you do, but we do it on my terms.'

'Why should I?'

'Because you haven't got any choice.'

'So what the fuck d'you want, then?'

'I want you off my back, Ray.'

'And why should I get off your back?'

'Because I can sink you. Because I've got Gatley's file.'

'And?'

'And I'm prepared to give it to you and go away for good if you'll forget all about me.'

'I'll think about it.'

'No, you won't, Ray. There's nothing *to* think about. You need that file, and you need me gone.'

'Maybe.'

'There's no other way. That's my only offer, take it or leave it.'

'All right, all right.'

'Good. Now, can you meet me tomorrow?'

'Where?'

'Somewhere out of the way. Somewhere quiet.'

'Where?'

'Can you do it?'

'Yes, I can do it. Now tell me where.'

'In good time. But you've got to promise me you'll come alone.'

'Of course I will, I don't want anyone else in on this, do I?'

'Except Carl and Becket are already in on it, aren't they? So don't get any bright ideas about bringing them.'

'Yeah, all right.'

'No Carl and no Becket.'

'Yeah, yeah, all right. I said all right, didn't I?'

'All right, but if it looks funny the deal's off.'

'It'll be just me. Don't worry, Crawley. This is between you and me. So, where d'you want to meet?'

'I'll ring you tomorrow morning on this number to tell you where.'

Sean hung up.

He lay back on the bed and stared at the ceiling. Tomorrow, then. Tomorrow it would all be over one way or another. And what would he have to show for it?

A headache.

It still hurt. It wasn't the crippling pain it had been, but it was always there, a general numbing throb inside his head. If he kept busy, he could almost forget about it, but when he stopped and tried to just sit and relax it was there, banging away at him. His eyesight wasn't quite right, either; it was still black and white. Actually, more sort of sepia; everything looked a muddy yellow-brown.

All that effort, to end up like this. No matter, he told himself. The headache would go eventually, it would slowly dissolve away and, like all other pain, he wouldn't be able to recall it. As for his eyesight, well, he'd never really been that excited by colour.

He tried some yoga breathing exercises that Lucy had taught him, but they didn't make much difference.

Lucy.

If only she was here, she could make him feel better. He pictured her, sitting in the converted stables, knitting and chatting to Luke. But that's all she was now, a picture. He wouldn't ever be seeing her again. She was already fading to a dim memory. The stay with her had been so unreal, and now it was like coming back after a long holiday and feeling you'd never been away.

And what about Sandra? He'd seen even less of her, and she'd looked after him too, in her own way, though she didn't know it. She'd be pretty pissed off, though. It would be evident by now that he'd gone and wasn't coming back. No note, no goodbye, no nothing. He realized that was a bit of a shitty thing to do, but he'd had no choice. He had to disappear. Tomorrow night he'd be at Heathrow, boarding a plane for Athens, and then as far as anyone was concerned Sean Crawley would cease to exist.

Ah, what the hell, he couldn't afford to feel sorry for Sandra, and she wouldn't want him to. Christ, he'd only spent three nights with her, she wouldn't miss him. She didn't know him. He didn't really owe her anything. He didn't owe anyone anything. He was his own man. Yes, a man. He could stop thinking of himself as a boy. He was a man, a man who could do anything he wanted. That's what he'd learnt, that's what he'd got out of all this, apart from his headache. He'd learnt that the only thing stopping you from doing whatever you wanted was yourself. Once you could kill the policeman inside you, you were free.

Shit. It wasn't working. He couldn't take his mind off the pain. He wished he'd brought some Disprin or something with him.

He decided to try the bathroom, see if there were any drugs there. He rolled off the bed, rubbed his temples and left the room. But, as he expected, the bathroom cabinet was empty. He ran some cold water instead and wetted the back of his neck. It didn't really help, but it killed some time.

He sat on the edge of the bath tub playing with the water from the tap.

He ought to try and sleep soon, but he wasn't tired. In fact he'd never felt so awake; his whole body was pulsing with energy.

Fuck it. He turned off the tap and went downstairs to watch television.

He couldn't concentrate, though; he stared at the screen and none of it seemed to make sense. The only thing on was a foreign thriller that had been badly dubbed into English. It was about plain-clothes policemen, and drugs, and cars and stuff. The only consolation was that one of the actresses in it looked a bit like Susan Gatley.

Susan. He wondered what she'd be doing now. Would she have stayed in the house in Canonbury Road? Stayed after finding Eric murdered in the kitchen? He doubted it. Probably her whole life had changed. Her drinks at the pub, her job at the theatre, her exercise classes, all the parts of her well-organized little life. How fragile it had been, as fragile as her husband's skull. But she still had what mattered; her eyes, her mouth, her luminous skin, her long neck. Her teeth.

He pictured her that first day, when his eyes had met hers. He tried to get back the excitement, but now, like Lucy and Sandra, she had become just another slowly fading memory. He pictured her naked, but it did nothing for him. It was over. It was always the same; he'd get obsessed by some woman, he'd have to have her, to fuck her. And then he would. And afterwards it'd mean nothing, she would cease to interest him. It was the same with Susan . . . Only he hadn't fucked her, had he?

He'd fucked Gatley. Ah well, it was all the same.

Why had she had to marry someone like Gatley? Short-arsed, bald git. All this was his fault.

He'd done her a favour, really.

He'd done a lot of people favours. He was quite a generous bloke when it came down to it. Gatley'd wanted to be famous, he'd got his wish. He was a very famous murder victim.

283

Gatley, Duke and Ken. All dead. And did Duke and Ken have their own Susans? Duke hadn't struck Sean as the marrying type, but Ken, Ken was definitely married. Would his wife miss him? He doubted it; she'd probably be celebrating, like Zara Mathews. All in all, there were a lot of people who should have been grateful to him, and now he had to go running off, running away to hide.

It wasn't fair.

But then perhaps it'd be fun, starting afresh. He could give himself a new name, a new character. He could be whoever he wanted and no one would be able to expose him. He could be and do whatever he liked.

Ian, Jim, Tony, Ray, Derek, Duke, shit, he could call himself Alphonso if he wanted, and nobody would know any better.

Hi, I'm Alphonso Redondo, I work for an independent film production company. Hi, I'm Tony Cooper, I'm a builder. Hi, I'm Ian Grant, I'm an accountant for Hackney Council. Hi, I'm Lewis Brogue, I'm in fashion knitwear. Hi, I'm Dave Scott, let me tell you about alternative medicine . . . It was a whole new world out there.

Yes, when it came down to it, it had all worked out for the best. His life had been non-existent before. Now he was a new man.

All he had to do was get through tomorrow in one piece.

But it was best not to think about that.

The woman in the film who looked like Susan got shot, which was a pity, and soon after that most of the rest of the cast got shot too and the film ended. It was starting to get chilly so he found a blanket, wrapped himself up in it and sat in the armchair. It was just like the old days in the outhouse.

He hardly slept at all that night. He dozed in and out of various programmes until, around five o'clock, it started to get light. He realized that it was pointless trying to sleep any longer, so he got up and turned the television off.

The first thing he wanted to do was have a good look round outside. He put on his new overalls and then, to be doubly safe, he tried on the wellington boots in the pantry. One pair was far too big, but the others were just about right. And so, with the black rubber slapping against his calves, he went out into the cold morning air.

The house was built half-way up the side of a small hill and was screened on all sides by woods. Down below he could make out green fields through the trees, but no other buildings. The drive wound out of sight up to the main road, and the trees here were well spaced, but behind the sheds and outhouses at the back of the yard was a tangled, untended wilderness. Sean hacked his way through brambles, bracken, saplings, fallen branches, weeds and straggly bushes until he found a small clearing.

He realized he was shivering. The morning sun hadn't yet penetrated the trees and his trousers were wet from dew.

He searched around for twigs and dead wood and piled them in the centre of the clearing ready for a fire. Then he returned to the house and made sure he knew his way around completely.

Apart from the front door, the only other way out of the house was from the pantry at the back, opposite which was a high wall and a small shed. The pantry itself was only one storey, with a roof which sloped up to a first-floor window.

Inside, everything looked slightly different in the daylight, but by six o'clock he was satisfied that he had a complete internal map of the whole house and its surroundings.

So now he had to get ready.

The first thing he needed was some tools. He decided to try the shed by the back door, as it was the only outside building which was padlocked. The door was so old and rotten that he had no trouble prising the screws of the lock loose.

Sure enough, inside were a few ancient, rusted farming and building implements, rakes, forks, hammers, chisels, a complete armoury. He picked out a large axe, a shovel and a sledgehammer. In one corner, under a tarpaulin, there was a neglected-looking rotovator and, next to it, a large can. Sean picked it up and shook it; it was nearly full. He unscrewed the cap and sniffed it. Petrol.

He took everything outside and fixed the lock up so that to a casual observer it would look untouched. Then he went back into the house and got the pink file, some newspapers and a box of matches from the kitchen. Then, with some difficulty, he carried them, the axe and the petrol back to the clearing in the woods.

He screwed up several sheets of newspaper and stuffed them under the pile of dead leaves and wood. Then he doused the whole lot with petrol and lit it. It burst into flames. He was pleased to see that what wind there was, was blowing away from the house. He took his notebook out of the file and the photographs of the Town Hall he'd taken on that first day. He smiled, it all seemed so long ago. He dropped it all on to the fire and watched it blacken and burn. He sorted through Gatley's stuff and burned the edges of a few unimportant documents before scattering them around the clearing. The rest he dumped in a pile well away from the flames, making sure there was no danger of them catching light.

He chopped some more wood, larger logs so that it would burn for some time, and stacked them for later. He watched the fire for a while, then checked his watch. Time was creeping by. It was only quarter to seven, but there was still a lot to do before he rang Ray.

The next thing was to deal with Ken. The wounds in his neck hardly looked like the result of a fight amongst builders; they'd have to be disguised somehow. He thought about it. Ray kills Turner, what does he do next? Yes. He destroys the evidence. Just like the file.

Well, that was easily done.

He took the axe and went to the pantry. He opened the deep-freeze and tried to lift the frozen body out, but it was solid and extremely heavy. He wrestled with it for a few minutes but he wasn't getting anywhere, so he fetched the shovel to use as a lever. Eventually he managed to heave Ken over the side. He fell to the ground with a loud clunk, like a falling statue.

Sean pulled the plastic bin-liner off the top half of the

body and studied Ken. His clothes had been removed and he'd been cleaned up, though there was no disguising that wound.

Sean took the other bin-liner off and rolled him on to his back. His naked body didn't look very pleasant, and his genitals had almost shrunk away. His knees were slightly bent and his hands were folded over his stomach with his arms at his sides. He looked like he was sunbathing.

Sean started with the head. He picked up the axe and began to chop, trying to make as many blows as possible land in the area of the wound. It was rather like chopping wood; frozen bits of flesh flew off in chips and the blade occasionally jammed.

He felt quite nostalgic. When he was young and the family had lived in the countryside near Reading, he'd quite enjoyed chopping wood. But it was hard going. It took about a quarter of an hour, until, at last, he cut through the spine and the head rolled free. He inspected the nub of the neck; it was so hacked about there was no way of knowing now exactly how Ken might have died.

Next were the hands, but first he had to wrench them away from the body. He had to use the shovel again and it was a tricky and lengthy process. They creaked at first, then cracked when he eventually managed to prise them loose.

The hands came off much easier than the head, and by the time he got to the feet he was getting quite good at it. The day was warming and he'd worked up quite a sweat, so, when he'd finished, he went outside for some fresh air and a bit of a sit-down before he tidied up.

It looked like it was going to be a lovely day, which would be a change after the bad weather they'd had over the last week or so. It was very pleasant, sitting there in the sun, listening to the birds and the rustling of leaves. He sat there for about twenty minutes before going back inside.

He wrapped up what was left of Ken, hoisted him upright on to the stumps of his legs, then, with a mighty effort, accompanied by a great deal of puffing and grunting, managed to topple him over and back into the freezer.

He went over every inch of the room with a dustpan and broom making sure he collected every bit of loose flesh. He wanted it to look like Ray had done a very thorough job. When he'd finished, he checked himself and tried not to think about it when he found a thawing gobbet in his hair, and another in the turn-up of his jeans.

He dumped the contents of the dustpan into another bin-liner he'd found in one of the dustbins, then dropped in Ken's head, hands and feet. Chopping up the body had made him think. He had intended using the axe as a weapon, but he'd been disconcerted by its bluntness and its tendency to stick. He thought he'd better find something else.

First of all, though, he wanted to get Ken's bits on to the fire. So he hid the axe in the bushes in case he needed it later and took the rubbish bag to the clearing in the woods.

The fire was blazing away now, and its centre looked quite hot. He piled on a couple more logs and watched them flare up, then emptied out the contents of the bag. The head, however, rolled off the logs. He was about to kick it back on when he had an idea. He ran back to get the sledgehammer and shovel; after all, he wanted it all to look authentic.

Smashing Ken's skull brought back unpleasant memories of killing Duke, and he tried not to look when the brains spilled out. When it was pretty well flattened, he shovelled the whole gooey mess on to the fire.

By now the other parts were beginning to cook. The smell of roasting flesh was disconcertingly appetizing and Sean's stomach growled.

On his way back through the woods Sean practised swinging the sledgehammer a few more times. It was nicely weighted, and not too difficult to handle. He was pleased to see how he could effortlessly splinter branches and dead trunks. And it had, after all, reduced Ken's skull to pulp in a few minutes.

He smiled.

Now he was ready.

It was half eight, time to ring Mathews again.

32

The phone was answered almost immediately, as if Mathews had been waiting by it.

'Hello?' he barked.

'Mathews. It's Crawley.'

'Good.'

'You're still all right to meet today?'

'Yes, but you'll have to tell me where, won't you?'

'The house.'

'Which fucking house?'

'The one in Suffolk. Where you took me before. It's out of the way and we can be alone. No danger of being seen. We can't risk London.'

'All right, but it'll take me a while to get up there.'

'Me too. That's why I've rung early. Now, I should be able to make it by, say, one o'clock – no, better make it two. Just to be on the safe side.'

'Whatever you like. You say.'

'I can definitely be there by two.'

'That's fine with me.'

'Right, that's settled then. And remember, no Carl and no Becket.'

'I remember.'

'Good man.'

Sean put the phone down. He noticed that his heart was racing. Good. Plenty of adrenalin, plenty of oxygen in his brain. It would keep him alert.

He calculated that if Mathews left straight away it would take him three hours at most to get there. But that was fine. Everything was set. He was ready. The sooner the better. Get it all done with.

He went around the house and put everything back just as he'd found it. He locked the front door, replaced the key in its hiding place and let himself back in by the pantry door. Then he turned off all the lights, unplugged the television and straightened the furniture in the sitting-room. He put his rucksack in one of the bedroom cupboards and hid it under a blanket. He needed to keep the wellington boots on for the time being, even if they were slightly awkward, so he stashed his trainers as well.

He checked the fire one last time. The burning flesh was now giving off an unpleasant stink, but you couldn't smell it from the house. He stayed just long enough to pile on the rest of the wood he'd cut.

He took the petrol can back to the house; he'd spotted a bucket in the yard earlier and it had given him an idea. He filled the bucket with petrol and hid it in the remains of the outside toilet. Then he took the key out of the unlocked back door and chucked it into the bushes.

Next, just as he'd done at Sandra's, he went around the house wiping all the surfaces, so that there was no possible danger of fingerprints. Even though, if it all went as planned, there wouldn't be much left to look for fingerprints on.

After that, all he could do was wait.

He sat in the main bedroom, which had the best view of the drive, and stared out of the window, the sledgehammer leaning against the wall.

He was ready.

Ready and waiting. He was good at waiting. He'd done a lot of it in the last few weeks. He could wait for as long as it took. Because this was the one last thing he had to do. After that he'd be truly free, one way or another.

And so he sat there, his eyes fixed on the road. Nothing else existed; he'd slipped out of any other reality, he'd cut himself off from time.

In the back of his head was the pain; he used it as a sort of mantra, to clear his mind of everything else. The pain, the drive, the yard, the sledgehammer, and somewhere in the future a big fire that would clean everything.

As the sun rose in the sky the shadows of the trees retreated from the drive, and the loose gravel glowed a bright yellow, but then the sun began to fade as clouds formed. The glow died and the day became grey.

After that, with no moving shadows, time had even less meaning. Sean slowed his breathing and sat there. And waited.

Just before eleven he heard an engine. Soon the familiar shape of the white transit van came into view. It rumbled into the yard rather too fast, and skidded to a halt.

Almost immediately the passenger door flew open and Carl jumped out. He was shouting and looked angry, as if he was in the middle of an argument. His left hand had a dirty bandage round it and there was a sling round his neck which he wasn't using.

Next out was Ray himself, also shouting, his face red and moist-looking. He came round to Carl's side, grabbed him by the lapels and slammed him against the van. Carl put his hands up in a conciliatory gesture, then looked sullen as Mathews let him go.

Carl opened the back door and helped Becket out. His left leg was in plaster up to the thigh and he had a pair of crutches. His hard face was set into its usual golem mask as he took the crutches off Carl and swung away from the van.

Good old Ray, he hadn't let him down. He knew that if he mentioned Carl and Becket enough he'd eventually get it into his head to bring them along.

Sean was glad of this chance to get another good look at Ray. He looked fatter than before, and older. His veneer of respectability was gone; his silver hair was untidy and it looked like he'd been wearing his suit for days. He had no tie and the top three or four buttons of his shirt were undone.

Sean took the sledgehammer and left the bedroom. He went down the landing and hid in the airing cupboard at the end, keeping the door open a crack so that he could see out.

For about ten minutes nothing happened, and then he heard voices and feet stamping upstairs. It was Ray and Carl. They went into the main bedroom. A couple of minutes later Ray came out, arguing again.

'Just check, all right? I don't expect you to find Ken's head, I just want you to find Crawley. The bastard's been here, and he's probably still here now. Check everything, even the loft.'

Ray thundered downstairs and Sean heard more shouting below. Carl hadn't reappeared yet, so Sean left the cupboard and got himself ready on the landing.

Carl strode out of the bedroom more pissed off than ever. For a moment he didn't see Sean, and when he did he jumped back in surprise.

'Fucking hell,' he said, his eyes and mouth wide open. Sean didn't give him a chance to say or do anything else, he let fly with the sledgehammer. It got Carl right in the gut and the air wheezed out of him in a sudden hiss.

His face went purple and he doubled over. Then he coughed a couple of times and fell to his knees. He coughed again and a thick rope of transparent slime oozed from his mouth.

He began to say, 'Oh, shit,' over and over again.

'I don't need to tell you what that was for,' said Sean, as he put down the sledgehammer and grabbed Carl from behind. He pulled him to his feet and manhandled him to the top of the stairs.

'Oh, shit,' said Carl, and Sean gave him a shove. He watched him tumble down, then he picked up the sledge-hammer and ran along the landing to the bathroom. The window was already open; he clambered out of it on to the roof of the pantry, rattled down the tiles and jumped to the ground.

His heart was really going now, hammering against his ribs, and he was gripped by a wild, scarlet excitement. He took a couple of deep breaths and moved as quietly as possible into the pantry. The boots made no noise on the stone floor. The only sound, apart from the gentle flapping of the rubber against his legs, was the buzzing of the deep-freeze.

The door through to the kitchen was open slightly and he peered round it. The kitchen was empty. He padded across it to the hall door. He could hear Becket on the other side, yelling.

'No, he's not fucking come down this way! He must still be up there.'

Mathews bawled something back from above them some-where.

Sean opened the kitchen door and saw Becket standing at the foot of the stairs, a crutch attached to each elbow. Carl was curled at his feet in an awkward position, blood drib-bling over his chin.

'Stay there,' Mathews roared.

'Too fucking right,' said Becket.

'Hey,' Sean hissed, and Becket spun round as if on a hook.

Sean retreated into the kitchen as Becket launched himself forward on his crutches. 'Down here!' he bellowed, clatter-ing into the room.

Sean grunted with the effort of swinging the sledge-hammer, but his aim was good. It caught Becket in his bad knee, and the plaster shattered. He sprawled into the oven.

'Owww,' he moaned, leaning over and clutching his bent leg. 'Why'd you do that?'

Sean took another swing at him, got him in the back, and he went down.

He could hear Mathews coming down the stairs, so he couldn't stay to make sure of Becket. He raced out through the pantry into the yard, dropped the sledgehammer and grabbed the bucket from the toilet. He'd only just got ready when Mathews came blundering out, brandishing a crow-bar.

He stopped when he saw Sean.

'What the fuck d'you think you're doing, Crawley?' he croaked, his voice broken and tired-sounding.

'I might ask you that, Ray. You were supposed to come alone.'

'I was ready to do a deal.'

'Bollocks.'

'You shit.' Ray lunged at him, but Sean easily got out of the way.

'I've had enough, Ray. I don't want to talk to you any more.'

'You fucking cunt, you've had your chance. This time I'm going to kill you.'

'No. It's all over, Ray. You shouldn't have fucked with me.'

Mathews roared and charged at Sean, his face twisted with rage. Sean side-stepped and hurled the contents of the bucket over him. Mathews spun out of control, rubbing his eyes and spluttering.

'Agh,' he spat. 'What the fuck's that?' He tried to look at Sean, but it was obviously painful keeping his eyes open.

'That was petrol, Ray,' Sean explained.

'What?' Mathews kept blinking his bright red eyes, then screwing them shut.

'Look,' said Sean, dropping the bucket, 'I said I don't want to talk to you any more, and I don't. I've had enough.' He took the box of kitchen matches out of his pocket and rattled them, but Mathews still hadn't understood yet.

'This is all your fucking fault,' he said, and spat a few more times, then tried to force his eyes open. His only thought now was to get at Sean with the crowbar. And as far as he could see, Sean had no weapon.

Sean dodged his first charge. He danced out of the way and struck a handful of matches against the box.

Ray never stopped to think.

'Goodbye, Ray,' said Sean, and as Ray came at him again, he ducked round behind him and threw the matches on to his back.

Mathews didn't notice at first, he was still too intent on attacking Sean, but then he suddenly stopped as he realized something was wrong. He turned round as if there was someone behind him, then let out a child-like shriek as the man-made fibres in his cheap suit-jacket began to melt and his hair caught fire.

He looked utterly bewildered as he hopped about for a second or two slapping at the flames.

'Help me!' he screamed.

'Come off it.' Sean picked up the sledgehammer.

Mathews staggered towards him, arms outstretched. 'Crawley,' he pleaded, but it was obvious that Sean wasn't going to help him, so he made one last mad dash at him. Sean gripped the weighted end of the hammer and held the blazing man away from him with the handle. Ray flailed at him, but it was too late. There was a sudden whoosh and he was completely engulfed. He grasped the handle and fell to the ground unconscious. He lay there, stretched out and holding the hammer in front of him.

Sean left him smouldering there and went to see if Becket was still alive.

He was.

He was sitting propped up in the corner. Somehow Carl was also still alive, and he'd crawled into the kitchen. Becket was cradling him in his lap and he was still muttering, 'Oh, shit,' over and over in a flat monotone.

Becket's face was drained of all colour and he was panting. 'You didn't need to do this,' he said hoarsely.

'Yes, I did,' said Sean. 'It was you or me.'

'I've never killed anyone.' Becket sucked air in through his teeth and closed his eyes.

Sean leant against the sink and stared at Becket. 'Yeah,' he said, 'but I have.'

'But me, I didn't . . . I've never done anything wrong.'

'It doesn't work like that.'

'Come on. We came here to talk to you. None of this was necessary. None of this.'

'You've got Ray to thank for all this, not me.'

'Where is he?'

'He's dead.'

'Oh, shit.'

'That's Carl's line.'

'Eh?'

'Never mind.'

'Help me, Crawley.'

'Why?'

'My leg, I can't move. My back, something's happened to my back. I can't stay like this. Would you, could you just phone for an ambulance? Ray's dead. That's what you wanted, isn't it? It's finished. This is nothing to do with me.'

'I never thought you'd turn out to be a coward, Becket.'

'I'm not a coward. It's just you don't need, there's no need, I mean . . . I'm very cold.'

'I've got no choice, Becket. You see, since this whole thing started I haven't had any choice.' Sean shut the door to the pantry and stuffed newspaper under it to block the crack.

'What are you doing?' asked Becket. His voice so husky now it was hard to tell what he was saying.

'I sort of almost liked you, you know,' Sean said. 'You were better than the others, but we don't have any choice here. I've just killed Mathews, and Carl doesn't look too well, and then of course there's Ken, and Duke, and Gatley. It's quite a list, and I'm afraid you're at the bottom of it. How can I let you live?'

'I won't tell anyone.'

'I'm not listening, Becket.' Sean opened the oven door and turned on all the gas taps.

'I can't move,' said Becket. Sean looked at him; he was crying. 'I've got into the corner here, and I can't move. Just help me.'

'I can't help you, Becket. You are what you are, and I am what I am. I can't touch you.'

'You're going to kill me, then?'

'It's what I do.'

'Please!'

'All of a sudden people are being nice to me, being polite, asking me for help, saying please. I must be doing something right for a change.'

'I can't move. I'll die. Why?'

'I'll tell you what this is all about. Duke took me to the zoo once, and we went to the insect house, and he showed

296

me the ants, millions of them, all swarming about the place, in this big glass cage. They lived there, lived in there, you see, eating, shitting, fucking, dying.'

'Ants . . . I don't understand.'

'Thing is, there were dead ants everywhere, and all the other ants just going about their business. And I'll bet if I went back there tomorrow it would look exactly the same, even though a million ants might have come and gone.'

'What are you talking about? What are you saying?'

'I'm saying it's a shitty world, Becket, and it's the best of all possible worlds, depending on which way you look at it. But, whatever it is, there's nothing you can do about it. The ants are behind the glass, doing what they do, and we can't change that. And you're sitting there, asking me all these questions, and in a few minutes you'll be dead, and there's nothing any of us can do about that. Not you, not me, not anyone. That's just the way things are. Now, I understand that for you that's pretty shitty, but for me, well, it's pretty good. Because you're the last. After you I won't have to do this any more. Look, I'm sorry, I'm going to have to get out of here. That gas stinks something awful.'

'Come on.' Becket's face was wet with tears. He tried to shift but the pain was evidently too much. His head dropped to his chest.

'You know what?' said Sean, holding a handkerchief over his mouth 'It's best not to talk too much, you know. Whenever I open my mouth I end up wishing I hadn't. As long as I keep it shut things are okay. But maybe, well, maybe I can talk to you, because it doesn't matter what you think of me, because, well, because you're dead.'

'You don't have to do this. Help me.'

'That's not my job,' said Sean.

'Oh, shit,' said Carl.

Sean left the room.

He wadded more paper under the kitchen door from the other side. He wanted to make sure he'd have plenty of time to get clear.

He went to the clearing and took off his overalls. He

dropped them into the flames and watched them sizzle and melt just like Ray's jacket. Then he returned to the house, got his rucksack out of the bedroom cupboard and changed into his trainers.

He checked his watch; he had plenty of time to get the next train. He took everything outside and had a look at Mathews. He'd gone out and was lying where he'd fallen, his eyelids burned off so that he was staring soulfully into the distance with scorched eyes. The sledgehammer was still clutched in his hands, for all the world as if he'd just been on the rampage with it. Only he hadn't quite managed to get away from the house before it went up. Poor old Ray, unlucky to the end. Luckily his legs were hardly touched by the fire, so Sean could get the boots on him without it looking odd.

He took Ray's shoes upstairs and threw them under the bed. Then he set light to it.

In no time at all the room was filled with smoke, and he hurried out.

He left the house by the front door and ran off up the drive to get his bike.

He didn't look back as he cycled off. In a few minutes the gas would go off, but he'd be well away by then.

As he pedalled down the road he thought he felt a spot of rain on his face.

Typical. After everything had gone so well, it would be a pain in the arse to get caught in the rain now.